Mountain Song

by
Exie Wilde Henson

PublishAmerica
Baltimore

First printing

ISBN: 1-4137-7778-3
PUBLISHED BY PUBLISHAMERICA, LLLP
www.publishamerica.com
Baltimore

Printed in the United States of America

DEDICATION

*With profound gratitude
and in
loving memory
of
my parents,*

Joseph Stokely Wilde, Sr. and Ethel Phillips Wilde.

Mountain Song,
a sequel to
Beyond This Mountain,
completes
— in fictional form —
the thirty-five-year saga of their remarkable lives.

Acknowledgments

My deepest love and gratitude to my husband, Gene, for his support and encouragement as I wrote this second book. Thanks, too, for taking the beautiful photograph of our North Carolina mountains, which is used for the cover of the book.

My love and thanks to our children, Melody and Steve Fifer, Rebecca Dobson, and Scott and Kristy Henson, for bearing with me through yet another book! Thank you, Scott, for designing—again—a beautiful book cover.

My love to our grandchildren—Amy and Kevin, John, Kelly, Matthew, Carrie, Anna, Ben, Ashley and Aaron—for the fun and fulfillment they bring to our lives.

As the youngest of nine children in the Wilde family, I am indebted to my brothers and sisters—Dorothy, Nell, Oneda, J.A., Marie, Stokely, Festus, and Kadez—for affording me opportunities they did not have, and for a lifetime of love and shared memories. They still claim me even after making their young lives—literally—an open book.

My love and gratitude to the unique individuals who were brave enough to marry into the Wilde family—Gene, Jennie, Naomi, Carroll, Helen, Paul, R.E., Edward, Fred, and Boone. What in the world would we have done without you?

My continued gratitude and love to Jerry Dempsey for her gift of true and abiding friendship, and for praying with me and for me across the years.

My love and appreciation to the people of the community of Lake Toxaway, N.C.—past and present—whose goodness of character greatly influenced me while I was growing up and who, after our being away for many years, welcomed us home with gladness!

My love and thanks to our many friends across the country who never gave up on my writing these books—and whose response to *Beyond This Mountain* is gratifying and encouraging.

My grateful acknowledgment to Dr. Dennis Hensley, my editor *par excellence,* who took the journey with me, word for word, through my first book, *Beyond This Mountain,* and through this sequel, *Mountain Song.*

My appreciation for the late Reverend Thea Rose for the inspiration of his life, which serves as a model for the young minister in both books.

The Wilde family is indebted to the late Frank and Mary Louise Inman, the designers and original owners of the big house where the Wilde family lived, and to the second owners, Mr. and Mrs. Carl Moltz. My thanks to Louise Aiken, granddaughter of the Inmans, and her husband, Ike, for information regarding the Inman family.

My appreciation to Joe Johnson who professionally prepared the floor plan of the house, seen at the front of the book, where the Wilde family lived.

My thanks to James and Judy Poe, the professional and personable photography team who took my photograph for the back cover.

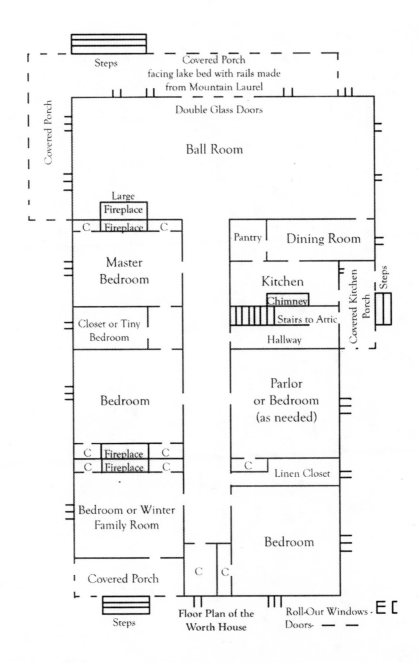

Steps

Covered Porch
facing lake bed with rails made
from Mountain Laurel

Covered Porch

Double Glass Doors

Ball Room

Large
Fireplace
C Fireplace C

Master
Bedroom

Closet or Tiny
Bedroom

Bedroom

C Fireplace C
C Fireplace C

Bedroom or Winter
Family Room

Covered Porch

Steps

Pantry   Dining Room

Kitchen

Chimney
Stairs to Attic

Hallway

Covered Kitchen Porch

Steps

Parlor
or Bedroom
(as needed)

C   Linen Closet

Bedroom

C   C

Floor Plan of the
Worth House

Roll-Out Windows   E C
Doors   — —

Chapter One

Justin was jerked awake by a heavy pounding on the door. He waited a moment to see if he might have dreamed it. No, there it was again! This time his wife, Laurel, sat up listening. He quickly lit a lamp, pulled on his pants and went down the hall to the back door.

An unshaven man stood unsteadily, blinking in the circle of lamplight.

"Are you the Justin Worth that used to run a loggin' camp?"

"I am. Moved here about a month ago. Who're you?"

"We heared you and your woman help sick people." The smell of liquor reached Justin as the words came out. "A woman's been knifed over in Terminal Town and I'm skeered she'll die if she don't git some help."

"Where?" Justin asked.

"Over where the sawmill is. That's what we call the place."

"Have you sent for the doctor?" Justin asked.

"No! No doctor! Doctors talk to the law." He lowered his voice. "But we cain't git the bleedin' stopped."

"Wait right here. I'll get my wife."

While Laurel got ready and checked her medical bag, Justin told Sarah and Adam, their two oldest children, to watch after the three younger ones. They understood because they had done this many times before. The hands on the kitchen clock stood at two as Justin and Laurel left the house. Justin was thankful he still had Jed Owen's farm truck, which he had borrowed to bring some farm equipment from their former place. They could get there quicker on wheels than on horseback.

When they entered the lumber shack, a frightening scene greeted them. A woman, bleeding from a stab wound to her back, was lying unconscious on the bed. Someone had turned her on her stomach and taken off enough clothes to find where she had been stabbed. Blood was smeared over the covers and had soaked a wadded-up rag someone had pressed against the wound. The overheated room intensified the sickly, sweet smell of blood.

No one said a word when Justin and Laurel came in. The white, frightened faces around the room seemed a blur as Laurel flew into action. She felt the woman's pulse and said, "Good! Her pulse is slow but steady, even with all this blood loss. Justin, wash out a pan and get me some hot water out of the kettle."

She pulled the supplies she would need out of her medical bag. She and Justin washed their hands with soap and dried them on a towel she had brought. She washed and rubbed disinfectant around the wound before examining how deep it might be. It was on the right side, just under the shoulder blade. If it had been on the other side, the heart would probably have been punctured. Laurel was happy to see that no blood was coming from the woman's mouth, so it looked like the lungs had escaped the knife. Only time would tell about the liver.

"How long has she been unconscious?" she asked the man who had come for them. He seemed to be the only person willing to talk.

"She passed out before I left to git you. She...she was drunk. I don't know if she even realized she'd been knifed."

"Then she's not out totally from loss of blood."

"She was real drunk, ma'am."

"Justin, I'll need your help. I want to open the wound and sprinkle some comfrey powder down inside it to help it heal. Then I need you to hold it together while I sew some stitches."

Justin did as she instructed and in a moment she inserted her needle and pulled the catgut thread through to start closing the gash. Fortunately, the woman didn't move. But someone in the corner did, in a hurry, muttering, "Lor', I gotta git outta here." Two or three others melted away before Laurel's sewing was done. Only the man who had come for them and a woman, standing in the shadows, remained.

"It's time we knew your name," Justin said to the good Samaritan.

"I'm Mack and this here's my wife, Gerta."

"We need you to help us bring her around," Laurel said. "Gerta, put on a pot of coffee. Mack, I need some cold water to bathe her."

Justin, meanwhile, didn't need to be told what to do. He chunked up the fire in the cook stove and added wood. Then he helped Laurel, very carefully, to turn the woman on her left side. As they saw her face fully for the first time, Laurel said, "She's pretty. What's her name?"

"Delilah," answered Gerta, speaking for the first time. "But she likes to be called Lila."

Gerta helped Laurel bathe her arms and legs, trying to revive her. When Laurel washed her face and put the cold, wet cloth on the back of her neck, Lila groaned and moved.

"Lila," Gerta called, "Lila, wake up!"

Lila opened her eyes and asked, "What happened?"

"You got hurt. Mr. and Mrs. Worth come to fix you up."

She looked from one to the other in confusion. Laurel smiled and said, "Let's see if you can sit up. Gerta's making some coffee. It'll make you feel better."

As they helped her sit up, the pain hit her. She opened her eyes and mouth wide, gasping.

"You've been stabbed pretty deep in your back," Laurel told her. "I sewed you up but I still want the doctor to come to check you."

"I don't remember gittin' cut," she said, her face contorting with pain. "Who done it?"

Mack and Gerta looked at each other, then at Justin and Laurel. "We don't know. Several people was here but they all was drunk and don't know what happened, or they ain't talkin'."

Lila looked around the shack. "Where's Brand? And the younguns?"

"Brand's sleepin' off his drunk over at our shack and your younguns is at the Devlins'."

Lila looked straight at Laurel. "I don't want no doctor comin' around."

"But you have a deep stab wound in your back," Laurel argued.

"If I ain't died yet, I ain't likely to. But it's hurtin' like the devil. Can you give me somethin'?" Almost every breath came out as a moan.

Laurel turned to Justin. "Let's step outside for a minute."

When they were alone, she asked, "What can we do? I don't have anything strong enough to ease her pain. It's like she's had surgery with no pain medication."

"You're not going to like my suggestion, but I don't think we have a choice. Let's forget the coffee and give her just enough whiskey to make her go to sleep again. That should help her until you go see Dr. Leighton and find out what to do. They're all scared of the law getting in on this. My guess is they've been in trouble before."

Laurel unhappily agreed. After she checked Lila's pulse and found it moving toward normal, she told her what to do. Lila was more than glad to drink the brew Justin held to her lips and drift into oblivion again. Laurel was relieved to hear the moaning stop. She and Justin left Mack and Gerta in charge temporarily. Mack was sobering up after several cups of coffee, and Gerta, who showed no signs of drinking, seemed to be responsible.

Laurel caught the mail truck to Deerbrook later that morning to see Dr. Leighton. After hearing her story, he assured her she had done everything he would have done. He gave her some morphine and general instructions for treating Lila for the next few days.

Then he said, "Let's talk about *you* for a few minutes, Laurel. How are you feeling?"

"I'm getting my strength back. It's taken longer than I expected, but I'm being careful and following your orders. Justin and the children keep me in line," she said, smiling.

"One part of me is pleased to see you busy taking care of people again, but another part says it's too soon. You lost so much blood, it's a miracle you're alive. Your body must have about a year to get back its reserves. Please don't get into full swing for a while."

His earnest tone made Laurel realize she had been too optimistic in her thinking of what she could do for the next few months.

"I promise I'll use caution in what I take on. I plan to go by and give Lila some morphine, then I'll go home and rest this afternoon. Sarah can keep the house running without me when she has to."

"How old is she now?"

"Seventeen. She graduated from high school in June."

"I heard about you moving to Lake Eagle Rest. Do you like it?"

"We love the house. It's wonderful after all those years in two-room lumber shacks. We don't know much about the community yet, but I'm sure we'll like it."

"What's Justin up to these days?"

"He's watching and working his crops at Mrs. Rapp's place. Bud and Toby, her sons who stay drunk most of the time, have finally stopped harassing him to leave before he harvests his crops. As soon as he finishes at the farm, he'll start looking for work in the timber business again."

Dr. Leighton looked at her in concern. "But…?"

"No. He won't start moving us around again. He says he'll work on a small scale. We all need the experience of living in a normal community where we can put down roots."

"Tell him what I said about your recovery time. I need him on my side in this, because…" He paused before continuing. "You know you're going to jump in every direction to improve conditions for people around you. I want you to do that again, Laurel. *But not until I tell you that I think your body is ready!*"

After she left, he sat still except for the drumming of his fingers on the chair arms, unwilling to call another patient just yet. He had some remembering to do. Was it just four months ago that he had given Laurel Worth up for dead? Had arrogantly announced to Justin that she would not—could not—live? Had asked Justin to do something that he couldn't scientifically explain—to talk to Laurel, to touch her, to review old memories, to remind her of their life together, to call her back to him and the children…?

Despite the impossible odds against her, she had lived. And it had caused a shift in Dr. Leighton's thinking. He had been humbled, had recognized a power at work beyond the physical, had been intrigued and challenged by the possibility that miracles still happen…and had made room in his neatly-catalogued scientific reasoning to acknowledge that fact.

But I did have a part in it, he thought, and sat quietly as he allowed the satisfaction to flow over him. *She's so vibrantly alive! I fussed at her, but I can hardly wait for her to swing fully into action again.*

He remembered Justin coming by to see him soon after Laurel had left the hospital. After Justin expressed his gratitude, he said, "I came by to work out a payment schedule for Laurel's surgery. I can pay you a little each month or I can sell a milk cow—we have two—and pay you more up front."

He had looked steadily at his friend to keep his emotions in check. The crash of '29 just five years before had stripped this man of his job, his home and his life's savings. Then, recently, his wife had collapsed, needing a hysterectomy, and had almost died from extreme loss of blood.

"You don't owe me anything, Justin. I can't take money for something I didn't do. I didn't save Laurel's life. We both know who did."

"You know I can't let it go like that, Doc. She's my wife. I have to pay you something."

"You and Laurel have already paid in advance. Look at all those years you saved me trips in bad weather by delivering babies and taking care of the sick. You know I'll be counting on your help in the future. And, as far as I know, neither of *you* has ever been paid for what *you* do for other people."

Justin looked at him as if he hadn't heard him and said, "I know what I'll do. I'll take pictures of the hospital and staff and of your family. We'll work out a schedule."

Dr. Leighton knew Justin Worth well enough by now to know when he had lost an argument. He held out his hand. "Since you're the premier photographer for Wildwood County, how could I refuse? Fact is, I *would* like that very much, Justin, and so would my wife and my staff." The pictures were now proudly displayed in his home and his office.

He had known and seen Justin and Laurel in action for about fifteen years and considered them good friends. During most of those years, while Justin was the supervisor of logging camps, Dr. Leighton had learned to trust Laurel's judgment in almost any medical situation. He had seen her deal with diphtheria; deter typhoid and hookworm; treat snakebites, panther attacks, and concussion; deliver babies. He had delivered four of their five children. He knew Justin was respected and liked throughout the county as a person to count on when someone needed help. Dr. Leighton admired him as much as any man he had ever met.

He had been surprised that a couple with their education and ability chose to do the type of work they did. Justin had finished college and was recommended to law school. Laurel had taught school several years before her marriage and had received some nurse's training.

Justin and Laurel Worth, he thought, *always seem to infuse life into the people around them. Lake Eagle Rest, you don't know it yet, but your quiet community is going to change! It's already started. And change means fireworks of some sort!*

He almost laughed out loud as he realized he was looking forward to it!

A discreet knock on his door brought him back to the present and reminded him that he had patients waiting. He stood to get back to work, in a very good mood, invigorated from Laurel's visit and his memories.

Laurel told Justin what Dr. Leighton had said about her recovery time. He agreed that she could continue nursing Lila through this crisis, but she would have to ride Tattoo, their trusted horse, instead of walking. He knew her well enough to know this challenge was invigorating to her, emotionally. So, for the next few days Sarah kept the Worth household running while Laurel helped Lila through her critical stage of recovery. Laurel enlisted Gerta and Mack to see that Lila didn't mix whiskey with her morphine doses.

The second day when Laurel asked where Lila's children were, Gerta explained, "I always take them over to the Devlins' when I know you're coming. They don't need to see how bad their mama's hurt."

Laurel wondered about the welfare of the children in such a home, but she knew she couldn't take that on now. She simply said, "You're a good neighbor, Gerta."

A day or two later Laurel arrived to find that Lila had sneaked some whiskey after all. She was slap-happy drunk, singing bawdy songs. When she saw Laurel she said, "I bet you know some church songs. Sing one with me."

She launched into a slurred rendition of "When the Roll is Called Up Yonder." She sang deliberately, looking slyly at Laurel, "When the roll is called up yonder, I'll be there," — pointing up as she said "up yonder" and pointing down as she said, "I'll be there." She collapsed in laughter over her wit.

Gerta, mortified over Lila's behavior, called Mack to help hold her still while Laurel changed the dressing on her wound. Laurel felt such pity for Lila that she asked Gerta not to let her know how she had behaved while drunk.

After a few days of fever and general misery, Lila started to mend. Her husband, Brand, was so evasive it was hard to get even a greeting out of him. He personified the atmosphere of Terminal Town. Laurel, after puzzling for a day or two, realized everybody was afraid. They didn't trust her not to bring in the law. She was sullenly tolerated, even by Lila, only because she was needed. Understanding this, Laurel still traveled several miles every day to check Lila's wound and change the dressing.

As she rode home one day, she patted Tattoo, their beloved Chestnut Bay, who had been part of the family since Sarah was a baby. There had been a running joke in the logging camps that Tattoo thought himself human instead of a horse because of the way Justin treated him.

"A month ago I couldn't have ridden one mile. Now I'm riding at least three miles a day!" Impulsively, she leaned over and hugged the horse's neck. "You're a good friend, Tattoo. You've seen us through good and bad times. I love you, you wonderful old horse!"

When Tattoo snorted and shook his head, she was certain he had understood her. As Justin once said, "He understands English and I understand Horse, so we communicate fine."

She continued, "I'm glad you finally have a house worthy of you, my friend. Your barn is bigger than some of the lumber shacks we lived in. And, I still think sometimes that our house is just a dream and I'll wake up in the shacks again."

As Tattoo carried her along, she allowed herself the pleasure of mentally walking through the house again. It still seemed too good to be true. Even through her haze in the hospital following surgery, she had heard Justin's promise of a house big enough for their family; no more lumber shacks and no more moving around every year or two.

Ethan Stewart, a young man who was like a son to them, who had lived with them and worked with Justin for about seven years, had found this house for rent. The owners, who lived in Atlanta, were not as concerned with a large rent payment as they were that a reputable family live in the house and keep it from falling into disrepair. When Justin, who had been hunting desperately for an adequate house for his family, was told the rent was only eight dollars a month, he had to walk away to get his emotions under control. He had rented the house on the spot.

Laurel had fallen in love, at first glimpse, with the house on its gentle knoll. The yard, full of oaks, maples, birches, and dogwoods, was comfortably covered with moss and natural ground cover that had learned to co-exist with the trees. It was a setting worthy of the sprawling, weathered, brown clapboard house with a roof of curling, mossy shingles where three large rock chimneys rose to a discreet height. And there were so many windows — tall windows — trimmed in white.

She and Justin and the children had walked through the front door and stopped, the family waiting to see her reaction. A wide hall ran the length of the house, almost like a hotel with rooms opening off each side. On the left side were three large bedrooms, each with a fireplace and tall roll-out windows. On the other side was a corner bedroom, a parlor, stairs to the partially finished attic, a kitchen and dining room. But that was not all. At the end of the hall, one large room — a ball room — spanned the entire width of the house. On one wall stood a huge rock fireplace. Sunlight poured through the row of tall windows on the opposite side. The room was so large, one of their logging shacks could have fitted inside it with room to spare.

Double glass doors led onto a porch that ran the width of the house and wrapped around one side. Ivy woodwork served as porch rails. They stood on the porch, looking across the valley to the mountain range surrounding them; one mountain ended as another began, with several sizes and shapes, dominated by a hogback. It was the ridgeline view that Laurel had learned to love.

Sarah and Adam had led them down a rocky path that wound through some large, aged oaks and maples to the edge of the sloping grassy yard. The path ended at a low rock wall, beyond which was thick undergrowth, such as berry bushes, shaded by many types and sizes of trees, stretching as far as they could see.

"The lake used to come to this rock wall," Justin explained. "This was the front of the house and this whole basin to that mountain range was covered with water."

"It must have been beautiful," Laurel said. "But I can't imagine it being more beautiful than it is right now."

Now, as she and Tattoo neared home, Laurel thought of the children, the months of turmoil they had been through with her illness, and their obvious delight in the big house. Sarah, seventeen, and a high school graduate as of May, 1933, had been like a mother to the younger ones through it all. Adam, fifteen, was just as much a support in his way. He had a big dose of his daddy's charm and could get cooperation out of the younger ones before they realized what had happened. Caroline, eleven, was at an awkward stage, not quite knowing where she fit, but she did her part, knowing that cooperation was an unwritten rule in this family. David, seven, was a serious little boy whose greatest joy in life right now was taking care of the animals. Alexis, three, was everybody's child. The four older ones each felt responsible for her, perhaps because of Laurel's prolonged illness when they had to take care of her. She was a happy little girl who returned their love in full.

When Laurel walked in the door after one more visit to Terminal Town, the children swarmed her. Sarah made her sit down and Caroline brought her some lemonade. Alexis climbed into her lap and snuggled. David gave his usual report about the animals, this time telling how much they liked it there. Adam was helping Justin harvest the crop at the Rapp farm, where they had lived and sharecropped before moving there. After a little while, Laurel kept her promise to Dr. Leighton and went to rest. Just before she dozed off, she thought, *Sarah must get on with her own life soon. She's taken care of us long enough.*

On their first Sunday in the Lake Eagle Rest community, Sarah and Adam had walked to the small Baptist church about two miles away on the other side of the lake bed, following a trail that Justin had heard about. They came home excited because they had met some young people their age. When Laurel and the three younger children went with them a week later, Laurel was pleased to see how many people they already knew. The Worth family was happy to be in church again, except for Justin, of course. It was established knowledge that Justin never went to church.

On the way home Sarah asked, "Mama, do you think we could invite the people our age over to our house?"

"Sure. Do you mean for a party?"

"We would have to play games or do something fun."

"We could play ball," Adam said. "That flat out to the side of our house near the road would make a good baseball field. We'd have to clean it off and set up the bases."

"We'll talk it over with your dad," Laurel said.

Justin thought it was a great idea. He and the children had the field ready for the first game by the next Sunday. Word had spread through the community and a group of fifteen young people, more than were in church, showed up about mid-afternoon. The game was launched with some good-natured teasing about who picked which girls and why. After a few innings, Justin and Adam carried out a pail of lemonade that Laurel had made from the cold spring water. When Sarah followed with a tray of sugar cookies, the game was halted for a while. The noisy, fun-filled afternoon passed quickly. Before the young people left, someone asked if they could come back the next Sunday.

That night Laurel said to Justin, "It took me a little while to understand why I sensed such a rightness about this afternoon. This is the way we spent our Sunday afternoons when I was growing up. All the young people gathered at our house."

"I'm proud of Sarah and Adam. They seem to have the knack for making friends wherever they go."

"Well, I just wonder where they learned *that*," she teased.

When Justin grinned, she continued, "You're good with young people. They seem very comfortable around you. Of course, I've never seen anybody who wasn't comfortable with you."

"Oh, there're a few people in this world who don't particularly care for me," he said. She could tell he wasn't too worried about it.

The next Sunday afternoon so many young people showed up that Justin hurriedly set up two horseshoe games, in addition to the ball game. Some younger children the ages of Caroline and David came. The grounds offered an ideal place for hide-n-seek and the big house presented a challenge to play ante-over, a game where one team yelled, "Ante-over!" as they threw a ball over the house, while the team on the other side of the house tried to figure where the ball would appear so they could catch it. The team that caught the most out of ten throws would win.

Before leaving, the young people again asked if they could come back the next Sunday. "Yes," Justin said. "Let's just plan for you to come every Sunday afternoon."

They left happy. They had a place to go and something to do.

When Laurel and the children went to church the Sunday after she and Justin had been to Terminal Town to take care of Lila, Laurel noticed a coolness toward them. The church people who had greeted them so warmly the first two Sundays barely spoke and some just passed by without speaking at all. She was further puzzled when just a handful of young people showed up for the Sunday afternoon ball game.

Embarrassed, some of Sarah's and Adam's new friends told them what had happened.

The word had spread that the new Worth family was hobnobbing with the people from Terminal Town, the part of the Lake Eagle Rest population that the long-term residents disliked, avoided, and even tried to pretend was not there. The gossip was that they had even given liquor as a medicine! But, the gossipers asked, what else could be expected? The Worths, for all their educated ways, had lived in logging camps several years before appearing in Lake Eagle Rest.

That night the family talked about it. Adam got right to the point. "Did the people want you to let that woman bleed to death?"

"No, I don't think so, son," Laurel answered. "I think they are reacting without knowing the facts."

"What can we do?"

"I don't know yet. You shouldn't have to pay this price for us helping someone in need. Justin, why are you so quiet?"

"Just thinking...It looks as if we have a choice. We can stop helping people who are labeled undesirable and be popular. Or we can keep on doing what we've always done and take the consequences. I believe these are basically good people who will get over the hysteria of the moment, created by a couple of busy-bodies. You children tell us which choice you would rather we make."

Sarah answered, "Daddy, you know we can't stop helping people!"

Adam added, "Yeah. That's what we've always done." He lowered his voice, "But I wish we could have our friends."

"I want our friends to come, too," Caroline said, and David nodded.

"Of course you do!" Justin said. "My advice is to ride out the storm as calmly as possible. Don't talk about it at school. I think you'll see your friends back in a week or two. And, of course, your mother and I will help whoever needs us."

Justin was right. The young people did come back to play ball and other games. Justin and Laurel believed they had ridden out the storm, not knowing that another one was brewing.

Chapter Two

School started in early September, bringing mixed emotions for the children. They dreaded having to start over in a new school, but they were also excited by the challenge. Adam rode the bus about seven miles to the Riverside High School, where he was in the junior class. Caroline started sixth grade and David started second grade in Lake Eagle Rest Elementary School, which had two teachers for seven grades. Sarah felt like a fish out of water, but didn't say anything because she knew she was needed around the house a little longer. She would take Adam's place and help her daddy finish gathering in the harvest at the Rapp farm, where they had lived and sharecropped for the past two years. Alexis stayed at home with Laurel, where she had her mama all to herself. She amused everybody by assuming the role of Laurel's caretaker, as she had seen the older children do for the past few months, telling her mother when she needed to rest or when she was working too hard.

Justin and Adam, as soon as the family was settled in the new house, had returned daily to the Rapp farm. The day after school started, Justin bumped along in Jed's old farm truck. Sarah had informed him that she would be helping him get the crop in, beginning tomorrow. Meanwhile, today, he was alone with his thoughts...

Those nine years in the logging camps had given them some of their best memories, in spite of the hardships and conflicts. They had worked together to operate the most successful and unusual logging camp in the area. The four families and crew of sixteen men had become more than a community; they had become like one family. Justin had talked Laurel into moving into that first camp by assuring her they could make good money fast—enough to buy a farm—and get out as soon as possible. They dutifully saved their money for a farm, but it had been in the Deerbrook Bank when the crash of '29 came. Suddenly, their logging business and their hard-earned money for a home were gone!

The years since have been the hardest, he thought. *The families and logging crew who were like one big family, were suddenly thrust apart to live however and wherever we could to make a living.* He had continued logging on a small scale, with Ethan Stewart's help, and had farmed enough to provide food for his family. His photography helped provide needed supplies. Fortunately, people never seemed too poor to want to have their picture taken.

When Ethan announced he was called to preach and had moved to the other end of the county to pastor a small church, Justin decided to get out of the logging business and try his hand at farming. Jed Owen, his former logging foreman, was farming and making a good living. Justin, two years ago, had entered into an agreement with Mrs. Rapp, a widow who lived with her married daughter, to rent her farmhouse and sharecrop her fields. The deal worked well the first year until Mrs. Rapp's two sons, Toby and Bud, had returned from the timber fields in Oregon, where they had lost their jobs because of drinking. Even though they had a place to live, they resented Justin living in their home place, and set about to get him out by harassment and threats. They weren't men enough to admit that Justin was supporting *their* mother. When they brought the sheriff out to try to force Justin off, leaving his extensive crops in the fields, even threatening to burn the house down on Justin's family, Justin leveled his shotgun at the three of them, ordering them to leave. Laurel, thinking he was going to shoot them, collapsed at his feet.

Justin realized suddenly that his knuckles were white from gripping the steering wheel so tightly. Laurel had been needing a hysterectomy, but all the other crises had taken precedence over her physical problems. Remembering her surgery and the time when they all thought she would die always brought a rush of terror.

When he realized she would live against impossible odds, Justin's fixed familiar world view had tilted and he realized it would never fit back into its former dimensions again. He had grown up, because of a religious, but mean-spirited and abusive stepmother, to believe that God, to whom she prayed loud and long, was up to no good. He had wanted no part of a God who trafficked with such a person as his stepmother.

But Dr. Leighton — and Laurel — had assured him that it was God who had brought her back to him. It did seem to be an absolute miracle. Doubts — *that he had been wrong all his life about God* — kept breaching the fortress he had erected in his mind. These doubts were leading him across a foreign and scary landscape. He hugged his self-sufficiency a little tighter.

Justin had felt the weight of three major problems before taking Laurel from the hospital. He had to find a place to live; Laurel must have special care for two or three months; and he must, somehow, find a way to gather his crop in spite of Toby's and Bud's attempts to destroy part of it and harass him in every way they could.

When Justin realized they could no longer live in the Rapp farm house because of Toby's threats to burn it down on them, Jed and Hannah solved their problem by insisting that the Worth family move into their spacious farm house with them and Nora, Hannah's sister. The farm had been left to Hannah and Nora five years before when their father died.

Justin remembered with clarity their discussion that night in the hospital. He realized that he, the boss and always the dispenser of charity, was being offered charity. His pride argued, quite verbally, until Jed looked him square in the eyes and said, "Justin, if the situation was reversed and *we* needed *your* help, what would you and Laurel do? You would've already moved us, that's what! You sure wouldn't be standin' around here jawin' about it as long as we have!"

Justin had laughed. He knew Jed spoke the truth. They were back on a good solid footing. Jed had just moved the checker where he could countermove without losing face.

Hannah clinched the deal. Standing firmly beside Jed, she said, "Justin, you know that Nora and me are going to take care of Laurel and the family anyway, so having all of you in one place will make it a lot easier. The other families from the logging camp will come to help."

Jed, he thought as he drove into the field where he would load corn, *what would we have done these last few months without you and Hannah and Nora and the other families from the camp?*

Two of his major problems had been solved and he was now working on the last one. Jed had firmly insisted that Justin use his truck for the daily trips from the Rapp farm near Riverside to Lake Eagle Rest. "You *will* use this truck to haul your produce. It's at least an eight-mile trip one way to your place from the farm. You'll still be hauling — come Christmas — with Tattoo and that wagon."

When Justin objected, reasoning that Jed needed his truck to haul his own produce, Jed argued, "We only have to haul from the field to the barn. Let them horses of mine earn some of that food they're eating."

After two more weeks of hard work, with Sarah by his side, Justin had his harvest gathered. He had a plentiful food supply for his family and animals, after giving Mrs. Rapp her share. His cash crops were sixty-five bushels of peanuts, thirty-five bushels of cabbage and several wagon loads of sugar cane. The small amount of money they brought — Depression prices — discouraged Justin. He had hoped to have enough money to buy shoes, clothes, and coats for the children before winter hit, with a little left over. He knew now that this cash would only be enough to buy staples and necessities. He had to get a timber job fast. It was a happy day when he left the Rapp place behind him for good, and could turn his efforts toward making a new life at Lake Eagle Rest.

But he was puzzled and said so to Jed, "I don't understand what happened to Toby and Bud. One day they were determined to destroy my crop. The next day they acted like they were scared to death of me. I haven't seen hide nor hair of them for weeks...Of course, I'm thankful!"

"I know," Jed said easily, "it's hard to figure out what bums like that are thinkin'. I'm just glad they've left you alone."

Justin didn't need to know that a group from his former logging crew had visited the two Rapp brothers one night, after they realized the two men weren't going to stop trying to destroy Justin's crop. Masked, armed with convincing knives, whips, and pistols, the seven men — with words only — had terrified and forced an oath out of the two brothers that they would not set foot on the farm again until Justin had harvested his crop and was gone.

The two blustering cowards honored their oath *only* because they were petrified at the thought of another visit from the masked men. They were not about to be caught around Justin Worth, anywhere, anytime!

During the weeks they had lived in Lake Eagle Rest, Laurel and Justin had begun to get a feel for their new neighborhood. Sam Parker, editor of the county newspaper, *The Wildwood Journal*, and a close friend to Justin, had given Justin some articles telling the history of Lake Eagle Rest in her glory days. The beautiful mountain-locked valley, with its man-built lake, had drawn the rich and famous who arrived in their private railroad cars to live in their spacious summer homes around the lake's edge. This idyllic way of life had ended a few years ago when the earthen dam gave way after heavy rains. Lake Eagle Rest, unleashed, cut a destructive swath to the south. Without the lake, most of the rich and famous lost interest in the community.

Some reminders were still there, however, such as the enormous hotel, the railroad that still brought a daily train in and took it out again, and the spacious summer homes around the edge of a lake that was no longer there. The Worth family was living, thankfully, in one of those homes. The others stood empty except for three or four families that came back a few weeks every summer to enjoy the coolness of the mountains.

It didn't take Justin and Laurel long to realize that the transient glory days of Lake Eagle Rest had been taken in stride by the long-time residents. The deep-flowing river of tradition, customs, religion, and neighborliness moved steadily along, while the capricious river had soon run its course. Lake Eagle Rest, without a lake, was certainly not a ghost town. Its essence seemed to be that of a sparsely settled but closely knit farming community where everybody knew everybody, and almost everything about everybody.

Perhaps because she was looking for it, one of the first impressions that Laurel received from the community was its sense of permanence. As she went to church or met the people under different circumstances there was an unspoken message: *Our grandparents and parents were here before us; we are here today; our children and grandchildren will be here tomorrow.* Permanence — stability — was a luxury she had almost forgotten in their transitory logging camp years and the past years since the Depression started. She allowed the concept and the hope to permeate her being like a healing balm.

She and Justin were amused but pleased to see how the upright population looked with tolerance, even affection, at those long-term residents who had a drinking problem and other shortcomings. They watched out for them. After all, that's what neighbors were supposed to do. This tolerance, however, did not extend to the inhabitants of Terminal Town, the hastily put-together sawmill area, which consisted of a company store, a hotel with a questionable reputation, a café, about ten lumber shacks and a holding pond for the logs.

After her experience with Lila and the few people she met, Laurel could begin to understand the hostility of the local people. Drinking, fighting, carousing, cursing, sullenness, and suspicion seemed to be the preferred manner of life for Terminal Town residents. Laurel was glad when Lila was well again and she could stop her visits. She left, however, with a feeling of unfinished business. She tried to express it to Justin. "I've never failed so completely in getting to know someone and establishing some kind of a relationship. They stonewalled me from the first encounter. They seemed resentful even as they accepted my help. I doubt they'll ever want to see me again."

Justin laughed as he hugged her. "Oh, but I imagine they will! You make a bigger impression than you realize, Mrs. Worth."

One Saturday morning in early September, Laurel had enlisted the children's help in peeling and slicing apples to dry for fried apple pies. They had found a perfect place to dry the apple slices on clean sheets on the flat roof of the kitchen porch. Caroline and David enjoyed crawling in and out of the attic window, and around on the roof, performing their tasks. Laurel would fill several flour sacks with the dried apples and hang them from the rafters in the attic. The fried apple pies were one of their favorite winter treats.

Sarah and Adam went back and forth from the barn, where Justin was working, to the house as they were needed. They had all sat down on the kitchen porch for a glass of lemonade when two visitors arrived. Laurel recognized them as two women she had seen at church. The obvious leader introduced herself as Gussie Turner.

"It's nice to meet you, Mrs. Turner. You're the pianist at church, aren't you?"

"Yes."

Turning, Laurel said, "And you're...?"

"I'm Irma Ricker. I've seen you at church."

"It's nice to meet both of you and know your names," Laurel said. "Please have a seat while I get you a glass of lemonade."

As Irma started to sit, Gussie Turner snapped, "No, Irma, we didn't come to sit and drink lemonade. We need to say what we came to say."

Everybody stared at her. Her hair was drawn back severely into a bun, stretching her skin to its limits. Her mouth was now pursed in disapproval.

Irma, a mousy looking woman and obvious "yes" person to Gussie, had been properly chastised. She quickly shook her head in confirmation.

Laurel, realizing this was not a social visit, said, "Please, come with me to the parlor where we can talk uninterrupted."

To the children, she said, "Please continue with the apples. We'll be finished soon, I'm sure."

As soon as they were seated, Gussie Turner sat forward on her chair and launched her case. "Since you are a newcomer to our community, Mrs. Worth, we felt it our duty to tell you that most people are disturbed at what is happening here on Sunday afternoons."

Laurel took a deep breath. "To what are you referring, Mrs. Turner?"

"The ball games. We don't believe in playing ball on Sunday."

Laurel looked from one to the other before asking, "Who are 'we'?"

Gussie, taken aback, stammered, "It's...it's the church and...all the people in the community."

Laurel sat up straight and asked, "Did the church and community ask you to come on their behalf to talk to us about this matter?"

"No. But we know how they feel."

"Do you? It's a big responsibility to be speaking for an entire church and community, Mrs. Turner. Was there some kind of meeting or survey to condemn playing ball on Sunday?"

"No. We didn't have to have a meeting or survey. We know the people in this community. You don't."

Because she somehow felt pity for the women, Laurel spoke

gently, "What you're saying is that *you* think it's wrong to play ball on Sunday. *You* have appointed *yourselves* as spokeswomen for the church and community without getting their permission."

Gussie, skilled in the art of intimidation, realized this was not going as she had expected. She glanced at Irma who ran her tongue over her thin lips and stared at the floor.

Laurel, in the same quiet tone, said, "Tell me why it's wrong to play ball on Sunday."

"It's a commandment. Remember the Sabbath day and keep it holy."

"So you think a ball game with young people having clean fun is unholy?"

"It's not showing proper respect," Gussie persisted.

"Then what would you have them do on Sunday? Sit around with their hands folded and look pious? They're young, Mrs. Turner. Do you have something better to offer?"

Gussie had no answer so she turned defensive. "Well, Irma and I tried to help you understand. If you refuse to listen, you'll just have to take the consequences."

Laurel stood. "Mrs. Turner and Mrs. Ricker, Jesus got in trouble all the time because of the things he chose to do on the Sabbath — healing the sick, raising the dead, plucking grain to eat because He and His disciples were hungry. Do you think it would have been better if He had sat with His hands folded on the Sabbath?"

Gussie was out of her depth. She stuttered, "I...I...But this is different..."

"Is it?" Laurel persisted. "The Pharisees were more interested in the rules than the good of the people. Jesus told them, 'The Sabbath was made for man and not man for the Sabbath.' That's what we believe, too. I'll tell my husband about your concerns, but I'm pretty sure we'll continue the ball games on Sunday."

Gussie stood. "Well, Irma, let's go! We're wasting our time." She swept out of the room and down the hall with Irma in her wake. Just before going out the door, she turned and leveled a parting shot, "Another thing! People don't like it because you're so friendly with that...that crowd in Terminal Town, either."

Laurel went back to the parlor and sat down suddenly because of the weakness in her knees. She was confused over this hostility. And she probably had handled it all wrong.

Sarah and Adam came tiptoeing in. Sarah's tone showed her concern. "Mama, they're gone out of sight. Are you okay?"

Adam, however, was full of admiration. "Mama, you took up for us! You told old Gussie-Fussy off."

Laurel laughed in spite of herself. "Adam, how did you hear all this?"

"Sarah and I didn't like their looks so we stayed in the hall and listened. Will we really get to keep playing ball?"

"We'll talk to your daddy tonight. I hate to go against the customs of the community, but I'm sure not inclined to let Gussie Turner tell us how to run our lives."

That night after Justin heard the story, he agreed with Laurel. "I think most of the parents in this community will be glad for their young people to have something fun to do on Sunday afternoons. It'll keep them out of trouble. And, Laurel, we're always going to have *somebody* who doesn't like what we're doing."

Adam asked, "So we still get to play ball this Sunday in spite of Miss Gussie-Fussy?"

"Who?" Justin asked.

"That's his name for Mrs. Gussie Turner," Sarah explained.

A smile flitted across Justin's face, but he said, "Yes, Adam, we'll play ball this Sunday. But, remember, you are to respect your elders."

Justin's words were prophetic. The crowd of young people continued to grow. The Worth house was the place to be on Sunday afternoon. However, after snubs every Sunday at church, Laurel realized that Gussie Turner was her enemy.

Adam was delighted when he came in one afternoon to find Justin reading the newspaper to Laurel as she finished supper. He hugged his mother as usual and when he gave his dad a hug, he said, "Now I know things are really getting back to normal in this family."

"Why?" Justin asked.

"I remember you reading the newspaper to Mama in the logging camp when we all lived together. Every time you came in from town you would read the news to her and then report it to the crew at supper that night."

"Are those memories good?" Justin asked.

"Oh, yes! I loved the forest and I loved having that big family of people. Sometimes I wish we could have lived that way, always."

"But you're happy here, aren't you?"

"Yes, sir. I love this house and I'm making friends at school and we have the ball games. The thing I'm happiest about is that Mama is well again."

"We all are, son," said Justin as he got up.

"Daddy, why don't you tell us the news at supper every time you get a newspaper, like you used to do? I'd like to know what's going on and I like the way you tell it."

Laurel looked at Justin and smiled. "I think that's a good idea."

Justin was pleased. "Okay, we'll start tonight."

At supper, after the blessing and everybody's plates were served, Justin said, "Adam has asked me to tell you the news of what's going on in the world, according to *The Wildwood Journal*. The paper tells about the 'Trail of Poverty' running through North Carolina — as in all the states."

"What's poverty?" asked David.

"It's when people don't have enough to eat, or enough clothes to wear, and sometimes don't even have a home."

All the children suspended their eating as they looked steadily at him, waiting.

"It's hard to explain so you can understand, but our country is going through a hard time where there aren't jobs for people to work, so they don't have any money."

"But, Daddy," Caroline said, "we've never been hungry, and we have clothes and a home. Why don't we have poverty?"

Justin and Laurel looked at each other. "Your daddy has worked very hard so we could have food and clothes and a home," Laurel said.

Justin said, "I've been fortunate. Lots of men would gladly do what I've done but didn't have a chance because they live in the city. They can't grow their food, like we do. The paper says that whole families have become hoboes, riding in the empty boxcars on trains, just to have shelter and, of course, look for work. There's danger, though, because they have to swing on board after the train is moving."

Adam said, "We have so much room in this house, and the little house is empty. It doesn't seem fair. Could we have some people come and live with us?"

Sarah spoke for the first time. "We have to take care of Mama right now until she gets her strength back. She can't take care of a lot of other people for a while. Dr. Leighton said she needs about a year to recover completely."

Justin nodded and added, "Sarah's right. Your mama took care of a lot of people for many years, but she knows she'll have to wait a while before she starts again."

"Before you keep discussing me as if I'm not here, may I say a word?" Laurel asked.

As they all looked at her, she continued, "I think it's good for you to know what's going on around us, and I'm glad you want to help. We'll find ways we can help other people who need us."

Alexis jumped out of her chair, ran to Justin and crawled into his lap. "Daddy, I'm glad I'm your little girl. I don't want to ride in a box."

Everybody laughed and the conversation turned to more cheerful subjects as the children told of some of their experiences at school and ended up discussing the ball games on Sunday afternoons.

Justin felt a keen sense of satisfaction that mingled with and helped control his anxiety about being so short of cash. In spite of his reassurances to the children, he knew they were at the poverty level in terms of actual money. The pitifully small amount of cash he had received for his money crops was steadily dwindling in spite of their frugal efforts. He had to get back to work in the timber business and he would start his round of photography again on weekends. However, he *had* brought his family through a tumultuous time and had found a house that was worthy of them. He looked forward to their future in Lake Eagle Rest.

The next morning he and Laurel lingered over a cup of coffee and discussed their financial situation. Justin plunged right in. "I know we're very low on cash and the first frost is just around the corner. We don't have enough to get clothes and shoes and coats for the children, do we?"

"Not all of them. Adam has outgrown almost everything. They all need shoes, socks, sweaters and coats."

He nodded. "I'm going over to Bradford Lumber Company today and talk to Mr. Bradford about a job nearby and I'll start my round of photography this weekend. The churches are having homecoming day during this month and I've been asked to come to several family reunions which are held this time of year."

"That's another thing I like about mountain people. They know it's important to stay in touch and to keep families close."

"Yes," Justin said. "And it's good for my photography business."

Laurel, realizing his burden of providing for the family, said, "We're in good shape, food- wise, for the winter — for ourselves and the animals. You worked mighty hard *and* fought a few battles to achieve that."

"Yes. I'm glad we're finished with the Rapp family."

"We have as big a store of canned goods as we've ever had, by the time Hannah, Nora, Bess and Alice got through dividing their jars." A wave of emotion gripped her as she remembered her friends from the logging camp faithfully canning vegetables, fruits, and jellies. Each one had set aside a certain number of jars for her family, as she lay in bed unable to help. If she started to protest, or even thank them, their standard reply was, "If the situation was reversed, what would *you* be doing?" This always silenced her. They all knew the answer.

Justin brought her back to the present, asking, "Is there anything we absolutely have to have for the house?"

She thought of her threadbare sheets and the care she had to take in washing them, but she answered, "No. Let's take care of the children's clothes first."

He was determined to work at something where he could stay at home. When he arrived at the office of the Bradford Lumber Company in Terminal Town, he found to his surprise that he was no stranger. When he introduced himself, Mr. Bradford stood with obvious pleasure, stuck out his hand and said, "So you're Justin Worth! Your reputation precedes you."

Justin laughed and said, "Now, that sounds a little scary. What kind of reputation?"

"Just that you're the best timber man in the area. All those stories from your logging camps keep floating around. Seems nobody ever got the hang of running a top-notch camp like you did in terms of production, camp regulations, and making a community."

"Did you hear that my wife was the prime force in making that community?"

"Oh, yes! We've heard enough about both of you to be happy to have you in Lake Eagle Rest. In fact, I need to thank you and your wife for helping with this last incident here. We have a predominately rough element right now. I don't like it but I have to have workers."

"I understand," Justin said.

Mr. Bradford was a dapper, rather fussy little man, not what Justin had expected. But Justin liked the gleam in his eyes and his firm handshake. Bradford motioned Justin to a chair and sat down again, himself. "Now, to what do I owe the pleasure of this visit?"

"I need a job," Justin replied.

The gleam in Mr. Bradford's eyes intensified. "Just what kind of job are you thinking about? I could make *you* several offers."

"I'll be limiting myself to work close by so my family doesn't have to move again. We've done enough lumber camps. And, of course, I'd prefer to work where I can stay at home."

"I was hoping I could interest you in setting up another camp, but it's in a remote area. Would you be interested in overseeing a group of loggers, just day work, no camp?"

"How many men?"

"Between fifteen and twenty. It's a big tract of timber."

Justin suddenly felt weary, just thinking of starting out with a new group of men after having Jed, Bulldog, Tom, Ethan and the rest of his crew all those years. He said slowly, thinking it out as he went, "I'd like to start with something small. My family has just come through a crisis where we almost lost my wife. Then we had to move because of circumstances beyond our control. They need my presence right now."

Mr. Bradford sat still, giving him time to get to the point.

Justin asked, "Do you have a need for cord wood? Frankly, I've never done it, but that may be the best way for me to start. I could start off with two helpers."

Mr. Bradford said, "Yes, we always need cord wood, and," he added dryly, "I think you may be able to handle the operation."

Both men laughed, then got down to business. When Justin left he had a job with Bradford Lumber Company on a tract of mountain land near the head of the lake bed. He would find two men nearby who would work with him. That night at supper he told the family about it.

Adam, always curious, asked, "What's a cord of wood, Daddy?"

"A cord is a unit of measure for a bundle of wood made up of sticks about the size of a fence rail. A bundle four feet high by four feet wide by eight feet long is a cord. It takes about twenty-eight to thirty-two cords to load a boxcar."

"What's it used for?" David asked.

"It's mostly ground up into a pulp to make paper and paper products. Sometimes it's used for fuel."

"Could I help you some?" Adam asked.

"Yes, when you're not in school. That's one part of the logging business you haven't seen yet."

That night in bed Laurel suddenly asked, "Justin, how are you going to manage a logging job without a truck?"

"Well, Laurel, what a question! Tattoo would be totally indignant if he heard you. He'll be glad to get back to the logging business after all that farming."

Laurel shook her head and smiled. "Don't tell him I asked."

She thought a minute, then continued, "So, Tattoo will be hauling wagon loads of cordwood to Terminal Town to load on the box cars. Will he have help?"

"I'll try to hire someone with another horse and wagon. It'll make production faster." He paused, then continued, "When our finances ease some, I'll have to buy a used truck if I'm going to make a living at this. But I'll need to work awhile first."

"It would be good to have a vehicle again. How long ago was it that we sold the T-Model Ford and went back to using the wagon?"

"Almost five years ago. Right after the crash of '29."

Laurel had another concern. "Justin, are you going to be happy dealing with cord wood when you've always had a big and efficient logging operation?"

"Yes. I'll be fine, honey. I want to be home more with you and the children. I'm doing what I choose to do for now."

After her breathing told him she was asleep, he lay beside her thinking. *Why didn't I jump for that big logging job? Laurel's changed since her brush with death, but I'm changing, too. It's a strange territory I'm in right now.*

Just before he slept, he remembered Mr. Bradford's remarks about his reputation. He chuckled and knew he would have to tell Laurel tomorrow. If they had a good reputation, she had certainly helped build it.

Chapter Three

Sarah, meanwhile, had become restless. She was making friends with some of the young women in the community and seemed to have a choice of which young man she would like to date, but she needed some direction for her life. She knew that Laurel and Justin had hoped she could go to college, but the Depression had put that out of reach.

Laurel sensed Sarah's unrest and knew it was time to cut the apron strings. One afternoon they were sitting together on the kitchen porch, stringing green beans on long threads to hang up to dry. The shells of the beans hardened, resulting in the name, "leather britches." Everybody in the family liked the pungent taste, when cooked with the right seasoning, as a change from ordinary green beans.

Laurel said, "Sarah, I want to thank you for the way you've helped the family through my sickness. You've had more than your share of responsibility."

"You're welcome, Mama. I'm glad you're getting back some of your strength."

"Yes. It's wonderful to be free from that weakness I had for a while."

Sarah looked at Laurel seriously. "You know you must do as Dr. Leighton says and not take on the world for a while."

Laurel smiled at Sarah's mothering and said, "I promise, but I want us to talk about *you*. It's time for you to feel free to find a job and start living your own life instead of taking care of all of us."

Sarah's brown eyes lit up. "Are you sure...?"

"Yes, I'm sure, Sarah. You must have your own life."

"But, I'm afraid you'll do too much if I'm not here to help."

"The other children will help and I will limit what I do outside the family."

"Will it be all right with Daddy for me to go to work?"

"You need to talk to him about it. He'll want the right thing for you."

The next week, as if on cue, a letter arrived from Laurel's sister, Emma, in Newport, Tennessee. She knew that Sarah had finished high school and possibly needed a job. She suggested that Sarah come quickly and apply for a job in the Green Canning Factory. They would start hiring next week. She offered for Sarah to live with them rent free, if she would help some with their two boys and the housework.

It was a time of mixed emotions when the family sat down to discuss whether Sarah should leave or not. Sarah was excited. Adam tried to be happy for her but couldn't imagine what life would be like with her gone. They had been buddies all their lives. Caroline, David, and Alexis didn't even try to be happy. They felt like part of their world would crumble without Sarah. Laurel had steeled herself for this time, because she knew the emotional havoc it would wreak on the others. Justin knew in his mind it was right, but his heart had to be persuaded.

Sarah, seeing her daddy's struggle, asked him to go for a walk with her. After a time of companionable silence, Sarah said, "Daddy, I want to thank you for raising us as you did. I can't think of anybody who has been happier than we have."

"But...Sarah..." he began, "I kept you in the logging camps too long, and the years since have...have been hard on all of us."

She interrupted, "No, Daddy! I won't have you telling me how bad our life has been!" Then she laughed as she said, "Do you know what some of my best memories are? Those days when you took Adam and me to school on Tattoo. You told us some of your secrets of the forest that we'll never forget. The snowy days were best. We rode along, wrapped warmly in our blankets, with your arms around us. You sang those silly songs and taught them to us. Do you remember the day we saw the great horned owl? You said when he blinked, you felt as if he were royalty, granting us permission to travel through his kingdom. Well, Daddy, Adam and I felt as if the forest was *our* kingdom! We loved it!"

He searched her face for a moment, then solemnly said, "I'm glad you feel that way, Sarah, and I'm so glad you told me. I've felt like I failed all of you terribly when the bank closed and we lost all our money for a home. I should have seen it coming in time to get our money out safely."

Sarah put her hand on his arm and scolded, "Oh, Daddy! You and Mama have given us the most important things in the world. I can't even realize all of it yet, but I do realize the love and fun and caring for other people."

"One of our chief regrets is that you can't go to college. Your mother would never reproach me for that but I know she feels it deeply and I'm afraid you do, too."

"I would like to go to college, and I know I would be going if it weren't for this Depression. You can't help that. You've provided your family with all the necessities, with some left over to help other people. You've succeeded, Daddy, and I won't hear another word about how you've failed us! You and Mama have shown me how to make a good life and I intend to do just that!"

"You're a lot like your mother, Sarah. She can always find a silver lining in any situation. And, if there isn't one she can make one up!" They looked at each other and laughed as they thought of Laurel's unfailing optimism.

"I've got a big dose of my daddy in me, too, sir! Of which I'm very proud!"

He couldn't speak so he turned and opened his arms. She went into them and they held each other in a bittersweet goodbye embrace, knowing an era had ended. They were quiet on the way back home, too full to trust themselves to speak again.

Two days after Sarah left on the train to Newport, Justin received a telegram saying she had a job making ten cents an hour, which meant four dollars a week. A letter followed saying she would be sending three dollars home each week, since she had few expenses. Justin was pleased with his first-born, but wrote back to tell her the family would accept half her salary until he got his timber job up and going. Laurel knew that this, together with a little of the crop money, would buy the shoes and clothes the children must have. With their food from the crops, including canned goods, she could run her kitchen on less than a dollar a week. She figured as she worked: fifteen cents for five pounds of sugar, fifty cents for a twenty-five pound bag of flour, ten cents for one pound of coffee, ten cents for a gallon bucket of lard and five cents for a box of matches.

Sarah's absence meant more work for the other children. After a couple of turbulent weeks of adjustment, their new routines were established. Each child had his or her own private reasons for missing Sarah and, after a week or two, realized they must now depend more on each other. They tried, in subtle ways, to help each other adjust to the fact that she was gone. Adam evidently decided that Alexis was one of his primary responsibilities. He never seemed too busy for her even though she dogged his footsteps when he was home. Caroline and David remained the buddies they had always been. Laurel knew that Caroline would soon be to the age where she would grow away from her little brother. But, thankfully, not yet.

Autumn's first cool spell in late September brought the nesting instinct to Laurel full force. Since moving in, there had been so much activity Laurel had not had time to think, beyond daily routine, about what she needed to do in the house. As she walked through the rooms, still amazed at all the space, she turned practical. The furniture looked sparse, with only a double bed and small lamp table in two of the bedrooms. Fortunately, each room had a good closet where folded clothes could be kept in boxes. She and Justin had a chest of drawers and Sarah's room had a trunk at the foot of the bed. She knew it would be awhile before they could get more furniture. As she looked at the tall roll-out windows, she realized that the owners of the house, even at its heyday, had evidently chosen not to have curtains. She would do the same, of necessity. There was no money for such luxuries.

She *would* have to make some new sheets as soon as possible, but she wouldn't mention that to Justin yet. Fortunately, they had plenty of quilts, worn as they were, to start the winter. She chose the Dresden Plate, the Double Wedding Ring, the Log Cabin, and the Stained Glass Window quilts to use as bedspreads until later when money was not so scarce. The quilts brought a rush of memories of the logging camp where she and the other women had quilted them. She caressed each quilt as she spread them over the beds.

She would plan some quilting parties in the big room when

winter came. It would be a good way to get to know her neighbors and, perhaps, Hannah, Nora, Bess, and Alice, her beloved logging camp friends, could come occasionally. As Alexis happily played with paper dolls, which Caroline had cut from the Sears Roebuck Catalog, complete with furniture, Laurel sat down with a cup of coffee and allowed her memories to continue...of her near-death experience in the hospital...

It was remarkable how clearly the details of her journey toward death...and back...were imprinted upon her very soul. Her peace and joy, constant companions since her experience, sealed with certainty the transaction that had taken place between her and God. She was walking through the beautiful meadow beside a stream toward the light at the crest of the hill, eager to arrive, when she had heard Justin calling her. And she could hear the children's voices in the background. She desperately wanted to keep walking toward that tantalizing light and warmth, but she stopped. Justin and the children needed her. She chose to go back...to live...but still hesitated because she knew she couldn't continue to live the way she had for the past several years. It wasn't just the endless hard work; it was her approach to life.

She saw with clarity that even though she had gone to church, had taught her children about God, had prayed, had even started a church in a boxcar — always wanting Justin to share her faith — *she* had been in control. *She* was responsible. *She* carried the load. *She* always needed to work things out. She realized with amazement that, for all her talk about faith, she had only wanted God's pat on the head as *she* plowed through the problems. She wanted His guidance, but she had never turned it all over to Him.

She would not — could not — play God any longer in her own life, in Justin's and the children's lives, in anyone's life! She deliberately let go of life as she had always lived it. If that meant dying, then she would die. It was a prayer without words.

At that point of giving herself...and everything precious to her...unconditionally...to God, she became aware of a Loving Presence in the hospital room. Had Papa come for her? She tried to lift her head but was too weak. She didn't hear or see anything. Yet, she knew the Presence was standing near the foot of her bed on the left side.

Love surrounded and filled her. She was aware of total love and acceptance at the center of her being. She *knew* she was of infinite worth to God just as she was. She didn't have to earn His love. And she knew she could never lose it.

Somehow, she understood that His transforming love had always been there, but she had been too self-sufficient to receive it. She had constructed her own little world where she was in control, and had kept Him on the fringe, at a comfortable distance to be called on in times of distress.

The Presence remained as she realized a transaction had taken place. She had laid down the control of her life and the Person who loved her unconditionally had taken over. A profound peace flowed through her, bringing wholeness and joy! She knew she would live to raise her children. And more...much more!

Alexis brought her back to the present with her concerned little voice asking, "Mama, why are you crying?"

Laurel lifted her into her lap and held her close. "Because I'm happy!"

"But, Mama," she instructed, leaning her head back and looking sternly at Laurel, "you laugh when you're happy and cry when you're sad."

"Sometimes you cry when you're happy, too, Alexis. You'll understand when you get older."

"Why are you happy?"

"Lots of reasons. One is that you're my little girl and I'm looking forward to seeing what a fine young lady you're going to be someday."

"Can I be a lady *and* a tomboy?"

"I guess so. Why?"

"Well, Adam calls me his tomboy and I'd rather be that."

Laurel squeezed her. "Okay, I guess you can wait awhile to be a lady."

As Alexis went back to her play, Laurel sat a moment longer. She was certain she had a destiny for which the hard years had prepared her. She was also certain that God would show her that destiny in His time. Meantime, she would continue to get her strength back and be ready. She had plenty to do with family right now. As she started fixing lunch, she thought, *It's so relaxing to know that I don't have to help God run the universe anymore!*

While the family was adjusting to life without Sarah, she was having her own adjustments. She was surprised, on her third day in the factory, when the woman working next to her said, "I hear you're Hunter Kingsley's granddaughter and have come from North Carolina to work."

"I am. I'm living with my Aunt Emma. You probably know her."

"Everybody knows the Kingsley family. Your grandpa taught several generations of us around here. He also performed weddings and helped people with their legal affairs and other problems. Their house was the place where everybody gathered — for fun or for help. It's like a light went out in the community when he died — with your grandmother following about two years later."

"I wish I could have known them better. We've lived in North Carolina all my life," Sarah said. "But I think my mother must be a lot like her papa. She and Daddy are always helping people."

The woman looked Sarah up and down for a moment, then seemed to make up her mind about something. "I'm Birdell Smith and I need to tell you something. There's a group of women here that's upset over you, a single girl, coming from another state and getting a job just because of your grandpa. They say there's so many women with children who need the work."

Sarah was astonished — and angry. "But the only reason I'm here is to send money home to my family! I have four younger brothers and sisters. My mother almost died a few months ago and we had to move. It's been a hard time. I'll tell those women *my* family needs help, too!"

Birdell looked at her with approval. "That's okay, then. But, *I'll* tell them about your family. Then they'll know they need to lay off bothering you. They don't call me Bossy Birdie for nothing!"

As she looked at Sarah's angry face, she added, "They're not mean people. Everybody is desperate for money."

Sarah's expression softened. "Thank you for helping me."

"You're welcome. I think you might have some of your grandpa in *you*, too."

The next week she had a more disturbing lesson on living in town versus living in the country during a Depression. The first afternoon she saw the train roll slowly through town, she had just crossed the tracks on her way home from work. The train, with boxcars as far as she could see, piled high with coal, clamored, clanked, hissed and whistled its way along the track. As she watched and listened to the horrendous noise, she saw a small boy — about David's size, only thinner — scurry up the metal ladder attached to one of the coal cars. Sarah watched, her heart in her throat, as he stood on the top step holding on with one little hand and throwing off pieces of coal with the other. With the train jerking, braking and swaying, it would be so easy for him to fall…

Just before his boxcar went out of sight, he climbed down and started back toward Sarah, picking up the pieces of coal and putting them in a flour sack that he evidently had pinned to his pants. Sarah moved back so he wouldn't see her, but she didn't need to worry. He was too intent on his task.

His little pale, pinched face — streaked with coal dust — is too old for his age, Sarah thought. *Daddy was right when he said this Depression is robbing children of their childhood.*

That night at supper, she told the family about it. Uncle Jim said, "It's dangerous but I'm sure that's the only fuel his family has. He's not the only one, Sarah. People are desperate for just the necessities."

"How often does that train come through?"

"Mondays, Wednesdays, and Fridays, always about the same time it came through today."

Sarah decided she was going to pack a bigger lunch on those days and…and she would bake some cookies…

She kept telling herself she was happy to be there with a job so she could send money to the family but a loud voice inside kept clamoring that she was needed more at home. Her letters told more than she meant for them to tell. In her third letter home, she wrote:

I like Aunt Emma and her family and my work is going well. I'll write more details later about my life here.

Mama, I've been wondering when you have time to rest since no one is there to watch Alexis during the day. Maybe you can rest awhile after they get home from school, before you start supper.

Daddy, I'm sure you and Tattoo are happy to be working together in the woods again. Give him an apple and tell him it's from Sarah.

44

Adam, I'll tell you something if you won't get stuck-up. You must be my best friend because I can't ever remember not having you with me. I miss you lots. I know you'll take care of everybody.

Caroline, you're growing up fast. Mama told me how much you are helping and that you are learning to cook. When I come home, you'll have to cook something for me.

David, I know the animals are okay because you're taking care of them.

Alexis, show someone the big fallen log we discovered on the hill. You can tell them how we pretended it was a big ship one day and a bucking bronco the next. Someone will take you to ride on it like I did.

Laurel's tears flowed over the letter, but no one knew. *Sarah sounds like the mother of the family,* she thought. *Cutting the apron strings is necessary — but painful — for everybody.*

When Justin read the letter, he immediately said, "She's homesick. The letter is laced with it."

"I thought so, too," Laurel said. But, seeing Justin's stricken face, she added gently, "She'll get over it and be stronger for it. She has some of her daddy's strength."

Justin, without a word, got up and left the room.

The magic of October was suddenly upon them and memory urged Adam to show the younger ones how to mix play with work. They made piles of leaves on the hillside and he taught them how to swing on a sapling and drop into the mound of leaves, as he and Sarah used to do. He swallowed his surge of longing for Sarah to be here as he helped the younger ones. After a few exhilarating rides, they carried burlap bags or rolled wheelbarrows of leaves to line the stalls for Tattoo, the two cows and Matilda, their nanny-goat.

When Adam suggested a Halloween party, Justin and Laurel agreed without realizing they were getting ready, again, to ruffle some feathers that had just gotten smoothed down. All the ball-game crowd came, plus some parents. Tubs for apple bobbing were on the porch off the big room. The favorite game was when the girls lined up behind sheets that had been strung from an arch in the big room, with only their feet showing. Each boy had to choose — from her feet — the girl he wanted to take for a walk. Since some of the girls had changed shoes and some had taken off their shoes, general confusion reigned with lots of yelling and laughter. Spin the bottle was almost as much fun because the boy got to kiss the girl the bottle pointed to. A kiss on the cheek, but still a kiss! They showed signs of staying all night until Justin tactfully reminded them it was time to go home. But, he did promise another party soon.

The next Sunday, Gussie Turner and her followers let Laurel know how they felt. Several women made it a point to pass in front of her with their noses in the air. Gussie, of course, couldn't resist having her say. "It looks like you're determined to be a bad influence on our young people. We heard about the boys and girls kissing and taking walks."

"Did a boy ever kiss you on the cheek, Gussie? In front of a crowd?" Laurel asked.

"Humph!" snorted Gussie as she hurried off.

That week Gussie let it be known, loud and clear, that trouble was ahead unless someone put a stop to the Worth family's activities. This time, however, she had some surprising opposition. The parents who had been at the Halloween party knew what they saw, and knew it was not as it was being portrayed. The community was divided into two camps and opinions bounced freely. Meanwhile, the Worth family — the unintentional initiators of the conflict — carried on with their lives.

The week after the Halloween party — and the aftermath — the family was eating supper when Laurel said, "I think we should have a special Thanksgiving celebration. We could invite Jed and Hannah, Nora, Ethan and Allison, Bulldog and Bess, Alice and Tom — and their children, of course. We could move the table into the big room and have a fire in the fireplace."

A chorus of "Yes! Yes!" coming from the children enveloped the table. Justin looked at Laurel with concern. "Do you think you're able?"

"Yes. Everybody will help with the dinner. I'm homesick to see everybody and some of them have never seen where we live now."

"I *would* like for all of us to be together again," Justin added.

So, it was decided and the word went out.

On Thanksgiving day the families who had lived and worked together for nine years in the logging camps gathered, with Ethan and Allison arriving first. They were immediately mobbed by the kids with hugs and questions. Ethan, who had been like a big brother for several years, gathered them close and whispered, "Let's go where we can talk without being bothered by any adults." They happily trouped off as the adults shook their heads and Allison said, "He's always happy to be with you."

"I hope so," Justin said, "since we're his family."

The other three families arrived together. The hugging, laughing, and teasing went on for a while, then everybody wanted to look over the new house and grounds. Finally, the women were able to get dinner on the table. After Justin had everyone gather around he said, "We're fortunate to have our own preacher in this family. Ethan, son, would you give thanks for our food and other blessings?"

Ethan's prayer included thanks for Laurel's life, for the love these families had for each other, for the special house that God had provided for Justin and Laurel. He prayed for Sarah, the only one missing, who would be homesick today. The women wiped their eyes on the corner of their aprons. Justin was determined not to pull out his handkerchief.

As the talk and laughter rose and fell around her, Laurel thought of that first logging camp: her desolation when she saw where they would live, her dread of working with people that were not of her class, her struggle with being totally consumed by the unending hard work of cooking for the families and the bunkhouse crew, her fear of what the primitive, isolated life would do to her children and to herself.

"Laurel," Hannah said, "you look like you're a thousand miles away. What are you thinking?"

"I'm remembering that first logging camp where I met all of you. I was scared and very angry at Justin. Then, the second morning we were there Nora walked in and started working her magic. When she took me to meet you, Hannah, I...I knew I was not alone."

Nora, Hannah's sister, was literally a giant of a woman. The victim of gigantism, she stood a head taller than the men, and her size matched her height. Laurel, in her mind, called Nora "Our Gentle Giant."

"What kind of magic did I work?" she now asked Laurel.

"Your no-nonsense, practical, gentle way of getting on with life, in spite of bad circumstances. You and Hannah pulled me along until I could get going on my own."

"Well, you sure got going and got the rest of us going," Hannah exclaimed. "You ain't never let us slow down since."

Bess, Bulldog Aiken's wife, grinned and said, "I wasn't much help that first year, was I?"

"No, Bess." Laurel smiled and shook her head. "When you arrived I wanted to leave all over again."

All the adults laughed as they remembered the sparks that flew between Bess and Laurel that first year. Until...until Joannie, their nine-year-old daughter, came down with diphtheria. Laurel quarantined herself with Bulldog and Bess and worked desperately to save her life. Joannie died, but Bess and Bulldog knew she had received the best loving care possible. After that, Laurel could do no wrong in Bess' eyes. They could have been sisters, the way they argued and loved each other.

"Then Alice and Tom arrived," Hannah said, "and we could tell Alice was expecting, so we all started mothering her."

"Yes, I was scared of everything, including my shadow. But you cured me of that."

"Yeah," Bess said, "since we joined up with each other, we've all been cured of one thing or another."

The talk moved on to their present circumstances. Jed's farming was going well, Bulldog and Tom were working together providing logs for a sawmill, and Ethan was pastor of a church. Justin told them about his new job.

"Thanks to all of you," Justin said, "we're here today in better circumstances than we've been for years. Laurel's getting stronger every day, we have this big house, and who knows what the future will bring for us!"

As if on cue, as they were finishing Nora's pumpkin pie and Laurel's egg custard, they heard footsteps running down the hall. Lila, from Terminal Town burst into the room, screaming, "Where's Miz Worth? My baby's real sick!" Her face was wet with sweat and her hair was flying. She held her baby tightly in her arms.

Bess reached her first and, gently, took the baby from her. Laurel went to her. "Lila, you're out of breath. Sit down here and drink some water."

"My baby," Lila repeated.

Bess and Hannah unwrapped the baby. They forcefully stifled their dismay. The beautiful baby girl in Bess' arms was dead.

Justin, seeing their expressions, said, "Ethan, would you and Allison take the children out. In fact, all of you young people need to leave." All the men except Justin left with them.

Lila took Laurel's hand and held on as if it were a lifeline. She was babbling and shaking with fright. "I shoulda brought her yesterday. She was havin' trouble breathin'. I don't know what it was. Can you help her get better? You got me better."

Laurel looked at Justin and he went to stand beside her as she faced her awful task.

Without taking her eyes off Lila, Laurel said, "Nora, could you get a warm washcloth and a hot cup of coffee?"

Bess walked around holding the baby as if it were asleep, but she had covered its face. Nobody seemed to move or even breathe as Lila washed her face and drank the coffee. She kept her eyes on Laurel, seeming oblivious to the others in the room. "Her name is Rose and she's six months old. We've got two boys but she's my only girl."

Then she straightened her shoulders, drew a deep breath, and said, "She's dead, ain't she?"

Laurel sat down in front of her and took both her hands. "Yes, Lila, she's dead. Do you want to tell me what happened?"

"She ain't acted like she felt good for a few days but I thought it was just a cold and she would get over it. I shoulda brought her sooner. What do you think it was that…that killed her?"

"Pneumonia, probably," Laurel said.

Lila asked, "Could I hold her a minute?"

Bess laid the bundle in Lila's arms. Everyone but Laurel and Justin left the room as Lila said goodbye to her baby girl. After she held her for a while, she looked at Laurel with her eyes full of anguish and guilt. "I have to tell you. I was drinkin' and…and I let my baby girl die." Justin took the little bundle as Lila collapsed into Laurel's arms.

Hannah laid the baby out in the corner bedroom and the other women helped Laurel get Lila to bed in another room.

She lay, wide-eyed, saying nothing while Nora wrapped hot flatirons in towels and put them to her feet. Bess sat down beside her and took her hand. "My only little girl died, too, Lila. She had diphtheria. I know how you're hurtin' right now."

Lila roused and asked, "Who are you?"

"I'm Bess Aiken and we worked with Justin and Laurel—Mr. And

Mrs. Worth—for nine years in logging camps. I'm a totally different person than when I met her. She told me about how much God loves me—and she showed me by her love. Let her help you, Lila. Listen to her."

Hope flared for a moment in Lila's eyes, then died as she said with flat certainty, "But God couldn't love me. I let my baby die."

"I can tell you for sure that He does. I did some bad things, too. But, He—and Laurel—loved me anyway. Now, I want you to rest awhile. You're worn out."

Jed rode to town to get Dr. Leighton, who confirmed the diagnosis of pneumonia, and Justin went to Terminal Town in search of Lila's husband, Brand. He found him sleeping off a drunk, not even aware that Lila and the baby were gone. Justin got him up, helped him wash his face with cold water and gave him some strong coffee to drink. Justin, then, went to find Mack and Gerta. He needed their help.

Justin's patience wore thin before they were able to make Brand understand that his baby was dead. Then, once he understood, it didn't seem to make much impact. When Justin asked him what they needed to do about a casket and the funeral, he said, "I ain't got no money for a casket and I don't know nothin' about funerals." Then he looked slyly at Justin and said, "If you give me a drink I might could think better."

Justin's anger spilled over. "Your baby is dead and all you can think about is a drink! Well, you're not going to get another drink anytime soon! Not until we know what to do about burying that beautiful baby girl named Rose!"

Brand struck back. "Who are you, comin' in here orderin' me around in my own house?"

"Do you remember Laurel Worth who doctored your wife back to health after somebody stabbed her in the back? Well, I'm her husband. Your wife came running into our house today carrying your dead baby in her arms. We're trying to do what has to be done, but you sure aren't much help!"

"I told you I don't know what to do," Brand whined irritably.

Justin had probably never wanted to hit a man as he itched to hit Brand. He turned, instead, to Mack and asked, "Can you find some good pine lumber around here that we can use to make a little casket?"

Mack nodded. "I'm sure I can. Where will you build it?"

"At my house. We have some friends there who can help me tonight."

"I'll get it and bring it over as soon as I can. And Gerta and me will find Brand's boys and take care of them 'til this is over."

"Thank you," Justin said as he left, not trusting himself to even look at Brand again.

Baby Rose may have been neglected in life, but she was not neglected in her burial preparations and her funeral. The casket, grievously tiny, was built with care by Justin, Jed, Bulldog, and Tom. Bess went back home just long enough to gather materials to line the casket and to make a white burial dress.

She announced to Laurel, as good friends do, "I'm stayin' with you 'til this is over. I'll take care of Lila. She and I understand each other." Then she added, "And this way I can see that you get some rest."

Ethan conducted the funeral with dignity and brevity. Most of the Terminal Town residents were there, plus a few of the established residents. Brand had a few drinks in him and looked warily at Justin, with never a word, when Lila thanked Justin for all he and Laurel and their friends had done for them.

That evening when the family gathered for supper, Alexis was missing. After they looked at each other a moment Adam said, "I bet she's in her tree. She's found on old oak down in the yard near the lake bed that has several branches growing out close together. It makes a comfortable place to sit and lean back. Go ahead and eat. I'll find her."

And there she was, with her face streaked from crying. Adam climbed up and sat down beside her. "Do you want to tell me what's the matter?"

"Adam, they put the baby in a box and put her in the ground."

"She died, Alexis."

"I didn't know babies die. I thought you had to be old to die."

Adam reached for her. "Come over here."

After she was settled in his lap, he asked gently, "Are you afraid that you might die?"

"Yes," she whispered. "I don't want to be put in the ground in a box."

"Alexis, you're going to live a long time and keep making everybody happy."

"Am I really?"

"Yes!" He hugged her. "And, now, let's go wash your face and eat supper."

Chapter Four

The greatest joy of Christmas was that Sarah came home—for a whole week! The family waited for her to get there before decorating the tree. Justin, Adam and David came in struggling proudly with a huge evergreen that would only fit into the big room. Popcorn ropes; paper chains made of red, green and white; prickly sycamore balls painted gold; and fragile colored glass ornaments soon adorned the tree, infusing the room with Christmas magic. Candles glowed on the mantle—in a bed of holly, turkey brush and pine cones. Adam sniffed and asked, "Sarah, what does that smell remind you of?"

"Our forest, of course. It's my favorite smell in all the world."

Christmas gifts were sparse until Sarah brought out her surprise. She had a gift for everyone. Laurel received an emerald green sweater that went just right with her auburn hair; Justin, a much-needed shirt and some Zane Grey books; Adam, a knife that had several blades like Justin's and a leather belt; Caroline, books and a hand mirror and comb; David, roller skates he could use in the long hall and big room; Alexis, a beautiful baby doll.

Laurel and Justin looked at each other, realizing she had probably spent all of her money, except what she had sent home, on these gifts. The happy faces and voices of their children helped them overcome their threatening emotions.

For Christmas dinner, the logging camp families came, of course. Among other things, they had to check up on Sarah. The newcomers this year were Lila and her boys, Vic, five years old and Ned, age three. In spite of Laurel's promise not to get heavily involved in taking care of people for a while, she couldn't forget Lila. She had learned that, following her baby's death, Lila had started trying to stop drinking, but this had only infuriated Brand, who was drinking or drunk most of the time. Laurel wanted them to have some kind of Christmas celebration. There were a few awkward moments after their arrival, but Bess gave her full attention to Lila, and David was soon talking a mile a minute to the two shy little boys. Laurel could relax. They were in good hands.

January brought a full-blown mountain winter. It was impossible to heat the big room comfortably, so for their winter family room, they moved into one of the bedrooms that had a fireplace. Justin moved the bed out to make room for the library table where the children gathered to study by the Aladdin lamp. Laurel's and Justin's rocking chairs were placed on each side of the fireplace. Since they had no extra sofa, Laurel covered a metal cot with a brightly colored quilt and propped pillows along the wall.

At night, with Justin resting while he read his "western," the children doing homework and Alexis pretending she was doing hers, Laurel mended or cut quilt squares or, sometimes, read. She started the custom of reading a Bible story just before bedtime. After several stories, Adam said, "Mama, I would rather you *tell* us those stories. Your stories are better than that book."

Laurel took the job seriously. She studied to get her facts straight, then plowed into exciting narrations of Abraham or Moses or Elijah or Jesus and the disciples. Even Justin had to stop reading and listen. Since he had never been to church with her, he had never heard her teach a Bible class. One night after a particularly riveting account of Elijah calling down fire on Mount Carmel to consume his sacrifice to the true God, ridiculing the prophets of Baal, whose god couldn't perform, Justin's admiration was evident. "Now I understand why the families in the logging camp braved that trestle and primitive conditions to sit in the box car, Sunday after Sunday! I don't think our children will ever think the Bible is boring."

The family settled into a pleasant routine. Caroline, after the initial shock of Sarah's absence and the realization of her new responsibilities, found she liked her new place of importance. She had sometimes felt almost invisible, between the two older and the two younger ones. Now she was definitely needed and noticed! She played dolls with Alexis; enjoyed learning to cook; and she still looked after David, who was beginning to rebel against her bossiness. She, more than any of the others, loved to read.

David, meanwhile, was happiest when he was with *his animals* — as he called them. Tattoo was everybody's favorite. When David rode him bareback, Tattoo seemed to know just how fast to go to satisfy an adventurous boy and how slow to go to keep him from falling off. After Laurel saw Tattoo slide to a sudden stop, in spite of David's "Giddy-up," just in front of a threatening empty clothes line, she stopped worrying. With Tattoo's record, he could certainly be trusted with a seven-year-old boy.

Chief, their tan and white, long-haired collie-shepherd, left no illusions as to who was really in charge of the place. The other animals instinctively knew he was boss. Among other skills, he knew how to herd a stubborn cow into the barn or a squealing pig into the pen. He would scout around with his long nose in the air until he was satisfied there were no enemies he needed to fend off. His vigilance would prove to save lives several times over.

But Matilda, the high-stepping white nanny-goat, belonged exclusively to David. Or, more accurately, David belonged to her. She had adopted David soon after Justin brought her home as payment for a picture debt. Cantankerous with everybody else, David could milk her, harness her to a little wagon and talk her into pulling Alexis, or coax her into shedding her dignity and romping with him.

One night after a satisfying ride on Tattoo, David interrupted the quietness.

"Mama, will Tattoo and Chief and Matilda be in heaven?"

Laurel looked at David as everybody else looked at her.

"I don't think so, son. I believe God created only people to live forever like Him."

"Then I don't want to go!"

Shocked, Caroline scolded, "Of course, you want to go to heaven, David! We're all going to be there!"

Justin looked up from his book and Laurel saw the play of emotions on his face: amusement...uncertainty...realization...

Adam, looking at David's stubborn face, comforted him. "Caro's right, David. As long as we're all there together, we'll be happy!"

Justin, hearing his children's earnest voices, kept his eyes riveted on his book, but not reading a word.

In March Justin bought a 1932 Chevrolet truck. He told Laurel he needed it for two reasons: his logging *and* his farming. Since their property had only enough room for a large garden, Laurel waited for him to explain. He had been to see Mrs. Thatcher, another widow, and had discussed share-cropping some good farming land.

"And, before you ask, my dear, this widow does not have grown, drunken sons. She has two highly respectable daughters who are married and live far away from here."

"Thank you, sir! I *was* going to ask! But, how can you do your logging job and farm, too?"

"Laurel, I'll *have* to do both if we plan to have enough food and clothes. I'll work it out. I may have to hire another man to help with the cordwood during the summer months. That way my helpers could use the truck while I take Tattoo to the field with me. Tattoo can't hold up to both jobs. He's getting old." He paused and rubbed his hand across his tired eyes. "The boys will help me in the fields and I can hire help for ten cents an hour, if necessary."

Laurel seldom saw any gesture of fatigue from him. She hugged him close and said, "I hope you'll take as good care of yourself as you do Tattoo."

The family was overjoyed in June when Sarah returned home to work in the newly-opened paper mill in Deerbrook. She and Adam soon initiated a full round of activities for the young people of Lake Eagle Rest. Besides the Sunday afternoon ball games, there were picnics and parties. After Adam took Justin to check out a swimming hole in the river that ran through the lake bed, swimming was added to the list.

Laurel braced herself for Gussie's attack at church on Sunday, and it came laced with more acid than usual. "Do you really want to be responsible for our young people going straight to hell! Boys and girls swimming together, nearly naked!"

"But they aren't nearly naked! Most of them don't own swim suits so they wear cut-off pants and shirts or blouses — the same thing they would wear to hoe corn."

Gussie, who never listened to common sense and who had to have the last word, sailed off with the parting shot, "It's a shame you ever moved here!"

Laurel, meanwhile, enjoyed the young people trouping through the house. *Space,* she thought, *is such a gift! They have room to have fun inside and outside!*

She expressed this thought to one of the parents who supported their activities with the young people. The mother answered, "Yes, the space in and around this house is wonderful, but the space in yours and Justin's hearts is even greater."

Laurel smiled at her. "That's a balm for Gussie's words."

"Oh! Don't pay no attention to Gussie! My husband says she looks like she has a sour pickle in her mouth all the time."

The next week at supper, Adam said, "Daddy, if we get our quota of work done in the fields, could we go camping Friday night? I need to get the feel of the woods again."

Justin looked pleased. "Who wants to go camping?"

A babble of voices answered. It seemed everybody did!

"Laurel, would it be too hard to get it together?"

"No. Everybody can help. And I would love it, too."

Their campsite was perfect—surrounded by trees, mostly pine, so there was a carpet of pine needles. A river was close by with a waterfall within hearing distance.

As soon as camp was set up and the fire going, Laurel and the girls started cooking supper while Justin and the boys gathered wood and, with Chief's help, scouted out their surroundings.

Fried potatoes and pork 'n' beans seemed like a feast. Adam held up a pine needle he picked out of his potatoes. "Is this what makes them so good?" Laurel's gingerbread finished off the meal.

Justin enlisted David's reluctant help in tying Chief to a tree near the family. "But, Daddy, he's not going to like it. He's never been tied up."

"It's better than getting mauled by a bear or a mountain lion. If he smells one, he'll feel honor bound to defend us. We're in their territory now, so we'll restrain him.

"And," he added, as he saw the others listening, "we don't need to be afraid. The animals are more wary of us than we are of them."

The campfire created a circle of light and warmth and security within the velvety blackness around them. "Daddy," David asked, "why does the fire make me all warm *inside*, too?"

"It's the forest *and* the fire, son. Listen to the night music. The river makes the melody. Now, let's listen to the accompaniment." Everybody sat perfectly still as Justin asked, "What do you hear?"

Quietly, they identified crickets, bullfrogs, hoot owls, and the popping fire. "It's the orchestra of the forest," Justin added. "There's no sweeter music in all the world. It warms your heart."

Justin, at Adam's request, launched into one of his ghost stories. At the scariest part, a scream, nearby, pierced the darkness. Chief growled and strained at his rope. Startled, the children scurried close to Justin, who sat placidly with a grin on his face. "It's just a mountain lion, sounding quite proprietary!"

"What does that mean?" asked Adam, a little embarrassed by his reaction. He had been out of the forest too long.

"It means he wants us to know we're in his territory and we're here on his hospitality."

Alexis had had enough talk. She tugged at her daddy to sit with a big tree at his back, then she climbed into his lap and cuddled. "Now, *nothing* can hurt me, can it, Daddy?"

Justin held her close and rubbed her hair. "No, punkin', nothing can hurt you when you're in your daddy's lap."

After he finished the story, they settled down, their bedrolls close together. After everybody was asleep, Justin piled the wood high on the fire and whispered to Chief, "Let me know if that cat comes close." Having been attacked by one several years before, he wasn't quite as easy in his mind as he had pretended to his family. He would keep that fire high all night.

The next day was spent playing in the river and soaking up the atmosphere of the forest. Justin gave each of them an assignment. They were to spend some time alone, just enjoying the forest, then to be ready to tell about it when they got home.

That night, just before going to their comfortable beds, with safe walls around them, they each shared enough experiences to satisfy Justin's determination that his children would grow up to cherish the nature around them. Sarah voiced everybody's feelings by asking, "When can we go again?"

Summer was a time of intensified work for everybody. Justin and the boys were in the fields early each day, carrying a lunch so they didn't have to waste time. Justin had bought a mule named "Stub" for a very low price and soon understood the name and the price. While Adam was making good time, plowing with Tattoo, Justin was prodding the mule along, with more stops than starts. Chief was the only authority Stub recognized, and that was because Chief applied a little pain. He would duck under the single-tree for protection and nip at Stub's heels. One day Chief abandoned caution, went over the single-tree and nipped. When Stub gave a good mule kick that caught Chief solid on the forehead, Chief collapsed like a bag of meal. Justin pulled him off the single-tree and called the boys. David fell down on his knees, crying, and started rubbing Chief and hugging him. "Is he dead, Daddy?"

"Let me examine him, son." He felt for a pulse and tried to tell if he was breathing. There seemed to be no sign of life.

David, sobbing aloud, jumped up, jerked Stub's bridle and yelled, "If Chief's dead, I'll shoot you right between the eyes, you dumb mule!"

Adam looked at Justin to see how he would react to such behavior. Justin held David's shaking body close and said, "Let's wait a few minutes, David. Chief's pretty hard-headed. I think he's just knocked out."

Chief lay motionless, and seemingly lifeless, while the three watched him. Justin and Adam had walked away a few feet when David yelled, "Daddy! I think his tail moved!"

As they looked, it moved, then moved again! Soon it was wagging!

David was crying all over again and smothering him with hugs. Justin said, "Son, move and let him get his breath and get his eyes open!"

They carried him to the shade and gave him water. Justin told David to watch him closely and, if there was any change, to call him or Adam. "He may have a concussion. That means his brain might swell some. So, he needs to rest a while."

Adam, meanwhile, had a talk with Stub. "You try that again and you'll be going to the glue factory, you troublemaker!"

Stub must have realized he was on probation. He cooperated the rest of the day.

"I never saw a family work so hard and play so hard!" commented one old-timer in the community. When they weren't busy in the fields, the children found other means of working.

Adam hired on to deliver the weekly paper, *The Grit*. He made the hefty sum of fifty cents a week. David and Caroline picked berries and sold them to the summer people for ten cents a gallon.

It may have been because of so much activity whirling around her most of the time that Alexis enjoyed playing alone. One of her favorite places was a playhouse that Caroline had helped her build under a tree at the lower edge of the yard. The roots that ran along the top of the ground separated the rooms in her house. It seemed an ideal, safe place. However, one afternoon as the family was coming in for supper, Alexis' screams and Chief's fierce growls catapulted them out the door to reach her. A fearsome sight froze them in their tracks. Only Justin moved — fast! Just a few feet from Alexis, Chief had hold of a long snake just below the head and was violently shaking it. The snake's body was lashing out in all directions. Deep, continuous growls expressed Chief's fury. Justin grabbed Alexis, who was frozen with fear, and left Chief to his task. As soon as Justin handed Alexis to Laurel, Adam handed Justin a gun.

Justin and the boys watched Chief's struggle; Justin was ready to shoot, if necessary. However, when Chief laid down his enemy at Justin's feet, the battle was over.

"It's a rattler — at least five feet long," Justin said. He quickly dropped beside Chief and examined his face and head. "Adam and David, help me examine him all over. Look for two little marks, close together. The snake could have bitten him before he got hold of it."

No marks were found and Chief had to submit to hugs and rubs and praise from the entire Worth family. "You're the bravest and smartest dog in the world," David told him.

Laurel wrapped Alexis in a warm blanket, held her close and rocked her until the stiffness and the dazed look were gone. Shivering, the aftermath of shock, loosened her tears, which Laurel took as a good sign. Some warm milk and Laurel's arms secure around her lulled her to sleep. Laurel looked at the anxious faces around her. "Sleep is the best healer. Maybe she can talk about it tomorrow."

That night in bed, Laurel shivered and said, "Death came close today."

Justin gathered her close to comfort himself as much as her. "We owe Chief a debt of gratitude we'll never be able to pay. We'll all need to be careful during snake season. But we know now that our children have a protector."

For the next couple of days, they stayed close and kept track of each other, especially Alexis. Everybody was subdued. The serpent had entered their Eden.

Laurel knew that, for her physical and spiritual health, she must have a quiet, restful time each day. Usually, it was in the afternoon before she started supper. Her chosen place was the porch facing the lake bed and the mountains beyond. One afternoon in July, as she allowed herself to be wrapped in the beauty around her and warmed by the western sun, her thoughts gave word to her feeling of contentment: *Summer time in the mountains...the fulfillment of winter's waiting and spring's promise...nature's season of full maturity. Flowers in full bloom, trees robed in lush green, warmth from the kiss of the sun, which lingered longer these days, as if enjoying the lavish annual pageantry. Long, full days unhampered by cold.*

Not unlike us, she thought. *Our springtime of waiting – new growth – promise – so much to learn. Then our summer of maturity and fulfillment – of working out our destiny.*

We're in the late summer of our lives – Justin and I. Soon we'll be heading toward autumn where we hope to see the harvest of our lives. Winter will eventually come to us. But, in the forest, we learned the value of all the seasons, so we don't need to dread any of them.

Her thoughts brought her to the great desire of her life: for Justin to become a Christian.

He was the best man she had ever known, besides her Papa, but she was aware of the great, unresolved conflict within him, intensified by her miraculous escape from death. Her prayer about Justin had changed since her near-death experience. Now, instead of begging and hoping, she claimed God's promise, *"Whatsoever thing you pray for and ask, believe you receive it, and it shall be granted to you."*

It was a new, exciting truth! Believe that you have it before you receive it. Claiming in advance of an answer. She had a *knowing* in her heart that, in God's timing, Justin would come into the Kingdom. She thanked God every day that this was going to happen. She was also fully convinced that God had a unique work planned for them to do together. One of the greatest lessons she had learned in the crucible was to give a problem to God and leave it there. She, all her life, had been prone to run ahead and open doors on her own. She was learning to leave the doors closed until God opened them. Her absolute trust in the goodness of God was the highway upon which she walked through her daily life and work.

At supper one cool night in September, Caroline asked, "Mama, are raw turnips good for you?"

"I think they would be better cooked. Why?"

"There's this girl in my class who eats raw turnips for lunch every day. She says they're good for you, but I can tell by the way she looks at my food that she's hungry. Today I gave her half of my fried apple pie. I wondered if I could take her something to eat tomorrow."

David spoke up, "Yeah. Some people in my class don't have much to eat either. One boy brings just a hunk of cornbread — and eats it by itself — almost every day. A girl who sits by me brings a tin pail of cold gravy. It looks real greasy. I don't know how she eats it."

Justin and Laurel looked at each other. Justin asked, "Laurel, could you send some extra food tomorrow?"

Instead of two lunches, she packed four. But, that wasn't enough. Caroline and David reported that several children were eyeing the extra food hungrily as they gave it away.

"What can we do, Mama? We can't carry enough food for all of them," David asked.

That night in bed, Laurel said, "I think I need to go to the school and try to find out about those hungry children. Is that OK with you?"

Justin pulled her close. "I knew this was coming by the expression on your face the other night. And you know it's fine with me. We can't let children where we live go hungry as long as we have any food." He laughed and added, "I know my woman!"

"And I know my man! You work hard for that food."

"We have enough to share."

The next day, Laurel and Alexis walked to the school after school was out. Laurel introduced herself to the teachers, telling them she had taught school several years ago and had taught the children in their logging camps.

The teacher, who also served as principal, said, "Oh, yes, we've heard about you. What can we do for you?"

"My children tell me that many of your students don't bring adequate lunches. They seem hungry. I wonder if you know about how many there are."

The teachers looked at each other. They agreed that about half of the students were in need of more food.

"How long has it been since you had hot lunches?" Laurel asked.

"Since soon after the Depression hit. People haven't had cash to pay for school lunches."

"Could you show me the lunch room?"

Both teachers accompanied her to the large room. "You can see we have tables and benches, the serving counter, a stove, sink, pots, pans, and dishes. Everything but food — and money to pay for the food and the workers."

Laurel's optimism took over. Her excitement flowed through her words. "This lunchroom could be scrubbed and put in operation in a few days! The children in this community could have a hot, nourishing lunch. At least one good meal a day!"

"But...how...?" The principal opened her hands, palms up, to express her frustration.

"I don't know *how* yet, but I believe this community can do it if we work together."

The quieter teacher spoke up. "I *am* worried about some of the children. They don't have enough to eat, or the right things to eat. You can tell by looking at them and the listless way they behave."

"Yes, hunger is a breeding ground for disease and can prejudice their future health. We must do what we can. I need to check out some things, then I'll be back in touch. Let's agree not to talk about this to anybody until we see if we can do it."

Laurel went to Deerbrook the next morning to see Erica Matthews at the courthouse. As clerk of court, she usually knew what was going on in the county — and in the government. She had been a staunch supporter of Laurel in the Women's Suffrage Movement years before.

After they had caught up on news about each other, Erica gave Alexis a piece of candy, sat back and said to Laurel, "I know you have something on your mind. Let me hear it."

"I was reading about the government commodities program last week. Does Wildwood County receive commodities?"

"No. But we haven't applied."

"Could you help me apply?"

Erica laughed. "I might. If you'll start at the beginning and tell me what you plan to use them for."

As she listened, she sat quietly holding the ends of her fingers together like steeples. She didn't even have to think about it. "Yes, I'll help you. I think it's a wonderful idea!"

Then she stopped and looked Laurel up and down. "Are you sure you're able to take this on? It'll take a lot of work."

"Yes. I'm able. It's been well over a year since my surgery."

"Okay, let's look at the application papers and see what kind of information we have to give." While they worked, Alexis sat on the floor in the corner and colored some pictures with her new crayons Laurel had bought before they came in.

An hour later, they were on their way to the county school office where Laurel received satisfactory answers to her questions. She realized she had her work cut out for her. This would have to be a community affair and she wondered if the community would cooperate. They were still considered newcomers by the old-timers, and their beliefs and behavior had stretched the parameters of community convention to an uncomfortable tension. She knew that there were two camps of thought in the community about what to do with the Worths.

Justin will know what to do, she thought. *He's a very persuasive man.*

After talking it through, they decided the quickest way to get the word out was for Laurel to make an announcement at church on Sunday. She would tell them just enough to get their curiosity up and ask everyone who was interested in a hot lunch program to meet at the Worth house on Monday night.

Most of the people from the church showed up, plus some families who didn't go to church. Both of the teachers were there. Some people sat on the floor and others stood around the walls. The huge fire crackled and popped and cast a warm glow over the group. Lamps added plenty of light.

After everyone was settled, Justin welcomed them. "I've met most of you by now, at our ball games or around the community. We welcome you to our home and hope this will be the first of many times we can use this room for community events. You've lived here a long time and are the leaders in the community. My wife and I are newcomers and we're not here to tell you what to do. We'll all need to work together to accomplish our goals for our children. Let's hear what Laurel has found out about a hot lunch program."

He's made it easy for me, she thought, as she stood to speak. She just needed to give the facts.

"We can apply for government commodities which include staples such as flour, meal, sugar, salt, shortening, dried beans, macaroni and rice. Some vegetables are available in cans. We can even get cheese and margarine."

"Are you sure this is free? Can they come back and charge us for it?"

"Yes, it's free. It's one way the government is helping people get through the Depression."

"I don't much like the idea of accepting hand-outs. I ain't never done that in my life," spoke up a man near Justin. From the murmurs and nods around the room, Laurel knew he had struck a nerve.

"What's your name?"

"Wayne Marshall, ma'am."

"Mr. Marshall, I know how proud and tough mountain people are. The rest of the country could learn a lot about survival from us. And I know that most of us here tonight probably have enough food to get by. But there are children in our community who are hungry and we must do our part to help them. In addition to the government commodities, the school board will pay two workers and provide limited funds to buy food. The men of the community may need to provide wood for the cook stove, but we'll talk about those details later."

"Will there be any charge for the lunches?"

"Yes. We have to charge a minimum of five cents a meal. I know many families don't have that kind of money now, so I plan to talk to some people who might pay for their children. We can't let even one child go hungry."

"How many children are we lookin' at feedin'?" Wayne asked.

Laurel turned to the teachers. "What is your enrollment?"

"Seventy-six students. About half of them will probably need help in paying for their lunches."

Laurel waited a moment, then said, "We need to decide tonight if we're willing, as a community, to try this."

After a brief silence, Wayne Marshall stood and said, "I'm willin' to try it. Mrs. Worth has already got us a lot of help and I think we can do the rest. I'd be ashamed to live in a community that let children go hungry."

That created a hubbub of comments, all favorable.

"We need to scrub out the lunch room and wash the utensils and dishes. If you can help, see me and the teachers after this meeting and we'll set up a time."

Everybody stayed awhile and visited, excited and proud to a part of this venture. After they were gone, Justin hugged Laurel to him in front of the fire and said, "Well, you haven't lost your touch. You've hooked 'em and they'll do right by this. Reminds me of when you got the logging crew to build those outhouses."

The children looked on, grinning, as she kissed him. "You charmed them into cooperating tonight before I said a word."

Laurel dressed carefully for her next appointment about the school lunches. She hadn't had a new dress for about four years, so her one remaining Sunday skirt and blouse would have to serve. She was thankful for her new green sweater. It gave her just the touch of confidence that she was suitably dressed.

She was going to call on Mrs. Winfield, a wealthy woman with an estate that had been built during the years when Lake Eagle Rest was an exclusive resort. She was the only one of the original residents around the lake who still chose to live there year-round. Laurel had sent a note asking if she could visit, to get acquainted and to discuss some important community matters. Mrs. Winfield's reply had invited her to lunch. Caroline would come home early from school to keep Alexis.

The Winfield estate was a mansion that fitted beautifully into its surroundings. The builders had allowed the lay of the land to dictate the flow of the house, resulting in several levels that hugged the knoll on which it sat. The mountain range rose behind and partially around it on each side.

Mrs. Winfield had a small table set in the library before a warm fire in the fireplace. Laurel looked at the elegant room surrounded by bookshelves to the ceiling, with a rolling ladder that gave access to the hundreds of beautifully bound books. She was surprised that she could look on this without envy. She knew now that she would never have the outer trappings, the material goods, that signified success. They would probably never even own a home. Parallel with that realization came the absolute knowledge that she had everything that mattered. Intact! She was unaware that her inner peace broke through to show on her face and in her manner.

The two women got acquainted while they ate. Mrs. Winfield let Laurel know she had heard of their Sunday afternoon ball games, parties, and about her visits to Terminal Town. Some of the local people worked for her and obviously had kept her up to date on the happenings in the community.

After lunch, over coffee, Laurel briefly told the facts about the proposed hot lunch program and finished by saying, "We have only one area of need not covered. Many of the children in the community can't afford to pay a nickel a day for their lunch. I came to see if you could provide lunch for them."

Mrs. Winfield had never had a request put to her straighter. People usually flattered her or floundered around with a lot of nervous talking before getting to the point. She liked this woman and her approach.

"How much do you need?"

"Ten dollars a week would pay for forty children to eat a hot, nourishing meal every day. I don't have the exact count yet of the children who need help. You know how proud most of these people are. It will take some tact and diplomacy to get them to accept help."

"You've taken on a hard task, Mrs. Worth. I appreciate your efforts and I will contribute ten dollars a week to the lunch program."

"I can give you a list of the children who you'll be helping, or at least the number. If ten dollars is more than I need..."

Mrs. Winfield interrupted. "Use any extra for unexpected expenses or for a treat for the children now and then. And, no, I don't need a list. You have enough to do. Just drop me a note or I would prefer that you come back for lunch once a month and give me an update on the success of the program."

As Laurel walked home, she made tentative plans for opening the lunchroom by the first of November, happily unaware that Gussie was out in the community working hard to undermine her efforts.

Chapter Five

In setting up the Hot Lunch Program, Laurel had asked some mothers in the community to visit the homes of the children who would need free lunches. They were asked to explain the program to the parents and to tell them that the lunches would start the first of November. One afternoon as she was working on orders for the lunchroom commodities, two of the mothers showed up, considerably upset. Gussie Turner, they said, had been visiting the homes of the pupils who needed help in paying for lunches. Gussie had reminded the needy families that it was not the mountain way to accept hand-outs, that everybody would look down on them if they let somebody else pay for their children's lunches. Most of the mothers disagreed, wanting their children to have at least one good meal a day, but many of the men were shamed into refusing the nickel a day per child. Only a few families had agreed to sign up for their children to eat free.

Laurel was so disgusted and angry with Gussie, she knew she couldn't trust herself to talk about it in a proper manner to these women. She thanked them, asked them for their lists and told them she would check on the families.

As soon as Justin got home, she poured out the story, asking, "Justin, why wouldn't she want hungry children to be fed?"

"Honey, this is not about the children. Gussie considers herself to be the leader of the women in this community. You are a threat to her, so she'll fight you any way she can. Even if it means children will go hungry."

Laurel's indignation, laced with a good dose of anger, was almost tangible to Justin as she paced the room. "But these children are suffering. Their growth will be stunted, they probably already have rickets, they're more susceptible to diseases, and nobody knows all the other effects of hunger."

She drew herself up to her resolute five-foot-four and declared, "Justin, she's not going to stop this program! I'll fight her over it!"

"Your ire and fire already told me that, honey," he answered dryly, not daring to smile. "I agree and I'm going to help you. But we have to have a plan. Let me give it some thought."

She knew that good physical labor would help her get over her anger so she worked steadily for the next hour. Then she knew she was ready to pray about it and ask God to guide them in their efforts to unsnarl this tangle Gussie had created. She asked that He help them use their energies toward finding a solution for the children, rather than focus on Gussie.

When the family was settled for the night, Laurel was ready to talk with Justin, using her head rather than her spleen. Justin got right to the point. "I think this is a case where men need to talk to men. You women have been doing your part. Now we need to do ours."

As she sat waiting, the firelight playing over her face, he continued, "I'll get Wayne Marshall and some of the other men who support this program to help me. We'll talk to the dads who wouldn't sign up their children."

"Oh, yes! That makes a lot of sense. Do you think you can convince them?"

"Straight men talk can be very convincing, Laurel."

She knew the matter was as good as settled. Justin would make it right. She got up and hugged him. "You're a good man, Justin Worth."

"Not necessarily," he said, grinning. "I'm trying to keep you from tarring and feathering a certain woman in the neighborhood."

They both laughed like kids, thinking how Gussie would look decked out in tar and feathers.

A week later, Justin handed her the list, with scribbles by each name. "All signed up, m'dear. Not a single hold-out."

"Justin, how…?"

"Different things. We made some deals with most of the dads. One is going to bring an occasional bushel of turnips, another some meal for cornbread, another a jug of molasses and so on. Several will provide wood for the cook stove. Two mothers will go and scrub the floors of the lunchroom once a week. Of course, you'll have to get all this organized."

Laurel felt the sting of tears and she sat down, putting her head in her hands. He understood and caressed her bowed head.

When she could speak, she said, "You helped them keep their pride."

"Mostly. Anyway, we worked it out. All the children will be fed."

He didn't think it was necessary to tell her the way he worked it out with a hard-head whose children were obviously sick from hunger. When the man wouldn't listen to reason about what hunger was doing to his family, Justin lost his patience and changed his tactic to one he knew the mountaineer would understand.

"I'm going to see to it that your children are fed! Now, if you don't sign that paper willingly, I'm going to fight you until you're ready to sign."

The man looked at Justin, astonished and confused. He dropped his head and swallowed. "You're willin' to fight me so I'll let my *own* kids eat at that lunchroom — free."

"Yes. I'm not leaving here without your signature — unless I'm carried off!"

"Well, I've finally met a man as stubborn as I am. I ain't goin' to fight you over my kids gettin' fed. Show me where to make my mark on that paper. I never learned no writin'."

Justin suddenly knew he couldn't just go, leaving this man stripped of his dignity.

He asked, "Have you ever worked around holding ponds or sawmills?"

"I've worked a little in timber," he said eagerly. "I'm sure I could learn."

"Meet me tomorrow morning at the sawmill in Terminal Town. I'm going to ask Mr. Bradford to give you a job."

The hope that flared in his eyes and the way he straightened himself and offered his hand strengthened Justin's resolve that this man would get a job, one way or another.

On the first day of November, 1936, the Hot Lunch Program at Lake Eagle Rest Elementary School was launched. Every child in school ate a nourishing lunch. Laurel and some of her faithful helpers were there to enjoy the sight.

That night at supper Laurel said, "I think Papa was smiling on us today. He would be very pleased."

It was the first time in awhile that she had mentioned her papa and it always touched Justin's heart. He said, "I'm sure he was, honey. I'm proud of you and I know some other people around this table are, too!"

She received hugs and kisses and comments from all the children. David closed the subject when he put it in a little boy's perspective. "I'm glad I can eat lunch now without feeling guilty."

When Laurel received a note from Erica Matthews, the clerk of court, asking if she could come to see her, she wondered if a difficulty had developed in receiving the commodities. When she walked in, Erica couldn't contain her excitement. She burst forth. "I've got a job for you! And you're the perfect person for it. You can't say no."

Laurel laughed and sat down. "I might not say no if you'll back up and tell me what it is."

"The Civilian Conservation Corps Camp—called the CCC Camp—in Pisgah Forest, needs a teacher. Many of the boys there can't read or write and those who can need further schooling. Could you take the job?"

"Slow down, Erica. I need to know some more facts. Tell me about the job."

"From what I can tell, the men will rotate in groups for classes. Of course, their primary purpose in being there is to work, but the 'powers that be' see this as a good opportunity to teach them some skills that will give them a better future. It will be basic schooling, you know, reading, writing, and arithmetic. A nurse has already been hired to teach first aid in caring for accident victims. You would work together. The CCC van will pick you up and take you home." She paused. "Frankly, Laurel, I'm a little nervous. Several women have applied for the job but you are, by far, the most qualified."

"When do you need an answer?"

"Tomorrow."

Laurel rose. "I'll talk to Justin about it and let you know in the morning. And, Erica, thank you for offering me the job."

That night Laurel and Justin included Sarah and Adam in discussing the pros and cons of her going to work. It would ease their financial straits, but they all knew it would affect the entire family. After Laurel assured them, on Dr. Leighton's authority, that she was fully recuperated and ready to assume her normal pace, their next greatest concern was Alexis. Who would take care of her?

Sarah came up with a ready-made solution. Her good friend, Molly West, who lived in a remote area of the county, needed a job.

"She would need to live with us during the week," Sarah said. "That way she could help some with the housework. I could pay her a little extra from my check. She could start supper and do some of the routine stuff."

Adam looked a little worried. "We'll have to make sure she knows how to take good care of Alexis."

Justin could sense Laurel's pent-up excitement. A part of him would like for her to always be at home; always available to him and the children. He liked coming in—for whatever reason—and talking over a mundane problem or just being with her. Her calmness and common sense would transmit to him, sometimes without specific words being spoken. Then he would be on his way again—comforted, grounded, focused.

Because he was a fair man, he also realized he was married to a woman of unusual vision and compassion, with the ability and pragmatism to implement her vision. She was a wife and mother, but she was more. She was an agent of change on behalf of the unfortunate, as her papa had been. He knew she needed to do this for her own fulfillment as much as for the good she would accomplish among the CCC men.

The details were soon worked out. Molly came a few days before Laurel started work so Alexis could adjust to her. Sarah prepared Molly for the job by telling her Alexis' favorite things to play. A very serious Adam surprised Molly by instructing her about what Alexis couldn't do. By the time Caroline and David added their concerns, Laurel said to Molly, "I don't think there's much else to say. As you can see, she's everybody's child."

Molly looked her straight in the eye and promised, "I'll take good care of her, Mrs. Worth."

Alexis automatically assumed, because of experience, that everybody loved her. She was content and excited to add Molly to that list. They would get along fine.

The night before Laurel was to start work, Sarah said, "I understand that Mama's work with the CCC Camp will be part of Roosevelt's New Deal. Daddy, what does that mean? Today at work the people were talking about Roosevelt's alphabet soup. It's confusing."

"Well, let me try to make it simple. The Depression—and you know by now what the Depression is—anyway, it started when Herbert Hoover was President. Since neither he nor the country could stop the slide, he was blamed for it. In 1932 the country voted in Franklin D. Roosevelt, who promised the country a 'New Deal.' He has made some sweeping social changes, emergency type programs, to help Americans get back on their feet, financially."

"What kind of programs?" Adam asked.

"One is the Civilian Conservation Corps Camps, like the one in Pisgah Forest where your mother will be teaching. These camps are set up all around the country for young men to work on projects that need doing anyway such as building roads, bridges, fire towers, and doing some flood control. The boys make about thirty dollars a month, I believe, and have their room and board provided, so they can send money home to their families."

"How old are the boys? Maybe I could work there," Adam said.

"Usually between eighteen and twenty-five, I think. You're not old enough yet, and your job, young man, is to finish high school." Adam understood that tone of voice.

"Another program the President started is the WPA—Works Progress Administration—which has created jobs for millions of men. They build roads from farms to markets, where none existed before. They build schools, hospitals, libraries and gymnasiums. They have a project close to us, too. They're building the Blue Ridge Parkway, a road that runs along the top of the Great Smoky Mountains.

"The CCC and WPA have helped keep many people from starving. Most mountain people would starve before they would go on the dole. These jobs have helped them survive *and* keep their self-respect."

The children had all listened intently. David asked, "But, Daddy, what about the soup with ABCs in it?"

Justin laughed. "All of the programs are known by their initials. I've just told you about two of them. There are many others, but we'll talk about them another night. I think it's time for homework."

Sarah got up to start clearing the table. "*Now* I'll know what people are talking about." She hugged her daddy before she picked up his plate.

Unexpected sights and sounds greeted Laurel when she first stepped into the CCC classroom. In the midst of much laughter and joking, half of the men were lying on the floor on their stomachs; the other half were on their knees straddled over the prone men, pushing on their mid-sections, urging them to breathe. Laurel stood in the door, absorbing the scene, as the instructor, in perpetual motion, seemed to be everywhere at once, demonstrating, suggesting, encouraging. It was like trying to take a picture of someone who wouldn't stay still. She was tall and thin with salt and pepper hair, cut in a bob with bangs.

After announcing a break, she walked over to Laurel and thrust out her hand. "Abigail Sinclair. My friends call me Abby. And you are Laurel Worth."

Laurel nodded. "I'm happy to meet you. The men seem to be enjoying this class."

"Oh, yes. Artificial respiration class is always fun — but they know it's also serious. Can be a matter of life or death." She rushed on. "I've heard about you from Erica, and Dr. Leighton told me about you *and* your husband. I'm looking forward to working with you."

Laurel edged in a few words. "I can already tell I'll enjoy working with you, from the enthusiasm in this class."

"We'll get better acquainted later," Miss Abby said as she turned and marshaled the men into position, changing the victims for the second half of the class. As she watched her, Laurel thought, *She's not physically attractive but there's so much enthusiasm pouring out, you don't notice her looks after first glance.*

When it was over Abby hurriedly introduced Laurel, saying,

"Mrs. Worth will teach you skills that you'll use every day and not just in emergencies." And she was out the door on her way to her next job — at the hospital.

Laurel, feeling somewhat as if a whirlwind had just passed through, realized that the next few minutes could make or break her acceptance by this group of taciturn, watchful, waiting young men in their work clothes and brogans.

"When we drove into the forest this morning, I felt like I was coming home. Our family lived near here in a logging camp that my husband managed. I have a lot of memories of the forest. One I will never forget is jumping into that whitewater just above Laughing Falls."

One young man interrupted, "But, ma'am, why did you do that? Cain't nobody git outta that water."

"My baby was in the river. I had to save him."

She had their full attention now.

"The wagon we were going to church in ran a wheel off the edge of the old bridge and my baby boy was bounced out into the river. I jumped off the bridge downstream to try to save him."

Nobody seemed to be breathing. Each one was imagining being in that tumultuous water, rushing toward the falls. "I was swept toward the bank where I caught hold of a low limb and prayed. The current brought the baby close enough for me to grab him. Then some men helped me get out." She added softly, as if speaking to herself, "But, of course, it was God who saved our lives."

There was a collective sigh of relief and another young man asked, "Would you tell us that whole story some time, ma'am?"

"Yes, I will, but now we need to talk about school."

"Ma'am, are you some kin to the Mr. Worth that takes them pictures?"

"He's my husband."

The easing of tension in the room was almost palpable, as if a current had passed through. Some nods and actual smiles appeared.

"Is he the one that puts his camera on that tall three-legged stool and covers his head with a big black cloth?"

"Yes, he's the one." Laurel laughed at this description of Justin. "The three-legged stool is his tripod and the black cloth keeps the light off the film until he snaps the picture."

"He used to ride that horse by our house. Always brung us candy. We called him the candy man."

Nods of agreement spread across the room. "He brung us some groceries once when my daddy broke his leg."

They were no longer lounging in their seats, sizing her up. They were sitting upright and ready to hear her. She was accepted right now on Justin's merits. She would have to earn her own as time went by.

She took a deep breath and dove right in. No need to tiptoe around what had to be done.

She had to call a spade a spade, but do it in a way that would preserve their dignity.

"I'm here to teach you to read and write and do arithmetic. I doubt if some of you have had a chance to go to school. It's nothing to be ashamed of, if you've never had a choice. But, if you have a chance to learn and don't, then you should be ashamed. Everybody who has good sense needs to be able to read and write and do arithmetic."

Everyone was silent as she moved around and looked carefully up and down the rows as if searching for something. She then declared, "Each one of you *looks* like you've got good sense, so let's get going."

She had them laughing and poking good-natured fun at each other as she divided them into two groups: those who had been to school and those who had not. She would divide them into smaller groups as she learned their abilities. She knew she would have several levels — from first grade up. As she worked, the atmosphere of the classroom enfolded her in its familiar embrace. She was back in her natural environment.

She quickly explained the alphabet to the non-readers and asked them to memorize the first ten letters, then to try printing them. She gave books to the other group and listened to each one read a few sentences. Their homework was to write their names and a short paragraph about themselves. When she left she believed they were off to a good start.

At supper Justin said, "So how was it, being in the classroom again after so many years?"

Laurel described Miss Abby and the artificial respiration scene.

"When Miss Abby left, there I was with thirty young men looking warily at me — like a calf looking at a new gate.

"When I told them my name, a couple of them asked if I was any kin to a mysterious man named Worth who used to ride by their house on a horse. He took them candy, it seems, so they called him the candy man. It sounded like he behaved strangely. He would set a camera on a tall three-legged stool and cover his head with a black cloth."

By now all the children were grinning and looking at Justin. "It was Daddy!"

"Yes, it was. And because they like your daddy, they decided to listen to me. We even got a little school work done."

She and Justin gave each other the special smile that their children loved to see. It was a big component of their security.

Sarah, in a totally serious tone, asked, "Mama, don't you need some help? Molly and I could go with you." She rolled her eyes dreamily. "Thirty young men...all in one room!"

"Oh, no, young lady! We've already got too many young men coming around," Justin teased. "I've been thinking about putting up a gate and keeping the key in my pocket."

Laurel had kept a low profile in church, mostly because she always felt that many of the people disapproved, in one way or another, of the things she and Justin did. *To be fair,* she thought, *we have tested their limits. We walked right over to the wrong side of the tracks when we helped Lila in Terminal Town. Then we had the actual temerity to play ball on Sunday, and have parties where boys and girls could have fun together. Then the Hot Lunch Program...*

Recently, however, she could sense a change toward her in the climate of the church. It seemed she had moved from the frigid zone to the temperate zone. People had conversations with her now. She believed it was due to the success of the Hot Lunch Program. The people felt proud of *themselves* for their concerted efforts to feed the children and looked kindly on her for bringing it to fruition. Gussie, of course, was her usual poisonous self. Laurel steered clear of her whenever possible. She knew she couldn't reason with her and she hated to leave church with Gussie's dirty looks or caustic words clinging to her.

One Sunday as they walked home from church, Adam said, "Mama, I wish you would teach Sunday school at this church like you used to do at the others. I bet all the young people who play in our ball games would come." He kicked a rock and made it skip along, then lowered his voice. "I'd like for my friends to hear your Bible stories."

She matched his serious tone with hers. "I don't know if they would want me to teach in the church, son. Your daddy and I have been in trouble one way or another ever since we moved here."

"But it's all for the right reasons. Would you let me ask the preacher about it?"

"He *is* a busy man, with another job and a large family. He might like help in getting the young people in church. Let's pray about it for a day or two and talk some more."

As Adam popped a quick kiss on her cheek with a "Thank you" and moved ahead to walk with Sarah, she felt a rush of pride and thankfulness for her son. Normally, she would have seen this need herself. She mused, *It's especially gratifying to have your child to remind you of the important things, when you've become too busy...*The joy that still surprised her seemed to give wings to her feet as she hurried toward home to prepare Sunday dinner.

The preacher, Noah Pierce, heartily approved of Adam's idea. "I haven't been able to get many of the young people to church but maybe you can," he told Laurel.

After Adam announced at the ball game that his mother would be teaching, the whole crowd showed up at ten o'clock the next Sunday morning. Pastor Pierce, flabbergasted, happy, and nervous all at once, got them settled in the back of the sanctuary—the only place big enough to hold them. Some who came just to be with the other young people soon fell under Laurel's spell. They were hearing things they had never heard before. God had been presented to them, primarily, as a stern taskmaster, eager to whop you over a minor infraction and ready to send you to hell over a big one. Here they were hearing about a God who loved, who cared, who wanted to be involved in their lives, who gave guidance and help. Of course, one had to come to Him on His terms: by believing that Jesus died on the cross to pay for their sins; repenting of their choice to live their lives on their own terms; choosing to turn from their own way and give themselves fully to

God. This was salvation. It was like being born again—this time, spiritually. It all made sense the way she described it.

One adjustment had to be made. The young people talked at home about what they were hearing from Mrs. Worth. A few of the parents decided to come early for church and hear for themselves; then a few more came. The preacher saw what was happening and asked Laurel if she would mind moving to the front of the sanctuary with the young people, then the adults who came early could sit at the back and not disturb the class. The church, however, kept filling up early. Most of the people started coming at ten instead of eleven. Laurel kept her lessons focused on the young people but was fully aware of the adults' interest and attention.

The pastor was delighted to see his congregation grow, but with it came a problem. Gussie accosted him with the fact that she needed the sanctuary to practice the piano, beginning at ten-thirty on Sunday mornings. She asked—insisted, really—that Laurel close down her class at that time. The pastor reasoned with her, "We've never had so many young people, and some of their parents are coming to see what's so interesting. I know you have a piano at home to practice on."

"It's out of tune," she argued, huffily.

"I'm not going to cut short the class where the young people are learning such life-changing truths. I'm sure your music will be just as good as it has always been."

It was the first time he had refused one of her directives and he knew he was stepping into contentious territory. He recognized anger, even if it was hiding behind a false smile, as she turned to go.

That night he told his wife, "We have a fly in the ointment at church, just as things are picking up. I'm sure I'll have further problems with Gussie over this."

Meanwhile, Laurel's classes at the CCC Camp were progressing better than she had expected. She often felt a clutch at her heart as she looked over the classroom. Some of the young men were awkwardly clenching little pencils in their big hands, intent on forming that A or C just as precisely as they would later hammer a nail; others were reading eagerly but haltingly, raising their hands to ask about a word. One morning after several days of rain, the sun broke through the

80

windows of the classroom, illuminating and warming the atmosphere. Laurel felt a rush of happiness. *This knowledge is illuminating their minds, chasing away the darkness of ignorance. And I'm allowed to be a part of bringing the light to them.* Their eagerness to push ahead challenged her and she realized her mistake. She needed to make a mental adjustment to teaching *adults* instead of *children*. Of course, they were more motivated and could go faster. She stepped up her speed, accordingly. The results were gratifying — to her and to her students.

She and Miss Abby were getting better acquainted, both liking what they saw and heard in the other. When she, on impulse, invited Miss Abby to spend the weekend with her family, the invitation was quickly accepted.

At supper they found out that Miss Abby lived in a big two-story house in Deerbrook where she took in boarders; she was a nurse, working regularly at the hospital; she taught first aid classes at other places in addition to the CCC Camp; she taught swimming at some of the local camps; she was organist at her church.

As the family was visualizing her dashing here and there, David asked, "What does your husband do?"

She answered briskly, "I don't have a husband. I never had a husband. Men take up too much time. I don't have time for one."

Justin grinned. "Some women think we're worth the time and trouble."

"I know, but I haven't been convinced yet."

She dismissed all mortals classified as men with a wave of her hand and said, "It's time I heard about you. Dr. Leighton said for me to ask you about some of the trouble you've stirred up since you moved here. He said that would give me a good understanding of the family."

That brought on a babble of voices until Justin restored order and promised each child he would have his turn to speak. As she heard about Lila and Terminal Town, the ball games, the parties, and the Hot Lunch Program, she sat back in her chair with a satisfied grin spread all over her long, angular face.

"Everything but an earthquake! And what other plans do you have for upsetting the people?" She was practically rubbing her hands in anticipation.

"But...we didn't do any of this just to upset the people," Laurel protested.

"Oh, I'm not criticizing. I'm applauding. It's a good thing to shake people up and get them living in the now! It's called progress!"

Adam sat forward and announced, "I know a good way to get in trouble again!"

They all looked at him as he looked at Miss Abby. "Mama has told us about your first aid classes with the CCC men. I know Sarah and I would like to learn some of that stuff and so would our friends. Could you come and teach us some of those classes?"

Sarah leaned forward and said, "Adam, sometimes your intelligence surprises me. It's a great idea!"

Justin and Laurel looked at each other, then at Miss Abby. The other children were shaking their heads in agreement.

Laurel said, "Miss Abby is probably too busy."

"I don't have anything on Friday nights. Could we do it then?"

All eyes were on Justin. He thought a moment, then said, "I can't think of anything more important that we could do for our young people. But we don't have any funds to pay you. We..."

Miss Abby interrupted. "I don't need nor want pay. I would have to spend Friday nights here. Would that be convenient?"

They assured her they would enjoy having her, so plans were made to start the classes the next weekend. By the time Miss Abby left, the Worth family realized a new force had entered their lives. They couldn't possibly have guessed the enrichment that would follow — for them and the community. And the enrichment would flow both ways. Miss Abby, who had no known living relatives, had found a family.

Chapter Six

The youth of Lake Eagle Rest flocked to the first aid classes on Friday nights. This was not entirely due to the fact that they had an overwhelming interest in learning first aid. It was primarily a social event: a place where the boys could see the girls and the girls could see the boys. Miss Abby, understanding this, waded right in with gusto, telling the group that she would teach them skills that may save their own lives or the lives of others. They would learn how to deal with broken bones, cuts, pressure points to stop bleeding, licks on the head, snake bites, burns, shock and near-drowning. She told them that other subjects would be covered as they went along.

"This is very serious business. We're going to start with artificial respiration. That's when you force air into and out of the lungs of someone who has stopped breathing. For example, it's used to revive persons who have nearly drowned or have been poisoned or have received an electrical shock. It's best learned by demonstration. Adam, you and Sarah each choose a partner. Girls with girls and boys with boys. Come up and we'll start."

After several clumsy efforts, they started getting the hang of it. The others, in pairs, were eager for their turn. Laughter lightened the intensity. Justin and Laurel watched from the back of the room, gratified that the boundaries of these young lives were being enlarged in yet another direction.

Following the public school schedule, the CCC Camp suspended classes from the end of May to the first of September, giving the crews the time they needed to work in areas that were not accessible during the winter. Laurel had agreements from the men that they would continue to read and write and not forget what she had taught them. She left them supplied with books, paper and pencils, provided by the CCC, and the promise that she would be teaching them again in September.

Laurel, realizing she had been out of the formal classroom for almost fifteen years, was eager to learn any new techniques that were available. She also needed to update her teaching certificate. Appalachian State Teachers' College in Boone offered a month-long course, from mid-May until mid-June. She could be through before canning time. The family went into one of its meetings, which always amazed Molly. She'd never seen a family work like this one. By the time it was over, each person knew what his or her job was while their mama was away. Justin, delegating his pulpwood operation for now, would be in the fields with Adam and David. Sarah would be at work during the day. That left Caroline and Molly to care for Alexis and do most of the routine housework. Sarah would plan the meals, keep tabs on everything and keep up with her own chores in the evenings.

It was a long, mountainous drive to Boone but when Justin left Laurel on Sunday afternoon, he told her he would be back to get her on Friday. He knew that the children — and he — would be needing to see her by then.

Laurel, knowing she had prepared her family for her absence, was able to practice what she had learned about actively trusting God to take care of a situation. She was at peace and could give herself up to the atmosphere of academia, soaking it all up like a parched ground soaks up a good rain.

Soon after moving to Lake Eagle Rest Justin rode Tattoo on several scouting trips around the lake bed just as he had scouted out the forest around their logging camps. He wanted to know what his family might encounter. Hundreds of acres of rich, fertile soil flourished with lush grass, laurel thickets, a variety of berry bushes and evergreen and hardwood trees. The mountain range at the head of the lake bed — steadfast, awe-inspiring, comforting — seemed to embrace the valley. Two rivers flowed from the heart of the mountains, winding their separate ways, watering the valley, before joining forces to plunge over a tiered waterfall of several hundred feet. In the western path of the sun's daily journey, the mountains furnished a stage for nature's lavish productions — rambunctious thunder storms or spectacular sunsets. *A wonderland of beauty*, he thought, thankful his children could grow up in such a place.

Since beauty cannot feed a family, however, the value of the lake bed took on a more practical consideration. It was a free stock range where people for miles around brought their livestock to graze. A clip on the ear of the cattle was the brand signifying ownership.

Justin took all this in as a veteran outdoors man accustomed to reading signs of nature. He saw where an occasional bear or panther had ventured off the mountain. He knew there were rattlesnakes, copperheads and water moccasins.

One sign disturbed him. Near a laurel thicket a patch of ground was torn up as if by a pitchfork. When he found, close by, that a watery depression near the river had been turned into a wallowing mud hole, he knew a herd of wild hogs were living nearby — their mean little eyes probably were watching him now from the dark depths of the laurel thicket.

Next to a snake, Justin feared a wild boar. With two sharp, upward curved tusks growing from its lower jaw, propelled by several hundred pounds of fierce strength, the boar was a deadly enemy. Justin had seen a boar rip open the belly of a dog in an instant. He was well aware of what one could do to a child or a man. He wanted his children to enjoy their surroundings, but he knew he needed to prepare them to recognize the dangers. That night he was thorough in his instructions and by the time he was through they knew, among other things, that they must keep their distance — and keep Chief away — from wild boars.

At dusk one summer evening Adam and Chief were herding in a stubborn milk cow when Chief started growling, his aristocratic nose raised, sniffing the air. Then he was off, barking furiously. Adam had never known him to leave an animal he was herding until they reached their destination. Curious, Adam left the cow, too, and followed. Chief was dashing back and forth, growling and barking, in front of an abandoned boathouse that stood on stilts in front but rested on a high bank at back. Grunts and squeals issued forth in response. Peeking through the gloom, Adam's skin prickled with fear. A huge wild boar, his herd around him, stood defiantly, his long tusks gleaming, and gimlet eyes glittering.

Adam knew the boar could charge at any moment, especially with Chief challenging him. After trying to calm Chief with his voice, Adam clamped his hands firmly around Chief's mouth, shutting down the barking. He looked into Chief's eyes and commanded, "No! Come!" He then pulled him, holding onto his front legs until they were out of sight of those eyes, staring out of the gloom. With every instinct in him straining to go back and take care of the danger, Chief still obeyed Adam, who took him straight to the barn and tied him securely.

Justin, when he heard Adam's story, said, "I'm proud of the way you handled that, son. I couldn't have done better myself."

The next morning, a Saturday, leaving Chief tied up, Justin set off with Adam and David. Justin knew he had to get rid of the wild boar before he homesteaded his herd under that boathouse, practically in their back yard. When Justin appeared with his rifle, pistol and a whip, Adam and David looked at each other with a mixture of fear and anticipation. Laurel watched them go, knowing the danger but knowing she also had a weapon. She started praying for their protection.

When they arrived, Justin instructed the boys to stay to the side of the boathouse out of sight of the boars. "Hopefully, I can stampede them," he said.

When he fired the rifle, the boar and herd rushed out of their lair. Adam moved slightly to see Justin's next action. The wild boar turned suddenly and charged straight toward Adam, his head lowered, those tusks aiming at Adam's stomach. Justin shouted, "Jump!" He couldn't shoot because Adam was in the line of fire. Adam saw a low hanging limb almost directly overhead and seemed to spring straight up, catching and holding on. The boar lunged, its tusks slashing at his legs. Adam, somehow, hung on as the boar turned and lunged for another attack. But Justin was there between him and Adam, already firing. The first shot hit the boar in the chest, but he kept coming. The second shot hit him between the eyes. His momentum carried him, a vicious quivering mass, to collapse at Justin's feet.

Adam dropped to the ground and Justin dropped beside him to

examine Adam's legs. David fell beside Adam, calling his name over and over. Justin was amazed. Both of Adam's pants legs were gashed half around but there wasn't even a scratch on his skin. The three of them hugged and clung together, then Justin asked, "What happened to the herd?"

David said, "Oh! I ran them off with the whip."

Adam and Justin collapsed against each other, laughing, as David looked at them. "They started after the old boar when he charged Adam, so I cracked the whip and turned them."

Justin put an arm around each son. "I've got quite a team. One son outwits the old man boar while the other takes care of the herd. Next time I can stay home."

As they got to their feet, two neighbors walked up with their rifles on their shoulders.

"We heard shots," one said briefly.

They looked at the boar, squatted and looked closer, then looked at each other.

"I'll be gol-darned! It's *him*!"

"Naw! It cain't be!"

Since their presence didn't seem important at the moment, Justin and the boys waited.

After some more examining and arguing, the men stood up and looked at Justin.

"It looks like you've killed Old Satan."

"Who?"

"Old Satan. He got the name because he was too mean and wise for us. He was a killer. Killed a man a few years ago. Killed more'n one dog. He was carrying several bullets in him. We got up hunting parties for a while to try to kill him, but never could get him." He paused to expertly shoot a stream of tobacco juice out the side of his mouth.

"What happened here?"

When Justin told them, one of the men said, "Both of you was mighty close to death today, or, at least, the boy could have been crippled for life. Good thing you're a good shot with a cool head."

The other man said solemnly, "Even with all that, somebody was watchin' after you and the boy."

Justin turned practical. "I guess it'll be okay to bury this brute right here. He must weigh four hundred pounds."

"Oh! You can't just up and bury Old Satan! We've got to git the word out. Everybody'll want to see for theirselves that he's dead. After that, we'll help you bury him."

Men kept arriving on Saturday afternoon to ease their mind that Old Satan was really dead. It seemed each group had another tale of the havoc the boar had wrought through the years. Justin was greatly embarrassed to find that he and the boys were considered heroes. When it was over and Old Satan buried, he was relieved.

He felt that he needed to put things in perspective for the boys, after all the praise they had received. "Adam and David, you've heard a lot of stuff about heroes today. We aren't heroes. We just did a job that had to be done and we were lucky. But I am very proud of the way you both conducted yourselves. David with your whip and Adam with your expert leap for that branch."

Adam looked very serious. "Daddy, I don't think I'm a hero at all. I didn't do that by myself. I felt like I was *lifted* up to that limb."

"It was your adrenaline, son."

"No, Daddy," Adam countered quietly. "I believe God took care of me 'til you could get there."

Justin just looked at him. He had no answer. But he allowed himself to think what would have been unthinkable before Laurel's escape from death. *Could it be that God had saved his son's life, too?*

Ethan showed up the next week where Justin was working in the field. He said, "I went to your pulpwood operation and the men told me where to find you. You're a busy man, as usual."

"I have to be. How are you and Allison?"

"We're fine. The church is growing. I heard about you killing that wild boar the people called Old Satan. I wanted to hear the story from you."

They sat down in the shade at the edge of the field and Justin told him. And — because it was Ethan — he even told him what Adam said about being lifted to that limb.

"Do you believe that's possible, Ethan?"

Ethan drew little marks in the dirt with a stick as he listened. He loved and admired Justin more than any man on earth, but he knew what Justin needed to hear from him. He also knew Justin was not going to like it.

"I not only believe it's possible, I believe it's probable. God has blessed you, Justin, with a wonderful family. You know he spared Laurel's life. He's blessed you with abilities and a compassionate heart. You're the best man I know."

Ethan paused, looked Justin square in the eye, and continued, "But you're as stubborn as a mule in one area. You've let one mean old woman — your stepmother — and her influence on your dad to dictate your thoughts about God for too much of your life."

Justin looked at him sharply, alarmed that he should bring up such a subject.

"Yes, Justin, I know about your religious, abusive stepmother. How she cowed your dad with her religious clap-trap. You told me about it in the hospital when we thought Laurel was dying, explaining why you weren't on speaking terms with God."

Justin went totally still, a gesture Ethan knew well. "This isn't church, Ethan, and I don't want a sermon."

"No, but this is God's green earth, as holy as any church building, and I am going to tell you a couple of things before you get yourself killed."

He shook his head. "I can just see you standing right in front of that charging wild boar. You either lead a charmed life or God is protecting you and your family. You're too proud to admit it, Justin. You think you can do it all on your own. Even though you can handle most things with ease, God has constantly handled the things you couldn't. And you've enjoyed the results of His care."

No one had ever talked to him like this and Justin stood up, not wanting to hear any more, but Ethan wasn't finished.

He stood up and faced Justin. "When I heard you'd killed Old Satan, a wild boar that had everybody spooked, you know what I thought? I thought, *Justin needs to get rid of Old Satan in his life, who has kept him hoodwinked all these years about the truth.* It would take the Devil, himself, to fool you this long, and he's done it!"

He saw a muscle twitch at the side of Justin's mouth and knew it was a sign of anger. He softened his tone. "I love you, Justin, as if you were my dad. That's what you've been to me since that day when I stumbled into your logging camp about twelve years ago when I was sixteen. You and Laurel took me in and gave me a home and — and love. That's what makes it so hard for you, I think. You're a better man than many Christians.

"The biggest single desire of my life is to see you come to a right relationship with God. Don't trample on His goodness any longer."

Justin didn't trust himself to speak and Ethan well understood why. Understanding that it was time to leave, Ethan turned and walked away. Then he called back, "Allison and I will be over this Friday night for the first aid class."

Justin was so stunned by what he had just heard, he sat back down and put his head in his hands. He willed his anger to seep away so he could focus on what Ethan had said. He knew it was the truth; he had just never had it vocalized before. He *had* mistrusted God; had not wanted to have anything to do with Him. He *had* been the recipient of the love of a good woman and had taken it as his due. He had never wanted to admit that his life was a result of God's goodness.

His thoughts in turmoil, he turned back to the plow, fixed his eyes on a tree on the other side of the field, and started cutting a furrow toward it. *I know there's a place where I need to go to get to God, but I'm not sure where it is nor how to get there. Wish it was as clear as that tree I'm headed for.*

Summer, in Laurel's mind, always meant canning time. Beans and corn and vegetables for soup came from the fields; peaches were bought in South Carolina; berries picked from the lake bed were made into jams and jellies. It meant ten-hour days of intensive work, but it was necessary if they wanted to eat well, come winter.

The first aid classes continued on Friday nights. Miss Abby arrived one Friday afternoon with a box full of swimsuits of different sizes for girls and boys. The first time the group tried them on there were squeals of laughter and calls for safety pins to help them fit right. For a couple of hours on Saturday Miss Abby and interested participants met at the swimming hole in the river, where she taught them different strokes and how to float. They were totally excited to add swimming to their list of accomplishments.

The third week of August—just before school started—was set aside each year for a revival meeting at Lake Eagle Rest Baptist Church. Pastor Pierce announced with enthusiasm, "The visiting preacher this year is one I've wanted you to hear for a long time. He's a young man, Ethan Stewart, whose church is growing by leaps and bounds."

That set off a buzz on the Worth pew that took a moment to run its course. Laurel thought, *How wonderful it's going to be to hear him preach again. I wish Justin would come.*

It was the main topic of interest at Sunday dinner. Justin, Laurel noticed, was quieter than usual.

Adam finally asked, "Daddy, aren't you proud of Ethan?"

"Yes, I am, son. Looks like he's making a name for himself."

The truth is that Justin was miserable. Had been ever since Ethan had laid the truth out for him after the wild boar attack. He didn't recognize it as conviction.

From the very first night, the preaching and the singing seemed alive with a sense of God's presence. When Ethan gave the invitation, several young people from Laurel's Sunday school class went forward to accept Christ. Every night others came. The pastor proclaimed on Sunday that the meeting would continue. Word spread and people from neighboring communities came. People were gripped with the knowledge that the Spirit of the Lord walked among them. Women met in groups to pray for their husbands and children. Disbelief turned to rejoicing as men, who had never willingly darkened the door of the church, came forward and knelt to enter the Kingdom. Two weeks, then three weeks—with penitents still crowding the altar.

When the invitation was given one night in the third week, Laurel felt someone grasp her arm. When she turned, Lila asked, "Will you go with me? I'm scared Jesus might not want me."

At the altar, after Laurel explained simply the steps to come to Jesus and what He gives in response, Lila repented and received the gift of salvation. Her joy in knowing she was accepted and loved was too powerful for her physical body to contain. She wept and praised God with the same enthusiasm with which, a few weeks before, she had cursed and sung her bawdy songs.

Justin stayed apart from it all. At mealtimes, which were taken up mostly with talk of the revival, he stayed quiet. No comments, no opinion, no interest. The children thought it strange, but Laurel knew better. She knew the *only* time Justin was *this* quiet was when he was working out a problem in his mind. *Could it be that he was no longer convinced he was right about God and was weighing the consequences, which must seem scary?*

She was holding fast her position of steadfast faith as she prayed for him. She knew Sarah and Adam were praying, too.

Meanwhile, Justin, working in the fields with Tattoo, was fighting the most intense battle of his life. His whole approach to life was being threatened. When Laurel had escaped death, a breach had appeared in the wall of his mental fortress—a wall built by assuring himself constantly that he didn't need God, that he could make it on his own, that God couldn't be trusted anyway—a wall that had admitted no good thoughts about God for most of his adult life. It seemed the breach had widened or the wall had collapsed altogether. Unbidden thoughts trouped in. Ethan's words came back in snatches. *You still think you can do it all on your own. But God has constantly handled things you couldn't and you've enjoyed the results of His care.*

His thoughts roamed, unwillingly, over some events he had not handled. *Laurel and Adam coming out of that whitewater above Laughing Falls...No one else he knew of had ever come out alive. His own confrontation with outlaws who were ready to pull the trigger...a panther attack that could have killed him and Tattoo...a lick on the head in the woods that should have killed him...And recently Alexis' escape from a rattlesnake and Adam's escape from a wild boar...*

His thoughts kept coming like a swarm of gnats he couldn't fend off. *He had the love of his family – a good woman and good children. A family that most men could only dream about.*

Another of Ethan's lines presented itself: *"You need to get rid of Old Satan in your life who's hoodwinked you all these years. It would take the Devil to fool you that long, Justin, and he's done it!"*

So, the Devil had fooled him! That rankled! But he had been willing to be fooled! That rankled worse!

A puny little man I've been – shaking my fist at God while receiving his benefits! What a sorry spectacle!

That afternoon, arriving home earlier than usual, he stabled Tattoo and took a path that led through some trees back to the house. He heard a voice and halted. In an abandoned canoe, leaning beside a tree he saw Sarah, on her knees with her head in her hands, praying.

He stood rooted in his tracks and heard every word clearly.

"Lord, please bring my daddy to You. I don't understand why he doesn't want to know You, Lord, but please have mercy on him. Don't let him go through the rest of his life without You. He's the best man I know. I ask you, Lord, to bring my daddy to You tonight."

Shaken, Justin slipped behind a large oak as Sarah finished and walked toward the house, wiping her tears. Justin walked to the canoe and sat down, his head in his hands, until he knew what he was going to do.

Supper was subdued and hurried. Everybody had their mind on getting to church; the revival was now in its fourth week. Each one kissed Justin goodbye and was out the door.

Ethan preached on the prodigal son to an overflowing crowd. On the invitation, just as the congregation got well into the hymn, "Lord, I'm Coming Home," Ethan suddenly left the rostrum, rushing down the aisle with his arms outstretched, tears pouring down his face.

Every eye turned to watch, including Laurel, who saw Justin coming forward to meet Ethan. The two men stood for a moment in a tight embrace, before Ethan led Justin to the altar. With the sound of "Lord, I'm Coming Home" resounding in his ears, Justin, like a child, said, "Son, I want to come home but I don't know how. Will you tell me?"

Laurel, tears flowing, sat down and started praying. Sarah and Adam were suddenly at her side and the other three were pressing close.

The pastor, realizing that something momentous was happening that claimed Ethan's full attention, continued the invitation as others kept coming.

Ethan, in simple terms, told Justin what he needed to do and what God would do in return. Justin understood, asked forgiveness for his arrogance, and believed with his entire being. He thanked God for His mercies and patience through the long years he had spurned His love. He rose from his knees, a whole man for the first time in his life.

Laurel saw him stand, his eyes searching the crowd. She and the children were around him in a moment; his second homecoming that evening was bathed with love and laughter and tears.

After everyone was settled back in their seats, Ethan, so full of joy he could hardly finish the service, asked for a word before the benediction.

"I want to tell you a story. I'm sure all of you know Justin Worth who came forward tonight, but you don't know this about him. I owe my life to him and his wife. When I was sixteen my pa was killed. He was a bootlegger and was killed by other bootleggers. My mother had died the year before, so I was alone and scared that the men who killed my pa would come after me so they could take over our still. I walked across the mountains from Gatlinburg, Tennessee, and ended up at the Worth Logging Camp in Pisgah Forest. I was so weak with hunger, I could hardly stand on my feet. They took me in and gave me a job. But they gave me much more. They gave me love and showed me how a family ought to love each other. In an abandoned boxcar where Mrs. Worth taught Sunday school, I first heard about a God I could trust.

"Justin, the man I love and admire most in this world, the man I consider my dad, came home tonight. There's great rejoicing in heaven over him and the others who came." As he looked at the faces around him he added, "And there's considerable rejoicing right here on earth!"

That night when the Worth family got home, Justin asked them to gather in the big room. Within the circle of light cast by the lamps, he said straight out what he had to say for his own peace of mind.

"I ask each of you to forgive me for being so stubborn and foolish and for waiting so long to make this decision. A man never had a better family, and I thank you for loving me and believing in me and just for being who you are!"

Laurel's happiness shone in her eyes. "You know we forgive you, Justin."

"Now you'll be a part of *everything* in our lives, including praying and church."

Caroline had hit the nail on the head. He had missed out on a whole section of their lives.

"Yes, I will. I have a lot to learn." His grin was back. "Will you teach me how to behave in church?"

94

Chapter Seven

Justin never did anything by halves. Whatever he entered into, he entered into wholeheartedly. It was the same with his newfound faith. If he was going to be a Christian, he was going to be a *real* Christian. A few days after his conversion he casually said to Laurel, "I'm going to visit Jed and Bulldog and Tom. I need to tell them what's happened to me."

Laurel knew that if anybody could influence them to become Christians, it would have to be Justin. They respected him, liked him immensely — even loved him — and deferred to him in most of life's decisions. He had started out as their boss and had become their friend. They would defend him with their lives. Their wives had become Christians in the logging camp, one by one, under Laurel's teaching.

Ethan should not have been surprised when, a few nights later, Justin walked down the aisle with Jed, Bulldog and Tom, bringing them home the same way he had come. These three tough woodsmen, with Justin, had taught Ethan the art of logging; the art of making the best of your circumstances; the art of looking out for each other; the art of being a man. They were a part of his extended family. He, again, was overcome with tears for a few moments before he could shepherd them into the fold.

The revival and the baptism service that followed were historic in numbers and in results. Seventy-five people — men, women and children — were immersed in the cold mountain water, in the river just above the falls where a pool had formed in a rocky basin to the side of the fast, flowing current. The baptismal group included

Laurel, who was raised a Methodist and had never been immersed. Sarah, Adam, and Caroline with most of the youth population of Lake Eagle Rest stood in the baptismal waters as Ethan explained that the immersion symbolized their death to the old way of life and their resurrection to live the new. Justin, wanting to record this event for the present and for posterity, set up his tripod and camera, showed someone how to operate it, and joined the group in the river for the picture. Ethan called in four other preachers to help baptize but he reserved the right to baptize his "family." It was one of the most rewarding days of his life.

When Justin invited the pastor, his wife and five children and Ethan and Allison home for Sunday dinner, Laurel was aware that their family had entered a new dimension—a dimension she had longed for—a dimension of harmony, of synchronicity. Even with their strong love for each other there had been a schism, a divide, with Justin on one side where none of them ventured. On their side, when they prayed or talked about church or spiritual matters, even though physically present and respectful, Justin would cross the divide to his other place. Their respect for each other had kept it in check, but it had still been a factor to be dealt with. The first time Justin haltingly said grace at mealtime, a sense of togetherness, of rightness, of wholeness, suffused the family.

The beginning of school in September was significant. Adam began his senior year and Alexis started first grade. Caroline, fifteen, and in the ninth grade, rode the bus with Adam to high school while David, ten years old, and a fifth grader, walked with Alexis to the elementary school.

Sarah, meanwhile, was enjoying this stage of her life. She enjoyed being with her family and was happy to be helping financially. She took great pleasure in buying some new dresses for Caroline and Alexis. It was a satisfying day when, after shopping with Sarah, Laurel went home with her first new clothes in several years.

Sarah had so many beaus on her string that things became complicated and comic at times. She had no serious thoughts of settling down to one young man. She was having fun playing the field. Justin and Laurel looked on with approval. Marriage would come soon enough.

After Lila's conversion, she would appear a couple of times a week with her boys, Vic and Ned. The first time Laurel noticed the bruises on her face and arms, she said nothing, not wanting to ask embarrassing questions. However, when she saw new bruises, she knew it was time to talk, embarrassing or not.

"Brand's mad as a hornet because I'm a Christian and won't drink with him no more. He's rarely sober so I can't reason with him. He beats me and the boys. Sometimes I'm afraid he'll kill us. I can tell you, now that you're my friend, that I'm almost sure it was Brand who knifed me, when you come and fixed me up. I was drunk but Gerta and the others have said some things. He's always been crazy jealous. I don't know what to do. I ain't got nowhere to go."

"You could press charges against him."

"What does that mean?"

"You could report him to the law. They would probably put him in jail."

"No! No! He'd kill me for sure if I got him in trouble with the law."

An idea was forming in Laurel's mind, but she needed to talk to Justin about it. She said, "Lila, we'll help work something out for you and the boys, but we need a little time. Will you promise me that, if Brand starts abusing you or the boys, you'll take them and go to Gerta's house?"

"Yes. I've done that before."

"Good. Now, let's ask God to help us with this problem."

After they prayed, Lila said, "You really think God cares about me and the boys, don't you?"

"I know He does! He'll help us know what to do."

"Good! We sure need some help."

Laurel's idea was to move Lila and her boys into the little house in their back yard. When she asked Justin about it, he sat down with a serious look on his face.

"We'd have to go into this with our eyes wide open as to the consequences. Brand is mean. Drunk or sober, he's mean. I'm not sure he even knows the difference anymore what is decent and what is not. I hate to get tangled up with a man like that."

"So, what can we do?"

"Oh, we'll help Lila and the children. We can't leave them to be abused. I was just talking it out."

Moving Lila and the boys into the little house became a community project. Gerta rounded up some furniture, including two mattresses, from the families in Terminal Town. Most of them despised Brand and were relieved to know Lila and the boys would no longer be at his mercy. The church people, now considering Lila one of their own, shared other necessities to get them settled. Lila took a job that came open in the lunchroom, which meant she could live apart from Brand.

"Did you see the people from Terminal Town and the church people working together to help Lila?" Laurel asked Justin. "That's different from when we arrived here."

"Lots of people have changed in this community. Including me," Justin answered.

Lila could hardly believe what had happened to her. She said so to Laurel.

Laurel answered, "Well, we asked God to help, and He did!"

"You did so much of the work yourself. Why do you give the credit to God?"

"Oh, I couldn't possibly have worked out all that happened, Lila. God is primarily responsible. I'm just His errand person."

Brand, coming out of his alcoholic daze, found out where his family had gone. His rage wasn't pretty to see. He took it out on the house since there was no person there to hit. Two chairs were broken and many dishes were smashed before he settled down. He would, however, find a way to make everybody sorry they had fooled him. *Especially the Worth family.* But, right now, he needed a drink.

Laurel's classes at the CCC Camp were proving to be a great success. She set up the practice of getting leftover newspapers from Sam Parker, editor of *The Wildwood Journal,* asking some students to read an article and summarize it for the class. Others read directly to the class. The men seemed happy to know what was going on in the world. Public speaking caught on. One day after a rewarding session where the men spoke on a variety of topics, she wondered how she had ever thought they were shy. Determined to keep her students reading, she visited the county school office and the county library and requested old books for grades one through six, which they planned to discard. Her reward was the men's gratitude. They were learning not only to read but to *enjoy* reading, which was one of the greatest gifts she felt she could give them.

One benefit for herself, personally, came from the first aid classes. She always arrived in time to participate in Miss Abby's first aid classes. She learned some new techniques and polished up some old ones. She didn't realize these were some final touches on her preparation for the work she would soon enter: the work she was destined for.

The Worth house was known as the place where things happened. None of the youth wanted to miss being there. It was the social gathering place, but other interesting events presented themselves. After seeing Laurel's skill at the CCC Camp, Miss Abby enlisted her help in teaching the first aid classes. After several weeks they believed they had taught the complete curriculum. When they gave out the certificates and announced the end of the classes, the young people moaned and groaned. "We won't have anywhere to go or anything to do on Friday nights, and we'll never get to see Miss Abby anymore."

Justin soothed the outcries by saying, "Give us a week or two and we'll see what else we can come up with."

One of the young men made a surprising suggestion. "How about some music lessons? We're all going to church now and we need to learn some of the songs. Could we sing some?"

That resulted in Justin bartering two hogs for an old pump organ, which Miss Abby would play. Two weeks later the walls were reverberating with a mixture of voices singing "I'll Fly Away" or "Victory in Jesus" or "I heard an Old, Old Story," using books that Miss Abby provided. Laurel requested some of the classical old hymns such as "The Old Rugged Cross." Justin's clear tenor voice seemed to set the tone for the others. The first night she heard him and saw his obvious enjoyment, Laurel had to slip from the room to get her emotions in check.

When she thanked him for making the singing lessons possible, he grinned and said, "I had a personal motive. I don't know those songs, either, and it's embarrassing for a grown man to be stumbling around trying to sing in church."

Nobody talked about it but they all realized this was Adam's last year at home. He had informed them that, after his graduation in May, he wanted to join the CCC and would request to go to a western state, to see the country. He was, after all, his father's son.

A party for every occasion was the result. The New Year's Eve party was one of their best ever. Ethan came and talked to them about their choices in life, then partied along with them. At midnight everyone gathered on the big porch to watch the new year come in. After the fireworks, Adam saw Alexis in a corner chair crying. He knelt in front of her and asked softly, "What's the matter? Did you get hurt?"

"I didn't see the new year come in. I tried but everybody was too tall and I couldn't see it."

He picked her up and sat down with her in his lap. Everybody sensed they needed to keep their distance. "Alexis, I'm sorry I didn't explain it to you sooner. You can't really *see* the new year come in. We just pretend we see it. We know it's a new year and this is the way we celebrate it."

She sat up straight and looked at him. "*You* didn't see it either?"

"No. None of us saw it. There's nothing that you can see."

"But how do you know it comes?"

"By the calendar." He walked over and took a calendar off the wall. "I bet you can read these names of the months."

She stumbled a few times but read every month from January to December. Then he showed her that they had to get a new calendar, because this year was all gone — as of a few minutes ago. She hugged him and whispered, "I love you, Adam."

He whispered back, "I know. I love you, too."

She skipped off, ready for bed, her problem solved again by her big brother.

Adam returned to his friends and the party.

Adam's graduation was bittersweet; another goal accomplished, by many means with many memories. Certainly, it was a time to celebrate, but a painful time of knowing it would never be the same again. Laurel, proud of her son and happy about his proposed plans, nevertheless often found herself close to tears as she went about her work. It was hard to give up his presence in the family.

Justin's sadness was tempered by Adam's obvious anticipation of travel and of facing new challenges. He was reminded of the intoxicating call of adventure and he believed Adam was ready to answer it. He saw a lot of his young self in his son. He also saw a big dose of Laurel's strength of character, for which he was thankful.

Adam spent time, individually, with Caroline, David, and Alexis — reminding each one that they needed to help all they could, especially since their mama was working. He and Sarah were such good friends, words weren't necessary to express their feelings. They would each deal with the mixed emotions privately. Alexis was the hardest one to leave. He passed the baton of her protection to David, saying, "You'll be her only big brother at home, so I know you'll watch after her."

David made a solemn promise he would watch after his little sister. That promise exacted a price from him a few times in the next few years.

After a farewell party, Justin loaded up a group of Adam's friends on his logging truck to travel to the train station. Appropriately, Adam had a boisterous send-off to Arizona and his new life.

Laurel was surprised when she received word that the school superintendent wanted her to come to see him. When she arrived he asked her to be seated and got right to the point. "Thank you for coming. I thought it would be better to talk to you face to face rather than send a letter. I want to offer you another job."

Laurel was startled and confused. "But I'm enjoying the CCC work."

"I know you are, and the boys are enjoying your teaching. How long have you been there now?"

"We just finished our second year."

"A change would be better now than in the middle of the year. The Wildwood County and Sylvester County School Boards have voted to sponsor an adult literacy program, as part of President Roosevelt's New Deal. As you know, a percentage of our adults can't read or write. We would like to offer you the job of going into their homes and teaching them."

"But what about the CCC boys? Who would teach them?"

"We can find someone qualified for that job much easier than we can find someone suitable for this one."

At her silence, he continued, "We understand the difficulties. First, you'll have to convince them that they *need* to learn. You know how fiercely proud and independent they are. The second problem is travel. These families are scattered throughout the hills and hollows. Some are in remote, rough territory. Frankly, we've hesitated in asking a woman to take on the job because of these conditions."

He paused and asked, "You do understand that it would be difficult at best and dangerous at worst?"

Laurel answered simply, "Yes, I understand."

Mr. McKenzie felt that he was over the hard part and was relieved that he could move on. "You've been highly recommended by several reliable sources and seem to be uniquely qualified for this work."

"What are the qualifications?" she asked.

"The formal qualification is a teacher's certificate, of course. But you and I both know that's the easiest to fulfill. The other qualities are harder to come by and don't come with formal training. They're less tangible.

"I understand that you've worked with these people successfully in your husband's logging camps. You probably know what it will take better than I do. Tell me what qualities you think are necessary for success."

Laurel smiled as she thought of the people who had become her larger family and how much her life had been enriched by knowing them. She sat back and began, "It may be a long list but I'll tell you as I have experienced it. First, they must be respected just as they are with no hint of condescension. They don't have formal schooling but their wisdom, approach to life, survival techniques, and sense of fairness could fill volumes. I can't begin to tell you all I have learned from them. It's a basic goodness of character.

"Secondly, they must sense that you *care* about them as individuals, that you have a sincere desire to help, to make their lives easier and more fulfilling. That this is more than just a job, it's a privilege. They need to know you *enjoy* working with them.

"Then, there's the common sense element on how to proceed in unexpected situations. This will not be a classroom where routine is established."

She laughed. "It's what they call 'gumption.' When I asked one of the loggers what gumption is, he said, 'It's what keeps a coon hound from barking at an empty tree.' A person must gauge the potential in a situation and proceed accordingly.

"Whoever works with them and gains their confidence must be willing to do battle with them when they *are* wrong. And they are wrong in some areas, such as not sending their children to school even when it's physically possible. They are passing on a way of life that has served them, but will not be sufficient for their children. This, of course, must be changed. But it will take some convincing."

By now Mr. McKenzie was smiling broadly.

Laurel asked, "Is that enough or shall I continue?"

"That's more than enough to let me know that you're the person for the job. Can you work out the transportation?"

"Yes. My husband and I will work on that. I do need to know which families are on the list and where they live."

"Yes. We have a list for you. We'd like for you to start in Sylvester County and work back to Wildwood County. Where they live is another question. They're scattered through the hills, often with no roads and no addresses. It's a matter of searching in a general vicinity for them. I know that's vague. We need to get someone to go with you and find the homes."

"The best person I can think of is my husband. You probably know he's a photographer and a woodsman. He's probably traveled through these areas on his horse. In fact, it would be hard to find anybody in the two counties who doesn't know him."

"Would he have the time? We would pay him, of course."

"I'll ask him and let you know. I think there would be an added benefit. Everybody likes him, so they would accept me more easily from the beginning if they know I'm his wife."

Justin *did* know the territories and he *did* want to go and help Laurel find the homes. "I was planning to do this anyway, m'dear. I wasn't going to have you riding off into unknown territory without knowing what you might encounter."

Laurel rode Tattoo, as she would for most of her work, and Justin rode the extra horse he had bought to help with his pulpwood. They systematically covered the areas, starting in Sylvester County and moving back toward Wildwood. Just as Laurel had predicted, every one knew Justin and welcomed him as an honored guest. Living up to his reputation, he had brought candy for the children. Almost every home had pictures he had taken of the family. They brought them out proudly to show Laurel. By the time they left, Laurel knew they would welcome her when she returned. Justin had prepared the way for her again.

After one visit to an obviously poverty-stricken home, she asked, "Justin, I know these people couldn't pay you for those pictures. How did you solve that?"

"I made it a point to spend the night with them and told them I had to take their picture to pay for my lodging."

Her heart swelled with love for him as he continued. "They had looked longingly on my camera several times when I had traveled through. I couldn't just ignore that desire."

"You got paid in good wages. You have their friendship, trust, and good will."

As the time approached for Laurel to begin her work, Justin wrestled with a mixed bag of emotions. He knew how much she wanted to do this, how much good she would do and how much fulfillment it would bring her. He, of all people, also knew the dangers of traveling alone in the remote areas where her work would take her: getting lost, having an accident, facing wild animals and snakes, confronting moonshiners. His solace came from knowing her common sense and courage and the fact that she would be riding Tattoo.

He extracted certain promises: that she would always be out of the woods before dark, and that if she got lost she would trust Tattoo to bring her out. She realized how serious he was when he brought out a pistol and required her to do some target practicing.

"But, Justin, I don't think I could shoot anything."

He took both her hands and looked her in the eyes. "Sometimes that's the only choice you have if you want to stay alive. Promise me that you will keep the pistol where you can get it in a hurry. And that you will shoot anything or anyone who is threatening your life. That's the only way I'm going to agree for you to do this work."

Seeing his worry, she answered solemnly, "I promise. I'll do what I need to do to keep safe."

They stood in an embrace, drawing strength and courage from each other — as they had done for many years.

Her destination the first morning was the home of a young couple, Nate Buchanan and his wife, Lark. They lived in Sylvester County, an hour's ride across the mountain. As she rode into the yard she saw Lark at the wash place beside a stream near the house. Nate was shoeing a horse beside the barn, with his two young sons watching. She and Justin had visited them so they knew her and came forward to greet her. Nate took charge of Tattoo while Lark led Laurel to the house. She noticed how clean and neat the place looked and was further pleased when they entered the shack. The furniture was crude but signs of pride abounded: in the jar of flowers on the table with a fringed cloth under them, in the hooked rug on the floor, and in the shining pots hanging above the stove.

Lark, obviously happy to see her, said, "Please sit down and I'll fix us a fresh cup of coffee. You probably need one after that long ride."

"Yes, I would like some coffee." She looked around. "You've made your home very comfortable and inviting."

"Thank you. I enjoy keeping house. I'm happy you're going to teach Nate to read and write. I went to school so I help him, but he's always longed for some schooling."

Nate came in with the boys. All three had washed their faces, slicked down their hair and were in need of a towel. After visiting a few minutes, Lark took the boys outside so Laurel and Nate could get down to business.

He was a likeable young man with hair that stood on end because he was always running his hand through it. His enthusiasm was a tonic to Laurel. "Do you think I could learn to write my name today?"

"Today?" Laurel echoed.

"Yes, *today!* All my life I've wanted to write my own name."

Laurel laughed. "Well, let's get going, then. I'll print the letters and tell you what they are. Then you can try printing them. But you have to memorize each letter as you go."

Soon he was laboring, awkwardly copying the marks that Laurel had given him, repeating the name of each letter aloud as he worked. His erratic scrawl finally became identifiable as letters. At last there they were in legible print—two magic words—his name! After printing his masterpiece five times, he grabbed the paper and jumped up, saying, "'Scuse me, Mrs. Worth!" He rushed out the door waving the paper and calling, "Lark! Lark!"

Laurel followed him to the porch. Lark dropped the shirt she was scrubbing and came to meet him, smiling. Nate flourished his prize before Lark's eyes and bowed.

"Ma'am, your husband can now write his name like you can. No more X's to sign my name like when we got married. I'm goin' to learn to read and write like normal people."

Lark had pushed her hair back and stood tall as she reached for the paper to see his accomplishment. She looked at him with pride in her eyes. "I'm proud of you! I knew you could do this because you can do most anything you set your head to do!"

The boys came running to see what all the shouting was about and looked bewildered that it was all about some markings on a paper. They turned back to digging red worms. Their daddy had promised to take them fishing. *That* was something to get excited about.

Before Laurel left she gave Nate an assignment to memorize and learn to print the alphabet up to M. Of course, he already knew the letters in his name. She told him they would soon start reading. She also explained the number system from one to one hundred and asked him to learn to count and write to thirty. She believed they could move fast because Lark could help him between her visits.

After she left the Buchanan home, she had a different task ahead of her. She needed to locate a house that she and Justin had not visited. Zach Barnes and his two almost-grown sons had just been added to her list of adults who couldn't read and write. She knew they lived in this vicinity and knew if she could visit today it would save her a long ride back over the mountain. Just as she decided she had missed it, she saw a shack down in a hollow off the beaten trail she was traveling. She soon found a path leading down to the house, slipped off and hitched Tattoo to a tree at the head of the path.

As she started down, she brushed the auburn curls from her forehead with her damp handkerchief, wishing she had a fresh one. The way down was steep and walled in with bushes and briars that clutched at her clothes and hair. She stepped carefully because exposed roots, some lying on top of the ground and others looping above the ground, threatened to send her sprawling.

The thrown-together shack stood apologetically in a clearing scattered with junk and litter. As Laurel approached, watching for the inevitable hound dog, she noticed a farm wagon, which sat askew because one wheel was missing. The other three wheels were rusty and the floor boards were rotting. On the other side of the yard a sagging clothesline carelessly held three pairs of overalls, the legs of one pair and the suspenders of another resting in the dirt below.

The place seemed deserted but Laurel walked sturdily forward and knocked on the crudely hewn door. The door had no knob but a rope that obviously controlled a latch on the inside. When a voice called roughly, "Who's there?" she stepped back quickly, fighting a momentary urge to run.

Her decision was made for her as the door opened slowly. A man, barefoot in dirty, wrinkled overalls and undershirt, a stubble of beard, dirty, uncombed hair and red, slightly unfocused eyes looked at her as he held on to the door. He would have been startled but didn't seem to have the energy.

She spoke first. "Are you Mr. Zach Barnes?"

"I ain't no mister. Do I look like a mister? I am plain old Zach — or what's left of him."

The contrariness in his voice lost its edge because of his weakness. She knew she was talking to a sick man.

"What kin I do fer ye, ma'am? We don't git no visitors much and I ain't no good with manners." As he spoke she noticed the red spots on his pale cheeks, and the trembling of his hand as he held onto the door for support.

She spoke quickly, "Mr. Barnes, I'm Justin Worth's wife. I'm sure you know him — the photographer. Everybody seems to know him."

He nodded his head up and down slowly and silently, waiting for her to continue, looking suspiciously at her satchel of books and papers. Laurel hurried on. "I'm working in two counties with a government program that teaches adults to read and write. You and your sons are on my list. I start with teaching you how to write your name."

Silent mirth seemed to seize him and shake him for a moment. He covered his mouth to keep her from seeing him laugh, and ended up with a spasm of coughing. As he got control again, he said almost in a whisper, "Old Zach's made his mark so many times and in so many ways, I don't know as I want to change, ma'am. I'm a thankin' you fer stoppin' by."

Laurel knew she was being dismissed without a chance to talk about the boys' schooling. She also knew now was not the time to bring it up.

She made a quick decision, swallowed hard and spoke. "Mr. Barnes, I thank you for your politeness and I don't want to be impolite, but you are too sick to stand. Please go inside and lie down. I'm coming in to see how I can help you. I know a little about taking care of sick people."

Something in her manner and voice was stronger than his stubbornness at the moment. He turned without a word and did as he was told.

Laurel followed him into the shack, talking to ease the awkwardness between them. "I'm going to fix you something to eat and drink."

His eyes on her as she looked around the kitchen area, he said, "Ain't you afraid? I'm known around here as a mean man."

Laurel, busy with her task of getting ready to prepare some food, answered absently, "Mean men get hungry, too. I see some meal here. Do you think you could eat some hoecakes?"

He chuckled before answering, "I see you're stubborn, too."

She didn't answer but stood looking at him, waiting.

He closed his eyes a moment, then admitted, "Yes, some hoecakes with molasses would be good. And some coffee would taste mighty fine, ma'am."

As she cooked she found out the names of his sons and their ages, but when she asked where they were his answer was vague. "They're out and about. Maybe they'll bring home some squirrels for stew tonight."

He ate the food as if he were, indeed, hungry. She poured herself a cup of coffee and sat with him while he ate, telling him about their life in the logging camps. After awhile he said, "Tell me agin about wantin' to teach me to read and write. I feel more like listenin' now."

After she finished, he said, "I ain't promising nothin' fer myself, but I would like fer my boys to learn what they can. They ain't never been to school."

"Would they be willing to try?"

"If I tell 'em to, they will. They may be about grown, but they know who's boss as long as they live here. Tell me when you'll be here agin and I'll have 'em here to talk to you."

"I'll come back day after tomorrow to check on you. In the meantime, I want your boys to bring in some Boneset or Indian Sage and make some tea for you. It's good for colds and flu. Do they know what plant that is?"

"My wife used them kind of plants and I'm pretty sure the boys know 'em."

"Don't take anything if you're not sure. We don't want to poison you. You need to rest and drink a lot of water to flush out your system. Eat what you can to keep up your strength."

He looked at her during her litany of instructions. "I thank you, ma'am, for the food and for your concern that I get better. Give your husband a 'hello.' Tell him it's from Old Zach."

By the time she left, Laurel knew she had gained entrance into a difficult situation. She didn't know until later that most people who knew the Barnes men would not label her visit difficult; they would call it dangerous.

Chapter Eight

Justin, busy cutting cordwood, farming or taking pictures, tried to analyze his newfound peace. He had always been of an optimistic turn of mind, usually able to see the upside of any situation. This peace, however, was deep and abiding. It came, he believed, from the knowledge that everything didn't depend on him—that Someone totally capable was now in charge. He could relax. He had never realized it was such hard work, holding himself up by his own bootstraps.

Joy was another surprise. A buoyancy, a strengthening, an empowering, seemed to flow—as from a fountain—in his innermost being. *Part of it, he reasoned, is finally having the missing pieces of the puzzle of my life in place – a sense of completeness – a finished temple where the Spirit of God can reign.*

He was a happy man as he came in for supper, wondering about Laurel's first day on the job. The conversation centered on family concerns during the meal, but later, with the children studying, he and Laurel quietly discussed their day.

He sat forward suddenly and said, "I worried today because I didn't warn you. There's one place I don't want you to go. The name is Barnes. They weren't on your list for today and I forgot. They're said to be...unpredictable...and even dangerous. I know they live close to where you were going today."

She laid her hand on his and said quietly, "I *went* to the Barnes' house today."

"Laurel!" His tone and volume stopped the studying. All the children looked at him.

"It's okay," she said, soothingly. "I found a sick old man and I fixed him some food before I left."

"You were in Zach Barnes' house? Where were his sons?"

"I don't know. He said they were out and about."

"Tell me what happened."

The children were listening as she recounted her visit, including the fact that Zach promised to have his sons ready for her to teach when she returned. She ended by saying, "I need to take him some medicine and some home-cooked food. He's a sick man."

Justin sat looking at her. She never ceased to amaze him. He wanted to be angry but he found himself laughing instead.

"So, you just walked in and ordered Zach Barnes to bed and started cooking! I wish I could've seen it."

"What's so funny about it?"

"They're not known to be neighborly. Usually warn people off with a shotgun if they're inclined to visit."

Laurel was genuinely puzzled. "Why?"

"Nobody knows! I don't want you around them!"

"But he needs medicine and…and he said he would try to learn to write his name."

"Okay! I'll go with you and meet him and his boys. Then we'll decide if it's safe for you to go back." He thought a minute then said, "Tomorrow morning would be the best time for me."

They carefully loaded the food — beef stew with vegetables, baked sweet potatoes and fried apple pies — into a basket that would ride behind Laurel's saddle. She added the medicines she thought Zach needed.

When they had tethered their horses and started down the path, Justin paused and called, "Hello the house!"

Sure enough, a burly young man burst through the door with a shotgun.

"Whatcha want?" he yelled.

Justin answered, "We came to see your pa."

"My pa ain't expectin' nobody!"

"Tell him the teacher's here with some food and medicine — and her husband."

The door opened and Zach spoke sharply, "Get inside and put up that gun!"

His son looked surprised but quickly did as he was told.

Zach called, "Didn't know it was you, ma'am. Come on in."

Once inside, Laurel introduced Justin. Zach allowed that he already knew about Justin, but hadn't met him face to face. He then introduced his two sons, Wolf and Keen, who sat stiff and mute with embarrassment.

Justin, covering the momentary awkwardness, observed. "You picked a pretty house place on a good flat piece of land with a stream running through it."

Zach almost smiled but it had been awhile and his face had to adjust. "My wife picked this place. She loved it." He was quiet with his thoughts, then added, "She's been gone now for about four years."

Laurel said, "You look like you feel better, but we brought some medicine that I think will help you." She spent the next few minutes giving him instructions on what he needed to do to get better.

Justin, meanwhile, engaged the boys in some talk about hunting coons and squirrels, moving on to talk about guns. Wolf unwound enough to show him his prize rifle.

Laurel said, "We brought some food that should help you get your strength back, but you need some coffee with it. I'll make a fresh pot."

Justin found nothing there to be afraid of but he was puzzled and decided to hit it straight on. "Zach, my wife wants to come here to teach you and your boys to read and write, but I need to know something before I'm going to let her come. Is there some kind of danger around here? Why did Wolf come to greet us with a shotgun?"

Zach and his boys grinned sheepishly at each other. "That's cheaper'n a fence to keep people out. The boys and me, we make a little brew every now and then to git us some cash. We cain't have folks wanderin' around."

"Your still's close by?"

"It's a ways through the woods."

"So you've encouraged the rumor that you're dangerous men?"

Zach nodded. "That way folks leave us alone." He added quietly, "A friend of your'n was by yesterday. Said to ask you if you remembered 'Abner.'"

Laurel and Justin both exclaimed, "Abner!"

"My wife was kin to his family. When I told him Justin Worth's wife was goin' to teach us to read and write, he told me some interestin' tales."

Laurel said, "Oh, I would love to see him and Rosalee and the boy!"

Zach was pleased. "We'll set up a meetin'. They're all comin' here one day when you kin come."

Justin said, "Abner's a good friend. He saved my life. Did he tell you that?"

"No. But he's the reason I told you about my still. He trusts you. Seemed real excited that he might see you again."

"Let us know when and we'll be here."

Justin's manner and tone then became urgent. "Before we go, I need to settle something in my mind. If my wife comes here regularly, will you give me your word of honor that there won't be any selling and buying when she's around? That you won't allow any of your customers to come while she's here?"

Zach straightened and sat taller in his chair. "It's been many a year since somebody asked me for my word of honor. It feels good…and I give it! I promise you that your wife will be safe here. In fact, we'll make it our business to watch after her when she's in this neck of the woods."

Justin stood and formally shook hands with Zach, Wolf, and Keen. "I thank you and I'll depend on you!"

The coffee started perking, the cheerful sound and inviting aroma invading the room.

After Laurel set out the food for their meal and worked out a time to return to start their lessons, she and Justin departed, believing they had made new friends, and they looked forward to seeing some old ones.

Adam's letters, bringing the joy of news from him but renewing the pang of missing him, were soon ragged from being read so many times by so many people. He was enjoying his adventure; he thought the country was interesting but wouldn't want to spend his life there; he had made some new friends; he missed all of them; he wanted at least one letter a week and he wanted to know *everything*. Each person had to deal privately with missing him, but they tried to support each other. When Sarah discovered that Alexis was carrying a letter to school and sleeping with another under her pillow, the family knew she was grieving. Sarah helped her print out her own letters to Adam, laboriously, telling him her news and a couple of concerns. Caroline played with her more after school and David kept her talking on her way to school and back. He knew he was trying to walk in his big brother's shoes. Sometimes he wished to be free from the responsibility, but mostly it made him walk tall.

Sarah turned twenty-one in May, 1938. She, at Laurel's encouragement, had started filling a hope chest for her own home. She spent some of her earnings buying linens, dishes and pots and pans. The chest itself was the old wooden flour and meal bin, with a middle partition, that Laurel had used in the logging camps when she had cooked for more than thirty people. Sarah treasured it for her memories of sitting on it when she was little and for the fact that her daddy had built it. It would be the first piece of furniture in her own home.

When Adam had left home, Sarah seemed to realize that an era had ended. The past four years in Lake Eagle Rest had been great fun, but she knew the time had come to look to her own future. She settled down to dating a young man, Roe Bradley, whom Justin and Laurel admired. His mother had died two years previously, leaving several children. Being the only son and oldest child, he shouldered a big share of the responsibility for his younger sisters.

When Justin and Laurel realized Sarah was getting serious, they shared their concerns about Roe. "I wish he had finished high school," Laurel said. "He dropped out to help with the family while his mother was sick."

"I talked with the foreman of the timber job Roe's been on for the past two years. Says he's one of the best he's got. Has initiative and common sense." He paused then continued. "Have you noticed him in the youth activities? He's quick to grasp the essence of most any situation and knows how to respond. The other boys seem to look to him for guidance in a new situation. And he's usually right."

"I like the way he treats his sisters. Reminds me of Adam," Laurel said.

Justin teased, "Oh! If he reminds you of your son, then the matter is settled. He passes inspection."

"*Our* son, Mr. Worth!" Laurel retorted. "And you're just as proud of him as I am!"

He hugged her and started out the door to go to work, hesitated and added, "Another plus for him is that he likes to read. He borrows books from me almost every time he comes. Always returns them, too."

As Laurel cooked supper on Friday afternoon, expecting Abby to appear at any minute, she thought, *The enrichment brought about by Abby's presence and influence would be hard to measure. Besides her vast reservoir of knowledge, her enthusiasm is contagious and hooks the young people into learning skills they would otherwise ignore. First aid, singing, and swimming are obvious results, but some of her more important gifts will hopefully stay with them for a lifetime: a sense of fair play; a sense of humor; seeing and responding to the needs of others; and an absolute enjoyment of life!*

Miss Abby's arrival was always heralded as befitted a family member. She, at Laurel's request, had started bringing books from the public library in Deerbrook — books for each member of the family. When she swung the canvas bag off her shoulder the Worth children scrambled to find what she had brought them this time. Classics such as *Treasure Island, Swiss Family Robinson, Little Women, Black Beauty, Alice in Wonderland* and *Uncle Tom's Cabin* were among the books she had chosen so far. Laurel, knowing that she would have chosen well this week, thanked her friend for bringing yet another enrichment into their lives.

As soon as the children had left with their books, Laurel and Abby sat down for a cup of coffee. They could talk for hours about improvements in childbirth techniques or treatment of different ailments or accidents, comparing notes about various natural herbal medications.

Justin and Abby always looked forward to their weekly after-supper argument about politics. She was as definite a Democrat as Justin was a Republican. They sharpened and honed their viewpoints and verbal skills all week to see who could win the Friday night contest.

It drove her to distraction when Justin criticized the concept of "big government" getting involved in so many social programs and providing so much welfare. He explained that he saw it was necessary under the present Depression, but once started on such a large scale, the government would find it hard to rein in or adjust the dole according to alleviated circumstances.

"Some people," he argued, "will feel entitled to continue being supported by the government—which is us, the taxpayers—even after they are able to find jobs. This stifles initiative and the American spirit."

"I don't have your perspective on the future," Abby replied. "I'm more crisis oriented to take care of the problems presented to us now. You see how the New Deal has helped the country. What would you have Roosevelt do, other than what he has done?"

"Roosevelt was handed the biggest problem this country has faced—probably since the Civil War—and has had to use extreme involvement of government. I'm not criticizing him. I *am* saying that I hope our future leaders will have the political strength and moral courage to steer the ship of state back to less government involvement in the daily affairs of her people."

"Justin," Abby said, "you'd better be thankful for government involvement. You and Laurel would be in daily quandary about the hungry children around you. As it is, the commodities bring the problem to manageable proportions."

"I know and I *am* thankful. I'm just airing my fears to someone who will listen and respond intelligently. Another concern is deficit spending. In our entire history, the government has spent what the taxes provided and no more. It has stayed within its budget. Deficit spending scares me because, once started, it's hard to stop. We'll be mortgaging the futures of our children and grandchildren."

"I can see that. Surely our subsequent leaders can correct that once this Depression is over."

The children were in and out and around while these discussions were taking place. After the first or second scare, at the sound of raised voices, that Miss Abby would never come back again, they realized that she and their daddy were thoroughly enjoying themselves. Almost unaware, the children were receiving different viewpoints on how a government should operate. They were also unconsciously learning that a person can disagree without being disagreeable.

Everyone agreed that Miss Abby kept the air stirring. One

Saturday after swimming lessons, she lingered, talking in the back yard in her shapeless swimsuit. When a logging truck pulled into the yard, Laurel called, "Abby! Get in this house right now and put on some clothes!"

Abby, in the middle of a sentence, grabbed a raincoat off a post, put it on and kept talking. The incident was forgotten until after she left.

Later that day Justin teased Laurel. "Why were you worried about the loggers seeing Abby in that swimsuit?"

"I was afraid, at a distance, they would think it was me," she admitted.

Justin enjoyed a good laugh before replying. "Laurel, between you and me, that swimsuit looks about the same on Abby as it would on a plank. No curves. Now you, my dear, not only have curves, they're in the right places. A man would have to be blind in one eye to confuse you with Abby."

Laurel felt inordinately pleased the rest of the day.

Brand Waters, for all his drunken boasting, was afraid to go around the Worth place to try to talk to Lila. His angry, befuddled mind came up with a solution that he was sure would succeed in getting his family back.

One afternoon as David and Alexis were walking home from school on a lonely stretch of road, he suddenly loomed in front of them, demanding harshly, "Are you Justin's Worth's younguns?"

Startled, David grabbed hold of Alexis' hand as he answered, "Yes, we are! Who're you?"

"My wife and boys is livin' at your place and won't come home."

"You're Ned and Vic's daddy?"

"Yes. And I want you to give *your* daddy a message. Tell him I said he took my younguns and, if he don't bring 'em back, I'll take *his* younguns. I could grab you and that pretty little sister any time I want! Like right now!"

David put his arm around Alexis, pulled her close and yelled, "Don't you dare touch my sister!"

"Oh, I ain't gonna grab you today 'cause I need you to take him my message. If he don't do what I tell him, I'll git you kids one way or another. Tell him that!"

"My daddy ain't afraid of you or anybody else! You'd better be scared of *him*!"

"He'd best be afraid—for his kids! Tell him I warned him." With that he turned, went down a trail and disappeared into the woods.

David and Alexis ran all the way home and almost fell in the door, pale and out of breath. Laurel calmed them down and finally got the story out of them. When Justin got home, David recounted the tale more coherently.

Justin knew Brand was mean enough to carry out his threat, and knew it could happen any time Brand had enough liquor in him to bolster his courage. He wouldn't allow himself to think of his children in the hands of such a brute.

Laurel knew Justin's calmness was for her and David as he hugged David and thanked him for being brave and for taking care of his little sister. Then he turned to Laurel and said, "I have to do some thinking. I'm going for a ride on Tattoo."

Seeing her expression, he hugged her and said, "No, I'm not going after him—yet."

His first spurt of anger urged him to find Brand, beat him within an inch of his life and force him to leave Lake Eagle Rest. As he rode Tattoo through the lake bed he also thought of going to the law. But that would involve Lila and the boys.

"Tattoo, I've never met a poorer excuse for a man. He seems totally worthless. He lives to drink and inflict abuse on others— mostly women and children. It seems he's beyond redemption."

That word "redemption" brought him up short. He was so startled by the thought he reined in Tattoo and sat totally still in the saddle. One thought chased another and another...

Could God be asking him to do *that?* To go to Brand with love instead of anger? To tell him about God's love and His offer of a changed life?

Could a real man do that, he puzzled, *in spite of the threats to kidnap and harm his children?*

The answer in his spirit was clear and uncompromising. "It would take *a real Christian man* to do that."

His whole self rose up in protest. *Brand doesn't deserve love; he deserves a beating. Besides, I'm not a very good Christian yet and I don't know how to do this kind of stuff.*

The answer, again crystal clear, interrupted his evasions.

Ethan!

He grew quiet and sat awhile with his head bowed. He knew when he had lost an argument and he knew what he had to do. Feeling somewhat as if the breath had been knocked out of him, he patted Tattoo and rode home.

"Laurel," he said, striding through the kitchen door, interrupting her cooking, "leave that with Sarah! I need to talk to you."

In their bedroom with the door closed, Laurel stood and looked at him while he paced. "I need to tell you what just happened to me and you need to tell me if I'm thinking straight."

He walked to the windows, his hands in his pockets. With his back to her, he spoke hesitantly, spacing his words. "I believe I just got instructions to take Ethan with me to see Brand and have Ethan tell him how to become a Christian."

He ran his fingers through his hair and turned around. "It's so confusing. One minute I wanted to beat him half to death and the next minute I wanted to save his soul. I'm...I'm not very comfortable with what's happening to me."

Laurel, half-laughing and half-crying, hugged him with all her might.

"Justin, that's the best possible solution. If Brand could change, they could be a family again. And, as for you, I think you're soundly converted! You're thinking like a Christian ought to think!"

"Well, I'm not exactly sure I like it! One part of me still wants to beat him up!"

"That's natural, too. God is working in you 'to *will* and to *do His* good pleasure.'"

Shaking his head as if he had been broadsided, he and Laurel went to join the family for supper. It was agreed that someone would take David and Alexis to school, pick them up, and watch over them closely until this was settled.

When Justin and Ethan arrived at Terminal Town the next afternoon a frightening sight greeted them. Brand, slap-happy drunk, was walking the logs in the holding pond, swaying and singing. Three or four men had gathered, looking on with consternation and fear. Each one knew of at least one logger who had drowned by falling off the logs and getting trapped underneath.

Justin and Ethan looked at each other with dread but with understanding. It had been years since they had walked the logs together but they knew they had it to do again. There could be only one outcome for Brand the way things stood. They would do their best to save him.

Each one picked up a long pole — that would hopefully help them keep their balance — and stepped out onto the slippery rolling logs, heading toward Brand from opposite sides. They believed they had enough skill together to manhandle him to safety. But Brand was having none of it! When he saw Justin he flew into a fighting rage and lost his balance.

The next few moments were filled with terror. Brand fell and slipped between two logs into the murky water. Ethan lay down on a log to try to get hold of him. The log rolled and Ethan was in the water, the logs closing over him. Justin, aware that two men from the bank were now with him, yelled for them to help him pry open the logs where the men had gone under. It was a death defying dance, but when they forced an opening of the logs, a hand grasped Justin's pole, then a head appeared. It was Ethan and he was clutching Brand with his other hand. Somehow, impossibly, Justin and his helpers maneuvered the two men across a couple of logs where they lay gagging and spitting up water. By now more help had arrived. Two men had roped a few logs together to make a raft to bring Ethan and Brand in.

Later in Mack's shack, Ethan and Brand got into some borrowed dry clothes. Brand fell across the bed exhausted but Ethan joined the men around the table drinking coffee. A festive atmosphere reigned — with good reason. They had cheated death again!

Mack said, "Justin tells us you're a preacher man."

"Yes. I'm pastor of Pleasant Valley Baptist Church."

"Never knowed a preacher who could dance the logs like you done today," one of the loggers observed.

"I've not always been a preacher. I used to log with Justin. He taught me that dance."

"I reckon I'll ask what everybody's wonderin'," Mack said. "Why did you'ns come over here today?"

Justin answered, "We wanted to talk to Brand."

"You'll have to sober him up first."

A voice spoke from the bed, "I'm sober! Getting' half drowned'll sober anybody!"

"Brand, come on over and drink some coffee," Mack invited.

As Brand came to the table the other loggers rose, saying they had to get back to work. They shook hands formally with Justin and Ethan. It was a sign of respect.

Brand did seem sober, to Justin's surprise, and his usual belligerence was gone. He looked from Justin to Ethan and back to Justin.

"Why'd you save me?"

The blunt question hung in the air, leaving Justin and Ethan without an answer for a moment. Then Justin said, "It's what anybody would do."

"No," Brand countered, "not just anybody. Why *you* and this preacher man?"

Justin decided he was sober enough to hear the truth. "I needed to talk to you. You threatened my children."

Brand interrupted. "And *you* took my wife and children off!"

"No!" Justin objected. "Your wife and boys left *you* because *you* stay drunk and *you* beat them. I've seen the bruises. *You* ran them off. My wife and I and the community fixed a place for them to live. *Because they're afraid to live with you!*"

Brand dropped his head. "The liquor makes me do crazy things."

Ethan leaned forward. "You may be getting some poison moonshine."

"And what would a preacher man know about moonshine?" Brand sneered.

"I used to help my daddy make it."

"You're a funny kind of preacher. I know why *he* came to see me but why're *you* here?"

"Justin and I came to talk to you about asking God to take over your life. You sure are making a big mess out of it by yourself."

In the silence brought on by that bald statement, both men stared at him. Justin thought, *Ethan, you don't fool around, do you? You know how to go for the gut!*

Brand looked at Ethan with misery in his eyes. "The liquor keeps away the pain."

Ethan's tone softened. "Tell me about the pain."

"It's knowin' that I'm no good. When I'm sober I'm ashamed of who I am. When I'm drunk, I forgit how bad I am."

"Do you want to change?"

"Sure. But I can't. I don't have whatever it takes to change."

"God can give you what you need."

Angrily, Brand said, "God ain't goin' to have nothin' to do with me! You ought to know that!"

Ethan spoke firmly. "Brand, look at me! God loves you enough that He sent His Son to die that you might have abundant life. Not this miserable existence. But you have to believe that and receive what He has done for you. He gives the power to overcome drink or whatever else that has control over you."

Brand, still trying to make Ethan understand that he was beyond God's reach, turned to Justin. "*You* tell him how lowdown you think I am. I've seen it in your eyes — like when our baby girl, Rose, died and I wouldn't help with the casket."

Justin's clear blue eyes held Brand's gaze as he said, "Brand, I had a different kind of problem. For years I thought I could live my life without God. I thought I didn't need Him. I hurt my family in a different way than you did. But God forgave me and they forgave me. Let this man tell you how to receive God's love and forgiveness and the power to begin a new life."

For the next few moments the rough lumber shack became a tabernacle as Ethan ushered a repentant Brand into the Presence where he asked for and received mercy — a package deal that included the power to become a child of God, with all the benefits, privileges and responsibilities thereof.

Brand, like a happy but bewildered child, asked, "Could I go home with you and talk some more? I know I'm goin' to need some help to understand all you told me."

After Justin went in search of Mack and told him Brand would be gone for a couple of days, they got some of his things together and were on their way. Brand surprised them when he asked Justin not to tell Lila about what had happened to him. "I want to do some talkin' with the preacher here and some thinkin' and maybe some prayin', if I can learn how. When I know I've really changed, I'll get you to ask her and the boys to see me, but not before."

Justin was greatly encouraged. It was the first responsible act he had ever seen Brand perform.

Terminal Town was all agog that Brand Waters was sober and was working regularly at the saw mill. He was even fixing up his shack. The preacher man, as they called him, was a regular visitor and took Brand off with him on weekends to go to church. It was whispered that Brand had "got religion." It was all a ruse, they reckoned, to get his family back.

Lila, of course, heard the talk but Laurel advised her to pray and wait for Brand to make his move. It was about a month before he contacted Justin to set up a meeting with Lila and the boys, asking Justin and Laurel to be present. His family and Justin and Laurel could hardly believe the handsome, clear-eyed, well-groomed man who appeared. *If the inward change is as great as the outward, we've got a new person here,* Justin thought.

Lila and the boys, alternating between hope and fear, gradually heard and sensed the difference. After much talk, they agreed that they would move back home with Brand the next day. Hope, love and curiosity mixed to form this decision. They all were eager to get to know this likeable stranger who was their husband and father.

Chapter Nine

From the moment Zach Barnes had mentioned Abner Riker, Justin and Laurel realized how much they would love to see him and his family again.

"How long has it been?" Justin asked.

"Since the day he escorted our logging crew and families safely through outlaw country — the day we moved from Locust Hollow."

"Let's see," Justin mused, "that was in 1930 after the Depression hit in 1929 and closed down our logging operation. It's been nine years. A long time to go without seeing a good friend."

"Yes, it is," she agreed.

"We'll have to meet him on his own stomping ground for his safety. He's probably one of the most elusive bootleggers in these mountains. His family's been in the business for two or three generations. It's the only way they know to make a living."

"I know," Laurel answered. "I hope they never find him."

"That's an interesting thing for a prohibition campaigner to say," Justin teased.

"I know that, too. I still hate what liquor does to families. I always will because I saw such terrible results when I was teaching. But Abner's a good friend. I wish we could help him get out of the moonshine business."

"That would be a big order. He sure brought some drama into our lives the day he kidnapped and blindfolded me to go take pictures of his still."

"He scared all of us but you half out of our wits. When Adam and Sarah jumped on him, I thought his masked men might shoot us all down right there in the road."

"It's strange how he and I liked each other from the beginning."

"Well, he knew you weren't afraid of him, even with his mask and his bluster. *I* could tell that. Then he realized your sense of direction in the woods in spite of being blindfolded. Somehow he knew he could trust you not to bring in the law even before he let you go that day."

"After you delivered their baby he felt he owed us a debt."

"Yes. I'll never forget that night! The baby was breech and couldn't be born the way he was turned. Rosalee was in such a dangerous state of exhaustion, Hannah and I thought we might lose both of them. The Good Lord helped us and gave us wisdom to do as He has many times."

They both were silent for a while, remembering...

After that birth, Abner gave himself the task of protecting the Worths. Locust Hollow, the small isolated community where the Worth Logging Camp operated, was located in the middle of rough mountainous terrain which served as a haven for bootleggers—and outlaws.

Laurel couldn't help but like Abner in spite of what he did for a living, but after he saved Justin's life *she* knew she owed *him* a debt she could never repay. Bill "Bandit" Butler, wanted for robbery and murder in several states, was hiding out with his gang in some caves near Locust Hollow. As Justin rode home one day, unsuspecting and unarmed, Butler made his move, thinking Justin was carrying a cash payroll. When his kerchief that served as a mask fell off his face, he raised his pistol to shoot Justin point blank in the chest. But he never pulled the trigger. Abner and *his* band of masked men, armed with rifles and shotguns, surrounded him and his partner, took away their guns and ordered the gang out of the territory. Justin knew that was not the only time Abner and his men had protected him and his family.

"It's time we renewed our friendship," Justin said. "Ask Zach to arrange a meeting on a Saturday so Sarah and the other children can go. He was one of Adam's and Sarah's favorite people."

Two weeks later, with much excitement, the Worth family arrived at the home of Zach Barnes to find Abner's family already there. Justin and Abner started to shake hands, then grabbed each other for a mutual bear hug. Their emotions choked any words for a moment. Abner recovered first. "I'm glad you've kept yourself alive, Justin!"

"I'm glad to see you, my good friend! I'm sorry it's been so long."

Meanwhile, Laurel hugged Rosalee and looked around. "Where is he?" she asked.

Rosalee understood. "Come here, Bryce."

A strapping young boy who was a younger version of Abner came forward smiling. Before Laurel could speak, he said, "Mama and Dad told me that you brought me into the world safe and sound. I thank you, ma'am."

Laurel held out her hand. As he shook it she smiled and said, "You look like you were worth all the trouble."

"I hope so, ma'am."

"I see he has his daddy's charm," Laurel remarked to Rosalee.

There was a general hullabaloo as everybody met everybody and started catching up on each other's lives. Nine years made a considerable difference in children's appearances, but Abner knew Sarah right away. He asked about Adam and talked with Caroline and David. He then asked to meet Alexis, the only one he didn't know.

Sarah pleased him greatly when she said, "I still have the eagle feather you gave me and Adam still has the bear tooth you gave him. Daddy put the tooth on a leather thong and Adam almost wore it out. He asked me to keep it for him when he left to join the CCCs."

Justin and Abner walked out into the yard where they could get caught up on each other's lives. Abner told him that his mother and dad had died in the past few years. He, then, voiced a concern to Justin that he probably never would have told anyone else. "Moonshinin' has been our way of life for several generations, but I want better for my younguns, Justin. I…I just cain't figure out how to make it happen. We seem to be stuck here."

"The children haven't ever had any schooling, have they?"

"No. There's no school close enough."

"We may be able to help you. Let me call Laurel."

When Abner repeated his comments, at Justin's request, Laurel smiled. "I can come to your house, Abner, and teach you and Rosalee and the children."

"How can you do that?"

"That's my job now, to go into homes and teach adults who need to learn to read and write. I'm teaching Zach and Wolf and Keen."

"He told me, but it's a good piece further to our place."

She turned to Justin for his response.

"You know I want her to come, Abner, but would she be safe from people who come to buy from you?"

"I would guarantee her safety. The word would go out that she's our friend and that she lives under our protection. Everybody in these parts knows what that means."

"Yes, I know, too," Justin said. "I'm alive because of it."

Laurel said happily, "I'll add your family to the list and we'll work out the details before we leave. Now I need to help Rosalee get our food set out."

Laurel and Rosalee had brought enough lunch for a bunch of hungry people. Zach and Wolf and Keen had cleaned up the place inside and out and surprised Laurel and Justin by being such good hosts. Zach, talking and laughing with obvious enjoyment and pride over his part in this reunion, was a different man from the sick recluse Laurel had found a few weeks earlier.

The day went fast as the young people talked, pitched horseshoes and played ball. The adults talked and reminisced as they drank coffee. Details were worked out about Laurel going to Abner's house to teach.

Before they left, Zach gave them one admonition. "I hope the word of this meetin' don't git out. I don't want my bad reputation ruined."

When Laurel added Abner Riker's family to her growing list for Mr. McKenzie, the superintendent of schools, she asked permission to start teaching the children as well as the adults. Mr. McKenzie agreed, on the condition that she teach the children after teaching the adults and that she ask the adults to pass on to the children what they were learning.

"This is primarily adult education and we must keep it so," he reasoned, "but this is a good opportunity to find the number of children in the area who don't go to school. We would need names, ages, birth dates and any amount of schooling they've had. If we find enough children, we can submit to the state a request to start a school in that area."

Laurel's eyes were shining. "Oh! Do you think that's possible?"

"We'll work on it with your help." He turned to the list again. "You seem especially eager to teach this Riker family. Do you know them?"

"Yes. We met them when my husband logged in Locust Hollow about ten years ago. Abner saved Justin from being shot in a hold-up by Bill Butler, the outlaw. Then I delivered their son, Bryce, who is now eleven."

She thought it wise not to mention that Abner had kidnapped Justin to take pictures of his still. That might be a little hard for a man like the superintendent to understand.

Mr.McKenzie had heard of the Rikers and the Barneses. He knew they were reputed to be bootleggers and to be dangerous. He asked no questions, however, because Laurel spoke *warmly* of them as *friends*. Evidently she would be in no danger from them.

He also knew, as Laurel did, that education was one pathway out of their generationally engendered, circumscribed way of life. Justin and Laurel Worth seemed uniquely to hold the key to open the door for future generations to escape to a better future.

He chose to say nothing of this yet. Keeping his excitement tempered, he merely said, "You seem to find a welcome into homes where most people couldn't or wouldn't go."

She nodded. "That's mostly because of Justin and his photography. He's been taking family pictures around here for years. Everybody knows him and likes him."

Turning back to the business at hand she said, "My CCC boys whose parents can't read or write asked me to go their homes, so I'm adding them to our list. I also have a special desire to go to the homes of some loggers who worked in our camps in Pisgah Forest several years ago. Do I have your approval?"

"Of course. We need as complete a list as we can compile. If it keeps growing we'll probably need to hire a helper for you."

Justin knew he needed to escort Laurel on her first trip to Abner's house. When Abner had given directions to Justin about a shortcut to his house, Justin knew it would take a seasoned woodsman to find his way in. Once they left the road, the trail took them down a mountainside through dense, dark woods, where sunlight could barely penetrate. When it became too steep, they followed a narrow ledge cut out like a shelf that wound around the mountain, always angling downward, with a steep drop-off of several hundred feet on one side. They heard a thundering sound before they saw a magnificent waterfall, several hundred feet high, leaping down the side of the mountain across the gorge. Justin looked back and smiled at her.

She, on Tattoo, continued to follow Justin, hugging the bank as he was, against the possibility of loose earth shifting along the edge, sending them and their horses tumbling into the abyss. She didn't want Justin to know how scared she was, especially where the trail had eroded. Tattoo handled it with his usual skill, but she knew they were in danger.

Justin's trust in Tattoo kept his fear for Laurel in check. No way would he ever let her come this way again. What happened next was vintage Justin.

He started singing, quietly and soothingly, his nonsense song that the children loved. "Kitty-mo-ki-mo, dow-wow, wid-a-hi, wid-a ho, wid a rumpa-stumpa-rutabaga, nip-at-katawinka. Sing some kitty wants a ki-me-oh!"

Tattoo jerked his head up and down and snorted. Justin asked, "What was that comment Tattoo made?"

Laughing, she answered, "He said, 'There he goes with that silly song again!'" Then she added softly to Justin's back, "I love you, Mr. Worth!"

Not daring to look back, he answered, "And I love you, *Mrs.* Worth!"

Royalty could not have received a warmer and more proper welcome, given the circumstances. The shack sat cosily in a clearing, at the foot of a wooded mountain. The yard was freshly swept. An old tin tub sat on each side of the steps with a profusion of tiger lilies and dahlias tumbling over the sides. A swing and two rocking chairs on the porch looked inviting to Laurel.

The entire family seemed to erupt out the door together, once they heard the horses. Abner took Tattoo's reins and helped Laurel from the saddle. She held on to him for a moment because her knees were still weak from riding that treacherous trail.

Justin swung off his horse, leaving it with Bryce, took Laurel's arm and led her to a rocking chair. Everybody hugged everybody and they all talked at once. Rosalee brought some order when she held up her hand and said, "Quiet, please! Don't talk them to death the first few minutes they're here!"

She turned to Laurel. "I know that's a rough ride. I've made some fresh coffee."

"Yes! That would be wonderful!"

They talked as they drank the coffee, which restored Laurel's usual equilibrium. Then she got right down to business by asking Bryce to bring her saddlebags where she kept her school supplies and books. They moved inside around the kitchen table for their first lesson. Since her first students would be Rosalee and Abner, Justin and the children went outside.

Laurel knew she was dealing with two intelligent people who had not had the privilege of a formal education. Wanting them to know how she felt, she said, "Abner and Rosalee, I'm going to teach you some skills that you need to know. In return, I want to learn some things from you that I would like to know."

Abner, mischief in his eyes, said in a serious tone, "I can teach you how to make a gallon of good moonshine."

Rosalee slapped his hand. "Abner!"

Laughing, Laurel said, "Thank you, Abner. If I ever feel the urge to learn, I'll know where to come. I was thinking more in terms of medicinal herbs and natural ways to treat illnesses and accidents."

"I'll share some of my remedies with you," Rosalee said. She was pleased that she had something to offer back. It gave them a more equal footing.

The lesson went well. Laurel explained and demonstrated how to print their names, teaching them the name of each letter. They followed her pattern and printed their names several times, repeating the letters aloud as they wrote. She then gave each an alphabet chart, teaching them the first thirteen letters, asking them to memorize them and practice printing each letter.

After a while of intense concentration and effort, Abner asked,

"Are you goin' to teach the younguns, too? They can help us remember these letters."

Laurel knew that was true. She asked, "Are you ready to show them what you've learned?"

"You want *us* to help you teach them?" Abner asked, not sure of himself.

"Yes, that's a good way to start. They may pass you up, but remember that you started learning first."

Rosalee called them and Justin to come in. Bonnie, two years older than Bryce, was an attractive girl. Laurel said, "Bonnie, you look like your mother, who is a very pretty lady, and Bryce, you're very much like your dad."

Both children were excited over the prospect of learning. Soon Abner was proudly showing Bryce his name and explaining the part of the alphabet he knew. Rosalee did the same with Bonnie. Laurel followed the same procedure with them until they could print and spell their names and knew the letters of half the alphabet. She asked them to say the alphabet over and over and print each letter until they memorized it. She promised to teach them the rest of the alphabet and start some simple arithmetic on her next visit.

When they finished, Rosalee and Bonnie flew into action to put a meal on the table. Laurel said, "I'm glad you asked us to eat. I've been smelling that beef stew ever since I walked through the door."

Served with coleslaw and cornbread, it was delicious. Rhubarb pie was served with coffee for dessert. The food and conversation was satisfying in more ways than one as Justin and Abner bandied a quiet hum of words back and forth with an occasional burst of laughter. Bryce was taking it all in.

Laurel noticed a brightly colored quilt on the wall opposite the fireplace. "That's a beautiful pattern, Rosalee. What is it?" Then they were off and running about quilting. Bonnie showed Laurel a quilt top she was sewing by hand.

It was difficult to leave, but they had to visit another family on their way home. At Justin's request, Abner led them out by another trail. It took a little longer but wasn't so hard on the nerves.

After Abner left them, Justin said, "I was proud of you on that mountain trail, Laurel, but I don't want you to ever take it again. Come around this way. I'll come back with you and make sure you know the way before I turn you loose to come by yourself."

"I'd love for you to come but what about *your* work?"

"We'll come on Saturday or even Sunday afternoon. I won't let you come alone yet."

Papa would like Lake Eagle Rest. The thought came unbidden as Laurel worked on lesson plans. She laid down her pen and sat back, trying to see the community through Papa's eyes. The Worth family had lived there for five years and now felt as if they, too, were wrapped in the strong, neighborly fabric that wove together the lives of the people here.

She smiled as she remembered the remarks made yesterday by her friend, Nettie Campbell. As they walked to check on the Hot Lunch Program at school, Nettie suddenly interrupted their conversation by saying, "That's the Bailey's cow! I bet they don't know she's wandered this far from home."

Laurel looked around, puzzled. "I don't see a cow."

Nettie laughed and said, "Listen."

When Laurel heard a cowbell tinkling in the distance, she asked, "But how could you tell?"

"Oh, I can probably tell the sound of every cowbell in the community."

Later that day, when they heard an unseen dog barking nearby, Nettie said absently, "I wonder why the Sloan's dog is carryin' on so."

Laurel marveled at the significance of these casual remarks. She was delighted that she and her family belonged to a community where a particular cowbell or the bark of a particular dog was recognized by sound only. She hugged the comfort of it to herself.

Papa, she knew, would like this sense of community: neighbors watching after neighbors; their response in crises; the way they pulled together toward a common goal, such as the Hot Lunch Program; opportunities they offered the youth, such as the first aid classes; their willingness to abandon ingrained ideas and adapt to change; the personal renewals brought about by the revival, which was bringing a corporate renewal, manifest in multiple ways. One was the change in attitude toward Terminal Town.

True, there were some holdouts. The Chandlers' daughter, Ailene, had come to Laurel last week. She was distraught because her father had refused to let her read *Little Women,* which she had borrowed from Caroline. He reminded her that the only book allowed to be read in his house was the Bible. Laurel advised her to obey her father and promised her that she and Justin would have a talk with her parents.

And, of course, it seemed that Gussie was there, always and everywhere! She had, as the pastor expected, given grief over Laurel's Sunday school class continuing in the auditorium of the church. She absented herself two Sundays in protest, leaving the church without a pianist. Except for a few, the congregation stood with the pastor and some even declared they liked the sound of the voices without the piano. When Miss Abby visited the church on the second Sunday that Gussie was absent, Justin invited her to play. The rafters soon were ringing as the youth surged forward and gathered around to sing as they did on Friday nights. The congregation was delighted. When Gussie heard the news she realized she had made a mistake. She hurried back to the piano bench the next Sunday morning. Justin was pleased his tactic had worked. The incident only increased her antagonism toward the Worths and all that they stood for in the community.

Winter fiercely gripped the mountains on its yearly visit. Laurel's home visits were curtailed but she had prepared ahead for this problem. She had taken books, alphabet charts, number charts, and simple arithmetic problems. She had shown them how to use grains of corn to add and subtract: tangible objects that gave substance to the strange numbers they were learning. She left simple instructions to keep them working when she couldn't get there.

Zach, Wolf and Keen had surprised her in their response. Zach, in spite of himself, was as pleased as a child with a new toy the first time he successfully printed his name. His self confidence zoomed to new heights, dragging Wolf and Keen along in his enthusiasm.

"I wish your mama could see us now. She'd be proud!"

"Perhaps she can see you," Laurel offered.

"Aw! You're funnin' us!"

"No, I'm serious! The Bible says we have a cloud of witnesses in heaven looking at what we're doing and how we're doing it."

"Where does it say that? Kin you show it to us?"

"Yes. Do you have a Bible? It's in the book of Hebrews."

Zach shook his head. "We buried her Bible with her. Ain't had one in the house since."

"I'll bring mine the next visit and show you the verses."

"It'd be comfortin' to know that she knows what we're doin'."

Nathan Buchanan was galloping along with his learning because he had Lark to help him. He was already reading simple first grade books and doing easy arithmetic problems. The excitement drew the boys' interest, so Laurel helped Lark set up a program where she and Nathan could begin teaching their own sons.

Abner preempted Laurel's need to make a decision about traveling in such cold weather. One morning Bryce showed up at Laurel's house, bringing their completed assignments and asking for more schoolwork, so they could keep up their momentum. Laurel introduced Bryce to the *McGuffey Reader* and was greatly pleased when she found that he could sound out simple words. She worked with him for several hours, realizing he could then begin to teach the others to read. This set a precedent and, in the coldest weather, Bryce or Wolf or Keen would gather the assignments of the families and travel to Laurel to get new ones. When she told Mr. McKenzie, he was surprised at their eagerness to learn and was further intrigued by her relationship with these people who had been considered unreachable.

Winter didn't seem to make too big a dent, however, in the comings and goings at the Worth house. Laurel found she could get three sets of quilting frames in the big room, so one afternoon each week a growing group of women gathered for a quilting party. If small children were present, they couldn't resist running under the quilts and pushing their heads up, making a little mound. They would squeal with delight when they were thumped on the head with a thimble.

Laurel had let it be known that Lila and her family needed some quilts. The women secretly agreed to surprise Lila with a log cabin quilt. She wouldn't know it was for her until it was finished.

It was difficult to keep the secret. Lila, irrepressible as always, would run her open palm over the quilt with autumn colors, exclaiming, "This is the prettiest pattern I've ever seen! Laurel, will you teach me how to do a quilt top like this?"

Laurel solemnly promised that she would. The women kept their heads down so she couldn't read the truth in their eyes. Gerta, Lila's friend from Terminal Town, felt her eyes go misty as she compared the former Lila with the present Lila, glowing with happiness. Gerta thought, *Lila's family is the talk of Terminal Town and Lake Eagle Rest in general. Brand Waters is a new man, causing some others, including Mack, who still find their comfort in the bottle to secretly wonder about the power it had taken for Brand's transformation. Someday, maybe we can ask the preacher man.*

The quilting went amazingly fast with so many needles making tiny uniform stitches that outlined the pattern. It was understood that they would quilt for the families in need first. Then each woman could bring a quilt top that she had pieced by hand to be quilted as they visited.

Lila burst in on the murmur of voices around the quilts. "I think we should do a quilt for Sarah. She showed me her hope chest last week."

The enthusiastic response warmed Laurel's heart. The women were off and running with ideas of what pattern to use. Laurel surprised herself by saying, "Let me show you a pattern *I* would like for her to have."

She spread out a quilt made of pieces of wool and velvet and silk. The browns, maroons, greens, reds, blacks, mingled with beige infused the various shapes with richness. Each piece was outlined with a thick, black briar stitch. As the women ran their hands over it and studied the pattern, Laurel said, "It's called a stained glass window quilt."

She felt a strong surge of emotion and for a moment could not continue. When she realized the women were waiting, she managed to continue. "That pattern would carry on a tradition and a memory of our years in the logging camps, *and* of a little girl we all loved who died with diphtheria. Her name was Joannie. Some of you have met Bess, her mother."

Lila said, "Yes, she was here when Rose died. Could she come and help us with the quilt?"

"I'd like to ask her and my other friends from the logging camp if it's okay with you."

They all agreed and Laurel sent word to Bess, Hannah, Nora and Alice. They soon were an integral part of the group.

One day when bad weather forced Justin to stay home, he worked in his darkroom in the morning developing pictures. He looked forward to a quiet afternoon and was surprised when women kept arriving. He found refuge by a fireplace at the other end of the house. That evening when he ventured out, he asked, "Has the Pony Express left?"

"Who?"

"The Pony Express. Neither rain nor sleet nor snow nor any other hazards…"

He and Laurel laughed together.

Justin offered the use of the big room, in winter, for prayer meeting on Wednesday nights.

It was agreed upon because the Worth house was more centrally located than the church and the huge fireplace gave forth a warm welcome. Everyone enjoyed a pleasant evening of singing and prayer with a middle-of-the-week encouragement from Pastor Pierce.

Occasionally, it didn't turn out that way. One Wednesday night a stranger showed up, saying he was Preacher Uriah Tanner from Tennessee and he would like to preach to the group. Justin welcomed him and introduced him. It wasn't long into his sermon before everyone realized they had a problem. His features were quite ugly with a hooked nose dividing a long, angular face. His expression, his flailing arms and thundering voice created a frightening atmosphere. It was his words, however, that dismayed Justin and Laurel. The God he portrayed was a God of wrath, delighting in seeking out sinners so He could punish them. Not one word of love or mercy or grace or forgiveness. Alexis perhaps spoke the discomfort of the listeners when she ran right in front of the preacher to find the security of her daddy's arms.

After awhile when the preacher showed no sign of ending his diatribe, Justin stood, walked to his side and laid his hand on his shoulder. It took the preacher a moment to realize that he was being asked to stop. His motions slowed and the thundering voice gradually leveled off, reminding Justin of a noisy machine coming to a halt. A moment of blessed silence followed, then Justin said politely, "Please be seated, Preacher. I want to say a few words."

A collective sigh of relief and shuffling of feet passed over the group. Justin said, "Preacher Tanner showed up this afternoon asking if he could speak to us tonight. I mean no disrespect for him but, since this is my home and I'm responsible for what you've heard tonight, I must make a statement."

He paused, looked around the room, and spoke clearly. "I used to have a low opinion of God, just like this preacher has. I lived my life believing He was up to no good. But I've found the truth about God and it has changed my life. God does hate sin but he loves the sinner. He is a God of judgment, but He is also a God of love and forgiveness. I couldn't let you leave here thinking I agreed with the picture of God that has been drawn here tonight."

He asked Pastor Pierce to come and dismiss the group. The pastor's prayer followed up on Justin's remarks, thanking God for His mercy and goodness.

Because of the unwritten law of hospitality in the mountains, the offensive preacher spent the night with the Worths. He was treated with respect but not much liking. When Justin left for work early the next morning, he made it clear that he expected the preacher to be on his way. Laurel was surprised when she came looking for David and Alexis to hear the man's voice exhorting her children that if they did such and such—a long list of offenses—God was going to send them straight to hell. He sounded pleased at the prospect.

When she entered the room and saw Alexis' and David's frightened faces, Laurel's natural courtesy fled and anger took over.

"I believe my husband asked you to be on your way. I thought you were gone."

His anger was thinly veiled as he smiled. "I was rebuked last night but I couldn't leave without these little ones knowing the truth."

"These children know the truth and it's not as you're telling it! Don't say another word to my children! I want you to leave my house right now!"

"But I'm God's messenger!"

"You're no such thing!" Laurel snapped.

He started to argue but his flow of words were cut off as abruptly as a spigot as he saw her pick up a broom that was standing by the fireplace. With a determined motion she slapped the broom up against his feet. He took a step. She swept again. He took another step. It was almost a dance before she had him out the door. He backed down the steps, pointing his finger to punctuate his angry remarks. When he started calling down the wrath of God upon the house, Laurel herded the awestruck children back inside and firmly closed the door.

Alexis hugged her mama tight around the waist, saying, "He scares me!"

David wanted to laugh in the worst sort of way, but he wasn't sure it was appropriate. Finally the laugh won and he sputtered, "Mama, you were so funny sweeping him out! He had trouble trying to stay ahead of your broom."

Laurel was still distressed over her children's exposure to such toxic religion. She asked them to sit down so she could explain.

"It's very important what you believe about God because you live your life accordingly. That preacher kept telling you that, if you do certain things, God will send you straight to hell. I heard him say that several times. You must understand that God doesn't send anyone to hell. God gave His Son so that no one has to go to hell. If a person goes to hell, it's because he or she chooses to go — in spite of all that God has done to keep them from going. Do you understand the difference?"

"Yes," David answered. "I don't think God likes what he says about Him. Do you, Mama?"

"No. It's not the truth. Alexis, do you understand?"

Alexis nodded her head. "God wouldn't hurt us. He loves us like you and Daddy do."

"Yes. He loves you even more."

Chapter Ten

April showers had softened the earth and plowing time was upon Justin. He found that he was eager to feel the plow cut through the earth, opening it to receive the seeds for another harvest. One glorious Saturday with dogwoods blooming all around the field, he was enjoying turning up a furrow, making a beeline for an oak at the other end of the long field. Suddenly, he saw Sarah and Roe making their way toward him, over the fresh turned, brown earth. He felt a moment of anxiety until he saw them laughing. No bad news. Then he stopped, totally still, knowing what was coming.

He fished his handkerchief out of his back pocket and wiped his face and hands. He took a drink from the flask he kept on his belt and used a trickle of water as he brushed his fingers through his hair. *That's as spruced up as I can get for my daughter,* he thought.

"Mr. Worth," Roe called, "we need to talk to you for a minute."

"I've been looking for some help," Justin countered.

"We came for *your* help, Daddy," Sarah said. Her happiness was tangible in her voice, her eyes, her confident stance. Their eyes met and she knew that he knew what was at hand.

Roe, for a moment, felt left out. Then he found his voice.

"Mr. Worth, Sarah and I love each other and we want to get married. We came today to ask your permission and your blessing."

"Sarah?" The single word carried a volume of meaning, but Sarah understood.

"Yes, Daddy, I love Roe. He's the man I want to marry." She laid her soft hand on his calloused one, as it rested on the plow handle, looked him straight in the eye and added softly, "He's the best man I know besides you."

Almost undone, he gathered her in his arms. They stood in a tight embrace. Words were unnecessary — and impossible.

Roe knew how close they were. He also knew he needed to present his case. "I know you love her, sir, and she loves you. I promise on my word of honor to love her and take care of her the way you'd expect me to."

Justin released Sarah and reached out his hand to Roe. "I've had my eye on you because I knew this was coming. I think you're a good man, like she says. If you both are sure in your own hearts and minds, you have my permission. Have you talked to your mother, Sarah?"

"No, not formally. We wanted your answer first."

"Go home and talk to her. You know how much I depend on her judgment and common sense. Then we'll all four talk when I get home tonight. We need to give you our blessing together."

The wedding was set for June. Sarah wanted a simple ceremony on the big porch facing the lake bed and mountain range. Ethan, of course, would officiate.

Mr. McKenzie, the superintendent of schools, looked through Laurel's reports on the Adult Education Program; he thought, *Laurel Worth doesn't understand how phenomenal her success is with these remote mountain people who have never learned to read and write. She and her husband seem to think it's a natural occurrence. Perhaps they're opening the door for a new day for the next generation.*

Laurel, riding through the mountains, enjoying the new life of spring about her, realized and relished the truth that this was the destiny for which God had been preparing her and Justin. *He takes care of all the details,* she thought, *when He prepares a person for a calling. Our work in the logging camps, learning to respect and love these people; my work in the CCC school; Miss Abby's common sense teaching of first aid; and, last but not least, Justin's relationship with these people fostered through the years. God knows what He's about! I'm so happy He's allowing us to be a part of it!*

The sense of destiny that rode with her did not inform her that her next visit would open a door that would have to be entered often in several homes in the next few months—before the door of education could even be considered. It was the door through which she would bring healing and survival. It was the door of destiny through which she would minister for the rest of her life. But, of course, destiny was too wise to tell her all that up front.

As soon as she saw Imogene Ryan, she knew she was faced with a very sick woman. The family, added to her list last week, was unknown even to Justin. Mrs. Ryan, a widow, was lying on a cot in the overheated main room of the shack. Her teenage daughter, Judith, was washing dishes. A concerned neighbor had asked for this visit and had prepared them for Laurel's arrival.

Imogene was so pale, her skin seemed translucent, like white wax. When Laurel asked, "Can you tell me how you feel?" her answer was so garbled Laurel couldn't understand a word.

Judith explained, "She can't talk plain. Her tongue is swole up and is real red. I think her throat's sore 'cause she has trouble swallowin'."

Laurel had a momentary panic, remembering the diphtheria that had killed Joannie. She took a deep breath, closed her eyes for a minute and breathed a wordless prayer. Then she was ready.

"Let me look at your tongue."

Laurel had to control herself to keep from recoiling at the sight of the blood-red, swollen tongue. It looked like a piece of raw beefsteak.

She asked, "How does your throat feel?"

Imogene whispered, "Burns."

"How long has she been like this?" Laurel asked Judith.

"She ain't had no energy for several weeks. Kin barely git out of bed. But her tongue just swole up a few days ago."

"Is she able to eat?"

"Not much with her tongue and throat the way they are. She don't want much 'cause it always hurts her stomach and she has to...to stay on the chamber pot."

Laurel was translating the girl's words into symptoms, which she could file into an orderly list and relate to Abby or to Dr. Leighton.

Smiling and speaking gently to the frightened girl, Laurel said, "I need to know what you and she eat most of the time."

"Since Pa died we've had a hard scrabble to keep food on the table. We eat mostly potatoes and cornbread. Our cow wandered off and I never could find her. She mighta fell and broke her leg or got lost. I...I'm afraid to leave Ma long enough to make a good search."

Realizing by now that Imogene didn't have the symptoms of diphtheria, Laurel said, "Judith, I know you're worried about your mother. I believe she'll get better when she has some good, nourishing food."

"Then she ain't gonna to die?"

"No. But she needs some help. I'm going to talk to the doctor and see what he says. I promise I'll be back tomorrow or the day after."

Imogene's eyes had let her know that she heard and understood. She reached out her hand. Laurel took her hand and Judith's hand and did what was to become a prescriptive part of her healing ministry in the years ahead. She said, "Let's pray together that God will give us the wisdom to know what is wrong and what we need to do about it. Then let's believe He'll answer."

Her simple prayer introduced hope into two lives where hopelessness had reigned for too long. After Laurel left, Judith, with hope edging out the fear, set to cleaning up and airing out the shack. Imogene asked for water to bathe herself and asked Judith to help her wash her hair. If that Mrs.Worth thought she could get well, they would meet her by doing their part.

When Laurel told Abby the symptoms, Abby said, "It sounds like a diet deficiency. Probably pellagra. I'll see Dr. Leighton at the hospital and ask him his opinion and what he recommends."

Dr. Leighton agreed that it was very likely pellagra, a deficiency brought on by not having any protein or vitamin in their diet. The patient needed fresh, lean beef, milk, or any source of protein, and yeast. He recommended niacin tablets until she could improve her regular diet.

Laurel returned two days later with her saddlebag filled with the foods that Imogene needed. Two quarts of beef broth, a cooked beef roast, a jar of canned green beans, a big bag of dried pinto beans, some flour and yeast and ingredients for making yeast bread. At the last minute she thought of blackberry jelly and butter to go with the yeast bread. She also brought a bottle of niacin tablets.

She explained about the diet deficiency and what needed to be done to cure it. Imogene drank a cup of warm beef broth and took two niacin pills. Since Judith couldn't read, Laurel gave precise oral instructions about her mother's diet for the next few days. She had Judith repeat them to her until she was sure she understood. She then asked Judith to watch her stir up the yeast bread. It took some ingenuity to explain about the bread rising and needing to be punched down to rise again. She showed on the clock when this was to be done.

On her way out she stopped by the Bonners, the neighbors who had reported their concern about Imogene. They had a small farm with chickens and cows. Laurel introduced herself and thanked Mrs. Bonner for sending word about Imogene. She told her what was wrong, which led, naturally, to ask Mrs. Bonner if she could spare some eggs and milk for Imogene and Judith. She also asked if the Bonners would look for the Ryan's missing cow.

Mrs. Bonner was relieved that it was not a "catchin' disease" and seemed pleased to know that she could help since she now knew what to do.

Laurel used her traveling time for thinking and praying. On her way back home, knowing she had started Imogene on her way to recovery, her thoughts turned to the children. Alexis was a happy third grader and David was in the seventh grade, his last year in elementary school. Caroline, seventeen and a junior in high school, had blossomed lately and Laurel believed it was partly because of Eli Wallace, a boy from Riverside, the nearby community where the high school was located. They had allowed her to go to some ball games with him.

Laurel knew Caroline had felt that she always lived in Sarah's and Adam's shadows. She was a more private person, quieter than the two older ones. She had a few good friends but not the crowd that Adam and Sarah drew. She cheerfully carried her share of the housework and spent time with Alexis. She and David, inseparable during their young years, now inhabited two different spheres. Seventeen and thirteen seemed a great distance apart, with diverse interests.

As Laurel's thoughts covered these facts, she found she had a vague, nagging concern that it was easy to leave Caroline in the background because she seemed to prefer it there. Or was it because she had just grown used to being there?

As Tattoo carried her through a trail where the foliage pressed closely upon them, she said, "Tattoo, I must give more attention to Caroline. Especially with Sarah's wedding coming up. I'll ask Abby's help and we'll figure out some things for her to do."

She didn't speak aloud the worry that Caroline was spending too much time and attention on Eli. There was something about him that Laurel didn't like.

Justin had kept up his practice of condensing the news and talking it over with the family at mealtimes, once or twice a week, whenever he got hold of *The Wildwood Journal* or *The Grit*. Germany, a faraway country, and Hitler, its dictator, had become familiar to the Worth household during the past year as Justin had viewed his concerns. Drawing information from the *Time* magazines, which Sam Parker, the newspaper editor, saved for him, Justin had drawn a word portrait of Hitler as a goose-stepping, hysterical, mustached little dandy, who was thoroughly evil. The family could imagine him strutting around, spreading terror and chaos.

Since taking control, Hitler had built up an army of more than half a million men, in direct violation of The Versailles Treaty of 1919, which spelled out the terms of Germany's surrender in World War I. The treaty limited the German army to 100,000 men. In further defiance of the treaty, Germany united with Italy and Japan, whose military aggression was alarming. Encouraged because Europe shrank from any action that might trigger another war, Hitler's troops marched triumphantly into Austria after Nazi collaborators had assassinated the chancellor. Czechoslovakia, alarmed at Hitler's swift conquest of Austria, knew they were next in line. They stood ready to fight, but Prime Minister Neville Chamberlain of Britain and the premier of France met with Hitler and Mussolini in Munich in September, 1938. In the name of appeasement, they agreed to give the part of Czechoslovakia known as the Sudetenland to Germany. No Czech representatives were allowed at the conference. Chamberlain announced to the world that the pact "meant peace for our time." Most of the thinking world, however, was realizing that evil on the march would only feel contempt for such compromises. A sense of guilt over standing by and allowing this aggression was at conflict over the horrible thought of another world war.

Now in May, 1940, Justin, on a world map he had pinned to the dining room wall, showed how Hitler, once in control of part of Czechoslovakia, had ordered his troops to occupy the remainder of the country. The disease of Naziism was spreading and no other countries seemed willing to help block its path.

"Daddy," David asked, "why can't America help?"

"Americans feel that this is Europe's problem. Every country has drawn in on itself since this worldwide Depression, just trying to survive economically."

When German troops smashed into Poland, Great Britain and France realized that appeasement had not worked. Hitler intended to conquer all of eastern Europe. Britain and France declared war on Germany on September 3, 1939.

That spring, Justin pointed out on the map that Hitler's war machine had turned north and invaded Denmark and Norway. Great Britain and France sent troops to help these countries, but were not prepared to provide sufficient air support. Germans drove the allied forces out.

"There's one hopeful piece of news today. Britain has replaced Chamberlain as Prime Minister. Chamberlain's appeasement policy has allowed Hitler free reign. Winston Churchill is now Prime Minister. He knows he's been handed a terrible challenge. In his first speech, the paper says, he told his people that he could promise them nothing but "blood, toil, tears, and sweat.""

Caroline said, "It must be scary living over there right now. Do you think they can stop Hitler?"

"He must be stopped. Civilization would enter the Dark Ages again if Hitler won Europe. I think America will get involved before this is over."

He and Laurel looked at each other, knowing each was thinking of Adam — and now, of Roe — going to war.

With that they moved on to other happier topics related to their every day lives. Sarah's wedding plans were progressing. Roe, whom Justin called "Highpockets" because of his height, was already becoming a part of the family. David introduced him to Matilda, the nanny goat, and Chief, the shepherd dog, telling them earnestly that Roe was going to be part of the family. Roe was amused to realize that *he* was the one to be approved, not the other way around. Often, as he and Sarah started walking to church or some other function, Alexis would be between them, holding their hands, swinging happily along. When Laurel offered to stop her, it was Roe who answered, "No, ma'am. She's fine. We like her being with us."

Miss Abby, after Laurel shared her motherly concerns, had invited Caroline to come to her house in Deerbrook one Friday night. When they went to see "Gone With the Wind," Caroline was entranced with Rhett Butler and thoroughly put out with Scarlet O'Hara. She was only slightly less excited by Miss Abby's big boarding house. Back at home on Saturday night, she related her adventure at supper, complete with a detailed description of Miss Abby's parlor, where a full-sized loom filled one corner by the fireplace. Then there was the pump organ and the piano and several bookcases, fronted with glass doors, where books were piled in disarray.

"Was there any place to sit?" asked practical David.

"Oh, yes, I forgot the two sofas and two arm chairs, with cushions and magazines scattered about, and two or three tables full of stuff.

"She rents a small apartment downstairs and three rooms upstairs. I slept in a small bedroom she keeps for her guests. People were coming and going all the time, kinda like it is here, so I felt right at home."

Laurel, who had been to Abby's house many times, was amused over Caroline's description. She would tell Abby about it.

Caroline finished by saying, "She wants me to come back in a couple of weeks. I told her I would check and see if you could do without me again, Mama."

"I think we could get your work done before Friday night if we try," Laurel answered.

Sarah's wedding plans happily brought Bess, Hannah, Alice, and Nora back into their lives on a regular basis. They arrived, complete with sewing machines and all the necessary paraphernalia, and set up the sewing area in one end of the big room where it could stay 'til they were finished. Bess, who had learned to sew in that first logging camp, had become an expert seamstress. She would make Sarah's wedding dress. Hannah, Alice, and Nora were determined that

Sarah, whom they considered partly theirs, would have a worthy supply of linens. They embroidered pillowcases and doilies. They sewed and embroidered three gowns of soft cotton.

Laurel, who had no time for sewing, was thankful for her loyal friends. She warned Justin, however, not to leave any of his clothes lying around. He might find them embroidered!

The wedding went according to the wishes of the bride and groom; their only regret was that Adam couldn't be there. They asked for a simple, private ceremony with their families—including her logging camp family, of course—and a few close friends. Even so, it was a large group that assembled on the porch on a perfect June afternoon to witness the wedding. Sarah was radiant in her simple white dress, carrying a bouquet of wildflowers with galax leaves on a bed of ferns. She, escorted by a solemn Justin, walked through the double French doors to take her stand beside Roe.

Ethan—handsome, capable, caring Ethan—infused emotion and meaning into the ceremony that reached everyone there, no matter how long they had been married—or if they weren't married.

After the reception, where hugs and best wishes and teasing abounded, Sarah and Roe left for a small house they had rented in Deerbrook. Sarah would keep her job at the paper mill and Roe would make the daily trip by train back to his logging job near Lake Eagle Rest.

Sarah had kept her composure until Alexis, holding on to her hand, asked, "Will you be gone forever and ever?"

Tears, which had been held at bay all day, filled Sarah's eyes as she looked at Roe. He quickly stooped and hugged Alexis. "No, no! We'll be back in a few days. We'll take you home with us one weekend. OK?"

Ethan, watching this exchange, turned to Justin. "I think that young man has what it takes to be a member of the Worth family!"

"You make it sound like a challenge."

"It is! But greatly rewarding," Ethan answered as he put his arm around Justin's shoulder. He, of all the people there except Laurel, knew Justin was silently suffering the age-old pangs of a father giving his beloved daughter to another man.

Laurel was determined to find Abe, Zeke, and Odell, three of the crew of their first logging camp. She still remembered the remarks they had made about wishing they could read, back when she was teaching the children in a corner of the mess hall. She was determined to enter their families into the adult education program. She heard that they were probably working with the local WPA, part of the Works Progress Administration, the basic economic and social program set up by President Roosevelt to give work to millions of Americans. Sam Parker, editor of *The Wildwood Journal,* told Justin the crew was building retaining walls and bridges along the Blue Ridge Parkway. Justin drove her to the work site, explaining that he couldn't let her have all that fun and excitement alone.

As soon as the foreman saw Justin, he asked, "Are you here to take a picture of my crew?"

"I have my camera ready and was going to ask you if I could take some shots, but we need your help with another matter first."

Laurel showed her papers to the foreman and asked if the three men were part of his crew.

"Sure are! Three of my best workers!" He turned to a young man nearby and told him to go tell Abe, Zeke, and Odell that they had company.

They were a happy trio when they saw Justin and Laurel—hugging and slapping Justin on the back, then taking off their work hats and inclining their heads to Laurel.

"Excuse us, Laurel, we're too dirty to shake your hand." Abe, it seemed, was still speaking for the three of them.

Justin looked them over and remarked, "Well, I can't tell that time has made you any uglier."

"That's 'cause we was ugly aplenty to start with," Abe replied, grinning. Then he said, "Laurel, you're lookin' like yourself again. You had us plumb scared when you was in that hospital."

"Justin told me how all of you came and stayed with him through that time. Thank you for being such good friends."

"Well, you've been good friends to us. How long has it been since we parted at Locust Hollow?"

"It's been ten years," Justin answered. "How're your families?"

"We've had some rough years like ever'body else we know, but we're survivin'. Our kids is gittin' grown up."

"Ours, too," Justin said. "Adam's in the CCCs in Arizona and Sarah got married last week."

Odell said, "We still talk about our days together in your loggin' camp, Justin. Them was some of the best days of our lives."

"We think so, too," Laurel said, "and we've come to finish some business we couldn't take care of while we were there."

All three men stared at her. "What kind of business?"

"Do you remember how many times you remarked that you wished you could write your name and read?"

"Yes, ma'am. I always wished I was one of them kids you was teachin'," Abe said.

"Well, we came to tell you that I can teach you now. It's my job to go to homes where adults can't read and write and to teach them."

They looked at her stupefied, as if a long desired but denied treasure was being offered. She explained, "It's a government program, like the WPA here where you work."

Justin added, "She's already teaching several families. Do you remember our favorite friend near Locust Hollow?"

"Abner?" all three men whispered his name, their unbelief in their expressions and voices.

"The same!" Justin answered. "She's teaching him and Rosalee and their two children."

Zeke finally spoke. "But we live a fer piece from you."

"How far do you live from the road where I would have to leave my truck?" Justin asked.

"Just about a mile through the gorge. We live close to each other, so one trip would do for all of us." They made arrangements for the first visit on Saturday, when Justin could take her.

Abe hesitatingly asked a childlike question, exposing their private fear. "What if...if we ain't smart enough to learn? What do you do then?"

Before Laurel could speak, Justin said, "Abe, you're smarter than a whole bunch of educated people I know! You and Zeke and Odell have skills way beyond what it takes to do reading and writing. You'll do fine!"

Their fears allayed, the three men got back to work. If Justin said it, then it must be so. They would depend on his word as they had for so many years.

While they were talking, the foreman had sent word around that Justin Worth would be taking some pictures. Setting up his tripod, and getting his angle right, he called to the group to be still before he covered his head with the familiar black cloth and got ready to push the shutter. He took several shots of different groups at work. Laurel helped him get the name of each man on a diagram to correspond with each picture. Then he took a group shot with the entire crew posing with their shovels and other tools.

"These pictures will make a full page spread in *The Wildwood Journal* next week. Be sure you buy a paper." As Laurel expected, all the men knew Justin and it seemed each one had to have a word with him before they could leave.

On the way home Laurel's happiness lit up the inside of the truck like sunshine. "Justin, isn't it wonderful when you've dreamed you could do something for a long time, and suddenly it happens? Your dream comes true!"

He laid his hand on hers for a moment. "I knew you were itching to teach that whole crew of men in the camp. I heard their remarks about it, too. Tell me something. Did you pray for this?"

Her smile was the one he loved best. "Of course!"

"Then it will happen as you prayed," he declared with complete conviction.

When Laurel and Justin got home, a pleasant surprise greeted them. The summer folks were back. Two families lived close: the Townsends, almost next door, and the Seymours, just around the bend. Now, coming toward them, smiling broadly, was Leanna, the Seymour's maid. She, an attractive, buxom black woman in her late fifties, had decided early on that Laurel was someone she wanted to spend time with — when she had a little breather from her duties.

"I heard I just missed a weddin'," she said, without preamble, as she embraced Laurel in her usual enthusiastic manner.

"Yes. I wish you could've been here."

Justin came around the truck and extended his hand. "Welcome back! When did you get in?"

"This mornin'. As soon as the missus took a nap, I nipped through the trail to let you know we're here."

"Come in and let's have some lemonade and catch up," Laurel said.

Leanna, from her first visit to the Worth home, had felt a certain comfort she couldn't describe just by being in Laurel's presence. Part of it must be that she could shed her maid persona, which—heaven forbid—she could *never* do in the Seymour household. She was treated with respect as a means toward getting needs met, but never as a *person*, with feelings and desires and hurts. With Laurel, she was just another woman, a friend who could drink coffee or lemonade and talk about her grown children or her life as a widow. She could be *herself*, an exuberant, laughing, outgoing woman. It was a pleasure to hear her rich contralto voice resonating through the house, bringing the children for their hugs and for her opinion of how much they had grown since last summer.

"I'm glad Sarah married Roe—out of all them beaus she was jugglin'. I liked him the best."

"We all did. We think they're right for each other."

"And Adam?"

"Adam seems to be enjoying his time in Arizona with the CCCs." Then Laurel added with a laugh, "He writes often and last week he sent a picture of himself with a girl he has met. Alexis was so alarmed she immediately wrote him a letter reminding him of all the pretty girls around here. She told him he didn't need a girl so far from home. It was quite a bossy letter."

"Well, Adam's belonged to her for a long time."

"She thinks so, anyway. I couldn't say it but I don't want him to get serious with anybody that far from home."

"He won't," Leanna said, soothingly. "He's too close to his family." After she, at Laurel's request, caught Laurel up on her own children and grandchildren, Leanna said, "One story they never git tired of hearin' is the time you was sick and I brought you a remedy in my umbrella. I'll never forget the look on your face. You was surprised! Nobody had ever give you a gift like that!" The memory brought forth that rich laughter that poured through the house.

Laurel laughed, too. "You were so serious and I was struggling to know what to do. I didn't want to hurt your feelings after you had smuggled out the medicine that you were sure would cure me."

"You explained, so ladylike, that you *personally* didn't like the taste of scotch whiskey. I still laugh every time I think of that tactful remark. Especially since I've come to know how you feel about it."

The only time the subject of color had come up was after Leanna had stayed to sing with the young people one Friday night. Her voice, enriching the many voices, caused every one else to stop singing and listen. After a moment she stopped, too. Justin spoke for the group. "Leanna, would you sing a few of your favorite songs for us? It would be a treat."

She conferred with Miss Abby about a few songs, then stood tall and proud. "I sing these songs for the young people at our church and I always remind them that these songs helped our people through the years of slavery. In the cotton fields or the cornfields I'm told that someone would heist a tune and the words would flow forth, words of comfort or delivery — if not in this life, certainly in the next. My grandma tol' me once that they were hemmed in on every side but *up*! Nothin' could stop their spirits from reachin' up!"

As "Swing Low, Sweet Chariot" flowed from her soul, the group was transported to that cotton field, imagining what it must have been like to have been *owned* by another human being, like a horse or a mule. It was a moment that revealed, even to their young minds, the physical, mental, and emotional cruelty of slavery. It also revealed the courage of the human *spirit*, refusing to be enslaved, rising above the physical circumstances to ride the winds of freedom on the words of a song.

Realizing their mood, Leanna next taught them the rousing song, "Joshua Fit the Battle of Jericho." With the words, "the walls came tumbling down," ringing in their ears, the young people left without realizing that a wall had come tumbling down that night, in their concept of a person of another color.

After they left, Justin, without thinking through his request, asked, "Would you consider coming to church with us and singing one Sunday?"

Leanna looked at him while gladness, then sadness flitted over her face. When she spoke it was matter-of-fact. "That wouldn't do, you know. Some people would be offended that a black woman was worshippin' with white folks."

"The people in Lake Eagle Rest are not that ignorant or small minded," he protested.

She was adamant, however, saying, "I'll sing with this group on Friday nights. That'll be enough."

Alexis, always looking for something to read, found *Uncle Tom's Cabin* in Caroline's room. Caroline had asked Miss Abby to bring it to her to help with a history report. Alexis was soon reading in her aerie in the big oak tree, not realizing what the book would do to her. As she read, unbelieving that such things could happen, a foreign and intense sadness gripped her. A trembling that she couldn't control started from the center of her being, spreading a weakness to the tip of her fingers and toes. She knew she had to get out of the tree before she fell out.

She made it to the kitchen where she fell into her mother's arms. "Mama," she whispered, "they sold Tom! He was the daddy and they sold him!" Stark fear was in her eyes and tears were rolling down her cheeks as she asked, "Can anybody buy our daddy and take him off?"

Confused, but realizing Alexis was almost in shock, Laurel called Caroline to bring a blanket and warm it in the oven. With Alexis wrapped warmly on her lap, she asked, "What are you talking about? What happened?"

"The...book," Alexis managed.

When Laurel saw the book lying on the floor, she realized the source of shock. "Oh, honey, you're too young to read that."

Alexis continued. "They tried to sell Eliza's little boy, Harry, but she took him and ran away. Could our family be sold away from each other?" Her eyes were pleading.

"No, Alexis! No! Never!"

"Why was their daddy sold?"

"That was a long time ago when black people were slaves. That means that other people owned them and could do what they wanted with them. But, Alexis, the slaves are all free now."

"They can't take families away from each other now?"

"No," Laurel whispered, rubbing her hair back from her forehead. "Now I want you to rest. We'll talk about this another time when you feel better."

When the trembling continued, Laurel gave Alexis a dose of paregoric to help her body ride out the sadness and fear. After awhile she slept but Laurel kept a close watch on her during the night. She didn't let her go to school the next day.

Justin, after holding her close and rocking her awhile before putting her to bed the second night, said to Laurel, "Alexis has always lived in Eden. She's been loved and cherished and protected. This was her first acquaintance with evil and the grief it brings. Her complete innocence and belief that everybody is good is gone forever."

"It's a painful part of growing up. I'm glad we were here with her. You need to tell her about the Emancipation Proclamation and President Lincoln."

For all the assurances to Alexis of how far our country had come from slavery days, Laurel was brought face to face with rank prejudice the following week. Leanna, with a rare free Saturday, went to Deerbrook with Laurel and Justin. The women's last stop was a small fabric shop on the corner across from the courthouse. Laurel and Leanna both made some purchases of cloth, thread and needles. As they left the shop, Leanna stooped to drink from a water fountain just outside the door.

The clerk, a small nervous man, rushed toward her yelling, "You can't drink from that fountain! There's a fountain for…for your kind at the end of the street!"

Laurel and Leanna froze as a crowd of people on the sidewalk stopped to see what the yelling was all about. Leanna, thoroughly humiliated, stepped quickly away from the fountain. She stood still as a statue, looking over everybody's heads.

Laurel's shock quickly turned to fury. She rounded on the flustered, cocky little man. "You ignorant, miserable little man! I'm ashamed that one person can treat another like this! You should've lived in the Dark Ages, not the twentieth century!"

Leanna, scared now, pulled at Laurel's sleeve. "It's okay! Let's go!"

Laurel, without taking her eyes off the clerk, said, "Leanna, get in the truck. I'll be there in a minute."

Leanna, with her head held high, an innate sense of dignity about her, crossed the street under the gaze of the crowd, and climbed in Justin's truck.

Laurel's anger, now in a slow burn, said, "Her money wasn't too dirty for you to touch. You handled her money and put it in the drawer with white folks' money as if there was no difference."

There was a twitter of laughter, then another. Justin, hearing

Laurel's angry voice, walked up just as the clerk, his cockiness gone, took out his handkerchief and mopped his face.

"What is it, Laurel?"

"This…this…" Finding no adequate, acceptable word to describe him, she pointed to the clerk and said, "*He* wouldn't let Leanna drink out of the water fountain, just after she had bought some things in his store."

"Why?" Justin asked him.

The simple, reasonable question stumped the man for a moment. Then he said, "It's what's expected. Them people has their own water fountain."

"Do you own the fountain outside your shop?"

"No…o…"

"Did the town officials ask you to decide who could drink there?"

"No…o…" A whine appeared in his voice.

"So, it's really none of your business, is it? That woman is a friend of ours and you just insulted her — made her feel less than a human being. A lowdown thing to do!"

Laurel, who realized that Justin's reasonable tone and message was much more effective than her anger, said in a quiet voice, "I'll never buy anything here again. And I'll ask my friends to go to the fabric shop down the street where we'll be free from insults."

With that, Justin took her arm and guided her toward the truck to join Leanna. The clerk turned back to his shop, astonished and scared. He had never seen anybody defend a black person so vehemently. He was sure the owner would hear about the altercation. If they started to lose customers, the boss would take it out on him.

Leanna, in the face of Laurel's and Justin's mortification at her treatment, was placid and even philosophical. "I learned a long time ago that that kind of treatment don't have nothin' to do with who I am. It shows the ignorance and meanness of the person who hands it out."

She straightened her shoulders and shook them slightly as if relieving herself of a burden. Then she smiled and said, "*Now*, let me tell you what I bought that special material and thread for. I'm gonna make Sarah a tablecloth with flowers embroidered in each corner. You need to tell me the size of her table."

Neither Laurel nor Justin found any words to meet this kind of wisdom and courage. Laurel turned and embraced her friend.

Chapter Eleven

Sunday dinner on December 7, 1941, would live in the memory of every member of the Worth family for the rest of their lives. They had enjoyed an inspiring church service and had come home hungry. As Laurel and Caroline hurriedly put the meal together, Caroline turned on the radio, hoping to hear some of her favorite songs. The upbeat messages of "Catch A Falling Star" and "Oh, What A Beautiful Morning" soon had her singing along. As the family gathered around the table and Caroline reached to turn off the radio, her hand halted in mid-air. The words coming forth were unbelievable! The Japanese had attacked Pearl Harbor! Everyone seemed frozen in place as the excited voice of the announcer told the story.

Laurel sat down heavily, put her head in her hands and started to cry. Justin was by her side in an instant. The children looked on, astonished.

"Laurel," Justin said, his own face stern, as he rubbed his hand over her hair.

"All our young men...Adam and Roe..." she said, struggling, "our Lake Eagle Rest boys...the CCC boys..."

The terrible words flowed over them, leaving fear and confusion on the faces of the children. Seeing them brought her back from her own anguish. She wiped her face on a napkin and said, "Sit down and let your daddy tell you what this means."

Justin sat at the head of the table, anger stamped on his face. "The sneaky cowards! I read where the Japanese ambassador is in Washington now, talking peace."

He explained in simple terms that this attack meant war for America.

David wanted to know more. "What did Mama mean about Adam and Roe and everybody?"

"If we have war, they're the right age to go."

"How old do we have to be?"

"*We?* David, you're fourteen. That's too young to go to war. You have to be eighteen or older."

"Where would Adam and the others go?"

"I don't know, son. Let's wait and see what our country does in response to this attack. Let's turn the radio off and eat dinner. Then maybe we'll hear some more details."

Everybody was subdued and there was little talk as they ate. Each child knew in his or her heart that the terrible event that had taken place far away would change their lives. It wasn't because they understood all the radio announcer had said, but because of the way their mother had cried and the set of their daddy's face.

The next day Franklin D. Roosevelt, President of the United States, declared war on Japan. Three days later Germany and Italy declared war on America. The United States Congress, then, declared war on Germany and Italy. World War II had begun!

Nobody seemed to be able to talk or think about anything else. At supper each evening Justin tried to simplify the complicated facts associated with going to war. His love for his country — and his absolute faith that America would win against *any* country foolish enough to challenge her — was contagious. That flame of pride in America that had been lit in him as a young man studying history by firelight had never dimmed, and never would. The torch bearing that flame was passed. His children were imbued with his patriotism. Just as their food nourished their physical bodies, love of country nurtured their spirits.

No one was surprised when Adam arrived home, set free from his CCC job, to *volunteer* for the United Stated Navy. He did *not* intend to wait for the draft. His visit was short and bittersweet. Justin and Laurel recognized that their son was now his own man; he was no longer the boy who had left two years before. The apron strings had been cleanly severed. But, thankfully, he was still Adam. He wanted to know everything that was happening to everybody, so he arranged time alone with each one, including Sarah and Roe. Alexis was allowed to miss a day of school just to be with him.

When he and David had their time together, Adam surprised David when he repeated a tale Alexis had told him.

"It seems you've done a great job of protecting our little sister. She told me about the bull chasing her and how you made her climb a high bank while you wrestled the bull into a ditch, twisted his head around and stuck his horns in the bank."

David looked embarrassed. "He wasn't a real big bull."

Adam laughed. "But he was a good bit bigger than *you* — and mad to boot! Alexis also told me that the bull couldn't get free and you went back and helped him get his twisted neck untangled and his horns out of the bank."

"Alexis talks a lot!" David said. They both laughed at the obvious.

David then continued. "I couldn't just leave him there helpless. I was ready to run when I pulled him free, but all the fight had gone out of him. He lumbered off in the opposite direction."

Adam put his hands on David's shoulders, looked him in the eyes and said, "I'm proud of you! You've grown a lot and you're already strong enough to wrestle a bull!" He squeezed David's muscles and pondered, "I wonder if *I* could've put that bull in a ditch!"

David, suddenly near tears in spite of trying to be so manly, said, "Adam, I wish I was old enough to go, too."

"Your job will be just as important as mine. I know you'll help Dad take care of the family while I'm gone."

One event that happened while Adam was home seemed to do him a world of good. It confirmed again the uniqueness of his parents. The family was gathered in the small, cozy, winter family room where a fire burned brightly, waiting for Justin to get home. They were concerned because it was a bitterly cold February night.

When Justin finally arrived, he wasn't alone. He came through the door with a firm hold on a ragged, dirty, unshaven man who was shuddering with cold in spite of Justin's coat around his shoulders. He seemed to have trouble standing up alone or focusing on his surroundings.

At one glance, Laurel and Adam flew into action. They helped Justin get him into a chair by the fire and wrapped a quilt around him while Justin knelt and took off his sodden brogans and socks, exposing his bare feet to the warmth of the fire.

Adam said, "Caroline, come help me heat up some coffee for him."

When they returned with a steaming cup of coffee, Justin handed it to him carefully, saying, "Barney, this is hot. Don't burn yourself."

The only sounds in the room were the fire popping and cracking, and Barney slurping his coffee. Suddenly, the air was rent with song. Barney's song. He threw his head back and, with great gusto, sang, "I lost my britches on the railroad track! Along came the train—choo, choo, choo—and cut my britches smack-dab in two!"

He hiccupped, laughed, and asked, "Justin, did you know I could sing?"

The younger children sat mute in wide-eyed astonishment. Alexis and David avoided looking at each other. They knew they shouldn't laugh.

Justin struggled to keep his own face straight. "That was a good song, Barney. Now, since you're warm, you need something to eat. My wife'll bring something."

"I ain't hungry but I could use a little nip," Barney announced.

"You've had enough this time, and, besides, I don't have any."

"Now, what kind of man would you be, without a little 'shine around?"

"Oh, I manage fine."

In spite of protesting that he wasn't hungry, when Laurel came in with some soup and cornbread, he ate happily and noisily. Then, suddenly, he fell asleep, his chin dropping on his chest.

Justin and Adam put him to bed. He was snoring before they got him fully covered.

Adam said, "He would've frozen to death out there tonight."

"Yes."

Adam felt a rush of love for his dad. *I wonder,* Adam thought, *just how many people like this he's helped through the years.*

When they got back to the family room Alexis asked, "Daddy, what was wrong with him?"

"He was sick, honey," Justin said.

"But if he was sick, why was he so happy?" she persisted.

Justin gave his head a little shake and gave up. "Actually, Alexis, he's drunk. That means he drank too much liquor or moonshine. It makes people act that way."

"I'm glad *you* don't drink moonshine."

Everyone laughed at the thought and things settled down to routine: homework for the school children; quiet conversation between Adam and Laurel and Justin.

The next morning at breakfast, Barney was sober but unembarrassed and still talkative.

"Justin, I mighta froze if you hadn't brung me home with you. I thank you!"

"You're welcome. You need to be careful in this kind of weather, Barney. Adam said he would take you home in the truck before I go to work. Wear one of my coats. He can bring it back."

It was a difficult but proud day when Adam left to join the United Stated Navy. A big group of the young people from Lake Eagle Rest rode in the back of Justin's logging truck to see him off at the train station. The party-like atmosphere, camouflaging deeper emotions, made it easier for the family. Even so, every member seemed to feel each other's hurt and tried to help. They were most concerned about Alexis, but she surprised them by announcing, "Adam said I needed to be happy after he left because he's doing what he wants to do. And he'll write us about all the exciting things he's doing. I promised him! So, let's not be sad!"

Laurel was glad when the weather improved enough for her to travel to the homes of her students. Zach, Wolf, and Keen kept their promise to Justin that they would watch after her. She noticed that they had cleaned up the yard, the shack, and themselves. They made her feel like an honored guest. The competition between the three of them amused and pleased her. It kept them going at a faster rate of learning. They reminded her of her classroom days when the boys tried to outdo each other.

Nathan Buchanan was probably her biggest success, and she knew that was because he had Lark's help. Laurel realized that she was only the catalyst to get this young family started toward an education. Because of their parents' excitement, the two boys explored the landscape of the "Three R's" much as they would have explored a new creek to fish in—and found it pleasing.

"Lark, you're a natural teacher!" Laurel exclaimed, when she saw how much progress had been made in such a short time. "If we find enough children to start a school, maybe you could take some courses and be the teacher."

Lark looked at her in wonder. "What would I have to do?"

"We could talk to Mr. McKenzie, the superintendent of schools, and find out."

Nathan, hearing this exchange, said, "Maybe we can help you find out how many children live around here. It would be good to have a school. *And*, Lark *would* be a good teacher. If she can teach me, she can teach anybody."

When Laurel arrived at Abner's house, she knew something was wrong when no one burst through the door with their usual welcome. After she called, "Hello," a couple of times, Rosalee appeared, distraught but very happy to see her.

"Thank God, you're here! You can help Bryce!"

"What's wrong?"

"We think he's got a broken leg. He's in a lot of pain."

Laurel felt an emptiness in the pit of her stomach. She had never set a broken bone.

Abner's worry was clear in his eyes and in his subdued manner as he greeted her. Bryce lay on the bed, his usual ruddy face was pale and covered with a sheen of sweat. His eyes showed his pain, but not a sound escaped him. Bonnie sat silently near his bed.

Abner explained, "He fell off the horse. The saddle cinch broke and his foot got caught in the stirrup. The horse was spooked and bolted. He said his leg was twisted backward, but he jerked loose anyway to keep from bein' dragged."

"Let me look at his leg," Laurel said.

As she ran her fingers gently over the area below the knee, she felt the break about half way down.

"It's the main bone. It needs to be reset as soon as possible, and splinted."

They moved away from the bed to the kitchen area.

"What can we do?" Abner asked.

Laurel considered for a moment. "It's too far—and we don't have transportation — to try to get him to a doctor. It would take hours for someone to ride for a doctor and get him back here. The other choice is for us to try to set and splint his leg, ourselves."

"How?" Rosalee wanted to know.

"I've seen it done. But you need to know that I've never set a broken bone, myself."

"We trust you," Abner said. "Just tell us what to do."

Rosalee nodded her agreement.

"Let's pray together first," Laurel said, and reached out to take their hands.

"Lord, You know I can't handle this without Your help, so I receive what I need from You right now. I go in that strength. Thank You in advance! Amen."

After her brief prayer, she became the nurse, talking through the details. "We need to get a splint ready before we set the leg, so we can stabilize it and hold it securely. Do you have any thin boards?"

Abner shook his head. "Not that small or thin. I could cut and split some."

A memory from their first logging camp surfaced in Laurel's mind — of an Indian woman telling her about how they would skin birch bark from a small tree and use it as a splint for broken bones. She asked, "Do you have any birch trees nearby?"

"Yes. Down in the flat by the river."

Laurel explained what she had been told. Abner understood immediately. "It'll need to be a sapling as near the size of his leg as possible. I'll go get some."

"Before you go — do you have any kind of pain killer?"

Rosalee answered, "Not for this kind of pain."

Abner asked, "Would a little moonshine help?"

Laurel looked at him quickly, but saw he was serious. "Have you used it before for something like this?"

"Yes. It helps the person relax, or dulls the senses somehow."

"Yes, I think it does. Justin had a woman drink some once after she had been stabbed in the back and I had to sew up the wound."

Abner went outside and returned with a quart jar of moonshine. He gave Bryce a tablespoon. "This is going to help you, son. We're getting everything ready to fix your leg."

The first swallow of moonshine gave Bryce a coughing fit. After he settled down, Abner gave him several more spoonfuls. He, then, went out the door saying, "I'll be right back."

Laurel continued with her preparations. "Rosalee, Bryce will need a thick, rolled-up washcloth to bite into when we set his leg. We'll also need some Vaseline and a soft cloth — maybe part of an old sheet — to wrap around his leg before we put on the bark cast."

When Abner arrived with the piece of birch bark, they looked at the size. He had stripped it off, leaving it to resume its natural shape. He wrapped it around Bryce's good leg and measured. He would now cut off the excess, so the bark would fit snugly.

When they gathered around his bed, Abner said, "Bryce, Laurel is going to set your leg and it's goin' to hurt. Listen to what she tells you to do."

Laurel placed the rolled washcloth between his teeth. "Your dad will hold on to you, Bryce. I have to pull your leg hard so the ends of the broken bone will go back together. When I start to pull, clamp down on the washcloth."

Bryce nodded that he was ready. Bonnie took his hand, but shut her eyes tight. Abner and Rosalee got a firm hold on him and Laurel asked, "Ready?"

When they nodded, she gave a strong jerk. Bryce moaned and, mercifully, passed out.

They worked quickly. Laurel, moving her fingers gently, felt a smoothness around the break, which indicated that the bone was set. She bathed his leg, dried it, then applied Vaseline. They wrapped the soft cloth first, then folded the birch bark around his leg from above his ankle to below his knee. Abner had trimmed it well, so it fit tightly. They tied it securely with strips of cloth. Just as they placed a pillow under his leg to reduce any strain, Bryce regained consciousness with a moan, which he quickly stifled.

Abner looked at Laurel and asked, "A little more moonshine?"

"Just enough to help him relax and, hopefully, go to sleep."

After Abner had given Bryce a few more sips, the adults left Bonnie by his side and gathered around the kitchen table for a much needed cup of coffee.

"Do you know of anything else we can do for him?" Abner asked.

"He absolutely cannot put any weight on that leg for a while. Could you make him some crutches or do we need to buy some?"

"I can make some."

"I'll ask Dr. Leighton for instructions before I come back next week. Meanwhile, be sure he gives that bone a few days to start knitting back together before he's even allowed on crutches. I prefer that you keep him in bed until I get back. Promise you'll come for us if you feel he needs more help."

Before she left, Laurel told them that she was going to start teaching Abe, Zeke, and Odell. This brought back the memories of their years at Locust Hollow.

Abner said, "The day I kidnapped Justin, I didn't realize all the good it would bring into our lives. Like you showing up today just when we needed you."

"Well, it goes both ways, you know! We still have Justin around because of you! You *did* save his life when Bill 'Bandit' Butler was ready to shoot him!"

When Laurel got home, Sarah and Roe were there. A visit during the week was unusual but Laurel didn't ask any questions. After supper, before anyone left the table, Sarah said, "Roe has something to tell you."

As all eyes turned toward him, Roe said, "I've decided to volunteer for the Navy like Adam did. I'd rather choose my place than be drafted, where I'd have no choice."

Justin said, "I think I'd do the same thing if I were your age."

Sarah said, "He wants me to move back home while he's gone. Would you consider taking me in?"

A chorus of "Yes! Yes! Yes!" erupted around the table.

Justin looked solemnly at Laurel. "That's a *difficult* problem. We'll have to think about it and talk it over and…"

Three indignant voices scolded, "Daddy!"

Alexis jumped up and ran around to hug Sarah.

Justin became serious. "Roe, we respect you for your decision. And, as you can see, Sarah will be *most* welcome to live here while you're gone. I promise you we'll take care of her."

Roe put his arm around her as he answered, "I know you will, sir."

Laurel added, "She can have her old bedroom back."

Sarah, in an uncertain voice, said, "I wondered if I could live in the little house."

When they all looked at her, she explained, "We have enough furniture for the little house. Otherwise, we'll have to store it somewhere."

Justin said, "I think that's a good solution."

Roe said, "Thank you, sir. I'll move our things and get her settled in before I leave."

Roe was one of hundreds of thousands of young American men going off to war. The United States Congress had enacted the first American peacetime draft law in 1940, with 6,000 draft boards across the country. Now, with the world at war, they set about calling men between the ages of eighteen and thirty-seven to register. As Justin faithfully read aloud the weekly list of enlisted men in *The Wildwood Journal*, the children understood why their mother had cried and their daddy had looked so grim when they had heard the announcement of the Pearl Harbor attack. All the able-bodied young men from Lake Eagle Rest and from the CCC Camp were among those called to defend their country. Roe was the second one from the Worth family.

While the United States was simmering with the turmoil of war, there was a good kind of simmering going on in Terminal Town. Brand and Lila were making a name for themselves. A totally different name! First, people noticed the difference in Brand at work, then in the way he treated his family.

Mack summed it up. "Brand's a changed man. It's great for his family and for him — and for the rest of us. It's almost scary to see the difference."

To give them credit, most of their neighbors were happy with the transformation — but, at the same time, felt threatened by it. That kind of transforming power wasn't easy to stop once it got started! Even though the men had not liked Brand's behavior, they had felt a kinship with him through his drinking. Now, their wives were commenting on how Brand had changed since he had quit drinking. The men understood the implied message. Some of their wives were attending church. Gerta, Mack's wife, had even joined.

And that preacher man seemed to be spending a lot of time around Terminal Town. When he came to visit Brand and Lila, he would usually walk around the saw mill, talking to the men — he knew them all by name—and sometimes would lend a hand with the work. The men couldn't help but like him. He knew as much or more about the timber business as they did—and he had earned their respect in the way he had rescued Brand from drowning under those logs.

Yet, he represented a way of life that they were scared of. They would have to give up too much, and they didn't believe they could "hold out" to be real Christians. Still, something drew them to him...Each one wondered, privately, and even wistfully, what it would be like to have what the preacher man and Brand and Lila had!

It was wonderful having Sarah back with the family. She busied herself with placing furniture, hanging curtains, and stamping hers and Roe's personalities on the three-room house that stood on the grounds near the big house. She used her precious Stained Glass Window Quilt as a wall hanging in her small living room. The rich colors, which she matched with curtains, made the room warm and inviting. She pleased Justin by having some of his pictures of their logging camp days framed and hung on another wall. Bookshelves held many books, showing Roe's and her interests.

She was the same Sarah toward the family; yet, she was, somehow, different. She was a young wife who had sent her husband off to war and she was lonely for him. All the love and attention of her family couldn't make up for his absence.

Laurel and Justin talked with Caroline, David, and Alexis. "We all must realize that Sarah is married and has her own home. Respect her privacy. Be sure to knock at her door just as you would at a neighbor's house. And, remember, she misses Roe very much."

She kept her job at the paper mill, riding to work each day with a neighbor. It was natural for her to take her meals with the family, so she took back her share of the cooking. Many nights she would ask Alexis or Caroline to stay with her.

The first morning that she was nauseated at breakfast, she thought it was just an upset stomach. After the third morning of the same, she believed she was pregnant.

She cried when she told Laurel. "I'm crying because I'm happy and I'm crying because I'm sad, and I can't tell which is which!"

Laurel held her and said, "I understand, honey. I know you're happy about the baby, but you're sad that Roe isn't here to share this time with you."

"Yes...and, Mama, I'm scared. What if...if he doesn't come home?"

"It's our job to hope and pray every day that he will."

"I'm glad I'm here with you and Daddy and the family while he's gone."

"We're glad, too! And looking forward to this baby is just what we need! I can't wait for you to tell your daddy and the other children!"

After his initial surprise, Justin rose to the occasion just as Laurel knew he would. He made Sarah believe she was the most special young woman on earth because she was with child.

He then grabbed his head and moaned, "Oh, no! I'll be living with a grandma!"

Laurel shot back, "That goes two ways, Grandpa!"

Justin said soberly, "I'm sorry Roe isn't here, honey, but you still have David and me."

David added, "Yes, I promised Adam and Roe."

Sarah nodded. "I know. I'm glad I have you both."

Caroline, busy with her senior year in high school, offered, "If you like, I'll move some of my clothes to your house and stay with you at night. That way, if you get sick, you won't be by yourself."

"Yes, I'd like that."

Everybody was excited about a new baby. Miss Alexis, however, had mixed feelings. She thought it might be fun having a baby around, but privately wondered if Sarah would still love *her* as much as she always had.

"Almost every family we know has a person going to war," Justin said. "Sometimes more than one. I saw Jed in town and he told me his and Hannah's boys left last week. Tom's and Alice's son is going soon. It's hard to believe it's been twenty-one years since we started that first logging camp and all the children were underfoot."

"Yes. I guess we'll always feel that they're partly ours."

They named the young men from Lake Eagle Rest and Laurel's students who had enlisted. Zach's sons, Wolf and Keen, had told her they'd be volunteering.

"We're thankful for the learnin'," Zach had told her. "My boys kin read and write now, and that's bound to help 'em."

The boys had followed her out to the road the last time she was there and asked if she and Mr. Worth would continue to visit their dad.

Wolf said, "He's like a different man since you'ns started comin' to see him. He'd about lost interest in life. Keep Abner comin', too."

She promised that she and Justin would keep a watch over Zach.

That same promise was exacted from Nathan Buchanan regarding Lark and his two boys. Laurel advised him to move his family closer to Deerbrook before he left. Lark could take some courses to become a teacher and his boys could enroll in school.

Justin and Laurel were determined to keep life going as naturally as possible, and not give in to worry. They would fight their own emotional wars privately. They had the weapons of prayer and faith.

It was a bleak day, however, when Ethan and Allison arrived to tell them that Ethan was volunteering for the Marines. They had thought he would be deferred because of his age.

"I've just turned thirty-seven," he said. "I barely got in under the line."

"I dread to see you leave your church. Many people depend on you," Laurel said.

"I know. But I can't let other men go fight for my country and refuse to go myself until they make me go. I know you'll watch over Allison for me. We've already asked Miss Abby if she can live in one of her apartments."

"I'm going to try to get a job in town," Allison explained. "It'll keep me busy while he's gone."

Justin gave his word, as he and Laurel seemed to be doing often these days. "Ethan, you know we'll look after her. We consider you our children."

Later that afternoon, Justin found Laurel sitting at the dining room table, her head in her hands. When she looked at him, he saw the tears.

Without a word, he sat down beside her and took her hand.

"Justin, there's something about Ethan leaving that shakes my foundations. Why?"

"Ethan's a symbol of so much good coming out of so much bad. God allowed us to have a part in bringing that about," Justin spoke hesitantly, dealing with his own emotions. "We're sending another son off to war."

Laurel nodded. "He'll be a good marine."

"Yes," Justin agreed, solemnly. "Yes, he will."

Caroline's visits with Miss Abby produced more than a good time. She brought home a new boyfriend. She had met him one Saturday when he had responded to a call from Miss Abby about a leak that had appeared in an upstairs bedroom.

Abby later told Laurel, "I sent Caroline up with him to survey the damage. When they didn't come right back down, I went up to check. There they were," she said, laughing, "standing on each side of the pail, with the leak going 'Splat, splat, splat,' talking up a storm. To them, the leak was nonexistent. They only saw each other."

His name was Brook Stanford, and the family liked him at once. With Caroline's curly brown hair, brown eyes and ready smile, and his dark good looks, they made an attractive couple.

Laurel was doubly thankful to have Sarah close. Caroline was a little giddy with happiness, and Sarah seemed to know how to share her excitement *and* help keep her on course with her school work and responsibilities. Her approaching high school graduation seemed more important to her family than to her. Her thoughts seemed focused almost exclusively on the fact that Brook was planning to volunteer for the Navy.

She voiced her concerns to Sarah. "How do you stand it, being apart from Roe? I feel like part of *me* is missing when I'm not with Brook."

"That's part of being in love. I do miss Roe terribly, but I'm still me without him. I need to be strong for myself and the baby and for the family."

"We've talked a little about getting married before he leaves," Caroline confided haltingly. She sat back and waited for Sarah's response.

"I think you ought to talk this over with Mama and Daddy."

"I'm afraid they'll try to talk us out of it."

"You need to hear it from their perspective, Caroline. Whatever they say will help both of you look at it sensibly."

Brook was around several times a week. One night at supper, Justin said, "I bet I know your folks, Brook. Is your dad the Joe Stanford that's a builder?"

"Yes, sir, I've worked with him ever since I graduated last year. He knows you, sir."

At the Worths' invitation, Brook's parents came for a Sunday afternoon visit. Justin and Laurel liked them immediately and believed the feeling was mutual. They were very complimentary of Caroline.

A couple of weeks later, Brook and Caroline, after Sunday dinner, asked if they could speak privately with Justin and Laurel. When they were alone in the parlor, Brook said, "I would like your permission to marry Caroline. We love each other and," he swallowed, "and we would like to get married before I join the Navy."

"Caroline?" Justin's voice was gentle.

"Yes, Daddy. I love Brook and want to marry him...*before* he leaves."

"Laurel?" Justin asked.

Laurel heard the determination in Caroline's voice, but she still had something to say.

"Brook, we think you're a fine young man, and we're not totally surprised. We do want Caroline to graduate from high school first. You're both young and haven't known each other but a few months."

Justin added, "Yes, we've seen this coming, but we didn't expect it so suddenly. Marriage isn't something you rush into."

"Life seems to be rushing *us*, Mr. Worth," Brook answered. "I need to join the Navy soon or I'll be drafted into something I don't choose. My one desire is for Caroline to be my wife before I leave."

Justin said carefully, "It sounds like your minds are made up." He turned to Caroline. "When is your graduation?"

"In three weeks, on the first day of June."

"And when do you plan to leave, Brook?"

"Probably by the end of June."

Justin looked at Laurel.

She spread her hands, palms up. "That means we'll have a lot to do in a short time—but we can do it!"

Caroline looked from one to the other. "Then you're not saying, 'No'?"

Justin looked at them solemnly and asked, "You both are absolutely sure?"

"We are!" they said together.

He hugged Caroline to him for a moment, then shook hands with

Brook. "Then I offer you our permission, our best wishes and our support. We're happy because you're happy!"

Laurel hugged Caroline, then Brook, and said, "Congratulations! We wish you great happiness!"

For Caroline, her high school graduation was just one more step toward her wedding day. For Laurel, it was one more promise fulfilled: a promise she had received several years ago, in the hospital, when she had amazed the doctors by surviving. She had come through her near-death experience with the *knowledge* that she would live to rear her children. Getting the third one through high school was a milestone for her. Only two more were left.

Her head told her to be happy about Caroline's marriage, but her heart kept arguing, "It's too fast. I'm not ready to give her up yet."

She knew Justin was suffering the same pangs, but they moved ahead together to grant Caroline's wishes. The wedding was set for the Sunday after graduation, the third day of June, 1942. The newlyweds would have almost a month together before Brook left to serve his country in the United States Navy.

Somehow, Laurel kept up with her work schedule, while getting ready for Caroline's graduation *and* wedding. She couldn't have done it without Sarah—and the rest of the family. Sarah helped Caroline stay focused on the two big events ahead of her, prioritizing as they went.

Laurel visited Dr. Leighton to tell him about Bryce's broken leg and to ask for advice. He had been very interested in the use of birch bark as a splint. He assured her that he couldn't have done anything better, gave her some pain pills for Bryce, and told her to keep him up-to-date on Bryce's progress, including how well the splint worked.

Justin returned with Laurel to Abner's house on Saturday to check on Bryce. The family had met this accident with the same fortitude that Laurel had come to expect. They simply saw what they had to do and did it. Abner had made a sturdy pair of crutches and Rosalee had padded the tops for comfort. They had not, however, let him out of bed. They were waiting for Laurel's permission.

Bryce looked and acted like himself again. He admitted that his leg hurt but said he thought the pain was getting a little easier every day. "I'd like to try out them crutches that Dad's been workin' on."

"Then, let's do it!" Laurel said, her relief evident in her voice. "Remember, you *must not* put any weight on that leg! If you do, the bone may come apart again."

Justin helped Abner get Bryce on the crutches and the two men stayed close beside him as he did a balancing act. After several awkward moves, he got the rhythm, then the confidence. After a turn by himself around the room, he was ready to lie back down.

Laurel had prepared some extra school work for him to do while he was in bed. Justin gave him two Zane Grey westerns and whispered, "A man can't work the whole time he's laid up. I bet you can read these by now and they'll help pass the time."

On their way home, they swung by to visit Zach. The difference in the man he had been a few months before and the man he was now was startling to Justin. This was a proud man. Proud because he could now read and write. Proud that his two sons were going to fight for their country. His pride showed in the way he had cleaned up the place — and himself.

He announced, "I'm givin' up the moonshine business, Justin. I promised my boys afore they left. I'll be lookin' fer another way to make a little cash. I used to work in the timber business."

"Come home with us and I'll take you to Terminal Town — Sawmill Town — in Lake Eagle Rest on Monday. I bet they could use another man. Several regulars have left for the service."

"Really?"

"Yes. You'd probably need to board in the rooming house."

"That'd be fine. This here place is lonesome without my boys."

Justin thought, *I do believe this old rapscallion hermit is ready to join the human race again.*

He patted him on the shoulder. "Get your things together and we'll get on our way."

Even with the short preparation time, Caroline's wedding was all she could have wished for. Laurel called on her logging camp friends, Hannah, Nora, Bess, and Alice, to help her. They were extended family, after all. Bess, the expert seamstress, made the dress from ivory satin. Caroline chose a simple style, without lace, that suited her slim figure. Her veil was ivory net attached to a band that nestled in her curls.

Hannah decorated the church simply, but beautifully, with rhododendron, mountain laurel, and ferns. Pastor Pierce believed a wedding ceremony should be brief and he kept it so. It was a poignant moment when he mentioned the loved ones not there: Adam, Roe and Ethan. It was fitting that they be mentioned, as well as many good friends of the bride and groom, who were already on their way to serve their country.

Nora, Alice and some friends from church helped with a simple reception on the wrap-around porch of the Worth home. The newly married couple left for their apartment at Miss Abby's house.

Justin had been pleased when Brook had approached him alone to talk. "Sir, I need your advice on what you think is best for Caroline while I'm gone. I know that you and Mrs. Worth have offered for her to continue to live with you. I appreciate that, but we would like to have our own living quarters established before I leave. Miss Abby has offered to rent us a two-room apartment and Caroline is going to try to get a job in Deerbrook."

"I think it's a good solution, Brook. This way, she'll learn how to run her own household. Of course, Abby is like family and Allison, Ethan's wife, is already there, too."

He put his hand on Brook's shoulder. "You know we'll watch after her. We hope she'll choose to spend some time with us, but it's right that you have your own place."

Later, he told Laurel, "I like that young man a little more every time I'm with him. He seems to understand what Caroline needs and is already taking care of her."

When Brook left on the last day of June, he felt like an old married man. In less than a month he and Caroline, with the help of both of their families, had made their small apartment into a cozy home. And Caroline, with the influence of Laurel's friend, Erica Matthews, got a job at the courthouse. She could walk to work.

Both families and a group of friends saw Brook off at the train station. Caroline's eyes were bright with tears, but she kept a smile on her face as long as she could see him waving from the window. She, then, allowed her tears to flow all over her daddy's suitcoat, as he held her close.

She asked Sarah to move in with her for a while. It would be easier for Sarah to go to work from Miss Abby's, and Caroline needed to become accustomed to life with Brook gone.

Miss Abby loved having the young women and took her role seriously as their chief encourager. Her philosophy was that if they were busy enough—"involved in life" she called it—they wouldn't have time to be lonesome or bored. She soon saw to it that "her girls" were helping at Red Cross Headquarters or with other war efforts.

"Thank God for Abby," Laurel said to Justin. "Nobody would dare be idle or bored in her presence. *And*, she even makes it all seem like fun!"

Chapter Twelve

Laurel always looked forward to the harvest, knowing full well the hard, sustained work it would take to get everything she wanted to preserve into jars and onto the pantry shelves. In the late summer of 1942, when it seemed that the whole world had spun out of control, including their family, she was especially thankful for the reminder of the faithfulness of God. A reminder of Who was still in charge of "summer and winter and noontime and harvest…" The baskets of corn or beans or tomatoes or other produce were also the fruit of Justin's and David's hard work in the fields.

"Now comes our part," she told Alexis, whose primary job was to wash jars.

The actual, physical war was several thousands of miles away, but it was ever present with them. Laurel knew that incessant worry did not honor God, so she placed their loved ones in His hands each morning and each night. In between, a vague dread, interspersed at times with sharp anxiety, would hit her as she went about her work. At first she felt guilty, as if she wasn't actively trusting God enough. Then, she realized that perhaps this was her part — her burden — to keep an attitude of prayer while she went about her life, to "pray without ceasing."

Justin agreed. "Laurel, within the last six months we've seen one son go to war and one daughter get married. Our two sons-in-law and our adopted son, Ethan, are gone. Many of your CCC students and adult education students have come by to tell you 'goodbye,' as they left for war. Our young men from Lake Eagle Rest who've been a big part of our lives for the past few years have come to visit us before they enlisted.

"Sarah," he continued, "is pregnant and is our responsibility while Roe is away fighting for our country. Caroline's a new bride whose husband is at war. We don't say it out loud but we know all of our boys are in danger."

He turned her away from the stove where she was stirring green beans, getting them ready to put in the waiting jars. As she faced him, he added, "Anybody with a grain of sense would be concerned, honey. I face it just like you do. I've figured out that I have to face up to the situation, pray about it, then carry on with life. It's my way of fighting the war here at home. Keep the home fires burning and the family going as normally as possible. That's what they're fighting for! Our freedom to live our lives and carry on the values of this country."

She put her arms around him and laid her head on his chest. "You're a good man, Justin!"

His arms tightened around her. "You, of course, know all that I've said. You've lived your life making the best of all kind of situations."

"It's still good to have your reassurance and to share each other's burdens."

Alexis, soon to turn eleven, had just completed two weeks of vacation Bible school at their Baptist church and was planning to attend another week at the nearby Methodist church. They were on the small kitchen porch one afternoon in July, with Laurel breaking green beans and Alexis washing quart jars in a tin tub, when Alexis turned her curiosity and sense of fair play loose on Laurel

"Mama, why did God tell Joshua to capture Jericho and kill all the people? Does that seem fair to you? I mean, it was *their* home."

Laurel, brought back abruptly from wondering where their boys were, thought through the unlikely question, then answered, "No, it *wasn't* their home! They had settled on the land and built a city on it, but the land *belonged* to Abraham's descendants—the group that Joshua was leading. God had given the land to Abraham many years before."

She struggled to compress the history of several generations into a few simple sentences. "Abraham's family lived there until a famine forced them to move to Egypt. His descendants became slaves, but

Moses delivered them. God called them to go back to the land He had given them. They called it 'The Promised Land.'"

Alexis, her small hand scrubbing the inside of a jar, persisted, "Okay, so he could've taken the land without killing everybody. Why did God want him to do that?"

*This child...*Laurel thought. She tried to formulate the answer before she spoke.

"Because they believed in false gods who, they said, led them to do some very wicked things. They even sacrificed their children to their gods — burning them alive or sealing them up alive in the walls around the city."

Alexis looked horrified but Laurel continued. God's reputation was at stake in a little girl's mind. "Their pagan religious practices weren't moral. That means they committed wrong acts against each other in the name of religion. God didn't want their beliefs to infiltrate His people."

Alexis gave a sigh of relief. "We studied about Joshua in Bible school and I've been worried about God ever since, wondering if He was as good as you've always said He is. I understand better now

Laurel got up to wash some beans and put them on to cook. When she returned, Alexis said, "Mama, I wish I understood how it all fits together in the Old Testament. I mean, there's Moses and Joseph and Abraham and David and...all the others. Could you tell me who comes after who?"

The teacher in Laurel responded. "I think I can. It would be a good review for me, too. Do you want to have a session every day while we're canning?"

"Yes! Then I'll know a lot of answers in the next vacation Bible school."

That night Laurel related all this to Justin, adding, "I'm pleased and surprised at her questions — especially about the character of God."

"They're good questions for a ten-year-old. Shows she's already had some good teaching."

"I think she really is interested, but her immediate motivation is to know the answers when she goes to Bible school."

Justin laughed. "That's okay. The important thing is that you'll be giving her a chronological knowledge of the Old Testament that she'll have for the rest of her life. Knowledge that most people don't have, including me."

So, while Alexis washed jars and Laurel prepared food for canning, knowledge and life-shaping beliefs were passed from a master teacher to a young girl with an eager mind, who had already begun her search — even when she was not totally aware of what she was searching for — as to what constituted the abundant life promised in the Bible. The kind of life her mother had!

Some of those learning sessions were "showing" rather than "telling" about faith and the power of prayer. One afternoon, just as they had finished preparing vegetables to be made into soup, a young girl, Eva Walker, whom they knew from church, ran into the yard, her breath coming in great sobbing gulps. Her mother ran a few yards behind her.

Laurel's stomach lurched when she saw Eva's face up close. She was obviously burned, but a gooey, yellow substance covered her face and was splattered in her hair. Laurel took her by the shoulders and set her down in a chair, saying, "Alexis, bring two glasses of water."

Mrs. Walker collapsed in a nearby chair and struggled to get her breath. Raggedly, she said as she panted, "A quart jar of corn blew up near her face. I thought you'd know what to do."

Eva sat moaning in pain and fright while her mother looked on the point of collapse. They had run more than a mile to get there for help. Laurel realized that Eva, a pretty teenager, could be scarred and disfigured for life. She felt panic — and even momentary resentment — that she was faced with such a challenge. Those negative emotions vanished, however, as she flew into action.

"Alexis, go get my first aid kit. I need some sterile gauze."

She quickly washed a small basin thoroughly and filled it with warm water from the kettle on the stove — water that had already boiled. She would take no chances on introducing infection. She, then, was ready to ask for healing — the part she couldn't do, the part that was up to God. She asked Eva and her mother to join hands with Alexis. Laurel, with one hand on their hands and one hand on Eva's head, prayed her simple receiving prayer.

"I believe, Father, that You desire to heal Eva's face completely from these burns. I ask You to take away the pain and heal her without leaving scars. I receive these requests from You right now and I will treat her as if You have already answered our prayers. Thank you in advance for Your faithfulness. Amen"

Eva, her eyes wide, gasped. As they stared at her, she added quietly, in wonder, "The pain is gone!"

Laurel grabbed her hands as she raised them to feel her face.

Mrs. Walker, tears running down her cheeks, turned to Laurel. "You drew out the fire!"

Laurel, startled, was quiet for a moment, then replied, "No, *I* didn't. I asked *God* to take away the pain and *He* did! Now, we have to do our part, believing He'll do what we can't do."

Knowing what was ahead, she said, "Mrs. Walker, go with Alexis and get a cup of coffee or a glass of lemonade. Then, wait for us in the living room."

At the mother's anxious look, Laurel added gently, "She's going to be all right. God is already at work healing her."

As soon as she and Eva were alone, Laurel set to work, gently sponging the corn off Eva's face. As Laurel knew it would, every stroke of gauze took skin along with the corn.

Eva sat patiently with her eyes closed. At one point she whispered, "It's feeling better. The corn was drying and was pulling at my face."

Laurel worked quickly with the cleaning, leaving scraps of skin and corn in Eva's hair to deal with later. As she started to apply ointment to the raw layer of skin, she hesitated, thinking, *I believe the skin needs to breathe. I'm going to try to keep it moist and wait about the ointment.*

When she laid a cool, wet cloth on Eva's face, the girl murmured, "That feels good."

Laurel breathed a silent prayer of thanksgiving that the pain had not returned.

Before calling Mrs. Walker, Laurel carefully removed the scraps of skin and bits of corn from Eva's hair. When Mrs. Walker looked intently at Eva's face, tears flowed again. "How does it feel, honey?"

"It's not hurting. It feels better since Mrs. Worth cleaned it."

Laurel said, "She's had a shock and needs to rest. Let's put her to bed here. When Justin gets home, I'll see if he can ride in to see Dr. Leighton and ask what else we need to do."

After they put Eva to bed in the corner guest bedroom and left her to rest, Mrs.Walker looked around her and saw the canning process that she and Eva had interrupted. Tomatoes, okra and corn looked ready to make vegetable soup. Mrs. Walker, needing to show her gratitude, announced, "If Alexis'll go to my house and tell the family what's goin' on, I'll help you finish gettin' this soup into jars."

Laurel protested, "You probably need to rest, too, after such a scare."

"Land's sakes, no! I'm too geared up to rest. I need to stay around to see how Eva does. Now, just tell me what to do first."

When Justin arrived home, Laurel had a note ready for Dr. Leighton, explaining what had happened, including the fact that Eva said the pain had stopped. She described the way the raw skin looked after her cleansing process. She asked for advice on further treatment, especially to prevent scarring.

Dr. Leighton sent word approving of her treatment so far. He advised her to keep Eva at her house for a few days, told her how to cleanse her face every day and apply vitamin E oil, which he sent.

Hearing this, Mrs. Walker went home just long enough to get some clothes for Eva and herself. She also regaled her family with the story of what had happened when Laurel prayed.

When Laurel finally went to bed that night, concerned about her part in getting Eva's face to heal without scarring, she was unaware, thankfully, that, in the eyes of the people around her, she had entered a new dimension. She had taken on the status of "Healer." The word went out, reverberating in needy homes and hopeful hearts, that Laurel Worth could "draw out fire." That must mean, they reasoned, that she could heal other hurts and ailments, such as the thrush that often plagued their babies. And, if her prayers were answered so promptly, perhaps they could take *their* burdens and have her pray over them.

After a week of treatment, Eva's face was healing nicely without scarring. Her mother or sister had stayed to help care for her. The pain never returned and Laurel, after detailed instructions, allowed her to go home.

By the first of August, Sarah was so heavy with child, Dr. Leighton advised her to take a leave of absence from work and to limit her time on her feet. "Looks like he's going to be half grown when he gets here," he added.

She returned from Caroline's apartment to the little house. Even though she had to sit, she stayed busy sewing baby clothes, helping prepare food for canning, and even helping Justin sort his pictures for delivery. When Laurel objected to so much activity, Sarah said, "Mama, this baby may think he can boss my walking, but he's not going to boss everything I do!"

Justin, hearing this exchange, laughed and whispered to Laurel, "Reminds me of another strong-minded woman I know."

Sarah saved some of her walking allowance to go meet Alexis each day, halfway down the spring trail, on her way home from school. It hurt Laurel's heart to see her awkward progress. It was Alexis' job to stop by the post office each day and to bring home the mail. If she saw Alexis running toward her, she knew she had a letter.

Roe was fighting somewhere in Europe. Sarah had no idea *where* he was nor *how* he really was. All mail was censored, so his occasional letters were brief, assuring her of his love and his happiness about the baby coming.

Adam, meanwhile, had been assigned to a troop carrier. His ship, with armored escort, transported thousands of American soldiers to Europe, and brought back the wounded. He, too, was limited in what he could share in a letter. When he read that candy and chewing gum was hard to get at home, he remedied the situation in typical Adam fashion, by mailing occasional packages of Hershey Bars and Teaberry Gum, always addressed to Alexis. Laurel cried over the first package, figuring that was his allotment from the ship's store.

Brook was faithful to write often to Caroline, but nothing of substance about where he was or what he was doing. He was on an aircraft carrier in the Philippines. Caroline was coming into her own as a young wife whose husband was at war. She came home almost every weekend. After her initial adjustment of sadness and loneliness, she seemed to square her shoulders and lift her personal load with grace and a strength that pleased her mama and daddy. When they told her so, she said, "I'd be ashamed to blubber and carry on, while Brook and Adam and the others are out there fighting for us. Besides, I have all of you."

Ethan was fighting the Japanese somewhere in Asia. Allison had surprised and pleased Justin and Laurel by coming "home" often with Caroline. The news over the radio and in the newspapers caused roller coaster emotions. The terrible downside was that Japanese troops had captured Manila and the Philippines. The upside was that Americans had won the battle of Midway Island, keeping Japan from seizing Midway as a base from which to strike Hawaii. It was a great victory for the Allies. Allison knew Justin and Laurel were greatly concerned about Ethan and she always shared her news. It made her burden lighter to know they were under it with her.

Hardly any family was exempt from the anxiety about a loved one somewhere in combat. The news was full of atrocities by Hitler's armies rushing across Europe toward Russia. It should have and would have discouraged some countries. But not America and not Great Britain! Americans were realists, but they were patriots! Anger turned into resolve and an absolute determination that evil would not win — that the warmongers would either be destroyed or confined to cages, where uncontrolled predatory animals *should* live. Americans, it seemed, were willing to pay the price for freedom, not only for themselves but for the world.

Laurel wasn't a secretive person, but she had a problem she wanted to check out with Dr. Leighton before she told Justin. She knew that if anything could unnerve him, it would be a problem with her health. For the past few months she had battled a puzzling fatigue—a weakness—that would hit her and not let go until she rested awhile.

More impatient than worried, she rode to Deerbrook with the mailman and went to see Dr. Leighton. He listened carefully to her symptoms, took some blood tests, and asked her to come back the next week for the results.

"Before you go, tell me about the young girl whose face was burned — when was it — about a month ago?"

"She's fine. Her face healed with no scarring."

"That's wonderful! Tell me again how you treated the burn."

"I kept her at my house for a week. When I cleaned her face and the skin came off with the corn, I had the impression that the next layer of skin needed to breathe. So, I kept it moist, but didn't put anything on it for two days. Then I started patting on the vitamin E oil you sent."

She hesitated, then forged ahead. "Do you believe that prayer can heal?"

"Why're you asking?"

"I prayed over Eva and asked for healing before I started cleaning her face. She was moaning with pain." Laurel paused, then continued, "Just as I finished praying, she went totally still and quiet. Then she said, 'The pain is gone.'

"I was startled and thankful, but a part of me still expected the pain to resume as I started cleaning the burn. But, she didn't seem to be in any pain from then on, even as the outer layer of skin came off."

She paused, then added, "I believe the Lord healed her right then and there—a miracle! He allowed me to do my part after He had done His."

She finished by asking, "So, what does a scientific doctor think about this story?"

A smile spread across his face. "*This* doctor believes the story as you told it. My scientific thinking crossed some boundaries and encompassed new possibilities when *you* survived, Laurel. You know that *you've* been a living, walking miracle for—how long now?"

"It's been nine years since my surgery."

"It seems logical to me that God might choose to honor your prayers for healing, since He chose, in the face of imminent death, to keep you alive."

She smiled. "You're a good encourager. Eva's mother has spread the word that I 'drew out the fire.' It scares me that I might get the credit that belongs only to God. I prayed, but God did the healing."

"But you were the tangible person with the faith to claim the healing. Even God works through human instruments."

After she left, Dr. Leighton did some praying of his own. He asked that this vibrant woman would not have major, life-changing health problems and that she would live—and keep enriching the lives of others—until a ripe old age.

To use one of Justin's terms, the war had "played hob" with Laurel's Adult Education Program. While waiting for the doctor's report, Laurel assessed the present status, to present it to Mr. McKenzie when school started in August. As she went down her list she smiled unconsciously as she thought of each family.

Zach seemed to be enjoying himself working in Terminal Town. He showed up to visit them occasionally when he had heard from Wolf or Keen. Laurel, Justin, or even David, would help him answer their letters when he needed assistance.

Nathan Buchanan, before leaving, had followed Laurel's advice and moved Lark and their two boys to Deerbrook, where the boys enrolled in school. Lark had already enrolled to take some teacher training courses.

Abner's family was the only one she had left near Locust Hollow. Bryce's leg had healed normally with the help of the bark cast and crutches. His only complaint was that it itched constantly and he couldn't scratch through all that bark. Laurel laughed and shook her head. "You men! You wouldn't dare complain with the awful pain, but it's okay to grouch about the itching." Bryce grinned, pleased that she had categorized him as a man.

Imogene Ryan and her daughter, Judith, had become good students since Imogene had recovered from her bout with pellagra. Laurel, following Dr. Leighton's instructions, had advised Imogene about the foods she needed to eat to stay healthy. For good measure, she continued giving her niacin pills as supplements.

The families of Abe, Zeke, and Odell were the next exciting challenge. She had barely got started with them when school was out for the summer. She knew there were other families around them that needed help.

Dr. Leighton, a week later, told Laurel that he believed she was suffering from pernicious anemia. For some reason, her body could no longer absorb foods containing vitamin B-12. She would probably need to take regular injections, supplying this vitamin, for the rest of her life.

He ended the office visit by saying, "I'm going to advise you, seriously, to do something that will be harder for you than taking shots. I want you to *slow down*. How old are you now?"

"I'm fifty-two."

"And Justin?"

"Fifty-eight! An old man!" she said, laughing.

"Yes. I've noticed how old and feeble he is! He can still work rings around most men half his age! You both go like a house afire!"

"How much do I have to slow down?"

"I want you to use your common sense. You should rest awhile every afternoon—a half hour to an hour. Then, think of a normal day and cut out at least one thing you planned to do that day. Those two things will help your mind start thinking differently about what you need to accomplish. *It won't be easy for you.* Do you promise me you'll cooperate, or do I have to tell Justin my orders?"

She saw that he was absolutely serious. "I promise I'll start making some adjustments."

"I'll expect to hear how it's going in two weeks, when you come in for your next shot."

Laurel decided the best way to tell Justin this news was to be casual about it. That evening after supper, during their usual talk about the day, she said, "By the way, I went by to see Dr. Leighton today. He says I have anemia and will need to take a shot of vitamin B-12 every couple of weeks for a while."

She had his full attention. "Why did you go see him?"

"I've been feeling tired lately and thought I might need some vitamins."

"And you didn't tell *me*?"

"I didn't want to worry you until I knew what it was."

"What else did he say?"

"I need to slow down some and rest awhile every day."

"Laurel," he said, reaching for her hand and looking at her intently, "are you telling me everything?"

"I am! You can go talk to him yourself."

At dinner a few nights later, Laurel surprised everyone by announcing that she wanted to learn to drive. Justin, starting to take a bite, laid his fork down with the food still on it. "You *what*?"

Laurel looked around at her motionless, staring children, and repeated, "I would like for you to teach me to drive the Ford car."

"When did you think of *this*?" Justin wondered.

"It's the sensible thing to do. Tattoo is getting old, and I have to walk or ask you to take me to the homes of my students, and…and I think it would help the family in general."

"I enjoy taking you to the homes of your students. They're my friends, too." Justin's tone showed some bewilderment.

"I know you do, and they love for you to come! You could still go when it doesn't interfere with your work." She smiled at him. "They'd probably go on strike if they thought you weren't coming back at all."

Justin suddenly realized that this was part of her adjustments to Dr. Leighton's orders.

So, walking a long distance or riding a horse was over — for now, anyway.

Sarah laughed. "I think it's great, Mama! Then *you* can teach *me* after this baby gets here!"

David, fifteen and already driving the Ford close around home, said, "I'll help you teach her, Daddy."

"Okay, son. I'm glad you're here to help me take care of these women."

Under the canopy of a bright blue October sky — with nary a cloud showing its face — Justin Roe Bradley made his appearance. He set up an indignant howl that was music to the ears of the listeners. Dr. Leighton had been concerned about Sarah's delivery, because the baby was very large for her small frame. His unease had come through to Laurel when he told her to be sure and notify him as soon as Sarah's pains started. It was a difficult delivery, but his and Laurel's combined skills brought Sarah and the baby through safely.

Justin Roe's daddy was thousands of miles away, fighting so that his son might live in freedom. The baby and his mother, however, had no lack of loving attention. Laurel and Alexis, of course, seemed ever present. Alexis' worry about Sarah's continued love for her dissipated the first time she was allowed to hold the baby boy. His little hand wrapped around her finger and she belonged to him. The first place David went every day after school was to check on J.R., as he called him.

Caroline came home with a couple of suitcases, announcing that she was moving in with Sarah for a few weeks to be with her at night. "I can't stand the thought of not being here, with all this excitement going on." She rode back and forth to work each day with a neighbor.

Justin could be found in the little house at odd hours, holding the baby on his lap, talking to him. Sarah was touched by her daddy's attention to her son and told him so. Justin replied, "I'm making sure he knows what a man looks like. Besides, he's a good listener. His eyes follow me like he agrees with everything I tell him. Makes me feel downright intelligent."

With their best efforts to notify Roe, it was still almost a month before Sarah heard that he had received word about the baby. The loneliness of not being able to share this important time with Roe would hit her most often at night. But, by daylight, she was ready to make the best of her circumstances. She was, after all, the daughter of two unique people who had modeled that lesson quite well.

"The war has done for the economy what the New Deal Programs couldn't do," Justin remarked to Abby, one Sunday afternoon when she was visiting. "The whole country has entered into the war effort producing weapons and machinery."

"Yes," Abby answered, "I read this week where a vacuum cleaner company had converted to making machine guns, and automobile factories are now turning out airplanes, engines, and tanks."

"The millions of young men marching off to war have created a job market not seen for many years in this country. There are more jobs than men to fill them."

Abby countered, "Yes. So, women are going — by the thousands — to the factories." She squared her shoulders. "We women may not carry a gun and meet the enemy face to face, but we're doing our part. Your Caroline has become quite a favorite at Red Cross Headquarters with her volunteer work. Makes me proud."

Later, Justin asked Caroline about her Red Cross work. "I enjoy it, Daddy. I help make up bandages and kits. We're starting the blood donor program soon. Miss Abby sees to it that our chapter keeps up with things.

"Allison and I laugh about Miss Abby, but we admire her greatly. For example, she gets up on Sunday morning early and goes to the hospital to check on her patients. Then, mid-morning she slips out and goes to church where she's the organist. She says the choir robe hides her nurse uniform. After church, she heads back to the hospital."

"Yes. She's one determined lady," Justin said.

He hugged Caroline and added, "Your mother and I are proud of you, honey. I know it's hard with Brook gone, but you're handling your own life well and are helping other people."

She laughed as she returned his hug. "I wonder where I got the idea that I should help people…"

Justin was so proud of America's response to the war, it was hard for him to stop talking about it. Patriotism — love of country — pride in being an American — was served with bacon, eggs, biscuits and gravy at breakfast. At supper, with whatever food was on the table, he served up another encouraging story about the progress the Allies were making in Europe and Asia.

The tide of the war was turning on all fronts. The German Sixth Army had surrendered to the Russians at Stalingrad. Allied troops had captured part of New Guinea from the Japanese. British forces captured Tripoli from Italian control. Each young wife, including Allison who was often present, wondered just where her husband might be — and tried not to visualize what it like in battle.

No one in the Worth family dared complain of any inconvenience the war caused, such as rationing of gasoline, fuel oil and even shoes. Nor was there a hint of criticism for President Roosevelt when he froze wages and prices.

"These are such small sacrifices compared with what our men are doing," Justin remarked, letting his family know what he expected from them.

When the government announced its urgent need for scrap iron and steel to use in the manufacture of machinery and weapons for the men on the front lines, the American people, in communities from coast to coast, responded with millions of tons.

Justin and the men from Lake Eagle Rest took their logging trucks around the countryside, gathering every piece of metal they could find. School children helped with the search. An ever-growing mound of scrap metal appeared in front of the elementary school where Alexis attended. For good measure, Justin took a picture of the children gathered around the scrap iron pile and sent it to Sam Parker, editor of *The Wildwood Journal*. As intended, this set up some competition with other schools in the county. The "Scrap Iron Drive" was something physical they could do to help win this war. With the slogan, *The man behind the man behind the gun will help win this war!*, efforts seemed to double. The United States produced an abundance of airplanes, tanks and ships. Americans, shoulder to shoulder — with a single united purpose — were showing the world that they *intended* to win this war!

J.R — the name David gave the baby stuck — was the joy and center of attention of the entire family. He had a sunny nature and favored each of them with his smiles and gurgles of pleasure. Everybody in the family was delighted that J.R.'s eyes were the same unusual color as Justin's — the wonderful hue of the October blue sky under which he was born.

Sarah, sad that Roe had never seen his son and was missing his baby stage, bought a small camera to record as much of his life as possible. She kept an album that chronicled the stages and events. When J.R. was almost a year old, weaned and walking, Sarah decided to go back to work. She hired a young woman well-known by the family to live with her and keep J.R. while she was at work. She discussed it with Laurel, who, understanding that keeping busy was an antidote to worry, encouraged her. "You know the baby will be taken care of. The whole family revolves around him."

Chapter Thirteen

David, a handsome, gangling sixteen-year-old, was determined to live up to Adam's expectations that he help take care of the family. True to his word, he helped Justin teach Laurel to drive the 1932 Ford. He was now giving Sarah driving lessons and knew Caroline was standing in line. He still found great satisfaction in taking care of the animals. Chief, their shepherd dog who was the indisputable territorial boss, was his humble servant. Tattoo, after Justin and Laurel, preferred him above all others.

When he heard that there was a mad dog loose in the vicinity, he warned Alexis not to go outside alone, then shut Chief up in the barn. It wasn't Alexis, however, that needed help this time. Caroline, home for the weekend, went to the spring to get two pails of water. When David heard her scream, he grabbed a hoe and ran. Caroline stood frozen with fear, staring at a large black dog standing above her on a rocky ledge behind the spring. The dog's teeth were bared, with saliva dripping, as he growled in rage. David had never been so scared in his life, but he didn't even break stride.

"Run, Caroline!" he yelled. "Run! I'll head him off!"

Caroline fled from the snarling dog as David ran toward him, circling above him, so the dog couldn't leap on top of him. They stood facing each other—the boy and the mad dog—as mortal enemies. David knew the horrors associated with hydrophobia. He had to win this fight.

He swung the hoe hard, aiming for the dog's head, but the crazed animal lunged, knocking the hoe to the ground. David kicked with all his strength, a heavy blow on the head, stunning the dog enough that he closed those awful jaws. David, seeing his advantage, grabbed the dog's head with both hands, holding his mouth closed. Saliva dripped as the enraged, snarling dog twisted and turned, trying to break out of the viselike grip. Just as David found his hold weakening, Caroline appeared with a big rock in her hand.

David yelled, "Quick! Hit him between the eyes! As hard as you can!"

Caroline lifted the rock high and brought it down with all the force she had. The dog fell and lay still. David hit him again for good measure. But he knew he wasn't through yet.

"Go get Daddy's rifle! It's in the closet in his bedroom! Hurry!"

As Caroline ran, David yelled, "Make sure you bring some bullets!"

Caroline was back by the time David had caught his breath. The dog still lay prone at his feet, but his tail was twitching. David said, "I'd rather you didn't see me shoot him."

"Okay," she said, turning away, "but I'll be right behind this tree — with another rock in my hands."

Laurel and Alexis were at Sarah's house when the sound of a rifle shot — close by — shattered the usual quiet. They all rushed down the spring trail, calling David and Caroline.

"Mama," David yelled, "we're okay!"

When he and Caroline met them and told them what had happened, Laurel asked, "You held his jaws together while he was slobbering?"

"Yes, ma'am."

She headed back to the house. "Quick! You have to wash your hands and arms thoroughly — with lye soap!"

When he had finished, she said, "Let me check you. Do you have any scratches or cuts?"

"I don't think so."

Laurel examined him closely, finding no cuts, but she still wasn't satisfied. "I want you to take a good bath, then I'm taking you to Dr. Leighton to see if you need a rabies shot."

"But, Mama, I need to bury that mad dog before some other animal gets to him."

Laurel realized that made good sense, but her priority was David.

"Caroline, you and Sarah find something and cover that dog until your daddy gets home or we get back. Alexis, you come with me and David."

David, reluctantly obeying his mother, instructed his sisters, "Pile rocks on top of whatever you cover him with."

Dr. Leighton listened closely to David's story, examined him and found no cuts or scratches. He chose, however, to give him a series of rabies shots because he had handled the dog. As he prepared the injection, Dr. Leighton observed to Laurel, "Looks as if we have a chip off the old block."

"What?" David asked.

"Son, I mean you remind me of your daddy. I've treated him for many years for all kinds of unlikely injuries. But, I don't think even *he* ever faced down a mad dog — with his bare hands."

By the time they got home from the doctor, Justin had already buried the dog well away from the house. He had to hear the story, in detail, from David and Caroline.

Hugging David, Caroline said, "He saved my life, I think. I was too scared to move and here he came running, yelling at me! He broke the spell and I was able to run."

"But you came back and helped. I couldn't have held his mouth shut much longer."

Later, when they were alone, Justin said, "David, there's not a soldier anywhere in the world that showed more courage than you did today. I'm proud of you!"

That night, the last thing he remembered before he went to sleep were the words, "Looks as if we have a chip off the old block." He was immensely pleased to think he might be like his dad — or Adam.

Characteristic of Laurel, when she was faced with a set of limiting circumstances — things she couldn't change — she set about to try to make the best choices *within* the circumstance. She followed Dr. Leighton's orders about resting awhile each day. She was surprised at how much difference it made and wondered why she hadn't tried it before. Sometimes, when her work kept her at the home of her students until the afternoon, she would rest at their house before she started home.

The first time she asked to rest at Abe's house after she had finished his and his wife's lessons, Abe, startled and scared, asked, "Do you want me to go get Justin?"

Laurel laughed. "No. I'm not sick. I promised the doctor I'd rest every day, if possible."

Abe, still fretting like an old woman, said, "If I let anything happen to you, I'd sure hate to face Justin."

The one truth that Laurel's mind kept skirting around was that she almost *had to rest* before she could finish her day. She wasn't ready just yet to stare that fact in the face. So, she kept pretending she had a choice. Possibly the hardest part was adjusting her expectations of what to accomplish each day. Her abundant energy had enabled her to keep going for long hours for most of her life.

She laughed and told Justin, "I must still be programmed by those years in the logging camps where our cooking shifts were fifteen hours or more a day."

Justin, not ready to tease about her health, said seriously, "Laurel, we have to talk about this. I know how much your education work means to you. One part of me would like for you to give it up, but, if you choose to keep working, we're going to make out a schedule where all of us will do more here at home."

"What do you mean?"

"I mean that David and Alexis and I, plus Sarah and Caroline — and whoever else happens to be here — are going to take on some of your housework. That's the only way I will be happy about you continuing to work with your adult education."

Laurel never knew when Justin talked to their children, nor what he said, but change was in the air. Caroline started arriving on Friday nights instead of Saturday afternoons. She said casually, "Mama, just plan for Alexis and me to do the weekly cleaning every Saturday. We'll change the beds and sweep and dust. She needs to learn, and I'll teach her the way Sarah taught me."

Washday was moved from Monday to Saturday. Justin built the fire under the black wash pot and filled it full of water. Sarah and David worked beside Laurel until the clothes were on the line. J.R., a toddler, was kept out of trouble, in the house, with Alexis and Caroline. Sometimes they switched jobs, but Laurel was never left to do the heavy jobs alone. They all wanted her to save her energy for cooking. Nobody could replace their mama in the kitchen. Alexis took over as boss of the dishwashing. They helped her, but she was the one who knew where her mother wanted things kept.

Because Justin watched her like a hawk and because of her family's help, Laurel cut down her demands on herself. She deliberately chose to enjoy it and not to fret.

Her work was becoming more demanding, not from an academic standpoint, but from people needing help with more basic matters. Her joy in finally getting to teach Abe, Zeke and Odell and their wives to read and write and do simple arithmetic was tempered by the conditions she found in the homes of the people who lived around them. Thankfully, the three men and their families had adopted her recommendations years ago about hygiene and nutrition. Their outhouses were built well away from the house and stream, with lids for the seats. The women had learned much about how to treat their children when they were sick. She was proud of them and told them so.

When she entered the homes a few miles from Abe, however, she found multiple problems. Malnutrition was evident, especially in some of the women and children. After visiting several homes, she realized that some of the young children had rickets. Pellagra showed its ugly face there, too, *and* she believed some of the people might even have scurvy. She couldn't expect to teach them to read and write until she tended to their physical needs.

She spoke to Mr. McKenzie about this. "I shouldn't be paid for these visits until I actually start teaching, and that'll take some time."

Mr. McKenzie disagreed. "We'll call this preparatory work toward literacy. You'll actually be teaching them life-saving and life-changing lessons."

So, again with Dr. Leighton as her advisor, she went forth to do battle with the sicknesses that blighted lives or snuffed them out. Having a healthy, rambunctious two-year-old boy at home helped her draw a sharp contrast with two little boys who she believed had rickets, a softening of the bones because of lack of calcium and vitamin D. She was determined to get help for them before their bones hardened into the curved shapes. Milk, green vegetables, cod liver oil and sunlight were all to be administered — in big doses.

Confident over her success with Imogene Ryan, she moved

quickly against pellagra with treatment of niacin tablets and a diet including fresh, lean beef and yeast products.

Scurvy, she knew, was usually thought of in terms of sailors, who lived on salt beef and dry biscuits for weeks at a time. She also knew the basic diet of some of these families was fried fat back — salt pork — and biscuits and gravy. When she talked to Dr. Leighton, he agreed that scurvy could very well be present. He told her they needed high doses of vitamin C, which came in tomatoes, cabbage, lettuce, carrots, onions, and potatoes. Oranges, lemons, and limes had massive doses in them.

"Do you know why British sailors are called 'Limeys'?" he asked.

"I have no idea."

"The British Navy, to combat scurvy, started issuing daily rations of lime juice to its men. Solved the problem.

"Get these families started growing the vegetables I've mentioned," he continued. "In the meantime, let's give them some vitamin C tablets. Also, take them some lemons to make lemonade. Tell them to drink it every day."

Taking in bags of lemons was easy compared to convincing them about a garden. She could tell some of the men were skeptical about her instructions, so she turned Justin loose on them. She was reminded again of how much she depended on Justin's way with people. Before he was through, he had them enthusiastic about planting a garden that included a wide variety of vegetables — a health store for their families. He gave the parents an incentive by promising them he would take family pictures — without cost — when everybody was well and healthy looking. And, of course, he had a pocket full of candy for the children.

When one has wished for something for a long time and it finally happens, there's an initial sense of unreality. Laurel and Justin were faced with these emotions one Sunday afternoon when Abner and his family came to their house to, in Abner's words, "hash out some things." Abner, true to form, jumped in with both feet.

"Rosa and me have decided we want to git out of the moonshine business. My family's been in it for a couple of generations and I felt locked in when I was young. But...but, you've shown us a different way to live. I want my younguns to grow up in *your* world."

Justin and Laurel looked at each other with broad smiles on their faces. "We've been hoping for a long time—and Laurel's been praying—that you'd make this decision," Justin said. They both hugged Rosalee and Bonnie and shook hands with Bryce and Abner.

"I wasn't free to leave as long as Ma and Pa was alive. And, it's still hard to leave the rest of the clan."

Justin reassured him. "I'd wager it won't be long 'til they follow you. There are jobs for people now, Abner, so they'll have other ways to make a living."

"You think so? Right now, they're agin me doin' this."

Justin realized the courage it must take to make this monumental move, but if anybody could bring out the other moonshiners, it would be Abner.

"Yes, I believe they'll come out. You're their leader. You've always called the shots."

The women, excited to talk about practical matters, went into the house. David and Alexis took Bonnie and Bryce off to pitch a game of horseshoes. As soon as the men were alone, Abner's fears came through to Justin. "I know it's the right thing to do but I'm not sure I can make it in the timber business. I'll be a total greenhorn."

Justin studied him for a minute and saw that he was serious. "Abner, ever since the first time I met you—with that mask on— you've been in charge. Even with the outlaws! You always land on your feet! You'll not only learn the timber business, you'll probably end up in charge there, too!"

Abner, embarrassed but pleased by these observations, shot back. "You sure know how to put the monkey on a man's back!"

"Yep! When it's needed. Now, let's go talk about a job in Terminal Town. I know they need some more men and I think a couple of the sawmill houses're empty."

Brand Waters, the most unlikely candidate a year or two ago, had become foreman of the sawmill work in Terminal Town. On Monday morning Justin introduced Abner and asked Brand to teach him the sawmill end of timbering. He assured Brand that Abner would be worthy of his time and attention.

Lila and Gerta took Rosalee under their wings, helping her get the small house in order. Zach, who had entered fully into Terminal Town life, was beside himself with pleasure that his friends were there and that he could help them get settled.

It was another satisfying day when Laurel went with Rosalee to enroll Bryce and Bonnie in Lake Eagle Rest Elementary School. The fact that grades four through seven were in one classroom enabled the two new pupils to fill in some gaps in their learning. They had primarily learned the skill subjects of reading, writing and arithmetic. Now, they were exposed to information subjects such as geography and history and science. Several other pupils their age and size were still at the elementary level, so they fitted in easily.

Bonnie, a pretty girl, shyly made her way toward acceptance. Bryce, however, with a big dose of his daddy's charm, soon became a popular leader among the boys. Being a good ball player helped.

Alexis reported on their progress at supper one night. "Bryce can hit the ball farther than anybody. And, Mama, when somebody told him he was a fast runner, he said, 'Miz Worth set my broke leg and kept me from bein' crippled.' Then he pulled up his pants leg and said, 'See how straight my leg is!'"

"He thanks me every time he sees me," Laurel said, laughing. "How do they seem to be doing in class? Could you let them know, privately, that if they need help, they can ask you?"

"They've *already* been asking me, and they learn real fast. Everybody likes them and tries to help them."

Laurel, in her monthly visit to Mr. McKenzie, was happy to report this latest bit of news. She told him she would focus on the community where Abe lived and still visit Imogene and Judith. Teaching Abner, Rosalee and Zach would be easier, now that they were in her community.

The Allies were winning the war on all fronts, at the cost of heavy fighting and heavy casualties. The war reports resulted in such roller coaster emotions, Justin suggested that the family wait until after mealtime to discuss them. He would then condense the news but keep it factual. When the word of D-Day broke in June, 1944 — calling it the largest single invasion force in history — Sarah believed that Roe would have been among those going ashore in Normandy, France. To ease her anxiety, she would tell J.R. stories about his daddy, reliving some of her memories. One of the first words she taught him to say was "Daddy." The two-year-old, who had never seen his daddy, nevertheless could be heard chanting, "Dad-dee, Dad-dee, Dad-dee."

Adam, they knew, was a radioman on that troop ship with its precious cargo, a prime target for the enemy. Brook and Ethan were fighting the Japanese somewhere in the Pacific. Their location couldn't be disclosed. Therefore, Caroline and Allison, like thousands of wives, imagined their husbands in *any* battle in that area.

When the November, 1944, election came, Franklin D. Roosevelt was elected to a fourth term as the President of the United States. Harry Truman became his Vice President.

The people of Lake Eagle Rest were bound by ties beyond the norm, as the families depended on each other for solace and prayers for their sons or husbands. Each family found that its burden of war was best managed if handled collectively with other families whose loved ones were fighting. Church services were special times when burdens were shared. A mother or dad could be heard praying for a neighbor's son as much as for their own. Normal aggravations or grievances or disagreements seemed suspended, or relegated to their proper places. Even Gussie, whose grandson had been wounded, seemed to mellow toward Laurel. Gussie had another enemy now — across the water — that she could vent her anger on. So, Laurel enjoyed a surcease of hostility from that quarter.

Abby liked to share her joys with the Worths, whom she considered her family. When she found out that one of her patients, Mr. Hughes, who had a summer home in Deerbrook, was an accomplished violinist and sometime composer, she asked if she could bring him for a Sunday visit. His music gave such pleasure that Justin asked if he could stay a week or two. They would invite the neighbors to hear him.

He agreed, asking if there was an isolated spot in the house where he might have some quiet time to possibly compose some music. He settled happily in the partially finished attic, where a bedroom had already been set up. It was for anyone in the family who might want privacy or for the steady stream of visitors — Abby called them "strays" — who gravitated to the Worth house.

Mr. Hughes' violin music ranged from classic compositions to fox trots, entrancing his audience. After Justin sent word to some nearby families who were known for their fiddle music, they appeared with their instruments to "heist a tune." Mr. Hughes was delighted at the opportunity to learn to fiddle. It was a blending of talent and culture. The soothing strains of a Strauss Waltz or Brahms' Lullaby would give way to foot tapping, hand-clapping mountain fiddle tunes. The sophisticated, accomplished gentleman, whose life had been devoted to music, enjoyed the mountain fiddlers, who had never had formal music lessons, but who could make their fiddles "talk." He envied their easy, unabashed enjoyment of their music.

Sitting in the attic, composing the tunes that came into his head, Mr. Hughes would become distracted by the sounds of the family. One rainy afternoon when a group of Alexis' friends came to play, his musical ear was perplexed by the series of sounds coming from below. Everything would be totally quiet for a little while, then there would be a yell or two, then several yells and laughter. He found himself jotting down the notes that would signify the quietness, then the occasional sound, then several sounds, then happy sounds for laughter. A few nights later — with pomp — he played his composition for the family, telling them that they had created the sounds and he had put them to music. He asked them to guess what the piece represented. As they puzzled over the answer, Alexis questioned, "Is it fair to ask which day and what time of day this was?"

"Yes. It was on Tuesday afternoon."

After he played it twice more, Alexis sorted it all out. "It's Hide-n-Seek! We were playing it inside the day it rained!"

Now that they knew, he played it with great enjoyment, knowing they could identify the various stages of the game. "I've named this piece 'The Romp.' I'll leave you a copy."

Before he left, he had one more gift for the family. It was a piece of music that flowed peacefully for a while, then a clatter or a bang, then several clatters, closing with the peaceful flow repeated. When they couldn't guess, he said simply, "Alexis Washing Dishes."

Alexis asked, "I sounded like that?"

"Yes. You were singing, but interspersed with your song was the clatter of the dishes and the clanging of the pots and pans."

When he ceremoniously presented her with the sheet of music, she objected. "But you worked hard on this."

He answered, "You made the music. I only recorded it."

For a fortnight the gift of music to the community — by unlikely partners — held in abeyance the cloying atmosphere of concern about loved ones at war.

Mr. Hughes, a lonely widower with no children, greatly enjoyed the give and take of the Worth family life. He was touched by their hugs for each other when leaving in the morning and again when coming together in the evening. It was a daily celebration of togetherness that affirmed and strengthened each person as they went about their individual lives. He thought of the proverb that declared, "A cord of three strands is not easily broken." The Worth family had more than three strands: a veritable tapestry of mutual love and respect.

When Justin tried to express his appreciation for his music, Mr. Hughes replied, "But, I am the one who should thank you! Your way of life is a song in itself. A mountain song of love and happiness. I've been greatly enriched."

Laurel's way of praying had changed in the years since her near-death experience. She now realized that, before her life-changing encounter, her prayers often had been simply informing God about what she planned to do, then expect His cooperation or His pat on the head. Sometimes she had pleaded, wondering and worrying if she had even been heard.

Now, she understood that God heard her immediately and answered her according to His wisdom and will in a matter. She trusted Him absolutely and completely to do the right thing, even if it wasn't exactly what she had asked for. Therefore, her pattern was to pray specifically for someone or for a situation, then express her trust that God would take care of it. She, then, left the matter with Him and went about her life, believing — actually, in her spirit, *receiving* — the answer in advance of any outward signs. This attitude was based on the promise that declared, "Whatsoever things you pray for and ask, *believe that you receive them,* and they shall be granted to you."

It was a triumphant way to live. Her spirit and emotions were usually at rest because she had passed her burdens on to the One who could do something about them. This left her free to expend her energy on the tasks at hand.

One May morning in the middle of the war, however, her normal praying procedures didn't suffice. She prayed her usual prayer for Adam, Roe, Brook, and Ethan, relegating them to God's care that day. She, then, started to get up and go about her work. On this morning, though, the burden didn't lift as it usually did. In fact, it became heavier. She quieted her spirit to try to understand what she should do. She didn't want to nag God or appear not to trust Him by repeating the same requests over and over, as if He had a hearing problem. After she spent some time in silence, waiting to hear impressions or instructions, she *knew* that one of the young men she had prayed for—one of their family—was in great danger. In the quietness between herself and her God, she believed that God was asking her to continue in prayer as long as the burden lasted. She also understood that her praying wasn't to convince God to do the right thing. It was as if God was showing her that the enemy forces of evil were great and the primary weapon against them was prayer. She was to prevail in prayer, to energize the angelic forces to fight the evil forces! This was spiritual warfare! God was allowing her a partnership in the fight!

Justin had stayed at home that morning to develop some pictures in his upstairs darkroom. When he finished and went looking for Laurel, he peeked in their bedroom and saw her on her knees by the bed. He went to the kitchen and got a cup of coffee, waiting for her to finish so they could talk.

When she didn't appear, he looked again. He became concerned that she had been praying for at least two hours without a let-up. He knelt beside her and asked, "What is it, Laurel?"

"One of the boys is in danger today. I need to pray until the burden is lifted."

He prayed with her until he could handle this news. He then took a pillow off the bed and asked her to let him place it under her knees. Because of the chill of the spring morning, he placed a sweater around her shoulders. After he brought a glass of water and placed it on the bedside table, he rubbed her hair back and said, "I'm thankful they have you to pray for them. I'll be close by if you need me."

As he left her, with his own heavy heart, he thought, *If anything on earth can save the one in danger, it's the prayer going up out of that bedroom.*

The day wore on with Laurel on her knees, sometimes quietly and sometimes audibly, praying for God's protection to be about the one in great danger. Sometimes she rebuked the enemy in Jesus' name.

Around noon Justin took her a glass of milk. She drank without comment and returned to her task. When Alexis, David, and Sarah arrived home that afternoon, Justin explained what was happening. Each received the news with dread, wondering which one of the family was in danger. They were a somber group as they prepared supper. Gradually, the dread began to be replaced by hope. They knew that their mother's prayers were powerful. Every member of the family believed that they would be answered, that the one in danger would be delivered.

Just as the family was gathering for supper, Laurel came into the room. She looked serene. "My burden is lifted. I believe the one I was praying for is safe."

Sarah, crying, hugged her first. "Thank you, Mama."

The others gathered around and hugged her. Justin guided her to a chair and put food on her plate. "You have to eat! No questions until she eats."

After they had eaten, she told them about the process she had gone through to know that she needed to continue in prayer until she knew she had an answer. It was a sober but powerful lesson for her children to know that God impressed her to fight the spiritual enemies that wanted to destroy — with the weapon of prayer.

She didn't tell the family but she marked the day on the calendar, intending to ask each one of their men, when they returned home, where he had been on that day. Actually, it was not necessary to mark it on a calendar. The day was inscribed clearly in the memory of every one in the family — for the rest of their lives.

In June, 1945, David got the wish he had waited for since December 7, 1941. The week after graduating from high school, he joined the Navy.

Justin reasoned with him. "Son, you don't have to go. The war is winding down. As you know, Germany has surrendered and it's just a matter of time until a Japanese surrender."

"Dad, you know I have to go! I'm not going to be the only man in the family who's the right age and still didn't go."

"I understand, son, and you make me proud." He embraced

David and, struggling with his voice, he said, "You've been my mainstay through these war years. I don't know what the family would've done without you."

Laurel understood that this was a passage that David had to make for himself — as well as for his country. She held him close before he left, knowing that when he returned he would no longer be the same. He would have an identity apart from the family. Her mind told her that was as it should be, but her mother heart suffered the age-old ambivalence of wanting to hold on to a beloved child and, at the same time, wanting to send him forth to live his own life.

Alexis put up the biggest fight. "I don't want you to go! I've always had a big brother to take care of me!"

It was Justin who took Alexis aside and explained, "David *is* your big brother and he's taken good care of you. But he's also a young man who has to live his own life. It's time for you to grow up some and let him go. Tell him so. Cheerfully."

Alexis' eyes filled. "Daddy, I sometimes wish we could just go on being the way we are and not have to grow up and go away."

"I know, honey. Your mother and I say that sometimes, too. But all of you must grow up and go away and live your own lives."

"Well, I'm not going far! I plan to stay close to you and Mama forever!"

Justin, looking at her earnest face, felt his heart twist a little. "We'll see."

Before he left, David reduced the family to tears talking about the animals. He quietly told some things each animal liked or didn't like, giving information and instructions about their care. He also had instructions for Alexis, making her promise him that she would take Chief with her when she was playing in the woods or going to a neighbor's house.

Everybody, friends and family, put on their best smiles and gave their heartiest waves as the train took him out of sight. Then they were free to cry. But not for long. He would expect better from them.

On a bright, warm day in September, 1945, church bells — all across the land — rang out the news that the war was over! America, the country unparalleled in the history of mankind, was still free! That freedom for itself and for the world had been purchased at a cost that could never be estimated nor fully appreciated. The Japanese had surrendered, joining Germany in defeat. Their designs to tyrannize the world were crushed by Allied forces who counted freedom above their own lives. The men would be coming home in the next few months! The Worth family knew they had much to be thankful for. Not one of their men had even been wounded.

J.R.'s third birthday in October was a true celebration. A little boy and his daddy who had never seen each other should soon have a reunion. Roe and Ethan, who had fought the Japanese in the Philippines, would hopefully be on their way home in a few months. Adam and Brook, who had seen action in Europe, would soon be discharged.

Laurel, meanwhile, was waging her own battles on several fronts. She believed she was getting rickets, pellagra, and scurvy under control, so she moved on to infant care and hygiene. It worried her that newborn infants slept with their parents where they could easily be accidentally smothered. She showed them how a wooden box or even a dresser drawer, pulled out and lined, would serve as a tiny bed for those first few weeks. She enlisted Alexis' help in making a model bed by padding a shoe box and lining it with soft flannel. Alexis asked if she could go with her to show the box to the mothers.

Since hygiene was the most sensitive issue she must deal with, she waited until she had earned the confidence of the people before she started her campaign. The placement of outhouses well away from streams and the construction, complete with lids for the seats, was her first plan of attack. Abe, Zeke, and Odell, humorously recalling the ones they had built years before in that first logging camp, were eager to help their neighbors. They explained how their families had been free from hookworm and many other illnesses since they had started following her advice.

Bathing, sterilizing dishes, keeping food away from flies, keeping ointments for cuts and burns, were all part of her battle against germs. After several weeks, believing the people might be ready, she invited Abby to go with her one Saturday to show them some first aid techniques. Abby thoroughly enjoyed her day, demonstrating how to bandage a wound, deal with a blow to the head, or apply artificial respiration to a person who had almost drowned or was having trouble breathing. She insisted that, if a bone was broken, they were to stabilize the victim and send for help. She had seen children unnecessarily crippled by inaction or the wrong action.

Apprehensive at first, Abby was impressed with Laurel's driving. Before the day was over, she made up her mind that it was time for her to get a car. She couldn't have Laurel outdistance her for very long in such a progressive skill.

Laurel was clearly impatient to get on with her literacy plans. Mr. McKenzie had indicated that the government program might be terminated before long, and she was determined to teach this last group. The improved quality of life she had brought to them drew forth their gratitude and trust. So, when she set out to teach them to read, write and do arithmetic, they put forth their best efforts. Even the men put aside their reluctance and fears and sat willingly with their wives to be instructed.

In a lifetime of teaching, Abe was one of her prize pupils. His enthusiasm — about finally being able to read — lit up Laurel's life. When he asked her to bring Justin for a celebration, she promised, knowing no details and asking no questions. Abe, in his customary take-charge mode, asked them to be seated. He then sat down at the head of the table, unfolded *The Wildwood Journal*, and began to read aloud. He paused at times and stumbled over a few words but it was evident that Abe Johnson had learned to read.

After a few paragraphs, he laid the paper aside and said, "Justin, I've dreamed of readin' the paper to you ever since we was in that first loggin' camp. I envied you when you'd set there readin' all them big words. And, Laurel, I envied them kids you was teachin'."

Justin was touched by the humility and pleasure that filled this giant of a mountain man. He was an intelligent, capable man who had been denied the privilege of a formal education. But he had never lost his dream and his drive. He had prevailed.

He stood and shook Abe's hand. "We're proud of you, Abe. You've learned a new skill. Just remember, though, that you've not always been the learner. You've been the teacher for many men in the timber business. I've learned a lot from you. Congratulations to you — and to Laurel!"

On the way home, Justin put his hand out to take Laurel's. "How long has it been since Abe was watching you teach those children in the first logging camp?"

"Twenty-five years!" she answered promptly. "I figured it up last week."

"A long time to hold on to a dream," Justin said, "for Abe — and for you!"

"Yes. I always considered it unfinished business. A dream I could never quite let go."

"Do you remember saying, years ago, that you hoped someday to be like your papa — in the way he helped people?"

"Yes. Papa's always been my model of how to live my life."

Justin squeezed her hand. "He'd be very proud of what you're doing."

She looked at him and smiled. "Yes. I think he would approve."

They rode along awhile in companionable silence. Then Laurel asked softly, hesitantly, "Do you think *our* children will want to carry on our way of life?"

He answered without reservation. "Oh, yes! I have no doubt that they'll carry on!"

Chapter Fourteen

Thankfully, just before the adult education program was phased out, Laurel was able to finish teaching the basic Three R's to the men and women in Sylvester County close to Abe's house. The day she gave her final reports to Mr. McKenzie, the superintendent of schools, he was in a talkative mood.

"It's just possible that we got our money's worth out of you, Laurel," he said, dryly. "Your contract reads generally that you were to teach literacy to adults in remote areas. It looks like you've taught reading, writing and arithmetic to numerous adults — I'll count the exact number for my final report — in several remote areas of Wildwood and Sylvester Counties. You've also taught some of their children. You've treated some serious diseases, set some broken bones, taught them that they must eat nutritional foods, and that they must observe certain methods of hygiene and proper infant care. You've saved some lives and brought health to others.

"You and your husband have encouraged some friends to change their way of making a living and..." When her eyes widened, he interrupted his train of thought. "Oh, yes! I knew they were moonshiners, but you spoke of them warmly as friends. You were our chance of finally getting to them. I understand they've moved to Lake Eagle Rest where their children can get an education."

She nodded, smiling.

He continued, "Lark Buchanan is taking some teacher training courses because of your influence and I understand her boys are doing well in school here in Deerbrook.

"I'm sure these facts are just the bare bones of the greater story of what you and your husband have done for these people. I understand he's busy taking pictures—free of charge—of the last group you helped."

"It sounds like somebody's been talking."

"Oh, I often see Dr. Leighton or Sam Parker or Abby Sinclair around town. They usually have a new story about the Worth family. I hope you realize that you've helped bring about positive changes that seemed impossible a short time ago."

He sat forward and asked, "So, what do you plan to do now that the job is ending?"

"I haven't had time to think about it. I'm sure I'll find plenty to do."

Mr. McKenzie shook his head and laughed. "I have no doubt."

He stood and held out his hand. "It's been a joy working with you. I plan to stay in touch. I don't want to miss any interesting stories."

Laurel's words proved true. Rarely a day passed that someone didn't show up with a need: a woman with a drunken husband and several children to feed; a young mother with a sick baby; the pastor asking for advice and prayer about a problem in the church. Somehow, along with the package of practical help, the recipients found renewed hope.

One evening just as they were sitting down to supper, a young woman appeared at the kitchen door. She was clutching a flour sack that looked like it was stuffed full of clothes. She was distraught, too exhausted to speak—and obviously pregnant. Laurel quickly got her to a chair and gave her a drink of water, signaling the family to leave them and go ahead to the dining room for supper.

When she could speak, the young woman said, "I'm not married and my pa run me off. He's ashamed of me." Her eyes filled as she placed both hands protectively over her rounded stomach. "My mama told me to come to you. She said you would take me in and would know what to do when my baby comes."

"Do I know your family?"

"No, but we know Abe Johnson's family and we've heard about how you helped the people in that community. I'm Camilla Bullock and my ma and pa are Leila and Oscar Bullock."

"Have you walked all the way from Sylvester County?"

"Yes, ma'am. I know a short cut across the mountain."

"How far along are you?"

"About six months, I think."

Laurel reached for her hand. "Camilla, come and lie down awhile. We don't want this baby to come tonight. After you rest, you'll need to eat some supper and I'll introduce you to the rest of the family."

Camilla gave Laurel a puzzled look. "You mean you'll take me in? Just like that?"

Laurel smiled. "Just like that."

Laurel, concerned that Camilla might lose the baby after that long hike over the mountain, insisted that she rest with her feet up for a day or two. Camilla, however, was a strong young woman conditioned to hard work. The second day she refused to rest any longer, saying, "I ain't never been still that long in my whole life."

The family, long accustomed to having other people in the house, made her feel welcome without undue attention. Alexis helped her get settled in the corner guest bedroom, showing her where to put her pitifully few clothes. At Camilla's request, Alexis showed her where the family took baths in one of the former bathrooms, using a big round tin tub. When she was cleaned up with freshly shampooed curly blonde hair, she was a very pretty young woman.

Sarah, almost at first glance, had known she was going to see if Camilla could wear some of her maternity dresses. Imagining how frightening it must be without a husband or family at this time, Sarah knew she needed a friend. She invited Camilla to her little house, telling her about some of her feelings during pregnancy and inviting her to talk to her if she needed someone. Soon they were just two young women caught up in discussing the mystique of motherhood. They ended up laughing over the way some of Sarah's clothes looked on Camilla. Only two outfits worked, but Camilla was delighted. The two young women struck up a friendship that was to last a lifetime. In the atmosphere of acceptance and friendship, Camilla soon lost most of her embarrassment.

One night as they were talking, Camilla stopped and looked at Sarah, as if trying to make up her mind. Then she blurted out, "You're my friend and I want you to know about the man who I was involved with."

Sarah said, "Only if you need to talk about it."

"I do need to voice it to somebody I can trust. I see now how ignorant and foolish I was. We talked about marriage, but when I told him I was expectin' I could tell he was scared. I guess he thought my daddy would come after him with a shotgun. Anyway," she stopped and took a deep breath, "anyway, I never saw him nor heard from him again. He ran off the next day and joined the Navy."

Sarah went totally still, trying to imagine such a betrayal. She whispered, "The dirty coward!"

Camilla shook her head. "Exactly! If I could marry him tomorrow, I wouldn't! I'd rather raise my baby alone than live with such a coward, plus some other names I could call him! I'm not in good shape — in more ways than one," she patted her stomach and gave a weak smile, "but I know I'm better off without him. And I believe my baby will be, too."

Sarah crossed the room and embraced Camilla. "You and your baby will be all right. I wish I knew — given the circumstances — that I would have as much courage as you have."

"You and your family have helped me gather up my courage," she replied, as both young women wiped their eyes.

The first time Camilla went to church with them, however, she halted outside the door, took Laurel's hand and said, "I can't go in. I'm too ashamed!"

The family waited as Laurel, kindly but firmly, said, "Camilla, this is the best place for you to start going out in public. Now, you're going to walk between Sarah and me. Justin and Alexis will lead us in. For now, you're part of our family."

When they entered the church, Camilla ducked her head, looking at the floor. Laurel whispered, "Bring your head up and look straight ahead. Remember, God loves you and we're in His house."

Camilla gave Laurel a startled look, then she raised her head and managed a brief smile. By now the congregation, made up of good people, didn't raise an eyebrow at who might be with the Worth family at church. They would accept this newcomer because it was the right thing to do and because of the family befriending her. They were unaware that their acceptance would play a big part in helping her to build a better life.

Justin, of course, was happy to help Camilla, but his primary concern was that Laurel would get enough rest. Laurel assured him that Camilla helped enough with the work to more than make up for the extra time Laurel gave to her. When Laurel took her to Dr. Leighton for an examination, he declared her healthy with the prospect of a normal delivery. He offered to come to help deliver the baby if Laurel would send for him.

Laurel, by now, knew better than to offer to pay him for the visit. He had told her one time that it was insulting to think that he couldn't do his part for the people she and Justin brought in, asking, "After all, who's paying *you?*"

After the doctor's visit, Laurel took Camilla to the fabric shop. "I want you to pick out some cloth for a new dress. Then we need to look at flannel and fabric for baby clothes."

"But I don't have any way to pay you back."

"You're a hard worker and you're earning your way. You don't need to pay us back."

Camilla glowed with pleasure over their purchases. On the way home, though, she fretted, "I don't know much about sewing."

"I'm sending for some good friends to help us sew. One is an expert seamstress. She'll let you help her make your dress and the baby clothes."

Bess, Hannah, and Nora showed up the next week and Camilla was soon caught up in the laughter and fun that always accompanied them. Soon they were deep into sewing. Bess was a patient and humorous taskmaster. She realized that her most important gift might not be the new dress, but the gift of teaching Camilla to sew. Hannah and Nora worked on baby blankets and diapers first; they then moved on to little gowns. Camilla was aware of the deep love and friendship between these women and Laurel. She sensed that they were, very tactfully, trying to see that Laurel paced herself and didn't work too long or too hard. It was an atmosphere of caring that touched her deeply. A determination germinated in her mind and heart to someday be a part of this kind of living. She secretly marveled at all the people who now knew her and accepted her just as she was — and were ready to help her.

The night Camilla's baby decided to make his entrance into the world, Laurel sent for Dr. Leighton, as promised. Sarah took on the task of sitting by Camilla, encouraging her, holding her hands during a pain, washing her face after a hard contraction, Camilla worked hard to cooperate with the doctor. Even so, everyone was exhausted by the time a boy arrived and immediately set up an indignant howl. Camilla named him Archer, a time-honored, noble name. She had confided in Sarah, "I intend for him to be proud of his name someday. Even if his daddy won't claim him."

Abe and his wife, who had secretly kept Camilla's mother informed about her welfare, now brought her to visit Camilla and Archer. It was both a happy time and a sad time as the mother obviously yearned to take them home with her, but wasn't allowed to by her obstinate husband. She was a shy woman but before she left, she said to Laurel, "God bless you for takin' care of Camilla and the baby. You're just like they said you was. I've been worried sick, but now I know she's okay with you."

Camilla assured her mother that she preferred staying with the Worths until she could, perhaps, find a job to support herself and her baby.

Hannah, Bess, and Nora had grown fond of Camilla with her determined, practical, even cheerful approach to her circumstances. They had resolved to be among her supporters. When Archer was about a month old they came visiting. Only this time they had a surprise with them. Thad, Hannah's younger son, had arrived home from the war and decided to make a visit to his extended family.

When they walked through the kitchen door, Laurel threw down her dishcloth and ran to hug Thad, then held him at arm's length for inspection. "Let me look at you! Goodness! You're handsome! When did you get home?"

Laurel had taught him and his brother, Jesse, their first three grades of school in the logging camp. He returned her hug and stood smiling patiently while she fussed over him.

"Our company got back in the states last week. I made it in home last night."

At that moment Camilla came through the door talking, "Mrs. Worth, I think..."

Her words broke off as she saw the visitors. Hannah, Nora, and Bess each hugged her. Thad, a handsome, muscular man with hair so blond it was almost white, went perfectly still and quiet, his eyes fastened on the laughing young woman with blue eyes and blonde curls.

212

When the hugging subsided, Laurel made introductions.

"Camilla, this is Thad Owen, Hannah's and Jed's son — and partly ours."

"Thad, meet Camilla Bullock, a friend who is living with us for a while."

Camilla shook hands and performed the normal social niceties. Thad did as well as could be expected of a man who was mesmerized.

Justin appeared and, after greeting everybody, mercifully whisked Thad away. He was having a problem with his logging truck and wanted Thad to look at it.

Bess laughed and said, "That's what I love about family. They haven't seen each other in about three years, but they pick up like it was yesterday."

She turned to Camilla. "Now! Let's see that youngun'!"

Each woman had a turn rocking him and crooning a little.

"He's a fine, healthy baby," Hannah said.

"I like his name," Nora added.

Two packages were presented to Camilla. She opened the first one to find three little boy outfits. She held them up one by one, saying, "Archer, look at your new clothes. You'll be so dressed up, you may have to preach Sunday."

The second package released the threatening tears. Bess had made a blue dress for Camilla. She held it to herself, tried to smile, but the tears won.

Practical Bess said, "Try it on. I guessed your size, now that you're rid of that big belly."

The dress fit. It also enhanced those blue eyes, as Bess intended. Camilla dried her tears, hugged each of them and went, like any woman with a new frock, to find a big mirror.

Unaware of Camilla's effect on Thad, the three woman talked freely about her and the baby on the way home. Thad was silent as he pieced together the situation from their conversation. He even felt his stomach tense a time or two. He told his unsuspecting mother that he was going back to the Worths' tomorrow to help Justin with a problem or two. He wanted to see her again. And he wanted to see Archer.

That night Laurel confided in Justin. "I think Thad is smitten with Camilla. When she came into the room, he looked like he'd been thunderstruck."

He laughed. "I remember the feeling well. That's what *you* did to me."

"Seriously, what do you think—given the circumstances?"

"I've been impressed with the way she's handled a difficult situation. I think she'd make a good wife. Thad must be close to thirty, so he's old enough to know what he's doing."

"Oh, I'm so glad you feel that way! Wouldn't it be great for her and for Archer to be in a family like that?"

"Laurel, you're matchmaking!"

"I know. I *do* like happy endings!"

It certainly was a good beginning with the definite prospects of a happy ending. Thad didn't let any grass grow under his feet in courting Camilla. His intentions were soon clear to everybody. He seemed almost as entranced with Archer as he was with Archer's mother. Camilla was the reluctant one. She faced him squarely with the problems he would be taking on with her and Archer.

He was a man of few words, but he knew when a speech was needed. "Camilla, I love you and Archer. I'm askin' you to marry me. I'm planning to be Archer's daddy. I'll adopt him and he'll have my name. I don't want to know the name of the man you were involved with. We don't ever need to discuss it again."

Justin spoke his mind privately and briefly to Thad. "I never met a finer man than your daddy and I believe you've got some of him in you. I'm aware that this is your private business, but I'm going to meddle anyway. If you marry Camilla, I believe you'll be man enough to respect her and never throw up her mistake. And I believe you'll care for Archer as your own."

"Yes, sir. We've already talked about it. I love both of them."

Hannah, in her easy yet forthright manner, told Laurel, "I know you're wonderin' what we're thinkin' about Camilla and Thad. Well, you already know what we think of Camilla and the baby. Jed and I trust Thad's judgment. Nora—and Bess and Bulldog—are tickled to think we'll have a baby in the family."

Justin had one more task he was determined to take on. He rode over to Abe's one afternoon and asked the way to the Bullock home. Oscar Bullock was surprised when he saw Justin get out of his truck. Like most people in the area, he knew and liked Justin Worth. He also knew Camilla was living with the Worth family. He went to meet

Justin, feeling skittish and guilty, not sure he wanted his wife to hear what Justin might say. The two men shook hands.

Oscar decided to meet this head on. "Is somethin' wrong with Camilla?"

Justin replied in kind. "Nothing that Camilla's daddy can't fix with a visit."

Oscar bristled. "Now, look here, Justin, you ain't got no right to drive into a man's yard and start givin' orders!"

"I'm not giving orders, Oscar. I'm here to invite you and your wife for Sunday dinner. Camilla's doing well and she has a fine, healthy baby boy who any grandpa would be proud of!"

"Did she send you?"

"No. She doesn't know I came and I'm not going to tell her. When you come Sunday, it'll need to be of your own free will and desire. It'll be a wonderful surprise for her."

"What if I don't want to come?"

Justin spoke softly, "You're a better man than that, Oscar. I know how much a daddy loves his daughter. Camilla made a mistake, but she's a fine young woman."

He turned to get in the truck. "Tell your wife that Camilla and the baby are fine. We'll look for you about one o'clock on Sunday."

He drove off, leaving Camilla's daddy feeling like he'd—very deftly—been pole-axed. He headed for the barn. He had some thinking to do before he faced his wife.

Sunday was a satisfying day at the Worth house. Camilla, surrounded by the family, took Archer to church for the first time. Living at the Worth house with people constantly in and out and all around had cured her of the impulse to hide. Now, with Laurel's coaching, she was able to keep her head up and, after church, to allow interested parties to see Archer.

When they arrived home, Oscar and Leila Bullock were sitting on the back porch, waiting. Camilla was astonished. She said in wonder, "Daddy came! Daddy came! Daddy came!" She was out of the car running, with Archer in her arms, before anybody could comment.

The family tactfully stayed in the car while Camilla and her daddy made their peace. Oscar was sitting in the rocking chair, awkwardly holding Archer, when Justin and Laurel stepped up on the porch.

"Welcome!" Justin said.

As the women greeted each other and went to the kitchen, Justin, looking at Archer, said, "You've got a fine grandson there!"

Oscar said, "Yes, I have!"

He paused and looked up. "Sometimes a feller gits a little confused about how to act. Seems I was. Thank you, Justin."

"Oh, you would'a figured it out. Your daughter was the happiest I've seen her since she got here, when she saw you on the porch."

"Well, I'm pretty happy myself right now."

He turned his attention to the baby in his arms who was looking at him wide-eyed. Justin, walking softly, left them to get acquainted.

After Sunday dinner, Oscar and his wife took Camilla aside where Oscar laid out his case. "I know I ain't done right by you and the baby. Your mama tried to tell me, but I was stubborn. I'm sorry, Camilla. We want you and our grandson to come home."

Camilla had gained a great deal of self-confidence from the way the Worths and their friends had treated her. Yet, she knew she had hurt her parents by her actions. She recognized an olive branch when it was extended.

"I know I hurt you, too, and I'm sorry." She paused. "Yes, I'd like to come home. I want Archer to know his grandma and grandpa."

Her parents waited on the porch while Camilla said a tearful goodbye to the Worth family. "I'll never, never forget what you've done for me and Archer. You've given me back my self-confidence and courage."

"No. It was there all along," Laurel said softly. "We just helped you find it again."

She hugged them and promised she would bring Archer back as often as she could.

She had one last private request of Laurel. "When Thad comes, please ask him to wait a couple of weeks before he comes to see me at Daddy's house. I need some time with them and I need to tell them about Thad before they meet him."

That night before going to sleep, Justin said, "Well, that just goes to show that we never know what a day may bring."

"It *is* strange. Camilla's been here about four months. I wonder what made Oscar change his mind all of a sudden."

Justin, in a level tone, said, "I guess he finally figured it out."

The next few months brought so many changes to the Worth family, even Justin and Laurel seemed disoriented at times. Roe was the first of the men to arrive home from the war. The entire Worth family, plus his dad and sisters, were there when the train pulled in. Everybody stood a distance behind Sarah, who had a squirming J.R. in her arms. Tears flowed unashamed on every face as Roe appeared and covered the short distance to gather his wife and son in his arms.

J.R., however, was having none of it! He first hid his face on his mother's shoulder, then pushed Roe away, saying, "No! No!"

Sarah, trying to greet her husband while holding on to her unhappy son, said, "It's Daddy! See? It's Daddy!"

"No Dad-dee! No Dad-dee!" The confused little boy shook his head and twisted away from Roe. Their families didn't know whether to laugh or cry. Justin stepped forward and took the boy from Sarah. "Welcome home, Roe! I'll take this bucking bronco so you can kiss your wife."

After Roe had been hugged and kissed and fussed over, everybody went back to the Worth house for a welcome home dinner. Roe wanted to know all the news about everybody, but Justin noticed that he didn't want to talk about himself or the war.

After some of the group left and J.R. grew tired and fussy, Laurel put him to bed in her and Justin's bedroom. Watching Roe look longingly at the little blue eyed, blond-haired boy, Justin said, "Give him a day or two, Roe. He'll get used to you in no time."

Laurel suggested, "Leave the baby with us and go on home. You need some time together."

Later that night, Laurel said to Justin, "Did you notice how thin Roe is? And he looks a lot older than the young man who left here."

"Yes. I'm afraid he's had a rough time of it. Probably fought hand-to-hand combat."

Roe set about to win J.R. over. It was both funny and sad to watch the process. Whenever Roe would hug Sarah or even get close, J.R. would rush up and scold, "No!" When someone mentioned "daddy," J.R. would get Roe's picture from the side of the bed, hug it and say, "Dad-dee!" Roe kept his distance, figuring this was a battle that may influence their relationship for the rest of their lives. He could afford to be patient a little longer to get to know this marvel of a little boy who was his son.

Nobody ever knew exactly what Roe did to earn J.R.' s trust, but one day J.R. approached him, put his hand on Roe's knee and asked, "Dad-dee?"

Roe said softly, "Yes, J.R.! I'm your daddy!"

J.R. lifted his arms. Very carefully, Roe picked him up and took him out the door. The toughened veteran didn't even try to hide the tears spilling down his cheeks.

They were a happy threesome as they moved back to Deerbrook to pick up the threads of their lives again. Roe would work at the lumber yard and Sarah would keep her job at the paper plant. A neighbor would keep J.R. while she worked.

Chapter Fifteen

When word spread that the men were coming home, the train station became the most popular place in Deerbrook. Every homecoming was a joyous, tearful celebration. Every man had to submit to hugs and pats and handshakes.

Brook was the second member of the Worth family to arrive, with family and friends yelling shouts of welcome. His face had changed in the four years of his absence; his youthful innocence was gone. A boy had left and a man had returned. Celebration dinners at both family homes helped him settle back into his peace time life. He and Caroline would continue to live in Miss Abby's apartment for a while. He went back to work with his dad in the construction business and she kept her job at the courthouse.

Ethan's arrival was heralded by a mixed crowd. His former church members and the tough timber-working men of Terminal Town mingled as they waited with Allison and the Worth family, watching the station clock. His weariness and gauntness were evident the moment he stepped off the train, despite his enthusiasm. Men who had never agreed to go to church were there, crowding around for a word or a handshake; all were comforted that the preacher man was back. After speaking to each person and promising to visit soon, he and Allison went home to their apartment at Miss Abby's house. They continued to live in Deerbrook, where, within a few weeks, Ethan was called to become pastor of a church.

Adam's arrival was delayed. He had written that he was needed on his ship a few months longer. He would let them know more later.

It was a new and joyful beginning for the young families. The men who had returned, however, were forever altered. Sarah told Justin privately, "The first time I touched Roe to wake him up, he lunged at me and yelled. He almost knocked me down. He apologized and asked me to stand well away from the bed and call him to wake him up. He said he would explain when he could. He won't talk about the war at all."

"Give him time, honey," Justin said. "I think he's been to hell and back. War wounds men emotionally and mentally, as well as physically. Those wounds don't show, so it's harder for us to realize they're there. Be patient and carry on normally with life. That'll be the best medicine for him."

Sarah's eyes filled. "J.R.'s the very best medicine, I think. I'm so thankful for that little boy. Roe's most like his old self when he's with J.R."

Alone at home one day, Laurel walked through the big house. Memories trouped along with her from room to room: the first time she saw the house — the years when the rooms and hallway rang with the happy sounds of young people coming and going — the community gatherings — their children's individual paths to adulthood — the people who had come for help...

Now, the quietness — the absence of people — the empty rooms — seemed foreign to her. Time had marched on relentlessly, marching two sons and two daughters into maturity. Four out of five were now launched.

She knew David was happy aboard ship. He was very proud to carry on the Worth tradition of helping staff the United States Navy. In one of his letters he mentioned that he was thinking of going to college on the G.I. Bill when he got out of the Navy, that he would explain more later. This, of course, generated some excitement for Laurel and Justin. They had envisioned early in their marriage that all of their children would go to college. The Great Depression had interfered.

They didn't dwell on it, but they felt the absence of Sarah and J.R. in their very souls. J.R. had brightened their lives for three years. The little house now stood empty, symbolizing an unseen emptiness in their lives. Justin, the ultimate extrovert, possibly suffered the pangs of transition more than Laurel. He stayed busy, as usual, but almost every afternoon he came through the door asking, "Did we hear from David or Adam?"

Thank goodness, Alexis was still with them!

It was never officially announced but was understood that Sunday afternoon was visiting time at the Worth house. Sarah, Roe, J.R., Caroline and Brook almost always came home for Sunday dinner. Neighbors and friends came most Sundays, putting their food with Laurel's to make the meal. Pastor Pierce and his family were usually present, as was Leanna, the Seymours' black maid and a good friend of the family. Alexis' friends were often around. It was the highlight of the week for Justin and Laurel.

Since it was an ever-changing, disparate group, with some not knowing the others, there were a few adjustments. One Sunday, Hannah, Jed, Nora, Bulldog and Bess arrived before Justin and Laurel got home from church. As had been their custom through the years, the women went to the kitchen, built a fire in the stove, sent the men to the spring box for Laurel's food and started adding their own.

They were totally startled when a tall, black woman suddenly seemed to fill the doorway. She stood with her hands on her hips and demanded, "Who're you and what're you doin' in Laurel's kitchen?"

Bess was the first to find words. "We're friends! We're just putting our food with hers and starting to warm it all up, so it'll be about ready when she gets home from church."

"Okay, then!" Leanna declared, as she relaxed her stance. "That good woman works hard! I didn't want nobody comin' in and eatin' up her food!"

She sounded so fiercely protective of Laurel, they liked her at once. They gathered around and introductions were made. When Laurel arrived home, she found them all working together in the kitchen, talking and laughing as if they had known each other for years.

When a neighbor approached Justin, wanting to sell him a forty-acre farm on the other side of Lake Eagle Rest, he was intrigued enough to go check it out. He was impressed with the level, cleared fields and the surrounding woods. Two spring-fed streams angled their way through the property. It was obviously a working farm, with outbuildings including a corn crib and smoke house. The barn, partly rock, was roomy and well built.

When he saw the small, primitive log house that went with it, however, he tamped down his enthusiasm and dismissed it out of hand. He couldn't—or wouldn't—ever ask Laurel to move back into a house that small. It would be almost like asking her to return to one of their logging camp shacks. He decided he wouldn't even tell her about it.

Later in the week he was surprised when she said, "I heard that you looked at a farm a few days ago."

"Who told you?"

"Lila. They were talking about it in Terminal Town."

"Yes. It's a good farm. All the cleared farm land we would ever need, with some good woods surrounding it." She heard the suppressed excitement in his voice. "But, the farmhouse is partly log. It's too small and primitive. I turned down his offer."

"I'd like to see it."

"Laurel, I know how much you love this house. I'm not going to ask you to move again. Especially to live in a house like that."

"I'd still like to see it," she persisted.

The next day when he and the owner took her to see the farm, Justin asked her to look at the house first, thinking that would put a quick end to things. She saw at once that the small house had originally been a one-room log cabin. Recent occupants had added some rooms, a rock porch, and a high-pitched tin roof.

The first thing she saw when she entered was a rock fireplace and large chimney that almost covered the entire wall at the left end of the living room. A window on each side of the chimney admitted the golden afternoon light.

It *was* primitive, as Justin had warned her. The walls of the living room were logs with cement between them. She walked straight through to the kitchen and dining rooms, which were add-ons at the back of the house. She then returned to the living room and went into the bedroom, which opened from the end of the room opposite the fireplace.

Justin and the owner, talking about livestock, left her to herself. She climbed narrow stairs to find a type of attic, one big room the size of the four rooms downstairs, with a steeply slanted roof on each side. The wide chimney almost covered one gabled end, leaving room there as downstairs, for a window on each side. A large window stood in the gable away from the fireplace. She figured that two large bedrooms would fit upstairs. She looked out on apple trees and a green field that was edged around with hardwoods. It was a pleasing vista.

The dirt cellar, which ran the length of the house, was next on the agenda. Bins, slatted to let air circulate, were built just off the ground, along one wall. A layer of hay cushioned potatoes and apples. On the opposite wall, wooden shelves held canned goods.

"The temperature stays the same winter and summer," the owner explained.

Laurel said, "We've needed a cellar like this for a long time."

The springs were the next item of interest. The one closest to the house was across the yard and down an incline in a grove of sourwood trees. As women do, Laurel mentally found a place for her wash pot and battling stump.

Justin and the owner talked about cleared acreage and wooded acreage while she surveyed the surroundings. The house was nestled near a vine-covered bank, with a small, level yard that had been shored up with a rock wall. Rock steps led to a higher level of yard, with trees on each side of a rock path. Apple trees and dogwood trees graced the grounds, front and back. A fir tree, as tall as the peak of the roof line, stood to the side, as a sentinel, as if guarding the house. It was a pleasant place.

Later that afternoon back at home, they sat down at the table with a cup of coffee to discuss the farm before Alexis arrived from school.

Justin, determined to make it easy for Laurel, asked, "See what I mean about the house?"

She laughed. "Justin Worth, you'd love to buy that farm! I can see it in your eyes and hear it in your voice."

He remained adamant. "I'm not going to ask you to move out of the house you love."

She put her hand over his. "What if I choose to move?"

"You'd be doing it just for me and I won't let you do that."

"I might be doing it for me, too."

He went still. "Tell me what you're thinking."

"I walked through our house not long ago — every room — and relived the memories of our past twelve years here. I think we were given this special house as a gift – *for as long as we needed it.* Half the rooms are now empty. I realized that we don't need a house this big for the next phase of our lives. I wouldn't face up to it that day, but, subconsciously, I think I started saying 'goodbye.'"

Justin looked at her, frowning in disbelief. "But, you've — we've — loved this house! I thought you'd want to live here for the rest of our lives."

"I'll always love it! We and our children will always love — and own — this house in our memories. But an era has passed and we must adapt."

"So, you're saying you'd be willing to move? To live in that small log house?"

"Yes. We'd have to do some work, but we could make a cozy little home out of it."

He sat, twisting his cup around and around in his hands, looking at her. "I'm so surprised, I don't know what to say."

"Just tell me what *you'd* really like to do. Totally from *your* perspective."

He spoke slowly at first. "Ever since we lost our money for a farm when the Depression hit, I've had to fight the knowledge that I let my family down. I've wanted to *own* a farm, where I would know I could always provide a living."

"According to the price you told me, we have enough money saved to pay cash, with a little left over."

"Yes. With Adam's allotment and both of us working, this is the first time we've been able to save a significant amount since the Depression hit. In fact, I was planning to talk to you about buying *this* place. The thing that's held me back is that there's not any farm land here. I'd have to keep on sharecropping. But we do need to own a home before we get any older."

When they heard Alexis coming through the door, Laurel quickly said, "Let's pray about this and talk tomorrow."

"We'd better not say anything to Miss Priss," Justin said. "She's going to have a definite opinion and we already know what it'll be!"

They felt like two conspirators as Alexis breezed into the room, giving each one a hug, talking at full speed, confident that they couldn't *wait* to hear all about what had happened at school that day.

The next morning as soon as they were alone, Justin resumed his argument. "It'll be hard to leave this house. Do you remember, in the hospital when I thought you might not live, I promised that I would find you a big house—a decent house—after all those years in the logging shacks. This house has been the fulfillment of that promise! I can't go back on my word! You deserve better."

"You kept your promise, Justin. Our family—and the whole community—has benefitted. Now, listen closely because I want you to hear what I have to say. First, I learned—after a while in the logging camps—that my happiness is not found in the type of house I live in. Secondly, as we get older and Alexis is gone, I think this house is going to be too big for me to take care of by myself."

For the first time, he believed that she really meant what she had been saying. That she wasn't pretending, just so he could have his farm.

"If we did move, what would you want done to the house?"

"I'd like the logs covered in the living room with dry wall or paneling. Then, we'd need to divide the upstairs area into two bedrooms. One for Alexis and one for Adam. The downstairs bedroom is big enough to add a small bathroom later."

"I think we'll have enough money for that."

After they agreed about buying the farm, they faced telling Alexis—a task they didn't relish. Her initial reaction, when Justin informed her, was disbelief.

"Oh, Daddy, stop teasing! I know we're not going to move out of this—*our*—house!"

Justin was patient but firm. "I'm not teasing, honey."

"But, *why?* We all love this house! I thought this would be our home forever."

Laurel helped Justin explain their reasons. When she first saw the log house, however, Alexis seemed too stunned to speak. Laurel, watching her, remembered her own dismay many years before when she saw their logging shack for the first time. She took Alexis through and explained the changes they would make, including the bedrooms upstairs.

Alexis realized they were serious and became silent—to deal with her conflicting emotions. She'd lived almost fifteen years and was unacquainted with personal grief. Thus, she couldn't put a label on the sadness that filled her. Later, Laurel tried to help her. "You're grieving over leaving this home, Alexis. It's the only home you can remember. You must figure out a way to say, 'goodbye.'"

In the midst of the turmoil about buying the farm, Adam arrived home unexpectedly. He had decided to surprise the family. Everyone was delighted and everything else was forgotten—including moving—for a few days while family and friends came to welcome Adam home. Alexis was especially overjoyed.

He was soon brought into the picture of his parents' plans, including a visit to the farm. He agreed that it was a good plan and suggested that they renovate the house before moving. He had some paid leave time saved up before he had to get a job. He and Justin would do most of the work, getting help as they needed it.

Without being told outright that Alexis was having trouble accepting this move, he tuned in quickly. On a Saturday afternoon, he asked her to go to a movie with him. As soon as they were on their way, he casually said, "You've been quiet about this move. Tell me what you're thinking."

This opened the floodgates, as he figured it would. He listened attentively to Alexis' reasons for *not* wanting to move, shaking his head in agreement every now and then. When she had finished, he said, "I understand exactly how you feel. I love the house, too."

"Then maybe you can talk them out of it!" she said eagerly.

"No...Alexis, I don't want to do that."

"Why?"

"Let's look at what's best for Mama and Daddy rather than what we want. Okay?"

She had depended on Adam to explain things to her for as long as she could remember. He didn't talk down to her and he never laughed at her. He always listened and respected what she had to say. Now she was willing to hear what he had to say.

"Okay."

"Let's take Mama first. She's getting older and she's not as strong as she used to be. When you leave home, she'll have to keep up that big house by herself. She and Daddy would rattle around in it with all of us gone. I think it would make them sad.

"Then, think about Daddy. He's wanted a farm for as long as I can remember, but couldn't afford to buy one. He's worked twice as hard because he's had to give part of his crop to the owners of the land he's sharecropped. He's been doing that for years, even before we moved here."

Alexis digested that, then said quietly, "I never thought of that."

"Well, you wouldn't because it's been a way of life ever since you were born. But, he's getting older, too, and doesn't need to keep working so hard.

"I know the log house looks bad after living in the big house all your life, but we'll fix it up to look better. You'll be through school in three years. I can see Mama and Daddy living there happily as they get older. They'll finally own a home. Do you understand?"

Alexis was subdued. She took a deep breath and said, "Yes, I understand. I think I've been acting selfish."

Adam reached over for her hand and squeezed it. "It's natural for you to want to stay in the house you love so much. Every one of us loves it—and always will. We've had some wonderful years there."

They enjoyed the movie and Adam took her to get an ice cream before they started home. On the way they talked about other things, including some girls whom Alexis thought Adam might be interested in dating. She never knew that he was greatly amused at her efforts to find him a girlfriend.

"What about you, young lady! Do you have a boyfriend?"

"I have lots of *friends* who are *boys!*" she retorted. "Daddy says I can't go on a date alone with a boy until I'm sixteen. About a year to go!"

"Daddy's right! And, remember, they have to pass *my* inspection, too!"

"I know!" Alexis said in a long-suffering voice. But she was smiling inside.

Just before they arrived home, she leaned over and hugged him. "Adam, I understand better now. I'm really glad you're home!"

One night after supper the four of them were in the big room gathered around the fireplace, where a cheerful, small fire warmed the chill evening air. Laurel, in her rocking chair with some mending on her lap, asked quietly, "Adam, I need to ask you a strange question about the war. If you can't answer, I'll understand. Do you remember where you were in May of 1943?"

Adam, who was standing looking into the fire, was quiet for a moment. Then he whirled around and demanded almost harshly, "Mama! How did you know about May, 1943?"

They all looked at him, surprised at his tone.

Laurel said, "I had a definite impression one day that I needed to pray for one of you men in the family. I prayed most of the day — until the burden was lifted late in the afternoon."

Adam stood looking at her, but somehow beyond her at a sight *they* couldn't see. He said, in wonder, "So *that's* the answer!"

Justin spoke quietly. "Can you tell us about it, son?"

Adam spoke slowly, haltingly...

"It was the most danger we were ever in, to our knowledge. We were transporting five thousand British soldiers across the North Atlantic to North Africa. Our two escort ships had turned back since we were nearing our destination. Suddenly, the captain called for our attention on the loud speakers. He had just received a radio dispatch telling him that we were directly in the flight path of forty German bombers who weren't but maybe half an hour away."

Adam paused, remembering. The only sound in the room was the crackling of the fire. He brought himself back to the present. "The captain called us to the battle stations. Even as we were getting the guns ready, he kept talking. He told us it had been an honor to work with such a crew and he knew we would continue to be sailors he was proud of...that we were to take care of the troops first. After he asked the chaplain to pray, he added, 'We're sitting ducks. If any of you men know how to pray, pray!'

"We all knew, of course, that *one* bomber, with a direct hit, could sink us. We couldn't possibly escape forty. And there was nowhere to go, no cover. The North Atlantic sky was clear blue with only wisps of clouds."

Justin, Laurel and Alexis were hardly breathing...imagining...as he slowly unfolded the scene before them.

"At a time like that, your training takes over. We manned the stations, planning to give them a fight, at least. We knew our jobs and prepared for the worst. And, Mama, I was praying, too! I'm pretty sure most of the men were praying — even if they had never prayed before.

"Then..." his voice wavered and he turned back to look in the fire until he could talk again. Tears were rolling down Alexis' cheeks. She dashed them away impatiently.

Adam turned back around to face them. His voice was still unsteady as he said, "Then...the most amazing thing happened! Fog suddenly rolled up off the water and engulfed our ship. We were blanketed with fog so thick we could barely see each other!"

By now Laurel's tears were flowing, too, and Justin had fished his handkerchief out of his back pocket.

"The captain quickly issued the order to cut the engines, saying, 'We're not here.' In a matter of minutes, wrapped in our cocoon, we heard the bombers passing over.

"We all seemed to forget to breathe until the drone of those engines could no longer be heard. The captain came on the horn again. He said, 'It looks like we've had divine intervention on our behalf!' He asked the chaplain to give thanks for our survival.

"Then he was all business again! He gave the order to blast the foghorn. We proceeded toward our destination by use of instruments. For once, no salty language nor complaints were heard about the pea soup that we were slowly threading our way through. We delivered the troops, picked up wounded British soldiers and headed back to England. It was the scariest and most amazing event of the war for most of us."

Reverential silence reigned while they each tried to absorb the impact of what they had heard. Distance seemingly made no difference to God. The prayers that Laurel had been constrained to offer in her bedroom had winged their way to their destination. God had heard and had called upon His limitless resources to answer. The lives of thousands of young men were saved.

Adam was the first to move. He stooped and kissed his mother on the forehead. "Thank you, Mama, for praying for us. I wish all the men could know about it."

"I'm sure many other mothers and dads were praying, too. It's God we must thank for such a timely answer."

After a prayer of thanksgiving, each one was still quiet. It would take awhile for them to come to terms, individually, with the story they had just heard. It was a landmark, however, erected in Adam's and Alexis' hearts—and in the other children's hearts as soon as they heard. A landmark to which they would return—if they sensed they were getting off course—for all the days of their lives.

As soon as they closed the deal on buying the farm, Adam and Justin got to work on the renovations. Roe and Brook came to help when they had a day off work. Ethan came as often as he could. Everybody, it seemed, wanted to have a hand in this project: Jed, Bulldog, Abner, neighbors whom Justin had helped. Adam said privately to Justin, "I never thought our biggest problem would be that we had too much help."

He hired carpenters to do what he felt they couldn't do right, especially since they had decided to put a dormer upstairs in the middle of the roof over the porch. It would add a third small bedroom and allow more light upstairs, breaking the solid, slanting roof line.

For a few days they wouldn't allow Laurel on the premises. They were working on a couple of surprises. After a few days Laurel noticed Alexis' change of attitude. One day as they were cooking dinner she said, "I believe you're feeling better about the move."

"Yes. Adam explained how much better it will be for you and Daddy."

"I'm glad. I want you to be able to treasure the memory of these years in this house. I don't want resentment over the move to rob you of that."

Alexis hugged her mother. "I'll *always* remember, Mama! I've been truly happy here!"

She went through their remaining days revisiting some of her treasured places. When they had first moved to the house, her mother had made a tiny, cozy bedroom for her in what had formerly been a large bathroom beside her parents' bedroom. Her single bed fit snugly into the spot where the tub had been and there was enough room on the opposite wall for a dresser. A tiny linen closet was made into a place to hang her clothes. She had long since moved to a larger bedroom, but now she sat awhile and savored the delectable sense of security she had felt there.

She spent time in the big, airy attic room where she had spread out school projects and vacation Bible school assignments, knowing her private place wouldn't be disturbed. She and her friends had passed many happy hours playing school. It was there that she had determined that, somehow, she was going to college. She was going to be a teacher.

She even visited the closet under the stairs where she had made a pallet the summer she read *Les Miserables* by Victor Hugo. While she read the book, she had pretended to be Cosette, the young girl who was made to sleep on the floor, part of the abuse heaped upon her by the family who was being paid to care for her. The wonder of her rescue always thrilled Alexis. Of course, Justin or Adam or David took on the hero's character who, in her imagination, rescued Alexis.

The last place where she spent some time was her aerie—her private place for reading or thinking. Her need for time alone, away from the constant stream of people, had been realized and nurtured in a grizzled old oak tree whose limbs had seemed to embrace her. Now, as she sat in the crook of several limbs—a natural seat—she knew she would recall this tree when she thought of certain books she had read or certain decisions she had made. She had learned to enjoy her own company and the energizing value of—sometimes—being alone.

The two surprises for Laurel in their new house, which were running water and an actual indoor bathroom, turned into three surprises when Adam learned that the Rural Electric Association was bringing electricity to the community of Lake Eagle Rest. He immediately hired men to wire the house. The day the lights were turned on, Adam was so excited, he could hardly contain himself!

"Mama, you're going to have a refrigerator, an electric stove and a washing machine! And, Daddy, you're going to be able to read your Zane Greys by electric lights!"

It was hard to tell who was the happiest. Laurel's eyes were shining as she turned the water on and off. Alexis went from switch to switch, turning lights on and off. Justin said, "I don't know if I can stand all this civilization!"

When the moving day arrived and everything was out of the big house, Alexis lingered, walking through the rooms by herself one last time. Tears coursed down her cheeks, but her memories trumped her sadness. Without realizing it, Alexis had learned one of her mother's secrets of contentment. She had learned about the power of choice within a circumstance not of her choosing. She deliberately chose to treasure the memories. Physically, she was leaving the beloved house—the setting of a happy, secure childhood—but the blueprint was forever engraved upon her heart. She knew that, for as long as she lived, her memories would walk with her through this treasured place.

The move went smoothly except they, again, had more help than they actually needed. It turned into a social event with neighbors bringing food. Alexis chose the upstairs bedroom with the window that overlooked the apple trees and the field. Adam took the one with the rock chimney forming part of the wall. The small dormer room would be for guests.

Justin was a happy man! Trying to be everywhere at once giving orders, it suddenly struck him that he hadn't done the most important thing. He yelled for everybody to gather around in the front yard. He then picked up a surprised Laurel and, ceremoniously, carried her over the threshold. The applause and laughter of their family and friends seemed the appropriate background music for this momentous occasion. After thirty-one years of marriage, they finally owned a home!

Chapter Sixteen

The next event seemed to place the seal of authenticity on this, their new home, as well as to serve as a harbinger of what they could expect from their life there. The crowd in the yard grew quiet and parted as two men brought a bloody man on a stretcher down the rock path, heading toward the door where Justin and Laurel stood.

With urgency, one man called ahead, "He's bleedin' bad, Miz Worth! We thought you might could stop the blood!"

At Justin's directions, they laid him on the dining room table, explaining, "It's Bill Moore. His double-edged ax glanced off a tree and cut his leg."

Laurel knew immediately that he must have nicked an artery. The tourniquet had slowed the bleeding but it still seemed profuse. Laurel applied pressure at the proper place. She then bowed her head and asked that the bleeding would stop, that she would have wisdom in knowing how to treat the wound. She thanked the Lord in advance for the answer she *knew* would come.

The room was totally quiet as she removed her finger from the pressure point. The bleeding had stopped! She set about examining the wound as Justin had brought boiled water in a basin and Alexis brought gauze bandages from her mother's ever present first-aid kit. Laurel carefully cleansed the wound and packed it with sterile gauze.

"Bill," she said, "the bleeding has stopped, but I want you to go to see Dr. Leighton in Deerbrook. You'll need to get some stitches."

The young man nodded. She gave him a drink of water and washed his face, then turned to Justin. "Could you make a bed in the back of your truck and you ride with him? Handle him very carefully." Justin knew that she was asking him to be sure to keep the pressure point closed if the jolting of the truck started up the bleeding again.

Justin nodded. "Yes, if Jed will drive."

He turned to the other men. "Follow us to the doc's office."

The subdued group of friends soon left. They were more elated than alarmed over the incident, and they were eager to pass the word. "It's true what they're saying. She stopped the blood just like she drew out the fire!"

Hannah stayed to wait for Jed and Justin to return. As they were cooking supper, she said, "Laurel, it sure didn't take people long to find your new house."

When the two men returned, Justin assured her that Dr. Leighton said Bill would be all right. "He was curious at first as to why the bleeding stopped, since it was an artery. Then he said, 'I shouldn't be surprised.'"

It was almost dark by the time the family — Laurel, Justin, Adam and Alexis — was finally alone. Adam had built a fire in the fireplace, against the cool summer evening. It was a definite occasion when Laurel, at Adam's request, flipped the switch to flood the room with light.

Justin sat down in his favorite chair, which had been positioned beside the fireplace, stretched out his legs and suggested that they thank the Lord for His blessings and ask Him to use this new home to honor Him and to help people.

When he had finished, Adam said, "Dad, I think the Lord got a jump on you with that request. You've only been here a few hours and you're already well into the answer to that prayer."

With the marvel of electricity, life became much easier. The refrigerator saved endless trips to the spring box for milk and leftovers. The washing machine saved hours of scrubbing clothes over the tin tubs at the washing place. The water running into the kitchen and bathroom may have been the greatest gift of all. The electric stove, however, had been looked upon with mixed emotions. Laurel didn't want to get rid of her old faithful wood-burning stove that had seen her through good and bad years. When she told Adam so, he laughed and got out his measuring tape. "I think we have room for both if we scoot the wood stove over a little."

He hugged his mother. "I'm glad you're keeping it. One of my first memories is sitting by this stove in the logging shack. It was the warmest spot in the house."

Alexis surprised them with the level of her involvement in the placement of furniture and the decorating of their new home. She told Laurel, "We don't need to cut out any light through the small windows in the living room. Let's buy a long strip of cloth and swag it at the top and let it hang down straight at the sides."

Laurel was pleased with her efforts and gave her a free hand. Alexis, engaging Bess' help, soon had the windows taken care of, with a minimum of curtain and a maximum of light.

With the major work finished on the new home, Adam got a job at the paper mill where Sarah worked. He dated several young women, with Alexis freely dispensing advice, expressing approval or disapproval. At twenty-seven, Adam was certain that he could find a wife on his own, but he never informed Alexis of that fact. He always listened as if her counsel was of vital importance to him.

Justin was a happy man. He finally had his farm. Adam walked the boundary lines with him, hearing his plans for, perhaps, clearing an upper field for bigger crops. Adam, in his off-handed way, reminded his dad that he no longer needed huge crops since he had fewer children to feed at home *and* since he didn't have to give part the crop away.

Justin's answer didn't surprise him. "I know. But the fields I was sharecropping belong to a widow with children to feed. They depended on the produce. I may need to continue to help her, plus a couple of other families who never seem to have enough to eat."

Adam opened his mouth to argue but fell silent. He didn't quite know how to gauge his feelings. He had hoped his father would slow down. At the same time he admired him for not doing so.

The lives of the Worth family settled into a pleasant pattern, which could never be called a routine. They were involved in too many lives, with unexpected happenings, for a routine to exist.

One such happening was a Sunday afternoon wedding in their front yard. Camilla and Thad, after Camilla had insisted that they wait a few months—to give Thad time to be sure—had asked if they could be married at the Worth home.

The couple—with Archer—had found acceptance and encouragement from Hannah, Nora, and Jed and the extended Worth family, which sometimes made Camilla's head spin. At first she would name them on her fingers: Abby, Ethan and Allison, Jed and Hannah, Bulldog and Bess, Tom and Alice, Lila and Brand, Zach and Abner and Rosalee. Then she found that didn't work. She always seemed to miss somebody who had just been added.

Ethan, of course, performed the ceremony, arched by two dogwood trees, on the rock steps that separated the levels of the Worths' front yard. The sense of family created a warm and appropriate atmosphere for the wedding—as arms opened for turns to hold Archer, who obviously felt that everyone there belonged to him in one way or another.

On their way home, Oscar Bullock, Camilla's dad, who had never willingly darkened the door of a church in his life, astonished his wife when he asked, "What would you think of driving over and going to church with Justin and his family on Sunday?"

Thad and Camilla had a little house ready in Riverside, a small community near his parents' farm. Thad worked at the tannery, which produced tannic acid from the bark of oak trees to tan animal hides sent from around the country. He also helped his dad on the farm. Camilla knew by now she and Archer were loved by Thad's entire family. She was now part of that circle she had once observed, with longing, from a distance.

Justin worked just enough at his photography and in the timber business to bring in some needed cash. The rest of the time he spent on the farm. One day as he was following the horse and plow across a wide open field, making a remarkably straight furrow, Alexis' curiosity got the best of her. She walked across the field, taking him a fresh jug of water, and caught up with him.

"Daddy, how are you going so straight? You don't have anything to go by."

He wiped his face with his handkerchief and drank the cool water. Then he said, "Come stand in front of me, behind the plow. Do you see that big oak over there? That's my destination. I head straight for that tree and make sure I stay on course."

She nodded. "Oh! Then you can go by the first row to keep the others straight."

"Yes, honey! If you know your destination, other things fall in line."

Almost every day someone who needed help was brought to Laurel. One contagious disease that she was trying to stamp out was Thrush, a painful infection in the mouth of infants. It was accompanied by fever, colic, diarrhea, no appetite, and difficulty in swallowing. Laurel, with Abby's and Dr. Leighton's counsel, taught the young mothers cleanliness techniques such as personal hygiene if nursing. If the babies were bottle fed she taught the mothers to sterilize the bottles and nipples as well as foods and milk. Since the disease preyed on weak and undernourished babies, Laurel was able to set out a regimen for good nutrition as further prevention.

Laurel, with one rare afternoon alone, sat down in the rocking chair on the front porch to assess the status of her *own* children. Feeling like a mother hen whose chicks had scattered in all directions, she tried to assimilate and digest all the latest information. Caroline and Brook, who came often, had informed her and Justin a couple of weeks ago that they were expecting a new arrival in a few months. Last week Sarah and Roe had told them that J.R. was going to have a little sister or brother just a month after Caroline's baby was due. David's letters indicated that his biggest concern about their move was that the *animals* would like the new place. This had brought about a great deal of joking, with Justin writing David to tell him that he had polled the animals and they sent word that they were happy—but would he please come home! David told his dad to tell the animals that he planned to be home in a few months. He also informed his family that he was corresponding with a nearby college about enrolling as soon as he arrived.

Laurel and Justin were very thankful to have Adam home again for a while, especially with a very active teenager in the house. Adam seemed to enjoy the supervision of Alexis' social life. He, with whichever current girlfriend, would take Alexis and her friends on adventures they would never otherwise have had: a hay ride for Halloween, a trip to the regional fair in Cherokee, a movie, a trip in Justin's truck along the Blue Ridge Parkway, a picnic in Pisgah Forest.

Laurel realized their time with Alexis at home was drawing to a close. She was well into her junior year of high school.

Laurel sat thinking about her youngest. Alexis, with her readiness to talk and laugh, *seemed* to be an extrovert like her daddy, but Laurel knew how much she treasured her time alone. She, like Laurel, needed regular periods of solitude to assess, re-orient, and to get re-energized. She expected everybody to like her, and if someone didn't, she thought *that* person had a problem. Laurel now smiled as she remembered Alexis' explanation of how she dealt with the *phenomenon* of a person not liking her.

"Mama, this girl in school doesn't like me. At first it hurt my feelings and I tried to be friendly, but she won't let me. I know I haven't done anything to harm her. *So,* I thought about it and decided it's *her* problem."

Laurel had answered, "Are you treating her right, even though she's not responding?"

"Yes. I know better than to be mean to *anybody.*"

With that statement, Laurel let it rest. Alexis wasn't being arrogant. She was living what she had learned.

Possibly because of growing up with her beloved brothers, she was comfortable around boys and boys were comfortable around her. She had many girlfriends, but when someone teased about the number of boys who came around, she explained carefully, as if the person were dull of understanding, "They aren't *boyfriends.* They're *friends* who are *boys.*"

When she had turned sixteen and was allowed to go on actual dates, the family noticed she juggled at least three boys. She would go to one event with one, another event with the other, and so it went...

Laurel and Justin were gratified over her academic achievements. She was never satisfied with less than an "A" in any subject. Yet, she wasn't considered a studious person. She didn't want too much studying to interfere with her fun.

Laurel figured it out. "Somewhere along the way, you've learned *how* to study. That's almost as important as the subject matter itself."

Laurel's reverie was interrupted by Alexis tripping down the walk, calling out ahead as she often did, coming in from school, "Mama, guess what...?"

Laurel, laughing at Alexis' joy of life, rose and came to meet her, waiting to hear all about it. This time Alexis had been chosen to receive a statewide journalism award. She needed to travel to Raleigh to receive it at the State Capitol Building. At supper, when Laurel told Alexis that she needed a new dress and new shoes, Adam jumped right in with an opinion.

"You probably need high heeled shoes."

Alexis wrinkled her nose in disdain. "Why?"

"Because this is a big honor and you are a young lady now."

Alexis looked at the three serious faces looking back at her.

"I'll probably fall flat on my face!"

Adam answered, "No, you won't. You'll practice walking in those high-heeled shoes around here until you pass inspection."

After purchasing the dress and shoes, they had a week to get her in shape to walk correctly to receive the award. Laurel and Justin were the audience, but Adam was the coach. He was relentless, encouraging but pointing out what she had to correct. The night she thought they almost had it whipped, he said, "Now we're ready for the stairs."

"The stairs?"

"Yes, my dear! You have to go up the steps to the stage to receive this award!"

For another hour she went up and down the stairs, balancing a book on her head. By the time they were finished she was tired but she believed she could walk in high heeled shoes — without clomping or falling on her face.

Laurel, without her immediate knowledge, had been elevated by the people around her to the status of a godly woman — a Healer. She was the person to see about almost any problem. Perhaps, because people hunger — even unconsciously — for a sign of God's presence in their midst, they eagerly embraced Laurel's answered prayers. It seemed that God took her prayers seriously. The proof was in lives all around them. Physical and spiritual healing — as well as wisdom to deal with the more mundane problems of life — was to be found in the presence of the lady whose auburn hair was now streaked with silver.

When she realized what was happening — aware of the privilege, and the burden — she tried to explain that she was only an instrument, that God was the Healer and the only One to be held in esteem. Her words fell on deaf ears.

Strangers, who were intimated by her reputation, were immediately at ease in her presence, embraced by her smile. Whatever they had expected, they found a humble, gentle woman in a simple, cotton dress—sometimes faded—covered with a small snow-white apron.

That was what people *saw*. What they *understood* and *counted on* was that she wore the mantle of a woman who walked and talked with God. They believed that God had placed it there because she had earned it. She had been chosen to represent the people to God and God to the people. This knowledge brought great comfort and security to those around her. Their part was to recognize and respond and give thanks. One of the ways they chose to do this was to shower love upon the one who had brought *God's* love into their lives.

They gave what they had—and what they knew would please her. Often, young boys would appear with a string of mountain trout, showing off their fishing skills, saying, "Mama told us to bring these trout and to clean them for you." Another day, another boy would bring a couple of rabbits, killed and dressed, ready to cook, saying, "Mama says you like rabbit better than chicken."

When someone heard that she loved wild roses and purple irises and tiger lilies, someone appeared with cuttings to plant for her. They enjoyed just being in her presence. One of Alexis' friends confided, "I'm always glad when *my* mama spends some time with *your* mama. She's always happier—and nicer to us—after they've talked."

Justin, in his unique way, had won his own place in the hearts of the people throughout the area. For many years, his trips with his camera had brought him upon situations that most people would have gladly left alone, saying it was none of their business. Justin meddled anyway, his steps sometimes taking him where a timid soul would not have trod.

When he found a family with children who looked hungry, he'd coax the mother into telling him what groceries they needed. If she was reluctant, he would look in the cabinets and even the bank house to find out for himself. If a recalcitrant father argued with him, Justin would save the man's pride by telling him he could come and work it out. Within the next day or two, groceries would be delivered. And the children could always count on candy — from the picture man.

Widows living alone understood that — before winter — they would receive a visit from Justin Worth with his sons or some of his helpers in his timber job. The result would be a huge pile of wood, cut, chopped, and stacked on the porch within easy reach when the snows came.

Adam and David, in their growing-up years, knew better than to complain about helping people. They had often wished their dad wasn't so free in volunteering *their* time. Their most dreaded job was slaughtering hogs. And, in autumn, the jobs had come with great frequency, as they went from one neighbor to another to help.

One old-timer after another, with a drinking problem, would happily relate how Justin had kept him from freezing to death when he picked him up and took him home to let him sleep it off. Each one spoke of it as an adventure to be proud of. One wrinkled — or pickled — old fellow, who had been rescued by Justin many times, remarked to a roomful of his cronies, "I've got a problem. You know I ain't never had much use for Republicans nor Christians."

When he fell silent, someone asked, "So?"

"Well, Justin Worth is both — and he's the best man I know!"

Then, because he had too much liquor in him to keep secrets, he revealed a longing that many of them would never voice. "I may talk to him about that Christian stuff...Justin's easy to talk to..."

Justin certainly was not a pious man, as one usually counted piety. When he became a deacon in the church, he brought his own approach to life — which included fun — to the office of deacon. At first some eyebrows were raised, then some adjustments were made. Hesitant steps were taken to accommodate this...this joy of life...this celebration...that somewhere, through the years, had lost expression. The songs he most loved — and sang clearly in his pure tenor voice — were songs of praise and joy and hope and love. Mournful dirges, sung by people with long faces, had no place in the house of the God he had come to know and love and serve.

He was a true friend to the pastor and to preachers in general, remarking that a man had to have common sense and uncommon valor to wear the shoes of the prophet successfully. His pastor once said, "When Justin comes into the room, it's like the sun has come out from behind a dark cloud. He brings his own celebration of life with him."

Alexis, after going to Deerbrook with Justin one Saturday, complained to her mother when she got home, "I'm not going to town with Daddy any more! He spends the whole day talking. Everybody knows him and is happy to see him. When I think we're getting on our way, somebody else yells, 'Mr. Worth' or 'Justin' or 'Uncle Justin', then they go at it again."

Laurel laughed. "What if you had a daddy whom nobody liked?"

Alexis smiled. "It's true, isn't it? *Everybody* likes my daddy!"

As she turned to run upstairs, Laurel thought, *And you, young lady, have a big dose of your daddy in you!*

The family became increasingly aware that Laurel's energy level was diminishing. Even with Dr. Leighton's treatments, she had to rest more often and for longer periods. Without words being spoken, Alexis took over the weekly cleaning and laundry. She looked forward to her time with her mother on Saturday mornings when they did the straightening, dusting, sweeping, and mopping. They also caught up on the important things in each other's lives. Alexis became quite proprietary about the way the house looked, and a few times overstepped her bounds.

Justin had the habit of leaving his tools and equipment on the front porch, an action that Alexis found totally inappropriate. After asking her daddy to find a different place to keep his tools and getting no results, she decided to take matters into her own hands. She put his tools in the dirt cellar, told no one and went off to school.

When she returned home in the afternoon, in Justin's words, "the fat was in the fire." Justin had spent a frustrating day without getting anything done because his tools were missing. By now, he had figured who the culprit was and was waiting for her.

Without even a greeting, he asked, "Alexis, where are my tools?"

His tone didn't encourage any suggestions, only facts.

She answered, "In the cellar. I thought that would be the first place you'd look."

Justin, who had rarely scolded her in her life, carried on, "I've wasted a whole day because you've got to have everything spic and span. A man can't live in peace in his own house."

Laurel and Adam were listening, amused, until Justin said, "You need to know your place, young lady."

When Adam saw Alexis' eyes fill and her chin come up, he thought it was time to intervene. "Dad, that's not fair! This *is* Alexis' place! She works hard with Mama to keep it clean."

Justin turned his temper on Adam. "Now I've got my son telling me what to do."

Adam replied, "Yes, sir, you do! The cellar's a good place for your tools. Let's go find 'em."

That was one of several conflicts over Alexis' way of keeping house. She enjoyed moving furniture around just to get the feel of something different. One afternoon when Roe and Sarah were visiting, she asked Roe to help her rearrange the dining room. They hoisted the pieces into their new places and stood back to look at the results. Justin appeared, took one look at his washstand where he shaved and said, "Alexis, I had that mirror positioned just right to get the light to shave by."

Looking from one to the other, Roe defused the encounter. "Don't worry, Mr. Worth, she'll have it rearranged before you shave again."

Justin shook his head, laughed and said, "I guess I can count on it."

Alexis' senior year of high school was a year crammed full of change for the Worth family. David, home from the Navy, was a man with a mission. After spending time with the family, getting oriented to their new home, and catching up with the animals, he enrolled in college. He was called to preach and he believed that was a call to preparation.

Even so, he asked to be ordained, so he could learn to do by doing. It was a solemn but joyous day when Ethan and Pastor Pierce did the honors of inducting David Hunter Worth into the Gospel ministry, by the authority that was vested in them by the Lord and by the local church. The immediate Worth family, their extended family, and scores of friends, present for the ceremony, viewed the occurrence with a sense of rightness. The phrase that reverberated in everyone's mind was, "To whom much is given, much shall be required." The Worth children had been given much, not in worldly goods, but in an infinitely more precious currency. Assets that were negotiable in this world and the next.

Adam, the first born son and self-appointed protector of his family, had finally settled down to dating *one* young woman by the name of Meredith Sumner. Of course, he had to bring her home to meet the family before they—especially Alexis—heard about her from another source. If Meredith, with her brown eyes, brown hair and a ready smile, realized that she was being inspected, she gave no sign of being nervous. Because Adam had talked a great deal about Alexis, she understood their close relationship. She could understand how Alexis might feel about someone else coming first in Adam's life. She set about to make friends.

Later she confessed to Adam, "I knew I needed to win Alexis over, but before I knew it *she* had won *me* over. We like each other. We're becoming friends."

Adam, who had heard a similar statement from Alexis, now gave Meredith a hug and said, "I'm glad. I was pretty sure my women would get along."

One cold February morning, about two o'clock, heavy knocking awakened the Worth household. The messenger was in a hurry. A neighbor's baby had chosen to arrive in a snow so deep the vehicles wouldn't budge. He had walked to get Laurel, but was puzzled as to how they could get her there.

Justin, worried about Laurel going out in the weather, suggested another midwife who lived in the community. The man said, "I sent somebody else for her. She'll be there to help. But the mama's callin' for Miz Worth with every breath."

Justin looked at Laurel. "If I wrap you up good, could you ride on the sled? I believe the horse can high step enough to pull the small sled over this snow."

By now everybody in the house was up and dressed. Adam went with Justin to hook up the sled. Alexis, concerned about her mama going out in this weather, said, "Mama, I'm going with you. You can tell me what to do and I'll help."

"A baby being born is not a pretty sight, honey. I'll have some help."

The men came in stamping the snow off their feet.

Alexis persisted, "*You* do it all the time. It's time *I* learned. In fact, you can just tell me what to do and *I'll* deliver *this* baby!"

It was such a confident, determined—and tacitly ignorant—declaration, that Justin, Laurel, and Adam dared not look at each other for fear of laughing. Suddenly, everyone got busy. It seemed they all were going. Adam would help his dad get the sled there with Laurel on it. Alexis would ride the horse to get initiated into the mystifying ritual of childbirth.

The humble little house was overheated, which intensified the smell of sweat and urine. Laurel realized the baby was coming soon and flew into action. Alexis, positive that she could learn to do what her mother did on a regular basis, was right by Laurel's side, a second pair of hands. When Laurel saw the baby's head crown she asked Alexis to hold the lamp close.

Just as the baby started to emerge, preceded by an issue of blood, Alexis went down like a stone. The other midwife, standing close, grabbed the lamp before it fell. Laurel called for Adam to come and get Alexis out of the way. She was in a heap at the foot of the bed where Laurel needed to stand to finish bringing this baby into the world.

Adam dragged Alexis' limp form away from the bed, then picked her up, carried her out the door and laid her on the porch, with her head in his lap. The fresh cold air would soon bring her around.

While he waited, a small wail, then a louder one sounded from the room. He couldn't help but smile. It must be rewarding to his mother to think of how many lives she had ushered into this world. He thought, *I wonder if she has kept a record. I'm going to ask her to name them for me.*

When his sister started coming to, she wasn't in good shape. She immediately slid over to the edge of the porch where she threw up rather vigorously while her brother held her head. When she finished, he took out his handkerchief, rubbed it in the snow to wet it, then gave it to her to wash her face.

Her eyes were big as she remembered. "The baby?"

"It's here! I heard it crying."

She sat up. "Oh, Adam, I'm so embarrassed!"

"I know. But it was really bad in there. It's way too hot and the smell about made me gag."

"Really? You're not just trying to make excuses for me?"

"No. It's bound to be better under different circumstances."

Alexis spoke with conviction. "I never, ever intend to do that again! It's awful! I don't think I'll ever *have* a baby!"

With no answer to this vociferous announcement, Adam was relieved when his dad appeared to tell them it was over and mother and baby were fine. Alexis refused to go back into the room, so Adam kept her wrapped in a blanket and waited with her until Laurel was sure it was safe to leave. They were quiet on the way home as the sled glided over the snow, glistening in the dawn of a new day.

The snow had cancelled school, which was good because Alexis couldn't have gone anyway. Laurel put her back to bed and obeyed Alexis' request that *she* should rest awhile, too.

When they got up to hoe cakes and coffee—made by Justin—Alexis repeated her opinion about childbirth to Laurel. Her mother said, "I know. I felt the same way the first time I helped. In fact, Alexis, I passed out, too. About the same way you did."

Alexis was so surprised she stopped eating. "Mama! You didn't! You're just trying to make me feel better!"

"Ask your daddy!"

Justin, understanding his cue, said, "Yes, she did! She gave them more trouble than Alice, when Tommy was born. I had to carry your mother home. She wasn't worth much for the rest of the day."

Alexis, looking from one to the other and to Adam, felt her humiliation evaporate. She was exonerated. If her mama...

Then a new thought struck her. "But, Mama, you went back and did it again and again! All through the years!"

"Yes, honey. I had to! I was all they had!"

Silence reigned for a few moments with everybody aware that Alexis was working all this out in her mind. They figured an announcement was imminent and they didn't have to wait long.

"*Well*, I may as well tell you now, Mama! I want to be like you more than anybody, but I'll have to be like you in some other ways! Will you be disappointed?"

"No, Alexis, I don't think you'll ever disappoint us."

Chapter Seventeen

Adam and Meredith decided on an April wedding. The church where Meredith attended near Deerbrook was banked with dogwood blossoms for the ceremony. Her pastor and Ethan did the honors. Rev. David Worth, brother of the groom, gave the benediction.

The young couple moved into an apartment in Riverside, near Alexis' high school. For the next few busy weeks before she graduated, Alexis was at their house almost as much as she was at home. If the newlyweds grew tired of the extra person, nobody ever knew. They continued to act as chaperones for the activities of the senior class.

Laurel and Justin had encouraged Alexis to check with her teachers about a college where she could work and earn her way. Her teachers, pleased over the request, had found a school that she could afford. A small but highly respected college in a nearby state offered a program that allowed students without college funds to work to pay for their tuition and room and board — everything except spending money. It would be a demanding schedule, with the student working and taking a full load of classes. Alexis — and her teachers — were sure she could do it. The teachers encouraged her to major in journalism. She smiled and was silent. She knew she was going to be a teacher. Like her mother. It was a satisfying day for the Worth family when Alexis' letter of acceptance came.

Laurel had believed for some time that she had a problem beyond the pernicious anemia. Dr. Leighton's vitamin shots helped her, but she still had spells when she almost blacked out and would have to lie down. Or, an extreme weakness would put her to bed.

She thought of what was best for the family at this time and decided to say nothing to anyone except Abby. Together they went to see Dr. Leighton who heard Laurel's symptoms, ran some tests, and consulted a specialist. His diagnosis was not encouraging.

"Your heart is enlarged, so the muscles are weakened. The heart isn't working as efficiently as it should. This slows down the blood flow, which affects all other body functions."

He paused, then with obvious difficulty said, "I know you expect the truth, Laurel. What you have is called heart failure, and it is progressive."

Laurel flinched, then brought her shoulders back. "What's the prognosis?"

"It's hard to tell. I'm giving you some medicine that hopefully will take some of the load off the heart. If you're reasonable about your activities, you could have a few years left."

"I don't want to be an invalid."

"I know you don't. Keep up some activities but not strenuous ones. No more going out in a snowstorm on a sled to deliver a baby. The word needs to go out that you aren't available to bring any more babies into the world."

The exchange had been kept strictly professional to block out personal feelings. As Laurel and Abby got up to leave, however, these feelings erupted from Dr. Leighton.

"What are we going to tell Justin?"

"Would it be wrong to wait awhile to tell him?" Laurel asked.

The three friends stood looking at each other. Each one knew how devastating this would be for Justin Worth, the man who could take on the world — and beat all the odds — as long as he had Laurel by his side. Dr. Leighton had already seen him when he thought he was going to lose her.

Now he said, "Okay, let's wait awhile. I think we've got some time."

"I don't want Alexis to know, either. She's enrolled in college and if she finds out about this, she won't go."

"Laurel, somebody in your family has to know. Abby, bring in Adam and Sarah. I'll talk to them."

After giving time for Adam and Sarah to talk to Dr. Leighton, then to share the information with Caroline and David, Laurel asked Adam to set up a time when she could meet privately with the four of them. Justin and Alexis were not to know about the meeting. Even though their world had been shaken, each son and daughter—who had wept and railed privately—now, after some inevitable tears, faced their mother with the maturity they knew she expected from them.

Laurel laid out her terms. Alexis was not to know and Justin could not be told for a while. They had some time to make the decision when to tell him after Alexis was safely away at college.

The four older Worth children, then, laid out their proposals. They all knew that, with Alexis gone, the house cleaning and laundry would fall to them. They had worked it out among themselves. If Justin and Laurel would sell them a corner of the farmland, Sarah and Roe would build a house where they would be a stone's throw away. Adam and Meredith would look for a house in the community. Caroline and Brook would come regularly to do chores as needed. David, of course, was expected to continue with his education. His college was nearby, so he would be home often.

And so the conspiracy was born. It was a conspiracy born of love and hopes and dreams for Alexis—the child, now a young woman, who had always been environed by their love—the one whom they would help reach for opportunities that had not been available to them.

It was also born of love and protection for Justin. They knew he would have to know in time, but no one had the courage or desire to say the words that had the power to dim or extinguish the exuberant joy of life that was uniquely his; yet, everyone understood that it somehow received its spark from Laurel.

Alexis, for all her exuberance about going to college, had major concerns about leaving home. She sought out Adam for his advice, telling him that one part of her wanted to stay home where she could take care of her mama—and her daddy.

Adam said, "Alexis, the best thing you can possibly do for mama and daddy is to go to college! They wanted all of us to have a college education, but the Depression interfered. Now, you and David *must* go! That'll sort of be for all of us."

"But, Adam, how is mama going to be able to do everything?"

"Alexis, we've seen this coming. Sarah and Roe have bought some land from dad. They're planning to build a house just around the curve. Meredith and I are moving to Lake Eagle Rest. We'll probably build close by, too. I give you my solemn promise that we'll take good care of mama and dad."

Her tears flowed freely with relief and with a measure of trepidation about leaving a loving environment for the unknown.

She had one last question. "Adam, do you think I'll ever be as happy — out there — as I've been here?"

"Alexis, you'll have a happy life. You carry happiness with you."

The day for her graduation arrived. Her valedictory address anticipated the future — the last half of the twentieth century — that beckoned each of the graduates to fulfill their potential. It also saluted the past — all that had been given to them to bring them to this door of opportunity.

Laurel and Justin, hearing her confident voice, each were full of their own thoughts. Justin, pleased by her poise and that special ability to communicate, thought, *She's her mother's daughter!*

Laurel thought, *Not one word has failed of God's good promises. He has allowed me to live to rear my children.*

She reached for Justin's hand and whispered, "Papa would like her, wouldn't he?"

"Yes! He'd like her *and* love her! She's got a good dose of the professor in her!"

Laurel's heart surged with joy. She smiled. "I know!"

The next few months passed quickly. Laurel learned to hoard her strength to show up best when Alexis was around. She had come to terms with her health problem and she believed she had some good years left. Her loving God had graciously granted her the wonderful years of rearing her children. She knew she could trust His timing as to when He called her home *and* she could trust Him implicitly with her family after she was gone. At any rate, death to her was not death in the way most people understood the word. It was only a gate through which one had to pass — and she had an advantage over most people. She had long ago been given a glimpse at the wonder that was waiting for her on the other side.

The day for Alexis to leave for college finally arrived. A day long anticipated — and dreaded. At her request, the family had said, "Goodbye" at the Sunday get-together. Adam wanted to get off work and take her. She refused, saying she needed to know he and Meredith would soon be moved in close by. She exacted a promise from Sarah and Caroline that they would call when the babies arrived. She instructed David to practice preaching because she expected to hear a good sermon when she came home for Christmas. She asked her daddy to take her, alone, to the bus stop on the curvy road near their home. She would ride ten hours or more through the mountains to reach her destination.

She had given her mother detailed and definite instructions as to what she could and could not do, and as to what she needed to leave for Sarah and Caroline and Meredith. She made her promise she would take care of herself. Laurel had agreed, keeping a tight rein on her emotions. She was privately amused at who was now bossing whom!

They both had steeled themselves for the task of saying, "Goodbye." Each tried to protect the other. Talking and tears were past. Their final embrace signified the bond that would always be there. It was a creative, life-giving bond. To the daughter it gave inspiration; to the mother it gave joy and fulfillment. They both knew that neither distance nor time — nor death — would diminish it.

Alexis, after all, had one last thing to say. "Thank you for all your love and for all you've done for me. I've probably been the happiest child in the world. I'll try to live out some of what you and Daddy and everybody has put into me!"

Laurel paused, astonished and pleased. She remembered saying almost those exact words to her papa a lifetime ago.

"I believe in you, Alexis. I'll pray for you every day. You'll succeed in whatever you choose to do."

She smiled. "And, now, you *have* to go."

As they drove off in his truck, with her trunk and suitcase in the back, Justin thought, *I've got three miles left with her before I send her off. It'll never be the same again.*

Silence reigned for a moment, then Alexis laid her hand on her daddy's hand where it rested on the steering wheel. "Thank you,

Daddy, for…for everything! I've had a wonderful — almost magical — childhood! It's been great fun!"

Justin squeezed her hand. "You brought part of the magic, honey, and the fun!"

He was determined, whatever he had to do, not to let her know about the sinking feeling in the pit of his stomach and the tears that were threatening to roll. He had to get through his next statement. "Alexis, I have one last thing to say. If you'll just try to be like your mother, you'll have a good life."

"I know, Daddy! Nobody else can ever be just like Mama! I *do* want to be like her — *plan* to be like her — as much as I can."

She turned her smile on him. "But, do you know something? Mama couldn't be the person she is without *you*."

Surprised, Justin protested. "But your mother's always been the one to help *me*!"

"Not any more than you've helped her! You've shared her and supported her — proudly — in helping other people. Lots of men wouldn't have done that. *So!* My next biggest job after school is to find a man like you! When I do, I'll marry him!"

By now Justin was laughing. "What if he doesn't want to marry you?"

"Oh, Daddy!" She was indignant. "Of course, he'll want to!"

The threatening tears had disappeared and his stomach was feeling normal again. This daughter of his was going to be just fine! He would look forward to future developments.

The bus arrived on time. Justin heaved the trunk and suitcase into the luggage department. For some reason, he still had laughter bubbling up in him and he knew he had to leave *her* laughing. He followed her onto the bus and saw her settled into her seat. He hugged her one last time and walked to the front of the bus. Then he paused and called back to her, "I'm going straight home and put all my tools back on the front porch!"

She raised up and said, "Daddy! Don't you dare!"

The people on the bus chuckled at this strange goodbye.

As the bus pulled out, there she was with the window down, smiling and waving. He would always remember that.

He hurried back to Laurel. She had asked to be alone when Alexis left, but Justin knew her conflicting emotions. Alexis, with her pronouncements, had brought him out of his turmoil and he would see if he could do the same for Laurel.

She was sitting on the front porch in her small rocking chair, waiting for him.

He sat down in the rocker beside her. "I got her off. She was happy. She's...she's going to be fine, Laurel."

"I know," she said, smiling.

Justin, suddenly serious, said, "But, Laurel, we have a real problem on our hands."

"What?" Laurel's tone was sharp.

"You and I, my dear," he intoned, slowly, "have not spent the night together—alone—in about thirty years. Do you suppose the neighbors will talk?"

She knew he was whistling in the dark for both of them, and she had never loved him more. They both were laughing as she stood and pulled him up for an embrace. No words were necessary. Together, they drew strength and comfort from each other as they had through the years. Together, they would face tomorrow.

Their aloneness was not to last long. They heard voices, then three young men came down the path, each carrying a hefty string of trout. It was Bryce, Abner's and Rosalee's son, with Lila's and Brand's sons. Bryce started talking before they reached the porch.

"Mama sent us on ahead with these rainbow trout. Said they're your favorite, Mrs. Worth. We'll clean 'em if you'll show us where."

"What do you mean, she sent you on ahead?" Justin asked.

Bryce talked in starts and stops like Abner. "Oh, they's a bunch of people comin'! Gonna have a picnic! They're bringin' food! Mama and Lila said *they're* goin' to spend the night and stay a day or two with you. Work in your flower beds. Don't want you lonesome with Alexis gone."

Justin and Laurel looked at each other and started laughing again.

Later, down by the creek, cleaning the trout, Bryce remarked, "Did you notice them laughin'? Ma and Pa say they're the happiest people they ever saw. I guess so—with all that laughin'."

Epilogue

It should have surprised no one that Justin — impulsive, adventurous Justin — went ahead on the final journey. He died with his boots on, on a mountain peak, with the world spread out before him. He had been employed to estimate the number of board feet in a remote tract of timber. When he didn't return home, Adam, David and Ethan found him. He was sitting with his back to a tree, his feet crossed. He had a surprised smile on his face. His right hand got their attention. It was resting on its side on his leg, with the thumb up, as if he were shaking hands. Adam remarked, "He was mighty pleased to see the person who came to meet him."

Laurel was strong for the family. Her grief was tempered with a sense of rightness. She said as much to the children and grandchildren. "This is something I can do for him. His greatest fear was that I would go first." She joined him two months later, going serenely in her sleep.

Their funerals, individually, were worthy celebrations of their lives. People streamed forth from the hills and the valleys to grieve, to express their love, and to give thanks for having known them. Ethan, David, Alexis' husband and a line of other preachers poured forth their tributes. The most memorable was from Ethan when he said of each of them, "We will not likely see their kind again. People like Justin and Laurel Worth seldom pass through this world. We have been honored and blessed to have been among their friends."

Justin would have been pleased to know that his pictures of the logging industry went on permanent display on the walls of the

Wildwood County Courthouse — history caught and distilled by the "Picture-Taking Man," clearly defining what a thousand words could never say. The legacy most treasured, however, was hundreds of photographs of *people* — individuals, family groups, gatherings. With almost every picture, handled lovingly, comes a story of how he — passing through — made life easier for those in his path.

Laurel's legacy survived the generations. Her story is still told and retold, reverently, lovingly, wonderingly, with new truths revealed to be treasured by her children...and their children...and their children.

Justin and Laurel had lived to see David finish college, get married and become pastor of a local church. They were there to celebrate with Alexis as she graduated with a teacher's degree, found the man who reminded her of her dad, and, of course, married him.

Alexis was the fledgling who traveled the farthest from the nest. Her husband, Adrian, a preacher, was an adventurer not unlike Justin. They traveled and ministered extensively, including missionary work in foreign countries. With all their exploits, she somehow managed a career of teaching. She was afforded the privilege of offering educational opportunities for her generation, and the next, knowing this would have pleased her mother.

They would say their greatest legacy was their children. Sarah and Roe, Adam and Meredith, Caroline and Brook and David and Julia remained in Wildwood County and raised their families there. They each chose to see and respond to life — and people — through the view-finder provided by their parents. They and their children, with few exceptions, carried into their generations the redemptive values that Justin and Laurel had talked and walked throughout their lives.

Justin's and Laurel's gravestone, standing stark white in a small cemetery on a mountain top, declares concisely and comprehensively: *Of such is the Kingdom of Heaven.*

Printed in the United States
64466LVS00003B/106